STRESS TO ZEST

STRESS TO ZEST

Stories and Lessons for Personal Transformation

ARITRA SARKAR

PENGUIN ENTERPRISE

An imprint of Penguin Random House

PENGUIN ENTERPRISE

Penguin Enterprise is an imprint of the Penguin Random House group of companies whose addresses can be found at global.penguinrandomhouse.com

Published by Penguin Random House India Pvt. Ltd
4th Floor, Capital Tower 1, MG Road,
Gurugram 122 002, Haryana, India

First published in Penguin Enterprise by Penguin Random House India 2024

10 9 8 7 6 5 4 3 2

ISBN 9780143465638

Typeset in Adobe Caslon Pro
Printed at Replika Press Pvt. Ltd, India

www.penguin.co.in

Dedicated to Mama and Baba

My origin. My ocean. My bridge. My achievement.

CONTENTS

PREFACE

The cobra and the anaconda are the deadliest snakes in the jungle. They kill in different ways. The cobra will bite you, injecting you with venom until you drop dead. The anaconda will wrap around your body, tighten its noose with calibrated pressure, and then apply a fatal twist when you are at your weakest. At that moment, you will die of suffocation.

Most books for stress management provide quick-fix solutions—the equivalents of antivenom sprays in the above context. At best, these 'medicinal' aids will heal the toxic effects of cobra venom, but they will not make you stronger, more agile, or more vigilant—qualities you'll need to cultivate to fend off the suffocating chokeholds applied by other dangerous species of serpents, such as the anaconda.

Among mental health predators, stress is at the apex. Your ultimate weapon for fighting off stress is yourself—through, the evolution of your consciousness.

I wrote this book to show you how to understand and use stress as fuel for growth. This book presents a collection of stories entwined with my learnings about the major types of stress we all face. The stories are set in different parts of the world and involve ordinary people who feel suffocated by the (stress) constrictor in everyday life. This book attempts to answer the following questions: Can anyone fortify themselves to become immune to the giant serpent's coil? Can they then go on to evolve in spite of being caught in its ferocious chokehold from time to time?

I hope you will take the lessons forward by applying them to overcome your primary barriers to growth. Nothing will give me greater pleasure than knowing that you, dear reader, have transformed your existence from stress to zest.

As someone who has changed careers thrice, experienced three failed business ventures, subsisted in a broken marriage for a decade, battled against body dysmorphia, struggled with addiction, fought against extreme pressure to follow their own heart, and constantly braved a bottomless pit of loneliness, I feel that I'm uniquely qualified to talk to you about stress.

Without further ado, let us march onwards to the training grounds where I will show you how to battle the mighty serpent.

WHAT IS STRESS?

Almost everyone juggles multiple priorities in life. Family, career, education, finances, health, grooming . . . the list of tasks is endless. In every sphere, we spend lots of time and energy trying to satisfy the needs and expectations of others. On the other hand, we seldom reflect on the question, 'Who do I want to be?' This central question of our existence—the purpose of life—gets relegated to the backwaters of our consciousness amid the noise and hustle of daily life. The absence of purpose can result in low self-esteem, make us susceptible to the diktats, control, or influence of others, erode our sense of autonomy, and lead us down the dank alleyway of harmful behaviour. If this happens, various negative feelings may creep into our minds, causing unhappiness.

Stress is a debilitating swirl of negative feelings—frustration, anxiety, depression and anger—induced by our compulsion to meet expectations. These expectations may be our own creations, or they may be foisted onto us by others. Stress that stems from trying to meet internal expectations is called 'inner stress'; while that which arises when we attempt to satisfy the demands of others is called 'external stress'.

Inner stress is the negativity that fills our hearts and minds when we feel unable to meet our own expectations regarding our performance, growth, or ownership. This form of stress is self-induced. Its origin lies in our mental conditioning. Most of us grew up believing that it's better to follow a path charted by others instead of carving out our own. Thus, we've become used to letting the words and deeds of others define our thinking and actions. Consequently, we never develop the self-confidence required to shape our own identity, nor to set our own benchmarks for happiness. Instead, we adopt goalposts from society, without thinking about whether or not they are right for us. Many of us are paying a steep price for our uncritical submission to the demon of dependency. Dissatisfied with the state of affairs in our life relative to our expectations, we are often so racked with anxiety, gloom and disappointment, that we find it hard to approach the future with an optimistic mindset. Four aspects of life that often give rise to inner stress are relationships, jobs, finances and health.

External stress is the negativity we experience when we try to meet the expectations of others. Unlike inner stress, this form of pressure is directly applied by people who frequently coerce us into accepting their demands and want us to meet their expectations. These may include our peers, family members, bosses and various other influential figures in society. From their perches, these individuals use their powers to impose a set of standards and expectations upon us, causing strife by forcing our lives to veer off in a direction away from our hearts. The most common external stresses are social, parental, and competitional stress.

Both forms of stress can be devastating to our well-being. However, they tend to manifest themselves differently. The difference between how inner stress and external stress affect us is explained with metaphors below.

Inner Stress

Imagine yourself about to run on a treadmill. You've preset it to roll at a specific pace and incline, but these settings can't be changed as long as the machine is in motion. Moreover, the duration of the run has been preprogrammed by the manufacturer and you can't see the timer. You've listened to numerous people who've all said that the only way to improve your speed and stamina is to run on that particular treadmill, at a certain pace and intensity. These opinions tend to override one's own instinct. 'What do *I* know about improving my well-being?' you ask. 'Being experts, these folks must be right,' you think. 'That thing sure looks unpleasant, but I'm unaware of a better option to improve my fitness,' you deliberate. Ultimately, you ignore your own opinions on treadmill running and decide to get on the machine. Following the advice of others, you then calibrate the settings to make your run uncomfortable and challenging.

Now picture yourself running in these circumstances. After some time, you'll surely feel exhausted. Your body will cry, 'Please stop!' But you'll find it hard to do that because you'll be worried about squandering the progress you've already made. At some stage, your mind will scream, 'That's enough!' You'll realize you've pushed yourself hard to pursue an activity you *really* don't care about. Fatigue will overcome you and leave you gasping for breath.

You'll feel jaded. You'll feel listless and in pain. These feelings will only intensify as you run for longer and longer, with no end in sight. You'll want to jump off that treadmill. But now you'll worry that by stepping off, you might end up letting everyone down. Anxiety and confusion will cloud your mind and make it impossible to act in your own best interest. Congratulations, you've set yourself up for a lifetime of misery!

External Stress

Now let's look at an example of how the pressure of external stress ruins one's mental well-being.

Imagine yourself running a 100-metre race against an army of faceless runners. Before you can say 'Usain!' the contest is over. Irrespective of the result, a gang of officials drags you to the starting line of another race as soon as you finish the first. There, you see another crop of faceless souls lined up next to you, keen to bag the next gold medal. In a jiffy, this one's over too. After that, you're dragged to another race . . . then another . . . and another . . . in perpetuity. Before you know it, you've got leaden feet! How would you feel enduring through the unending races?

As you run a series of races (whose results are preordained) against a continuously changing pantheon of competitors, you will feel anxiety. As you compete in a race over which you have no control or influence, you will feel frustrated. Weighed down by the cumulative force of all that mental negativity, you will tell yourself in resignation, 'I either have to put up with the system or quit the stadium altogether!'

That's external stress for you. Stress is the toxic by-product of the modern, mechanical life. It's the life we've embraced—abandoning our true calling in order to ensure certainty of income and a certain standard of living. By letting these strains into our system and giving them free rein to pollute our hearts and minds, we run the risk of turning into emaciated husks.

The characters in the stories presented in this volume lost their well-being and joie de vivre because of the noxious effects of stress. Can they overcome stress and find peace and joy? Read on.

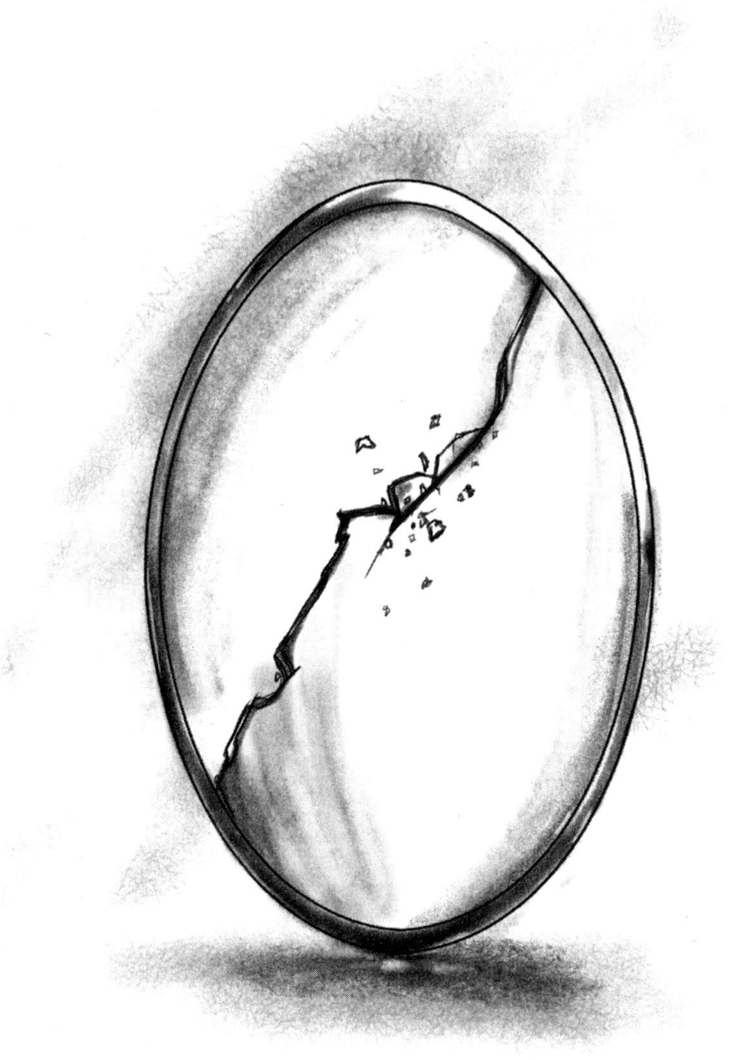

1

OVERCOMING RELATIONSHIP STRESS

UNDERSTANDING RELATIONSHIP STRESS

Borrowing the metaphor presented in the previous chapter, we live in an age of the treadmill marathon. This is an era when we are constantly running as fast as possible for as long as we can, managing deadlines, targets, appearances, trying to keep up with potential rivals. We run because we want to win a prize. This could be wealth, material objects, fame, or somebody's appreciation. We think this prize will solve all our problems and make us happy. That's what we've been taught since childhood, so that's what we believe without question. However, let's just pause for a minute and ask ourselves: 'How does this race make me feel?' What would the answer be? Our likely response would be, 'Extremely stressed'.

Stress is a result of inner pain from not meeting our or others' expectations in a sphere of life that's important to us. It's a toxic by-product of our drive to pursue external standards of accomplishment at the cost of inner peace and happiness. In our quest to meet or surpass these standards, we put in tremendous efforts—studiously avoiding activities and connections that could potentially make us happy.

Our relationships can be hurt by this relentless pursuit of standards. This is because we often extend these to our personal lives and then force or manipulate our partners to conform to them, even if that's not what they really want. In response, our partner expresses resentment by trying to impose their standards on us. This creates conflict that can easily spiral out of control and destroy the relationship. Here is an example of how unaligned expectations led to stress for Sonny and Ankita, who are caught in just such a quagmire. After three years of stonewalling one another, they'd grown cold and distant.

Relationships are often mime shows for showcasing our expectations. Most of the time, we don't express what we want to our companions because we are afraid it might lead to conflict and alienation. So we postpone important discussions until a time comes when we are forced to reveal what we want. By that time, there's already a trust deficit between the two. Anxiety, suspicion, and disappointment in our relationships permeate every aspect of our lives. In such a scenario, the revelation of a vast chasm between our expectations serves as the final blow to the relationship.

The bond between the two protagonists of the upcoming story was strained because of unaligned expectations about who they wanted to be. How will they overcome their relationship stress?

THE BIRYANI BAND

Biriyani was Sonny's favourite comfort food, something he hadn't enjoyed with Ankita in years. In fact, they hadn't enjoyed *anything* together in years. One day, a chance came to rectify the situation, but little did he know that underneath the aromatic flavour and polished texture of the signature delicacy laid a mound of rotting flesh.

At 7 p.m. on a Friday night, Sonny Kapoor was watching an advert for an upcoming international cricket match on his mobile phone. The logo of a restaurant sponsor was printed on the ad. He grinned. 'Finally, a chance for some extended private time with Ankita. Sports and biryani included . . .' He was hemmed in from all sides by fellow sardines in the overcrowded compartment onboard the rush-hour train from Chhatrapati Shivaji Terminus, but the smile never left his face. He opened his photo folder and saw a picture of a young woman with short hair, wearing jeans, kissing him outside a multiplex. The timestamp of the photo was from two years ago. He smiled ruefully. *After two years . . . Gosh, I guess we never imagined what we'd signed up for!*

He walked the half-mile distance from the station to his home with a spring in his step. An hour later, he reached his apartment in Andheri (West), Mumbai, to discover his girlfriend hosting a karaoke musical rehearsal with her circle of friends. The sight of the unplanned gathering in his TV den made him so angry that he ripped off his badge that read 'SHRAMAN KAPOOR, RELATIONSHIP MANAGER, ACCENT BANK' from his blazer's front pocket and threw it onto the floor. He then flung his jacket on his (thankfully) unoccupied recliner in the TV area, and shouted, 'Ankita, couldn't you find another day to host your stupid meet-up?'

One of the guests, a slender man in his late twenties, wearing a T-shirt with the slogan 'Save Mankind from the Right', looked at the young woman seated next to him on a lime-green sofa. 'Err, Simran, maybe we should cut short our practice, huh?'

'Yes, Pulkit. We should leave now,' agreed the young woman, who was wearing a traditional Maharashtrian sari. The two guests started to pack up their portable audio equipment.

However, Ankita was not willing to let them go just yet. She signalled them to stay, and looked at Sonny defiantly. 'We have lots to do. They can't leave yet.'

'Why not?' Sonny placed his hands on his hips.

Just then, someone rang the doorbell. Sonny opened the door to see a skinny young man, wearing a Swiggy food delivery uniform, holding out a bunch of greasy, piping hot bags. 'What the hell! Who ordered all this food?'

The man handed him an invoice and smiled. 'Three orders of Hyderabadi biryani, right on time.'

In a haze, Sonny signed the receipt, took the six plastic bags, and slammed the door in the delivery boy's face. Ankita grabbed the packets and taunted, 'They can't leave now. Who's going to eat all this food? Your siblings? Your best friend?'

She placed the food packets on the dining-room table and arranged four sets of plates and cutlery items. Sonny's brows drew closer together. *A full-blown dinner party with a bunch of strangers at the time of our special date? How inconsiderate!* He observed that the amount of food ordered was significantly more than the group could consume in one night.

What a waste of food! None of my friends would eat something like this before our bumpy, two-hour road trip to Khandala tomorrow.

'They definitely can't eat all of this,' he grumbled aloud.

The aroma of his favourite food wafted in the air and entered Sonny's nostrils, cooling his head a bit. However, Ankita added more gasoline to his rage. 'You should join us, too. I'm sure you could enjoy a piece of mutton or two.'

Sonny clenched his teeth. *Who does she think she is? An empress? A goddamned diva? Who does she think I am? Her fucking stagehand?* He raised his voice at Ankita and gesticulated wildly with his hands. 'This is totally uncool. Not telling me in advance that you were organizing a private party. I had plans, too.'

'What plans? To watch a T20 cricket match between New Zealand and Bangladesh?' Ankita quipped.

Sonny's face turned red. 'Is it wrong to enjoy some downtime after a gruelling day at the bank, cold-calling hundreds of people to sell them consumer loans? Given that you return home at five after your shift at credit card customer care, isn't my demand for some R&R legitimate?'

She waved her arms towards the door. 'If that's how you feel, go to Khandala with your stupid gang. Count me out. I'm fed up of your constant snide remarks and condescending attitude towards my passion.'

A prominent vein popped out of Sonny's neck. Simran spotted the signs of a looming storm and hastily urged Pulkit to pack up their accessories and leave before things got ugly. 'It's time to leave. We can reschedule for Monday,' she whispered to Ankita.

Ankita looked at her friend, filled with anger. 'The regional karaoke zonals are next week. We've got to practise. Nobody's going anywhere.' She looked sternly at her boyfriend of three years, unmoved by his entitlement to the shared TV, and snapped, 'You're forgetting that I too pay rent.'

Her karaoke mates looked at each other, totally confused. Sonny gazed at her with a surly expression. Ankita narrowed her eyes. 'Like you, I too graduated with an MBA from Sardar Patel University. Unlike you, however . . .' Her eyes shifted to his name badge lying on the floor. She picked it up and placed it inside a cabinet near the living room, housing Sonny's collection of classic dance music CDs. 'I actually want to be more than a greasy clerk. That's why I forego the lucrative overtime pay at the bank's customer hotline so that I can put a few hours into music practice every day.'

Sonny waved his hands as though dismissing her dream. 'Huh! For what? You've been saying you want to be a playback artist for years. And what have you done about it? Have you composed your own songs? Have you pitched your music to any recording studios? No, you haven't. All you do is waste precious time on this karaoke bullshit.'

At that moment, Simran, who had grown to be Ankita's closest friend through their shared passion for music, recalled a conversation they had at the apartment after their second meet-up, two years ago. Simran had caught Ankita emerging from the bathroom, her eyes red from crying.

A Confession

'What's wrong, honey?' Simran had asked, concerned.

Ankita wiped off the telltale signs of grief. 'Oh, nothing! I'm just stressed.'

When Simran pressed, Ankita sniffled. 'I'm sorry. But I've been upset all night. It's Sonny. Last night, he came home after our first rehearsal wrapped up. Instead of asking me about my progress, or you guys, or how I felt about reconnecting with my passion, he mocked me for returning home early and "wasting time". He told me I should be logging in more work hours and try to compete for a promotion. He treated me like a loser and said I'll never amount to anything. His utter contempt towards my passion upset me so much that I cried all night in the toilet.' She blew her nose.

'What's his beef? Isn't he aware that music is your passion?' Simran asked.

Ankita shrugged her shoulders. 'I thought he was. In college, he would tag along with me as my biggest fan and cheerleader. But once we moved in . . . after our graduation . . . he changed.'

'How did he change?'

'In college, we were so chilled out, without a care in the world. We were so supportive of each other and encouraged each other to shoot for the stars. We had all these dreams—we wanted to change the world together; to do something great.' Ankita hung her head. 'It all disappeared after we moved in together. Daily survival and building a future hit us like twin sledgehammers. I found my refuge in nurturing my passion alongside my job, while he continued with his relentless pursuit of corporate success.'

Simran's mind harked back to the early years of her marriage, and a lump formed in her throat. 'I was married at twenty. I had two kids by the time I turned twenty-two. For the next five years, I struggled to balance my domestic responsibilities with my passion for music. When I saw your event advert on social media for a karaoke get-together, I felt liberated. Finally, a chance to rekindle my passion. Fortunately, my husband took leave from work to look after the kids, making it possible for me to come.'

Ankita squeezed her friend's hand. 'You're lucky to have found a supportive partner. But Sonny? Well, he . . . it's not that he's socially conservative or bigoted. He's just risk-averse. He wasn't always like this. He was an excellent dancer at school. He honed his talent and even performed at college events, where we sang and danced as a couple.' Ankita's voice rose in excitement. 'We often daydreamed of becoming a performing duo like Fred Astaire and Ginger Rogers. Then, in the last year of college, his father died, and he became so serious, all of a sudden. That was when he quit dancing.'

Simran nodded.

'Life started feeling like a battlefield to him, with imagined enemies homing in on him at all times. From being a happy-go-lucky, supportive boyfriend, he turned into a morbid control freak, always critical of everything—of me, of my friends, of my performance at work. He measured happiness in the currency of dollars and titles, instead of friendship and passion.'

Ankita took out a photo album and turned its pages to a photo. It was a picture of Sonny and her wearing '80s-style disco outfits at a dance festival. 'This picture was taken at a college fest. We performed a duet on that occasion,' she said, wistfully.

'You guys look so sweet together,' Simran gushed.

Ankita pointed to a beaming, moustached man in his mid-fifties with his arm around Sonny's shoulder. 'That's his father, Drona. He was really supportive of Sonny's passion for dance. Despite being a modest-income clerk at the income tax office, he always paid for his son's lessons and allowed him to participate in contests. He was conservative and should have frowned upon our teenage romance. But he allowed Sonny to see me only because I shared his own passion for singing.'

Simran cupped her chin. *That is so different from my dad, or for that matter, any parent I've ever known.* 'Why did he do that?' She appeared puzzled.

Ankita looked wistfully at the picture of the short, slender man wearing a striped green kurta and pajamas. 'About ten years ago, when I was in my final year in high school, I'd gone over to Sonny's place. We were supposed to perform together at a rehearsal, later that evening. Sonny was changing in his room. Drona sir greeted me and offered me a cup of lemon tea. After a brief chitchat, he gave me a beautiful compliment.' She paused for effect. 'He'd heard me singing in a musical, two years earlier. He told me my voice was utterly enchanting and that I should become a theatre artiste.'

Simran clapped her hands in delight. 'You must have been thrilled!'

Ankita shook her head. 'Upon receiving the commendation, I blushed. However, instead of basking in its gorgeous sunlight, I doused myself with the cold shower of reality—how would I make ends meet if I were to follow my dreams? Reminding sir that there are millions of aspirants who end up wallowing in failure, penniless and destitute, I said that the pursuit of passion was too risky. I couldn't afford to take such a big risk in my life. To that, he said something I'll never forget.'

Simran furrowed her thick eyebrows. 'What did he say?'

Ankita smiled nostalgically. 'He told me, "The support of one's parents is vital for the pursuit of dreams. Your parents aren't forcing you to be an accountant, a banker, a lawyer, or something like that. You have the freedom to be who you want to be. Don't shortchange yourself by taking the secure path. Don't waste your precious freedom. You'll regret it someday."'

Simran's eyes lit up. *He wanted to live his dream through his son.*

Ankita put away the book of memories. 'With his father's untimely death, Sonny lost his best friend and guide. Slowly but surely, the passion inside him died. Today, all that's left are its embers. We don't do anything meaningful anymore. All we do now is argue over small things like bills, family events and household responsibilities.'

Simran shook her head. 'It seems your relationship has just lost its spark. But it's up to you to rediscover it.'

'The spark's gone.' Ankita paused and looked sadly past her friend at the only blank space on the wall. 'It will never come back. How can it? I'm not his father. I can never connect with him at a deep, spiritual level. I can never inspire him. I can never rekindle his passion for dance. How can I ever change him? And even if I could, should it really be my responsibility?'

The Rearview Mirror

At that very moment, the interior of the apartment transformed into the bedroom of a different flat. The colour of the paint changed from fuchsia to teal. The first-edition poster of *Grease*—framed and hung on the wall opposite the main door—

morphed into a painting of a woman looking out of a window. Ankita felt dizzy. 'Uh . . . where are we?'

Simran held her hand and gave her a reassuring gaze. 'In the bedroom of my house. Come with me. I want to show you something.'

'Huh! What? Where?' Ankita asked in confusion, scarcely believing this spooky juxtaposition of parallel lives.

Simran slowly moved her palms downwards. 'Calm down! I understand what you're going through because I've been through the same thing . . . a long time ago. There I am.' She paused and pointed to a younger version of herself—ten years younger, jet-black hair down to her shoulders, wearing a lime green salwar kameez, sitting at a desk typing furiously on a computer. 'Look at me. Wasn't I such a prude? That's ten years ago.' Simran giggled before her voice became serious. 'The second year of my marriage. The most difficult period of my life.'

Right then, a nanny with two wailing infants stormed into the room. 'Ma'am, the children haven't stopped crying since you retired after lunch. Can I leave them with you for some time?' Her voice was frantic, her eyes pleading.

Simran rolled her eyes and let out an annoyed huff. 'Come on, Manasi. Don't tell me you can't hold the fort for two hours, for God's sake! I've been with the twins for six hours straight. I'm really tired, and I have other important things to do.'

The babysitter ran out of the room with the children, a frightened look in her eyes.

Simran held Ankita's hand and narrated her domestic saga. 'I had two puppies right off the bat. But I was so young and had all these ambitions. A year into my marriage, I became scared. Did I tie the knot too early? Was this the end of my freedom? I worried I'd never be able to do those things that I really wanted.

Life would become a perpetual compromise, spent at the altar of duty and tradition.'

She closed her eyes and took a deep breath. Then, she showed Ankita a niche in the wall near the bedroom door. Lo and behold! There was Lord Ganesha, the Elephant God, garlanded with flowers and surrounded by incense sticks. Ankita was surprised by her friend's fervour, 'Gosh! I didn't know you were religious.'

With a matter-of-fact nod and pursed lips, Simran proceeded to say, 'You're right. I've never been into rituals or worship or things like that. I'm agnostic, but I view myself as spiritual. My in-laws, on the other hand, are extremely religious. My husband? Not so much. However, Gulshan—who'd chosen me over a dozen other eligible matches arranged for him—was desperate to assure his parents of my pious creds. So he insisted we fill our home with shrines, including one in our bedroom, of all places.'

'My God! I could never bear such encroachment on my private space!' Ankita shuddered.

'During that period,' Simran continued, 'my husband colluded with my in-laws to bind me in a straitjacket. I couldn't decide what to eat, when to wake up, who to meet—nothing. The list of restrictions was endless, nonsensical and humiliating. Nonetheless, I had to follow them, no questions asked. Two years into our marriage, I just couldn't take it.' She approached her younger self, who was typing away—unmindful of the spirits watching her.

Ankita could see the logo of the travel site yatra.com displayed on the monitor. There was an Indigo Airlines e-ticket on the screen. Startled by the words 'one-way' on it, Ankita blurted out in shock, 'What were you doing?'

Simran gave her friend a gloomy look. 'I was about to run away. I'd booked myself a ticket to Dharamshala. I'd decided to become a Buddhist and live in a monastery forever.'

The two women watched as young Simran prepared to click on the 'Confirm Purchase' button. Suddenly, she seemed hesitant and then a banner ad for an inter-corporate badminton competition caught her eye.

'Why did you stop?' Ankita tilted her head to the side.

Simran cleared her throat. 'As I was set to bid adieu to my oppressive life, I was gripped by a question. Did I hate *everything* about my life? I remembered the faces of my kids, full of smiles in the evenings during cartoon hour and grief in the mornings during the nappy change. I remembered the faces of my friends, bursting out in laughter when they surprised me with a party on my twenty-first birthday. I remembered the face of my husband, creased with earnest concern on the night I told him about my pregnancy before he dashed out into the empty streets at 3 a.m. to buy a painkiller. I remembered the faces of my in-laws, their eyes sparkling with joy on my wedding day as they bathed my feet with milk before I entered this home for the first time. I love them all, bag and baggage included. God bless their souls. I guess the only thing I really hated was the vacuum inside my soul. The vacuum no person, no object could fill. Freedom. The time and space to follow my passions and to be with the people who share them.

'Freedom was the one thing missing from my life. I wanted the freedom to be my true self . . . so, so badly. Yet, the pursuit of freedom for its own sake could incite a bushfire of opposition and leave a trail of misery in its wake.' Simran leaned closer to her friend. 'Could the pursuit of freedom be inclusive? Could my detractors turn into cheerleaders? What if my husband embraced his passion and became supportive of my desires? What if my in-laws accepted that a family could only be truly happy if each and every member is happy? I could then have it all. I could *really, really* have it all. Did I need to throw it *all* away?'

Ankita watched the alter ego's mouse hovering on the 'Register' button. 'You decided to take a chance on your husband . . .' She glanced at her inquiringly, 'You'd try to persuade him to change his mind instead, right?'

Simran nodded her head vigorously. 'Exactly. My hubby was an avid badminton player in high school. He'd given up that sport during the final year of college so he could focus on his career. But what if he took it up again? Would he then understand my desires? Would he then support my thirst for freedom? I didn't know. But I was prepared to take a chance.'

Their conversation was interrupted by the abrupt swinging of the door. A tall, well-built, bespectacled and bearded man in his mid-thirties entered the room. He was wearing a beige shirt with a red tie and dark, formal trousers. Ankita gasped and hid behind the curtains, but Simran pulled her out and gestured for her to remain silent. Oblivious to their presence, the gentleman ventured towards the desk. The young Simran glanced at the door with a startled expression, then swiftly clicked on the banner ad. The site for the badminton contest opened up.

'What are you working on?' The man rubbed his nose and looked at her suspiciously. The younger Simran showed him the details of the contest. 'Err . . . Gulshan! I wasn't expecting you back so soon. Anyway, now that you're home, let me show you something. Here! This is an ad for an inter-corporate badminton contest sponsored by Tata Steel. I thought you might like to join in. After all, you were such a good sportsman back in the day! I'm sure this will bring back happy memories. Generate positive vibes. Help you unwind after enduring the horrible stress from working for those heartless slave-owners at your bank for so long now.'

The man's eyes lit up. An approving smile appeared. 'Wow, so thoughtful of you! That's exactly what I need right now. But how did you come up with such an amazing idea? I think I mentioned my passion for badminton once . . . on our first date, if I recall correctly.'

The young woman squeezed his hand and lightly patted his shoulder. 'You think I'd forget something so beautiful, so deeply personal?'

The man looked fondly at the pictures of a group of corporate tycoons lifting a trophy on the webpage. 'That was such a long time ago.'

The younger Simran then stood on her toes and kissed him sensuously. She gazed into his eyes. 'This is not about winning or losing; it's not about proving a point. It's about being yourself. It's about letting go. You know you'll never be happy until that part of you has emerged into the light.'

He caressed her face with his fingertips. His voice quivered. 'Oh God! You've never looked at me with such love. You've never spoken to me with such candour. You've never touched me with such electricity. You've never kissed me with such passion. All this time, I've been doing my duties as a husband and a father, only to be at the receiving end of your cold, distant, uncaring gaze. I thought you had no feelings for me.'

Ankita felt a tear running down her face.

'Oh, Gul baby, I love you! I really do. I wouldn't have married you if I didn't, you fool! But you must understand . . . I haven't been myself this whole time. I've been feeling suffocated in our marriage because I can't do the things I love. I can't be with the people I care about. How can I give my all to you when my greater half is packed away?'

Gulshan took a step back, looking startled. His expression changed and he looked suddenly relieved. He sighed. 'Phew! Thank God! I thought you were cold because you didn't love me. Each night, I go to bed with this hollow, sinking feeling in my chest. A feeling of emptiness. Right now, I feel so light that I could fly.'

Simran embraced her husband as tightly as a recently released prisoner would. Gulshan broke down in tears. 'All this time, I should've shouldered your burden of my family's tradition. It's so unfair. I've held you back. All along, we've starved each other of love, of freedom. From now on, let's support one another to reach for the stars.'

Simran closed her eyes and caught her breath. Instantly, the two friends were transported back to Ankita's apartment, two years ago.

Redemption Redux?

'After that day, we never looked back.' Simran's eyes twinkled after the two regained their bearings from the time jump. 'Gulshan became so loving, so supportive. His new aura affected his friends, parents and colleagues in such a positive way that they changed their behaviour towards both of us completely. I was amazed to find them acting kind and supportive instead of cold, hectoring and judgmental. That's how I've nurtured my passion for music. That's how I've won back my freedom without having to compromise on my family's welfare. And it all started with a simple yet powerful word.'

'What word?' asked Ankita.

'Badminton.'

Simran held her friend's hand and persuaded her to open up about her feelings for Sonny. 'I have a feeling the passionate person he once was is still hiding inside. When that dude comes out, all hell will break loose.' She gave her friend a smile. 'How do I know? One look at his maniacal, Travolta-esque photos, and I just did. However, speaking from personal experience, you must recognize he's never going to make the first move. It's best you make the first move. Change starts from within. Maybe you should start by opening up first. Maybe that will make it easier for him.'

'"Maybe" is just not good enough for me to risk it,' Ankita said in a flat voice. 'He's long gone. I know he'll never open up to me. But if I open up to him, he'll pounce on the opportunity and humiliate me further.'

To Tame or Not to Tame?

The memory of that private, heart-to-heart exchange from two years ago, faded. Now back in the present, they were standing in Ankita and Sonny's living room, Pulkit and Sonny also there.

'Redemption is possible, but it's not in my hands,' Simran muttered. She glanced at Ankita. 'You guys should work out this issue candidly, in private. Pulkit and I shouldn't be here.'

Ankita recalled Simran's advice from two years earlier, and considered, 'It's true. Sonny is less likely than Gulshan to dramatically transform his mindset. But surely, he can be made to see that I'm also a living human being with my own burning dreams and desires. Surely, he'll understand that I'm never going to be a stationary prop in his life. He must understand the value of 'we' over 'me' because if something doesn't change between us right now, we won't make it.' Ankita looked at her friend with sadness.

We have to change the way we behave with each other. We have to learn to listen and not to talk over each other. We have to stop brushing our issues under the carpet, hoping and praying the debris will disappear and be forgotten forever. But the fact is indisputable—our approach of avoiding and glossing over the big issues is just not working. After three years of being stuck in this rut, it's time for us to open up. It's time to share our dreams and goals. It's time to talk about our values; about the things that are important to us. It's time to bare our souls to each other. To just talk. I do need to go first.

Ankita indicated to her guests that she wanted them to stay. 'You guys are my family, my circle of passion. I want you to stay.' She softened her combative tone. 'Sonny, don't you want to know why this rehearsal is so important to me?'

Sonny turned up his nose in contempt. 'Hmmph! Probably because you have to work hard and you can't handle the pressure. Or is it the diva inside you craving attention? You tell me. I'm not a psychologist.'

Ankita took a deep breath. *I can't let his hurtful comments rattle me.* She looked at him steadily, 'I know you want me to be a typical corporate worker wife someday. A dutiful VP's spouse who will attend formal company events as his excellent co-worker. Someone who will go out of her way to make your parents happy. A conformist who will shake hands with your friends, act gullible and agree with all their views, make small talk about their kids and the weather. But that person's just not me,' she said resolutely. She pointed at the TV den where the bemused Simran and Pulkit stood in front of the karaoke setup. 'This is me.'

'*You're* upset? What about me? Do you care about my feelings? How do you think I feel after I tell my family and friends for the umpteenth time that you aren't joining us at Khandala? How do you think I feel when I see them arm-in-arm with their companions, in a loving embrace, in perfect sync, while I sit there alone?' Sonny's volume increased with each rhetorical question. 'How do I justify your absence to them? By telling them that it's more important for you to rehearse your playback singing than to spend time with them? Am I supposed to blindly support your aspirations while you refuse to support mine? Where is the justice in that?'

Sonny advanced closer to Ankita. Simran lunged forward and stretched out her arms, creating a barrier between the two. 'It should be absolutely clear to you, Sonny, that she wants different things. She's a free spirit, not a caged bird. If you truly love her, you'll let her be. You'll support her passion and not try to mould her into your lifeless ball of clay.'

'How dare you poke your nose into our private lives!' Sonny's eyebrows furrowed together. The corners of his lips narrowed like the edges of a river before it descends into a whirlpool.

Simran gazed at him with an expression that could freeze a block of iron. 'That's not how your father would want to see you look.'

Sonny's eyes filled with anger and a vein popped in his neck. 'How dare you speak of him! You know nothing about him. You know nothing about *me*!' He advanced towards Simran, his right fist clenched. Frantic to save her mate from Sonny's violent temper, Ankita caught his fist in mid-air.

Simran glared at him and warned, 'You beast! Touch me even once, and I'll have you thrown into Tihar Jail immediately.'

Ankita gestured to her friend to calm down, then turned to Sonny. 'Simran's absolutely right, Sonny. That's exactly how you make me feel—every day of my life. Like a lifeless lump of clay.'

Sonny backed up a few steps and mumbled defensively, 'Err . . . I never meant to make you feel small. All I wanted was for us to be a team.'

'A team to work towards what?' Simran threw her arms to her sides. 'Your goal to be a corporate tycoon and make pots of money? Does she share it? If so, why does she lock herself in the bathroom every night and cry until she falls asleep?'

Sonny's expression betrayed the horror he felt at hearing about this revelation. 'What? I didn't know that . . .'

Ankita burst into tears. 'What's happened to us, Sonny? What have we become? I'm hurting so badly right now that I can't think straight anymore.'

Sonny's voice quaked. 'I . . . I had no idea you were hurting so much. None at all.' He approached her, his arms extended to offer a conciliatory embrace, but Simran prevented him from getting closer.

She hugged Ankita before pointing an angry finger at Sonny. 'She's been suffering for the last two years, and you had no idea?! Are you so caught up in that selfish, ugly world of yours that you never even saw her for who she is? Do you know who *you* are?'

Sonny felt his heart dropping ten flights to the basement of his tummy. *She's right. I've never even looked at myself in the mirror and answered that question. Who am I? Let me see. A leader of a small team of loan officers. A hoarder of sales leads. A manipulator of customers. A manager with an abrasive attitude. A boyfriend who's emotionally absent. That's all that I've been reduced to. But who am I meant to be?*

Death of Innocence

Right then, the plush sofa set from Stanley's morphed into an antique table and chair set from the Mumbai wholesale market, Chor Bazaar. The framed poster of *Batman* in the TV den turned into that of the 1975 film *Sholay*.

'I'm home,' Sonny called. Then he shuddered in shock upon recognizing the living room of the place where he grew up. Astonished and disoriented by the unexpected time travel, Sonny struggled to maintain a balanced gait. 'My parents' cuckoo clock?' he noticed. Suddenly, a pesky mechanical bird popped out from its hideout to screech, 'It's 3 p.m.'

'That's the one Uncle Deepak got us from Scotland when I was two,' he said in amazement. 'But where is everybody?' he asked.

As if in response to his words, the outlines of two figures etched themselves onto the chairs in front of him like on an animation storyboard, and two saucers magically appeared on the table.

'What the hell!' Sonny yelled, feeling as befuddled as a character from *The Twilight Zone*. Seconds later, the two figures had been fully formed. 'It's my father and me. I was so young,' Sonny said, his jaw-dropping. At that moment, as if to further bewilder him, a calendar appeared on the wall and flipped open to the month of July, where a single date was circled in red. 'This can't be happening. 4th July 2006? That was seventeen years ago!' he exclaimed. The memory of that day played out in front of him like a movie.

The younger Sonny sobbed hysterically before his father. 'Oh, God! We ranked last among all the contestants. I'm so ashamed. I'm a miserable failure,' he cried, his tears drenching a bandana clutched between his fingers.

His father, Drona, reached out his hand to protect the accessory. 'Son, the judges rated you poorly. But the 500 viewers who saw you perform at the inter-school dance contest today thought you're a star. Now, I can stay and console you all night while you pour your heart out. But I can't just sit still and watch you sully the symbol of your hard work. Let me keep this bandana for now.'

Sonny looked at him like an athlete throwing a tantrum at his coach. 'I don't understand you. Why do you keep feeding me all these lies about my talent? Why do you encourage me with false hope? Today, I got jolted back to reality. It was brutal. The competition's insane. I thought I was the best in my school. But that's like being a large rat inside a sixty foot construction pipe. In the city swamp, there are massive alligators who'll eat me for a snack. This is hopeless! I'm better off quitting this pipe dream and doing something safe like accountancy or computer science. At least then I won't be starving in a Dharavi slum.'

Drona raised his arms like a football referee. 'Sonny, don't be so hard on yourself. The performance standard at the city level is definitely high. But it's not unattainable. Plus, you aren't too far from that level. A little more practice, a lot more devotion, and you'll be ranked among the top three pretty soon. I know it. Plus, you have the secret sauce no one else does—your chemistry with Ankita. It's way off the charts. Anyone can see that. Stop focusing on just the negatives.'

'Oh, come on! You know Ankita was carrying the show. Everyone in the stands was cheering for her. Don't you realize how humiliated I feel?'

His father nodded. 'Your pride's hurt. But ask yourself: what's worse—to be outclassed, or to be carried on someone's shoulders?'

Sonny responded churlishly, 'Sometimes, I just don't get you.' He couldn't admit that the question had confused him.

Drona wiped his glasses on the fabric of his kurta. 'Anger and disappointment are twin brothers. If they both jump on your back together, you should have the sense to kick at least one of them away.'

Sonny's tone reeked of disgust, 'I have no time for your aphorisms. I'm going to burn my dance memorabilia today and dedicate my life to something that I can banish from my mind each night.' He tossed the bandana to Drona and stared glumly into space.

Drona smiled for a moment as he folded the headband and then placed it in his pocket. Leisurely, he sipped on his cup of herbal tea. After a few minutes of uneasy silence, Sonny sneered. 'So, what's your inspirational catchphrase this time?'

With a half-smile, his father replied, 'Son, failure's just the begin—' Suddenly, he stopped short and his face turned white.

'Dad, what's wrong?' Sonny grew nervous. Meanwhile, the present-day Sonny caught in this weird space-time warp, closed his eyes and groaned, 'Oh God! I can't watch this.'

The old man gasped for air and his hands trembled. The cup and the saucer crashed onto the floor and smashed into many pieces. Young Sonny realized that something was badly amiss and leapt forward to help his father. Before he could support his father's frail body, Drona fell off the chair and smacked his head on the floor with a hollow thud.

'Dad! Dad! Wait, I'm getting help!' screamed Sonny. He ran to the kitchen. There was nobody there. The cook and the cleaner had left for the day. He dashed for the cordless phone. Frantically, he dialled the emergency helpline. 'Please! Please! Help us! My father's had a heart attack, I think. Please send an ambulance right now. We need help! Now! This is urgent!' He waited for the operator's response. But all he heard was a soft static sound. His anxious eyes roved around the apartment and fell on a picture of himself with his parents on a vacation at a hill resort in Shimla. They were all twenty years younger in it. He looked at his mother's image and said, 'If only you were here!'

Phoenix or Mirage?

Right then, the interiors changed and he was jolted back into the present. He repeated the existential question he'd posed to himself just before his space-time dalliance: 'Who am I meant to be?'

Sonny's introspection was interrupted by the sound of the doorbell. He opened the door to see that, for some reason, the Swiggy delivery boy had returned.

'Sir, you didn't tip me for the order. The bulk of my earnings come from commissions and tips. I hope you understand,' he said, deferentially.

Sonny nodded his head and tipped him ₹300 using the app. The deliveryman's phone pinged, notifying him of the same and he beamed at the amount, walking off with a spring in his step towards the elevator. While he waited for the lift to arrive, he hummed the song '*Ek ladki ko dekha toh aisa laga*' ('I saw a girl once, and it made me feel so . . .').

When he heard the tune through the open door, Sonny froze momentarily. 'Wait . . . I know that voice,' Sonny whispered to himself.

He swung open the door as Ankita asked, 'Hey! Is everything okay?'

The delivery boy was at the far end of the hallway, waiting for the elevator. His voice majestically crooned the song from the Bollywood movie, *1942: A Love Story*. He spotted Sonny from the corner of his eye and smiled.

'That song. That voice. That day,' Sonny whispered, trying to remember a very special day in his life. The pieces of the puzzle from his memory pieced themselves together onto the delivery boy's face to form his father's visage. 'It's you. It can't be,' Sonny gasped in disbelief.

At that moment, the surroundings and its various characters froze in different states of suspended animation. *What's happening?*

The delivery boy was also motionless. *Is this a new virus? Has everybody been incapacitated by a deadly chemical weapon?* Sonny panicked, his mind conjuring various alarming possibilities. *But if that's the case, why am I still awake?* he pondered, dismissing the conspiracy theories. As he tried to arrive at a logical explanation, a sphere of white light enveloped the delivery boy.

'What's going on?!' Sonny furrowed his eyebrows. However, there was no reply from the Swiggy employee or anyone else. Instead, a radiant, tubular figure emerged from the delivery boy's body.

'What the hell!' Sonny shouted, about to make a run for it. However, the bright tube changed into the outline of a human figure, reminding him of his earlier quantum escapade. 'Wait!' he shouted. 'I've seen this before.' Then, before his eyes, it transformed into the figure of a person: a man wearing a lime-green churidar kurta. 'Papa!' Sonny exclaimed in shock.

The incandescent glow faded as the full form of Sonny's father appeared. There he was, standing right in front of Sonny, in the pink of health, wearing the same clothes he'd worn on his last day on earth—and looking not a day older. Meanwhile, everything and everyone else remained frozen, including the delivery boy, who continued to stare at the elevator door without blinking, his right index finger planted on the button of the lift.

'You're alive! How's that possible?' Sonny shrieked.

The old man removed his glasses and wiped them on his kurta. 'I never left this world,' he replied with a smile, putting them back on.

'Huh? What do you mean?'

'I only left *your* world.' Drona's eyes twinkled.

Unable to fathom the otherworldly logic, Sonny broke down in tears. 'Oh, God! I thought you were dead. All this time, I thought you were dead. If only you were here, I could have been somebody.'

His old man approached him and touched his face. The sensation felt as real to Sonny as any contact with the living would. 'You're real. You're here,' he cried with sorrow and joy.

Putting his hand on the boy's shoulders, Drona explained his current existence in the universe. 'I left your world because you'd banished me from your heart. I left your world because I died in your dreams. Nonetheless, I am still present in the universe. I am here, everywhere and nowhere.'

Sonny gasped. 'Are you God? Is this heaven?'

Drona burst into laughter. 'Hahaha! I'm definitely not a supreme being. But I've merged with Him at the origin of the universe. I'm now a part of the celestial energy chain that shapes and connects all beings.'

Perplexed but mesmerized, Sonny asked, 'Why are you here now?'

The old man plucked the stationary flower out of midair, closed his eyes and inhaled its fragrance. As the scent of the rose permeated his being, he replied, 'I want to show you something.'

'What do you want to show me?' Sonny shrugged his shoulders. 'I'm dreaming, right? I'd be a fool if I didn't believe that.'

Drona shook his head. 'That's not it. Quite the opposite, actually.' Sonny held his breath and stared at his father with anticipation. The old man then placed his hand on his son's temple and said quietly, 'For the first time in your life, you're fully awake.'

As Drona's hand touched his forehead, a not-so-old-but-forgotten memory was triggered in Sonny's head. His mind rewound to a time when he was in high school, fifteen years earlier. He'd just attended the annual Parent-Teacher Association meeting with his father. After the event, Sonny went down to the school canteen with his dad. It had been bustling with people ordering tea, samosas, patties and other snacks. Amidst the chaos, Chef Shoaib Murtaza—a portly, bald fellow in his fifties, with a bushy moustache, who was famous for his mouth-watering munchies—had been entertaining the crowd with jokes and funny stories. A kid then drew people's attention to another of Shoaib's formidable talents, 'Shoaib! Sing something. Please!' With a gaggle of students egging him on, the multitalented canteen cook burst into song.

'*Ek Ladki ko dekha toh aisa laga . . .*'

His melodious voice reverberated across the canteen and filled the hallways of the school like a majestic orchestra at an opera house. Eyes sparkling, his fifteen-year-old son also joined him. With the father-son duo in full chorus mode, another student made a different request. 'How about a number from our dance-meister, Sonny?'

'Oh no! I can't,' an embarrassed Sonny refused, accompanied by a chorus of 'Oh No!'. Sonny slinked away from the canteen.

Suddenly, a third voice joined the duo, making him stop in his tracks. The voice was his father's. To the amazement of everyone present, Sonny's father—who'd been silently observing the incidents—spontaneously picked up from the next line of the song.

'*Jaise khilta gulaab, jaise shayar ka khwaab . . .*' ('Like a blooming rose, like a poet's dream . . .')

Then more people joined in the chorus. Before long, nearly fifty parents and teachers were singing along. At that moment, Shoaib's son turned on an old audio cassette player kept in the canteen for the children's merriment, and played a popular dance number. Sonny relented and together with Drona, broke into a dance to the track, their bodies in perfect harmony with the voices of Shoaib and his father. Then, to everyone's surprise, the canteen manager's son joined Sonny on the makeshift dance floor, adeptly in step with his dance moves and egged on by the ever-expanding, appreciative crowd.

Later, as the cheers of the crowd faded, Sonny once again found himself face-to-face with his father in the hallway of his world that was frozen in time. With a quivering voice, he stammered, 'That day . . . that day . . . that was the only time in my life when we performed together.'

Drona gave a sly wink. 'Do you see the truth now?'

Sonny burst into tears and hugged the old man. 'I understand. I finally understand. You died with my own soul.'

Drona crossed his fingers. 'You tried to banish me from your consciousness because you were too afraid to follow your passion without my guidance. But, do you want to know the real truth?' As Sonny looked at his father nonplussed, Drona opened his palm to reveal a heap of white dust. He blew the powder into his son's nostrils, and smiled. 'I've always been within you.'

Sonny immediately felt woozy. Everything shook, swivelled and rotated like the seats in a 4D movie theatre. Then, everything and everyone—except for Drona and Sonny—transmuted into illuminated doughnuts before merging into a giant hemisphere of light. Finally, Drona transformed into a skein of light himself, and got sucked into the glowing object. The gargantuan sun-like thing then exploded. A massive trail of energy emanated from the sphere like a river of lava and reached Sonny.

To his horror, Sonny felt his entire body turn to dust. His breath faded. The paranormal magma moved further up his body, causing an asphyxiation-like feeling. His voice lowered to a whisper. 'I see you now,' he gasped. Magically, the fiery trail turned into ice. 'I believe in you,' his voice started cracking like that of a man in his dying moments. At the sound of those words, the ice became vapour and entered his nostrils, rendering him unconscious.

When he finally awoke in his 3D world, Sonny stepped out of the apartment and shouted, 'My papa sang that song ten years ago at our school canteen.'

The delivery boy nearly fell over with surprise. 'That song—that was *my* father's song,' he stuttered.

Joining the dots in his mind, Sonny clicked his fingers. 'You're the son of Shoaib, the cook at our school canteen. It was you singing with my father and your dad that day. It was you who danced with me,' he said, incredulous.

The Swiggy delivery man nodded. 'Yes. I'm Kalim, Shoaib's son.'

'How's your father? Is he well?' Sonny asked, fondly.

'He's alive. But he has throat cancer from smoking. His voice is gone. He's so ill that he can't work anymore. So I've been supporting my family for the last few years, doing various odd jobs,' Kalim said with resignation.

A look of sympathy filled Sonny's eyes. 'That's terrible. But at least he's alive. The same cannot be said of my father.'

Shocked, the delivery boy looked down on the floor, unable to express his condolences. When he finally mustered the strength to look his client in the eye, he saw that tears had welled up in Sonny's.

After an uncomfortable silence punctuated by suppressed sniffles, Sonny requested in a breaking voice, 'Can you please sing that for me again?'

That was Kalim's cue to pick up from where he'd left off. Hearing his haunting voice, Ankita came out of the flat and started to sing. Pulkit and Simran also joined in. Soon, all five of them were immersed in the song. Sonny called a time-out and rushed back into the flat, hurrying out with a portable speaker. Asking everyone to continue, he played a remix track and started break-dancing to it.

Amazed, Ankita remarked, 'What! Where did that come from?'

'It never went away. It just got lost in the maze,' Sonny replied with a wink.

By then, the noise had spread to the other apartments on their floor. The neighbours came out to see what was going on. Ankita looked at the stern, no-nonsense face of the residential committee's president. 'Oh my God! There's Mr Saxena. We'll be hauled up by the building association for violating noise restrictions,' Ankita whispered in fear.

But instead of pointing fingers at them, the grumpy old man joined in the fun, matching Sonny and Kalim step-for-step.

'You didn't actually think running the association is my true calling, huh?' he ribbed.

Before long, a queue of residents had formed behind them as they danced and sang their way down the steps of the building and onto the community lawn. Ankita and Sonny later invited Kalim, Pulkit, Simran, Mr Saxena and several other closeted dance buffs from their building to dine with them. Over the sumptuous meal of biryani, they decided to form a musical troupe of their own and christened it 'The Biryani Band'.

Coalescence

A year later, Ankita was lying in a private room at the Lokmanya Tilak Hospital, recovering from an operation. Sonny sat next to her, holding her hand, their eyes glued to the TV set, where a repeat telecast of the recently held Filmfare Awards was on—they had missed the original broadcast because of the operation. After the host announced, 'Here's The Biryani Band, India's hottest musical sensation,' the group was seen performing their hits that had taken social media by storm that year.

'Ankita, isn't it amazing how far we've come since that day? The day we had that blow-up?' Sonny kissed her forehead, scarcely believing the magical turn their lives and their relationship had taken in the past twelve months.

Ankita glanced at her wedding ring fondly. *Yes, we've come further than we'd ever expected. If someone had told me then that we'd be married in six months and that our belief in each other would skyrocket, I would never have believed that person.*

Sonny raised her hand to his mouth and kissed the ring. 'I'm so happy I listened.'

'Listened to whom?' Anika asked, a puzzled expression on her face.

Sonny let out a sardonic laugh. 'To myself. That one guy I've been shutting out my whole life.'

A knock on the door interrupted their conversation. A nurse entered, holding a baby in her arms. She handed the child over to Ankita. 'Congratulations, Mr and Mrs Kapoor. Here's your son.'

Right then, the door exploded open and several familiar figures barged into the room. 'Look at the little one. He looks just like Ankita,' Pulkit said.

'But his eyes and his mouth look just like Sonny's,' Kalim gushed, holding the little baby's finger.

'I can't wait to take you under my wing and put you in your proper place,' Mr Saxena said, mimicking an ancient, crusty professor.

Simran waved her fingers at him. 'Oh! Stop it! You'll give him a lifelong phobia of dance.'

Unnerved by the noise, the baby whimpered. The nurse, afraid that the din would overwhelm the newborn, ordered the group to clear out. As the band members departed from the room, the baby started crying hysterically.

'He must be hungry. Why don't you feed him?' suggested the nurse. However, the baby refused to partake of his mother's breast milk.

'Wait! Everybody, stay! Let's try singing to him. I'll go first!' She burst into the song that had started it all. As the lyrics of

'*Ek Ladki ko dekha*' filled the room, the baby's mood changed and he began to gurgle. The nurse looked confused and Ankita squeezed Sonny's hand, 'He was missing passion and human connection like his parents, not milk.'

REFLECTION: OPEN UP TO BUILD TRUST

Do you feel stressed because your aspirations are in conflict with your partner's?

Life constantly throws us into uncomfortable situations. These are moments when we have to choose between doing what we really want, doing nothing, or doing something to satisfy others. Our actions in these moments determine the future direction of our lives and the state of our happiness. If we choose the second or third option, it is usually because we are driven by fear or the struggle to survive. Our actions involve compromising on who we really are. These compromises ultimately lead to a state of inner distress in the long term—a state we constantly try to mask from others. Splitting our beings, we put on a happy face for the world, and an unhappy one we only see in the mirror when we are alone; this only deepens our dissatisfaction over time. I don't have to go far—my own marital problems attest to this fact!

I was married for ten years. During that time, doing nothing or doing something for the satisfaction of my ex-wife were always my go-to choices for conflict resolution. For the entirety of our relationship, we never spoke candidly about the issues that really mattered: our dreams, goals and ambitions. For the first half of our marriage, this felt inconsequential. I was enjoying the high-flying life of a corporate tycoon and wanted to share it with her. My focus was on keeping her content so that I could project an image of stability to both myself and the world. To achieve this objective, I did everything possible to make our lives comfortable.

She, meanwhile, dutifully focused on managing the house and maintaining our relations with friends and family. We never sat down to talk about the future or other important topics. We were so busy with the perfunctory inanities of daily life that we coexisted without ever taking the time to build a real connection. However, this inauthentic approach only masked the rot that had set in our bond. In the seventh year of our marriage, we finally settled down permanently into a new apartment. One day, we became embroiled in a huge fracas—a fight over a rather trivial issue. I wanted her to attend a cocktail party hosted by an organization of young business leaders with me. But she didn't want to. Soon, the conflict escalated into a full-blown argument and she vocalized aloud, for the first time ever, her distaste for 'posers, sycophants and phonies'.

'I want a simple life . . . a nice backyard, a cozy home, a few close friends. I don't want this life in this shithole of a place,' she yelled.

I was mortified. I'd thought both of us wanted to be jet-setting globalists until then, and that we attended such events to network and expand our horizons. At that moment, it became as clear as FIJI water that we wanted totally different things from life. Our gulf could not be bridged. Chastened by the revelation, we spent our first night in separate bedrooms. That became the first of many—signalling the end of our union.

Shortly after my divorce, I was fortunate to meet a wonderful woman. We sparked off an amazing connection right from the outset. This time, I was determined not to repeat the mistakes of the past. I opened up about my goals and dreams, and allowed her the room to do the same. When we discovered we wanted the same things, we became more comfortable with sharing deeply personal stories and facts, things we had never shared with anyone, not even close friends. As openness took root in our relationship, we were able to build a sturdy foundation of trust, one that has only deepened and solidified with each passing day. A decade hence, as I look back at how far we've come, I realize the initial bedrock of trust has been crucial in helping us navigate the stresses and tribulations of life. It enabled us to negotiate the uncertainties of a long-distance relationship. We have tremendous faith and belief in each other, and our love for one another has only deepened as a result.

Thus, based on my personal experience, I can confidently say inaction and compromise are not viable in relationships. At the same time, though, we recognize there's nothing harder than being open about our thoughts and feelings. How do we counter their threatening looks, icy glares and aggressive body language when we confront our partner with a jet stream of our heartfelt words and emotions? How do we overcome that knot that forms in our stomach when we think of how they might react negatively to our vulnerabilities? How do we stay committed to the truth in the face of nasty judgment, and possibly violent reprisal? Before answering these questions, we have to understand the root cause of our fears.

We are afraid of losing the other person because we are possessive about them, as if they were a treasured object, rather than a human being. However, we forget we are all independent spirits belonging to the universe, not to anyone in particular. Our journey of life is unique with the common purpose of ultimately merging our consciousness with the universe. This journey of 'attaining oneness' is a deeply internal and personal one. It entails following a spiritual path of one's calling—such as the pursuit of passions, the practices of any religion, meditation practices, daily activities of life—without any attachment to the result. When we accept the above statements, we realize the following:

We all have the power to choose and act, leading our own journey of growth. When we make choices and take actions based on a higher purpose or inner calling, it builds confidence, letting us stay present without getting too caught up in the results. This mindset helps us handle challenges that come our way.

Going back to the characters of the story in the previous chapter, Ankita knew in her heart that music was not just a hobby for her. It was her passion. The pathway to inner fulfillment, not just external rewards. With Simran's help, she realized that in order to be true to herself, she had to stand up for her passion and emphasize its meaning and importance to Sonny. This realization bolstered her sense of purpose and helped her remain staunch while defending her principles in front of her partner. At the same time, she was also able to dilute her ego, listen to Sonny's point of view and communicate her true feelings to him. Over time, her authentic actions injected positivity into the environment and gave Sonny the comfort of opening up. Similarly, if we follow our passion without attachment to the result, we will deepen the connection with our inner self by overcoming fear and lust for personal gain, diluting our ego and becoming more open overall. This will not only earn us the trust of our partners but also help to create a more positive environment. This is why it's necessary to do the more difficult thing which is better for the long term.

If we choose the first option and express what's truly in our hearts, we might face resistance from others, even our loved ones. But if we stay committed to this path—the path of authenticity—we feel a sense of empowerment coursing through our veins throughout our journey. At the same time, our partner will also feel closer to us, knowing that we've given them a part of us no one else has. The surge of self-belief enables us to take on the steeper challenges that lie ahead. We will thus be able to lead our lives with confidence, fearlessness and a clear conscience. This transformation of our mindsets leads to happiness in the long run.

Nowhere does the challenge to be an authentic person surface more often than in the sphere of relationships. Since we spend the most significant moments of our lives with our companions, it's important that we bond in heart, mind and spirit. However, this won't happen on its own, even when there is a deep connection. We have to work to make this bond deeper and everlasting.

The first step is to work on ourselves to gain self-awareness. To do this, we must introspect to understand the barriers to our evolution and discover our passions, values, needs and other facets of our identity. But self-awareness alone is not enough. It must translate into meaningful and disciplined action. Once we have gained self-awareness, we must behave with each other in a manner that's consistent with our identity. We must talk honestly and openly about our dreams, values and needs. This may cause conflict, but over time, could also lead to the discovery of a common purpose—a purpose that unites us and propels us forward towards the accomplishment of that goal. As we move in sync, we earn our partner's trust and understanding.

If we succeed at this, it will surely lead to a deeper love forming due to the realization that we're both sailing in the same boat; a love so powerful, it can weather the worst of storms and uplift us to reach for the stars. That's what we learn from Sonny and Ankita's story. They did the hard thing and bridged a deep fissure in their relationship, coming out stronger and happier by connecting with and expressing their authentic selves. Learn how they did it and you will believe you can, too.

2

OVERCOMING PARENTAL PRESSURE

UNDERSTANDING PARENTAL PRESSURE

In our daily lives, we have to deal with people who have power over us. These individuals can be our friends, family members, colleagues, as well as influential figures in society or industry. To serve their own interests, they may often railroad us into doing things that are out of sync with our dreams, goals and preferences. This pressure can be devastating for us because it can force us to lead a life that's not aligned with our true calling.

Family pressure is one such example of psychological force exerted by people—in one's circle—to further their own interests. Because of family pressure, one is often forced or manipulated into adopting a way of life that's not of one's choosing, getting stuck in an unsatisfying career, relationship or lifestyle. Parental pressure is the most potent form of family pressure because parents are the 'heads' of the family and hold the greatest sway over our lives. Due to their roles as breadwinners and emotional pillars, they exercise enormous influence over their children's life choices. Their authority permeates every aspect of their children's lives—lifestyle, education, careers, travel, friendship, finance and romance. Parental authority is difficult to challenge because it's been firmly entrenched in the minds of people over centuries through various institutions. This social conditioning compels a person to seek their approval when making important life decisions. Should they refuse to support their child's aspirations, denying them either funds or permission or both, or even simply voicing their disapproval, children tend to feel pressured to compromise on their original intent to win that approval, accompanied by guilt for not acquiescing.

The protagonist of this next story suffers grave emotional hardship because of parental pressure. Will she overcome this barrier and find joy?

THE DAISYLAND MURDERS

The relationship between Birgitte Larsen and her daughter was polarized by the differences in their identities. These differences seemed insurmountable, and it seemed only death could bridge the gap between their souls.

'Freya, have you heard back from the admissions councils?' Birgitte glanced at her daughter as she poured herself a bowl of cereal. 'All day, parents in my Orestad High Facebook group have been posting messages about their kids' college admission results.'

The eighteen-year-old woman was engrossed in her cell phone and didn't look up at her mother. 'All of them rejected me. But there's no reason to despair yet because one result is yet to come.' A thick layer of sarcastic butter permeated her voice and her head bobbed up and down like a rudderless boat.

Birgitte set her bowl of cereal down on the countertop with a thud. 'Which one? You applied for social work studies at five colleges: Copenhagen, Aarhus, Aalborg, USD, and—'

Freya nodded. 'Skive College.'

Birgitte looked a tad disappointed. 'That was your last choice . . . Well, I suppose you'll get in. After all, *everyone* gets in there.' Her voice sounded condescending.

Freya looked at her mother with a bitter expression and raised her voice. 'All I'm good at is doing drugs and sleeping around with degenerates. I'll never live up to your "Mrs Suburbia" role model: a loyal company worker, faithful wife, or whatever dolled-up paragon of Mrs Denmark you have inside your head. I'm a real disappointment to you, aren't I?'

She's a few short steps away from being permanently ostracized by civil society! That said, I just remembered . . . Birgitte rifled through the contents of her handbag to check whether she was carrying an important document for a meeting with the branch manager of Danske Bank later that day. She found the letter bearing her official letterhead and the subject line, 'Request for the release of government college funds for Freya Larsen'. She noticed there was no other document stapled to the letter and realized she had forgotten Freya's progress report and recommendation from her school's principal for the 3.30 p.m. meeting with the banker, Mr Jacobsen.

Birgitte frowned at the number of Fs on Freya's progress report. She quickly scanned through Principal Andersen's comments, which would be the focus of the discussion with the banker. The events from three months earlier floated in her consciousness. That day when she prized open a can of rotten secrets. The day she received a phone call from the principal about her daughter's progress report.

Anderson's tone was heavy with a sense of resignation. 'Freya has persistently underachieved in academics throughout her school career. This is because her attitude towards studies is lackadaisical. She is aloof towards her peers and hostile to her teachers. I am concerned that she's developing antisocial tendencies. Several times this year, she was caught with drugs in her locker. She was also spotted kissing an alleged drug dealer on school grounds. Her lack of interest in any discipline—academic or creative—is unusual for a student at this high-performing academy.' Andersen continued, 'There is a silver lining, though. Last month, she volunteered for three days at the Cultural Assimilation Centre, teaching refugees about the history and language of Denmark. A relevant initiative—both politically and socially—I must say. So I feel she'd be well-suited for a career in social work. I recommend she graduate in this discipline.'

Later that day, Birgitte had confronted Freya about the damaging report. 'The principal said that you're doing drugs and associating with dealers,' she said in the sternest voice she could muster.

Freya shrugged her shoulders. 'He's biased against me.'

Birgitte held out a packet of weed and said, 'You're lying! I found this under your mattress. Do you realize that you could be sent to a juvenile detention centre? Are you aware that I could lose my job?'

Freya rolled her eyes as if it were a trite matter. 'So what? Jail would be a whole lot better than living with you.' She glared at her mom accusatorially. 'Over there, no one will stop me from associating with the inmates I want to meet. Or from participating in the activities and causes that I care about.'

Birgitte snapped back, 'How can you say that I stop you from doing these things?'

'Mom, do you deny that you stop me every time I want to break the rigid monotony of school life? Last year, you didn't sign my parental approval letter authorizing me to travel to Brazil and join the protest movement against the destruction of the Amazon. Six months ago, you refused to accompany me to a cultural awareness dinner organized by the Islamic Society of Denmark.' Freya stuck out a finger for each accusation. 'Last month, you refused to host my transgender friend and her family for dinner. These were all important issues to me—all important people in my life. I lost the only friends I had and all my goodwill because of your narrow-minded provinciality. At least be honest and admit that you don't approve of my life choices.'

'Approve of your life choices?' Birgitte scoffed. 'Certainly not. Not when you lack the maturity to distinguish between a war zone and a picnic garden . . . between the fact of Islamic radicalization and the fiction of assimilation . . . between cheap self-publicity and genuine compassion.' She grabbed a framed picture off the mantlepiece—a photo of Freya snuggling up to a young man with olive skin, a goatee and dreadlocks—and threw it at her daughter. 'How can I value your judgment when you can't distinguish between a drug dealer and a saint?'

Freya managed to catch her precious photo with one hand. Her voice was shrill with resentment. 'You always look down on me. You don't approve of the man I want to be with. You don't approve of the things I want to do in my life. Well, you can just stuff your supercilious attitude up your ass. I want to do great things. I want to be around exciting people. And you can't stop me from leading the life I want.'

That day floated away from her memory. Birgitte reiterated to herself, 'This letter is her salvation from a life of crime and delinquency.'

Freya saw her mom carefully stapling the document to the funds release letter, and couldn't resist the urge to remind her, 'If you forget that, they won't release my college fund and I'll turn into your worst nightmare. A single druggie, a jobless bum.'

Birgitte turned away so she wouldn't escalate the disagreement and slipped her Copenhagen Police Department badge into her front pocket. Right then, the doorbell rang.

'Letter from Skive College,' the mailman announced, handing the document to Freya, who perused it while Birgitte held her breath.

Freya heaved a sigh of relief and turned back to face her mom. 'You should be relieved that I won't be turning into a welfare leech.'

'Or a radical troublemaker,' quipped the mailman before departing.

'Phew! The news has come at the right time,' Birgitte said. 'It will make it much easier to secure the grant.' She donned her jacket and clipped her gun to the rear pocket of her trousers. Preoccupied with the upcoming day at her job as lead investigator, Birgitte caught a glimpse of her daughter's sullen face and realized she'd been really mean to her.

She put her arms around Freya. 'Honey, I didn't mean what I said. You know that. It's just that I've been so stressed, trying to solve the murder of . . .' Her voice trailed off.

'My dad, I know,' Freya said, 'and I really and truly admire you for your relentlessness. But you've got to wake up and smell the coffee. There've been no new leads in that case for ten years. No clues, no new suspects. The police department is about to close the case. Isn't it time to move on?'

With a glint of bitterness in her eyes, Birgitte retorted, 'You were barely two years old when he died . . . his body was sliced and diced and packed in an ice container like a consignment of meat and deposited in a carton along Highway 21. Just before Holbæk,' she said, her voice rising in volume with each phrase. 'That was the long, dark winter of 2003. You have no memory of him. How can you possibly understand the depth of my sorrow? How can you possibly understand my need to solve this crime?'

Birgitte glanced at a framed picture of a happy young family—her husband, baby Freya and herself—on a vacation in the Norwegian fjords, and struggled to contain her tears. 'As long as I'm alive, I'll never abandon my quest to bring my husband's murderers to justice.'

Freya moved her arms up and down as if she was trying to shake open something. 'Why must you cling to the past? Nothing will bring him back. You must accept that his death was bound to happen.'

Birgitte clenched her teeth. 'Bound to happen? How dare you say that!'

Freya dispassionately recited the facts she had memorized over the years, like a television newscaster. 'After his body was identified, a search of his emails revealed he'd actively participated in the drug smuggling activities of the same ring he'd been assigned to bust. According to *Politiken*, he was planted as an undercover agent by the police department to bust a national drug syndicate that was linked to a global cartel. However, he became attracted to the twin prospects of earning money from the drug trade and accolades from the PD for pulling off a few minor heists. He played both sides.' She stared at her mother coldly. 'You know that's true.'

Those words pierced Birgitte's heart like a medieval joust. She studied her deceased husband's face in the photo and then whispered, 'Magnus, why did you do this? Why did you drag the family name through the mud? To this day, I have no answers.'

Despite knowing that Freya's facts were indisputable, Birgitte slapped her. 'In your eyes, he's a snake . . . a piece of sordid history, not a living, breathing person. You never knew him. That's why you can remain so detached and unemotional. That's why you swallowed everything that the press reported. But you are forgetting one thing. He was and will always be my husband. And I—' Tears rolled down her cheeks as she said this, 'I loved him. I loved him so much. You'll never understand.' Brigitte buried her face in her hands and sobbed.

Freya groaned in frustration upon seeing her mother continue to romanticize a proven criminal. *I can't bear to see her holding so much grief from the loss. Her sorrow is so great she can't lead a full life. In her mind, he's still alive and she needs to find him.* Freya mentally ticked off the negative results of her mother's obsession. *She doesn't want to date others or pursue other cases. She's rejected so many opportunities to further her career over the years because all she wants to do is solve this case. And she's turned me into a living sponge for her grief by making my life miserable . . . by manipulating the direction of my life . . . by discouraging me from meeting people I wanted to connect with. Magnus, you fucking bastard! You're responsible for turning her into a controlling monster. You must have manipulated her heart while you were alive. I hate you.*

Before Freya could articulate a response, Birgitte looked up. 'He'll always be your father. Don't you ever forget that!' she shouted before storming out of the house.

Freya waited for the sound of her mother's car speeding away before she studied the framed photo Birgitte had glanced at earlier. 'Dad, I'm sorry I said all these horrible things about you to myself,' she said to the image while staring into her father's intense blue eyes. 'In truth, I don't feel anything for you. I hold no love, hate, anger . . . nothing in my heart for you, personally. But I'm angry at you because of what my mom's become. I'm angry because she may have behaved differently with me had you not succumbed to your greed. Perhaps she wouldn't pressure me to follow the safe path of academic pursuit, a conventional life with marriage and children, a life of safety, comfort and conformity. A life that's not true to my calling. What sort of life do I want? I don't even know. But if you were around, perhaps she'd encourage me to find my own way. Perhaps she'd support me in quenching my thirst to see the world, to meet people who are not like me, to lead an unconventional life. Perhaps she'd be my guide in exploring who I want to be.'

She took out a totem she always carried with her for making difficult choices. *Anyway, all that is wishful thinking. The reality is that I'm on my own, and I need to chart my own way. Mom can stuff her hopes and aspirations for me down her stinking toilet. Her plans don't matter to me because finally, I've found my path. Now that she has the paperwork, the principal's recommendation and the admission letter, securing my college funds from the government will be a breeze. Tough luck, I won't be using it quite for the purpose that she intends!* Freya's lips curled in a wry smile. *But then, this is my life, and I have the right to make my own choices.*

She put away the totem and flicked open her phone. The screensaver was a photo of the same man from the photograph her mother had flung at her, snuggling with her on a hiking trail. 'My love, thank you for showing me the way. I can't wait to run away from this horrid life with you.' Her mind rewound to an afternoon three months earlier.

She was spending an intimate afternoon in her bedroom with her boyfriend, RM (short for Richard Mustafa), while her mother was out. After a bout of rough sex, they were curled up in each other's arms. Craving intimacy, Freya lovingly stroked his sweaty dreadlocks.

'Stop doing that,' RM grumbled as he removed her hand. 'You know I find it annoying.'

Taken aback by his brusque response after such a passionate moment, she said, 'Oh, darling! I just find your hair so beautiful. Especially after we . . . um . . . we do it. It's so soft and it glistens, and that makes me want to touch it.'

The young man took out two nugs from a plastic packet and rolled them into a joint. He offered it to her, 'Want to smoke a joint?'

'Sure. Why not?' She opened the window for ventilation.

As they smoked the weed, Freya raised a question that had been on her mind for the last six months. 'Have you decided where to live after your parents' divorce gets finalized?'

RM shrugged his shoulders. 'Dad is moving back to Marrakesh to work with his brother at the olive plantation. Mom won't be returning to her native Hawaii because she has nobody there anymore. She'll be moving to LA, and I'm going with her.'

Freya grew pensive. 'That's a huge change for you. After spending your life in Denmark, you'll have to readjust to a whole new world . . . new school, new friends, new everything. Sure you can handle it?'

'Oh! That's no problem,' RM said, flicking his hand dismissively. 'I'll manage. I'm sick of this place anyway. I'm sick of being in a country that doesn't value enterprise and disruption. I'm sick of living in a place where my faith and race make me an undesirable outlier.' He grimaced.

Freya pecked him on his cheek and shook the packet of weed in his face. 'You mean, you're sick of living in a country that refuses to legitimize your passion for drug dealing?' she teased.

RM pretended to take offence to her cheeky remark. 'You're not serious. I know you look down on this sterile, hobo system as much as I do. It's galling that I provide a vital service for kids to escape the boredom and mundanity of their lives, yet I'm at constant risk of incarceration. In LA, on the other hand, the police are only bothered about serious crimes and I can run my enterprise selling cannabis cakes and muffins in relative peace.'

Freya furrowed her eyebrows. *What will become of our relationship?* She stroked his arm. 'I suppose we'll have to do the long-distance thing for a few years. Once I graduate from college with my degree in social work, I'll join you in LA. I'll pursue a master's or get a job.'

'Why don't you join me in LA in three months? You can go to college there.'

Freya shook her head. 'That's impossible, given my financial situation. College in the US is super expensive. My meagre government tuition fund will not even cover a fraction of the costs. Plus, my mom will never pony up the extra funds.'

'Don't you have someone who can loan you the money? Grandparents? A rich uncle somewhere? Wealthy friends?' RM pressed.

'Nope.'

RM pondered different options for avoiding a long-distance relationship. Silently, he looked around the room, his eyes sweeping past the posters of anti-establishment musicians from different eras, such as Eminem, Sixto Rodriguez, and Axel Rose, and landing on one of Bob Marley playing to a raucous crowd on a beach. Suddenly, an idea germinated in his head and his eyes lit up. 'Freya, who says you have to go to college?'

The teenager raised her eyebrows. 'Huh? What do you mean?'

The young drug dealer grabbed her hand and squeezed it hard. 'Run away with me to LA. We can live together on Venice Beach. We'll manage my business together. We'll be a team. Why do we have to follow a conventional path?'

Freya felt like she'd been struck by a bolt of lightning. She contemplated her options. *Isn't that the life I've always dreamed of? A life full of adventure, mystery and passion? A life where I can aspire to reach the sky? A life where I can do whatever I want and be whoever I want to be? A life where everyone I meet will have values different from my own?*

RM threw a few more logs into her roaring fire of excitement. 'That $10,000 the government owes you for college, you can invest it in my business. You'll get to live and eat for free. Everything will be swell,' he promised.

Freya stroked RM's thick dreadlocks and considered his proposal. Her gaze landed on a photograph of herself with her mother. It had been taken at an awards ceremony to commemorate Birgitte's valour for tracking down a suspected suicide bomber. She studied the photo for a moment, looking at her lone sullen expression in a sea of appreciative faces. 'Let's do it, RM. In three months, I'll receive an admission letter from a college. Mom can take it to the bank and furnish it as proof for releasing my college funds into my account. Then we can take the money and run away to LA.'

Freya reminisced about that afternoon as Birgitte made a quick call to the bank manager, Mr Jacobsen, to advance their meeting. 'Mr Jacobsen, I have some urgent paperwork to file at the station today. Are you free to have the meeting now?' she asked.

After a twenty-minute drive from Vanløse along the Ørestads Boulevard, she reached the branch of Danske Bank near Freya's school. The branch manager received her immediately and ushered her into his office. He leafed through the documents while she bit her nails. 'They documents seem to be in order.' He looked at her reassuringly. 'I'll go ahead and sanction the funds. She's going to start her first semester next month, right?'

Birgitte nodded and wiped her fingertips with a tissue.

After signing the letter, Mr Jacobsen logged into the banking portal and keyed in some commands. 'The money's in her account now. In two hours, it will automatically be wired to the bursar at Skive College,' he confirmed.

Birgitte heaved a sigh of relief. *Finally, she'll lead a peaceful life, something my husband could never experience in his lifetime. Neither could I. That's why I've tried so hard to keep her on the straight and narrow . . . to make sure that she's never cheated off it. Despite all my efforts, though, each day I wage a losing battle because she keeps pushing her boundaries and keeps on challenging my common sense. Finally, my efforts have borne fruit! Now she can have a life without the looming dread of destitution and death. A life of stability and contentment. A peaceful life. Something I'll never have. Is there anything more valuable than that?*

Jacobsen said empathetically, 'I know how tough it is to be a parent these days. So many bad influences. So much danger everywhere. So much decay of our cultural and moral norms. It's heartening to see a troubled soul like Freya finally on the mend.'

Their business concluded, Birgitte left the bank and headed towards the police station, calling Freya to relate the good news as she drove down the express boulevard. As she waited for her daughter to take the call, she spotted something by a clump of bushes ahead on her right. It was a rabbit struggling to escape from a ball of barbed wire. She slowed down her car and peered closely at the suffering animal. Before she could think of stopping and freeing the trapped creature, Freya took her call.

'The money's in your account now. It's done, at last,' Birgitte announced triumphantly. Freya disconnected the line without a word of appreciation. 'Well, thank you, too,' Birgitte mumbled bitterly as she sped past the squealing rabbit, its fur ripped by the sharp nails.

Meanwhile, Freya's mind raced with possibilities. *It will take two hours for the funds to get wired to my college. I have a short window between now and then to withdraw the money, go to RM's place, and get the hell out of this country together. I need to act now.*

After shooting RM a quick SMS instructing him to be ready to leave, she put on her overcoat and scarf, and ran to the nearest bus stop on Jernbane Allé, near Vanløse Station. Five minutes later, she alighted at a bus stop opposite the closest Danske Bank branch in the Vanløse district. She approached the teller and requested to withdraw 70,000 DKK (about USD $10,000)—the entire amount of her collegiate grant.

'Use it for the greater good,' advised the teller as he finished counting the cash and handed it over.

Freya collected the money in a neat envelope and took a ten-minute bus ride to RM's neighbourhood, Tingbjerg. She was about to disembark at the ghetto when the bus driver asked, 'Are you sure this is where you want to be? It's a rough neighbourhood.'

She ignored the question, got off the bus and walked for five minutes to RM's apartment block.

The door to his apartment was wide open. 'RM, are you there?' she asked, shutting the door behind her. There was no response. 'Mr Mustafa?' she called, hoping RM's father would answer. Again, no reply. When she entered the living room, she saw several artifacts from the Middle East and Africa, trophies RM's father had collected over the years, scattered across the floor.

The stuffed head of a big cat lay on the floor with a knife plunged into its skull. *Who damaged the cheetah?* A hanging tapestry of a fifteenth-century Persian rug—hailing from the court of the Safavid Shah—had been ripped off the wall, torn to shreds and dumped on the floor. She felt a shiver run down her spine. *The flat's been vandalized. I've got to make sure my darling's okay*. She banished the contradictory urge to run away. Gingerly, she tiptoed towards the adjoining kitchen.

In front of her, two bodies were slumped face-first in the kitchen sink, their backs towards her. Spray-painted on the wall next to them, the phrase 'ANTINATIONAL DOGS'. She moved closer so she could try to recognize their faces. The victims were RM and his father.

'Oh my God!' she shrieked.

She lifted her boyfriend's face from the blood-soaked ink.

As Freya processed the horrific details, she felt dizzy and weak in her knees. She was about to collapse under the sheer weight of the brutal revelation when the door of the apartment was thrown wide open. Several people burst in, shouting, 'Over here! They entered through here!' The officers spotted Freya in the apartment and rushed towards her. 'Police! Drop down on your knees! You're under arrest!'

Freya knelt and raised her arms in surrender. Suddenly, a familiar voice shouted, 'Freya! What the hell are you doing here?'

A pall of haze blanketed her vision. A single figure emerged from the posse of obfuscated officers. 'Mom, is that you?' she asked before passing out.

When Freya awoke, she found herself lying on a hospital bed. Her mom was by her side, looking worried. 'You've been out for four hours. How are you feeling now?'

Freya shrugged her shoulders. 'Okay, I guess. What happened?' Suddenly, the memory of the traumatic incident resurfaced in her mind, making her cry out, 'RM! RM! He's dead. They killed him!'

Birgitte placed her hand on her forearm. 'I'm so sorry about RM. The attack was pre-planned. The Daisies targeted Hicham Mustafa because he was extremely active at the Cultural Awareness Centre, helping to spread awareness about Islam among the general population, trying to build a cultural bridge between the locals and the immigrants. The perpetrators—and we have proof there were a few—entered the flat just before you and butchered them both. Thank God you weren't caught in the crossfire.'

Freya looked at her mother coldly for a moment and then cried. 'I know you didn't approve of my relationship with RM. You think he's a drug dealer, a criminal. But I love him. It hurts so bad.'

Birgitte stroked her daughter's hair. 'I know, baby. I know. You loved him. Enough to . . .' She took out a sheaf of currency notes from her handbag. 'Enough to leave home for good.'

Freya saw RM's face in her mind and broke down, howling, 'Oh, God! Why didn't I reach there sooner? We'd have left the country by now.'

Birgitte stroked her daughter's shoulder. 'I wish I could say something right now to make you feel better.' Her hand moved above Freya's right palm and hovered for a moment like a helicopter looking for a landing spot. The next moment, they joined. 'But I can't. I'll only say this: I know what you're going through.'

Suddenly, Freya saw the hospital room turn into RM's apartment. RM was chopping vegetables by the kitchen sink. He saw her approaching, smiled and invited her to join him. However, she felt rooted to the spot, unable to move an inch forward. Then, a shadow emerged from her body—wielding a knife. It advanced relentlessly towards the boy. RM backed up in fear, but the intruder kept coming. It cornered him at the sink and then stabbed him several times in his neck until he stopped breathing.

As the nightmare faded, Freya's eyes wore a steely look. 'Mom, finally, I know how you felt after Dad's death. Finally, I understand your rage, your bottomless pain.' A glint of red illuminated her eyes. 'I want nothing more in life than to see those white nationalist pigs dead.'

As she looked into her daughter's bloodshot eyes, Birgitte saw a younger version of herself, a version soaked in vengefulness.

After I saw her father's body carved up into pieces, I went into a public toilet at the nearest truck stop and smashed the mirror with my fists. In the shards of glass, I saw my broken self. Her face looks exactly like mine did that day, she remembered, shuddering as she recalled that pivotal moment of her life—the moment she dedicated her soul to the pursuit of law enforcement.

While Freya reeled from the pain and trauma of RM's death, a list of recent life decisions came to her mind. *Drop out from college. Run away from home. Live a bohemian lifestyle in LA.* She considered those choices for a moment. *It would be selfish of me and disrespectful to his memory if I followed through and ran away.* Freya mentally tapped her conscience's 'delete all' button. *I need a purpose in life*, she acknowledged and then vowed aloud, 'I will remain in this country to send his murderers to the gallows.'

Birgitte saw Freya's right hand repeatedly going from quivering to closing into a clenched fist. It reminded her of her own reaction upon being confronted with the news of her husband's death. She whispered under her breath, 'Freya is about to embark on a self-destructive path. She must be turned away from it.' Her mind recalled the moment in her own life when her anger had turned into a driving force to provide selfless service. *She's not aware of it yet, but her true passion is waiting to get unlocked. If she doesn't find and follow it soon, her anger and grief will destroy her.*

On the day of that deadly discovery—right after she'd broken the glass, as blood had gushed from her hands, she had looked around to find a cloth to dress her wounds with. She couldn't find anything. She felt terribly weak as she tried to tear a piece of fabric from her clothes, but her hands wouldn't move an inch. Suddenly, she felt lightheaded. She stumbled and collapsed on the floor with her back against the wall. Her life flashed before her eyes in the form of vignettes on the mirror. Right then, an unfamiliar voice rang in her mind.

A janitor had entered the WC. She took out a bandage from a drawer in her cleaning cart, and quickly secured Birgitte's wound. Then, she pulled up the almost-unconscious woman and made her sit on a toilet seat. 'I've called emergency services. They'll be coming soon.'

Despite the haze, the young woman somehow saw her saviour. She was a middle-aged woman wearing a hijab. 'I'm Nahima,' the janitor introduced herself.

Birgitte groaned, 'Why did you bother to help me? Just let me die.'

Nahima glared at her and scolded. 'Go ahead and die. You'll join your departed ones in heaven. Maybe. But know this: there are millions out there like me who have to survive for the sake of our father, mother, husband or children. Think about our living death because people like you don't have the balls to fight for people like us.'

The paramedics arrived and carried her outside. Birgitte saw the shadow of a man next to Nahima, and groaned. 'I've got to fight. I've got to live . . . for my baby . . . for everyone out there. I will be a law enforcement officer.' Then, she fell unconscious.

As the memory of that momentous night flashed like a shooting star across her mental night sky, Birgitte resolved, *Freya needs help to discover her passion. I must help her.*

Freya looked at Birgitte, who appeared to be lost deep in thought. *Maybe she's thinking of something to say to put my mind at ease. Maybe she wants to convince me that everything will be okay in the end, or some such cliché. Maybe she'll try to impress upon me the need to stick to a life of discipline or some rubbish like that. Or she'll advise me to suppress my bad memories and grief because a lifetime of forgetting and moving on is infinitely preferable to one consumed with revenge. Maybe she'll say I need to see a trauma specialist and heal myself. She can say whatever she wants, I'll never back down on my hunger for revenge.*

To Freya's surprise, Birgitte did not propose the path of diligence and rectitude. Instead, she took out Freya's overcoat from the closet and instructed, 'Come with me, Freya, there's something we need to do together.'

Freya squinted her eyes. 'What is it? Will the doctor allow my release?'

With an enigmatic but determined look on her face, Birgitte said, 'Your vitals are stable. Your blood work's perfectly normal. In my eyes, you're fit enough to hit the road of uncertainty.'

Fifteen minutes later, the two women walked out of the hospital. 'Are you crazy? Where are we going?' Freya gazed at her mom perplexed as she escorted her towards the car.

After driving for twenty minutes on the highway, Birgitte pulled over by the side of the expressway.

'Why are we stopping here?' Freya asked.

Birgitte pointed to a clump of bushes about twenty yards away. 'Follow me,' she instructed and led her daughter towards the green patch. When they reached the spot, Freya was surprised to see a rabbit caught in a prickly mesh of wiring. Its fur was bloody and its eyes droopy, which Freya knew meant that it was growing weaker from the loss of blood. However, it remained very still. *It appears to have survived by avoiding resistance, thereby judiciously conserving its energy*, she inferred internally.

Freya reacted instinctively. 'We must rescue it.'

'I knew that's what you'd say,' Birgitte said. She took two pliers from her handbag and handed one to her daughter. 'When you said you wanted revenge, justice, your eyes had the same look I wore on the day I saw my dead husband. The day I looked into the mirror and couldn't stand to see my own reflection. You feel the same way. The anger. The hate I felt towards myself and his killers. Back then, I had a spiritual encounter with a stranger. An unknown voice told me that to survive, I needed to fight for something. For justice. Not to destroy lives. That's why I became a law enforcement officer. A crusader of justice.'

Freya nodded and accepted the pliers. 'I wasn't aware of my passion. That's why I was trying to hold onto something in my life. Anything to give me a sense of identity . . . without thinking about the consequences.' She cut through the thorny wires around the rabbit's paw.

She continued, 'Now I've found my passion. It's law enforcement. It's the only thing that will bring meaning to my life. Thanks for helping me hear my own voice.'

The two worked together for a few minutes without speaking. 'Freya,' Birgitte said finally, 'I realize I've misunderstood you all these years. I thought you were rudderless and could be easily swayed by a false breeze. I thought the only way to protect you was by making sure you stayed on the safe path. I was wrong. The truth is . . . I needed support from someone to overcome my grief. I never searched for that support. That's why I couldn't bear to lose you, too. So I trapped you in a cage and refused to accept you'd want to run away. But now I do accept you.'

By then, Freya had cut through the wires. The rabbit finally escaped from its trap and hobbled into a hole in the bark of a tree.

'I'm sorry I wanted to run away,' Freya said. 'But, really, truly . . . I was just running from myself.'

Birgitte saw Freya gazing at the free bunny. 'How do you feel now?'

Freya let out a deep sigh. 'I feel so light. So happy that it's safe . . . that it no longer has to suffer.'

Birgitte caressed her daughter's hair. 'The joy of saving lives is what keeps me going every day.'

A tear welled in Freya's eye, and she gave her mother a hug. 'Mom, all this time, I thought you were a police officer only because of your grief for Dad. But now I realize the truth. You have a higher purpose.'

She understands. She accepts, Birgitte thought, as tears of happiness flowed from her eyes. She hugged Freya back. 'I swear to pursue law enforcement to serve and to protect others, as you do. I swear to work on my anger. I swear to never give in to hate,' the young woman promised. Birgitte wiped her eyes, 'I can finally see who you really are. Now go, follow your passion.'

Dragonflies

After an extended period of counselling, Freya attended the Copenhagen Police Academy to specialize in criminal law and forensics. She graduated top of her class. Two years later, she received her license and accepted an invitation from Birgitte to work as her partner at her own private detective agency. The two set up their office in a secluded cottage located on a rolling hill in the countryside, an hour away from the main city. A place called Gilleleje. On Freya's first day at work, Birgitte announced, 'Want to catch the bastards who killed the people we loved?'

Freya's eyes lit up with a bonfire of joy, fury and determination before mellowing down a few notches. 'But the murders of Magnus and RM aren't connected. Plus, their cases have been closed due to lack of evidence.'

Birgitte shook her head. 'You're wrong. I was informed by the PD that they have fresh evidence linking RM's murderers to Magnus's.'

'What evidence?'

'A daisy. Actually, part of a single flower petal, similar to the one you saw in RM's flat, was spotted by detectives last month in a box of Magnus's possessions. All those years ago, nobody in the PD had noticed it when they had confiscated his belongings. However, when the case was about to be closed, a final inspection of the evidence was commissioned. This time, someone spotted the petal. After a thorough inspection, forensic specialists and botanists concluded that it was from a marguerite daisy. The same flower species that you found in RM's flat.'

Freya's cupped her face with her hands, her mouth agape. 'The symbol of the Daisyland Society. This means they were killed by members of the same white nationalist group.'

'That's what it looks like,' Birgitte agreed with a nod. 'If we find the leaders of the cult, it will inevitably lead us to the murderers.'

'So what are we waiting for? Let's go catch these bastards,' urged Freya.

'My thoughts exactly.'

The two women proceeded towards their car to drive to the police station and shortlist suspects for interrogation. They had stepped five yards out of the door, when two men wearing suits approached them from a distance. Freya peered at them. *Who are they? What do they want?* A few minutes later, they were coming down the hill and the midday sun highlighted their faces. 'Principal Andersen?' blurted Freya, recognizing her high school principal.

'Mr Jacobsen? What are you doing here?' Birgitte exclaimed at the same time, recognizing the bank manager.

The two men did not answer. They stood silently about twenty feet away from them. Soon, they were joined by three other men.

Freya's eyes lit up like a detective's upon discovering a vital clue to an unsolved mystery. *I know them all. The mailman. The bank teller who handed me the money. The bus driver who took me to RM's neighbourhood.*

'What do you want from us?' asked Birgitte. Her inquiry was met with silence once again.

'This is weird. Why are they all standing and staring at us?' Freya whispered nervously to her mother.

Birgitte frowned. 'I don't know. This is really strange.'

As the two women tried to make sense of the situation, twenty men appeared, striding down the hill. They wore working-class uniforms and were from several professions—law enforcement, plumbing, carpentry, aviation and more. They arranged themselves silently next to the early arrivals, forming a neat line.

'Who are you?' Birgitte shouted at the men. 'What do you want? Why aren't you answering me?'

The eerie silence continued as the twenty men, none of whom appeared to be carrying any weapons, simply stood there and gazed at the two with icy stares.

'If you don't leave our property right now, we'll arrest you,' threatened Freya.

An ominous silence filled the air, which was soon broken by the patter of heavy boots. Birgitte then saw a larger group, of about fifty men, also dressed in working-class uniforms—from public transportation to sanitation to banking—marching down the hill from different directions. She turned around and gasped in shock. The ever-swelling group had surrounded the cottage from all directions.

'Notice something?' Freya asked Birgitte. 'They're all male, white, probably native-born, ages fifty plus.'

Even more men had started congregating, swelling the group of outsiders to more than 200 people. The two women could see there was no way to evade them. Nowhere to run. Birgitte feared that foul play was imminent. 'If you don't leave right now, I'll shoot.' Her voice was loud and severe. However, the mob stood its ground, refusing to back off and showing little interest in complying with her order. In desperation, Birgitte reached for her gun, only to discover she'd left it inside the cottage.

Freya gave her mother a panicked look. 'They're going to kill us.'

Birgitte glanced behind at the cottage and estimated that the distance between them and the main door was about twenty feet. 'On my signal,' she whispered, 'make a dash for the door. Grab the weapons on the desk and blow these motherfuckers' brains out.'

They stood still, waiting for the right moment to make a run for it. A soft breeze whispered from the woods, kissing their necks and faces with its icy lips. Then, the wind grew stronger. A clump of dead leaves blew towards them from the distant woods. Birgitte hoped that the floating stock of foliage and dust would distract the seemingly malevolent group. 'Now,' she whispered.

Freya made a dash for the house. Five seconds later, they were both inside. They looked around as they quickly loaded their guns, relieved that no one had followed them in. No one was banging on the door. 'Shall we wait for them here?' asked Freya, nervously.

Birgitte gritted her teeth and shook her head. 'And be sitting ducks? No way. I didn't see any weapons on them. Let's take our chances and go outside.' They ran out to confront the enemy, only to find that they'd all disappeared.

'How many were there?' Birgitte's mind visualized a forest teeming with the angry masses. She shuddered.

'There must have been at least 500. How many more would have joined them in the next hour? I don't know. The entire city? The whole country? Nothing's out of the question.' Freya voiced the horrifying possibility that an army of disillusioned natives was about to overrun society, legitimizing oppression and discrimination and suspending the fundamental rights of minorities. They walked towards the top of the hill to check if the intruders had departed. Before they reached the top, Freya pointed into the distance. 'There's something over there by the top of the hillock. A trail.'

They looked out from the peak of the hillock in every direction, but couldn't see a soul for miles. However, they did see a trail of identical flowers scattered around the periphery of the house. A ring with a perimeter of 350 feet. A flowery trail to mark the presence of the unmasked men.

With a feeling of dread, Birgitte picked up a flower to ascertain its identity.

It was a marguerite daisy.

REFLECTION: FIND THE THREADS THAT BIND US

Are your parents pressuring you into leading a life that's not true to your calling?

The pursuit of meaning necessitates the cultivation of close relationships. But often, we end up shooting ourselves in the foot. For instance, after an argument, we tend to demonize the other person. We focus on our differences, rather than our similarities. These differences are the aspects of our identities that don't match, whether they are values, opinions, aspirations, or lifestyles. Our minds magnify these identity differences and create emotional distance and barriers. While the walls that go up enable us to nurse our hurt egos in the short run, in the long run, these differences can cause permanent rifts in our most important relationships and prevent us from maintaining closeness with the other person. We might end up losing a crucial potential ally in our pursuit of meaning, as a result.

To turn this on its head, we should keep in mind that more than differences, we share similarities with our parents. Similarities of traditions, culture and genetics. In the heat of conflict, we are often unwilling to accept that we have anything in common with the other person. And even if we do, we don't want to go looking for them in that tense moment. We feel that that is tantamount to endorsing the other person's view over our own. Our egos cannot handle such a retreat from preconceptions.

This is especially true for parents and children. With the rapid democratization of technology and education around the world, children are more knowledgeable, skilled and socially conscious than their parents had been at their ages. By using the rich arsenal of tools, resources and connections at their disposal more effectively and dynamically than their parents, the values of children have become far more progressive, their interests more specialized, and their connections more global. Consequently, their identities have become more multifaceted. This divide has always existed between parents and children, but in this 'turbo-polarized' age, the generation gap has become more pronounced than ever before.

In the lives of young people, the identity divide between them and their parents poses a huge obstacle to the pursuit of meaning for either party. This divide expresses itself most often in the form of parental pressure. Parents tend to direct their kids towards their own aspirations, that may belong to a different time and social context which are no longer suitable. Kids who succumb to this pressure, ultimately compromise on their true selves and experience a deep lack of fulfillment in the long run.

It isn't easy for a parent to build a connection with a child who is suffering from parental pressure or a more deep-rooted psychological challenge. The first step for them is to be empathetic and listen without judgment. Children often reveal the source of their angst, only for parents to recognize that they had also experienced similar feelings at some point in their lives. Thereafter, an honest and heartfelt exchange can lead to the discovery of common ground. In this story, Birgitte connected with Freya on the pain of loss. Parents can make use of opportunities when they and their children are facing similar emotional challenges to forge bonds that could last a lifetime.

In the long run, the identity divide can be bridged if parents and children have an open conversation about the deeper facets of life such as sharing their hopes and dreams with one another. During this necessarily two-way exchange, both parties may realize that they want all the same things, just in different packaging. By sharing their aspirations, they also speak candidly about other personal aspects that have contributed to their identity-formation process—experiences, inspirations, passions, strengths, weaknesses and relationships. This promotes comfort and might even result in them giving the other loved one access to their warehouse of personal memories, which parents often aren't able to do. It's likely they both uncover many common threads in these vast, rich storehouses, to weave into a beautiful blanket that provides them with comfort, love, understanding and joy, especially when the going gets tough.

The protagonist of this story overcame brutal psychological pressure from her mother to listen and lead her life led by her own true calling. Learn how she overcame parental pressure, and you will believe that you can too.

3

OVERCOMING SOCIAL PRESSURE

UNDERSTANDING SOCIAL PRESSURE

If you want to lead a happy life, it's very important to have a supportive circle of friends and colleagues. We expect members of our peer group to help us grow and help us lift ourselves in times of distress, while doing the same for them. However, our actual experiences with our peer group aren't always in alignment with these idealistic expectations. Rather than supporting us, they might stifle our individuality and growth aspirations, many times.

Social pressure is feeling compelled to meet the standards of our peer group in particular, and other forces of society. These include goals that every member of the collective might be striving towards, based on often unstated principles and values they share in common with us. To win the approval of the group, everyone must be seen to be working towards these standards; by extension, it becomes unacceptable for one to underachieve or strive towards one's own standards. If we are constantly compared to our friends and peers, who are using their own yardsticks to map our progress, our life satisfaction may be adversely impacted. If we are unwilling or unable to meet their standards, we may be ignored, humiliated or even excluded by them. This can result in anxiety, depression and social withdrawal, among other issues.

Social pressure has existed for as long as society itself. It serves to maintain order within collectives. Over centuries, its impact on people's well-being has progressively worsened because of the changes in technology, lifestyle and diversity in social values.

Before the advent of the internet, one largely found peers—friends and colleagues—in the place they lived. These peer groups were homogenous in lifestyle, income, education levels, and consequently, identity. Moreover, people had lower aspirations for a better life because they had less access to knowledge, resources and connections. In this environment, it wasn't difficult to keep up with the Joneses. Consequently, not everyone felt it impossible to cope with the mental stress arising from social pressure, except on occasion.

In the modern, borderless world of social media, peer pressure has become amplified, and standards are harder to achieve. These days, therefore, social pressure is taking an almost crippling toll on one's life satisfaction.

One's circle is not only confined to one's own geography, but also includes connections from social media. These peers may live in different countries around the world, having different levels of wealth, knowledge and achievements. Thus, the contemporary peer group is more heterogeneous in identity than peer groups of the past. By extension, the standards also seem loftier and harder to attain. Narcissistic and superficial behaviour is rewarded more than it would in everyday life and the pursuit of this group's validation can be so addictive, that the quest for meaning might take a backseat. In the absence of genuine mental and emotional connections, inauthenticity and one-upmanship run riot in such groups. Everyone seems to have a hefty bank balance, high social status, attractive appearance, solid professional accomplishments and fulfilling close relationships. It seems as if everyone is leading a happy life. No wonder then that the level of pressure to match peer standards today is unimaginably higher—it can be almost traumatic to try and keep up with the digital Joneses.

The protagonist of the following story faced great emotional distress from social pressure. Will she overcome this barrier to happiness? Read on.

FORGOTTEN WINGS

Most young women at her school believed that wrestling was an obscene and comical pursuit—but Valentina Perez believed it was her road to salvation.

She was performing a weight-training drill with a set of heavy kettlebells in her bedroom, when her exercise routine was interrupted by a loud car horn and shrill voices.

'V, come down. It's time to hit the Pi Kappa Phi party in Fort Lauderdale,' hollered a woman from the vehicle.

Valentina rolled her eyes and groaned. 'Oh God! Not today. I only have three months to prepare for the wrestling regionals.' She wiped the sweat off her forehead and went over to her window. A familiar red Mercedes convertible was parked outside her house. The driver was in her early twenties—tall, with long, straight, dark hair, high cheekbones, a perfect tan, and wearing a short red dress with a plunging neckline that barely concealed a freshly implanted pair of breasts. She got out of the car and shouted in a rasping voice, 'Come on! We don't have all day.'

Valentina furrowed her eyebrows and yelled back, 'Hey, Jackie! I thought the Miami Dade College frat parties were suspended because of alcohol abuse and molestation.'

Almost instantly, the car sunroof opened. Two women sprang up from the backseat like jill-in-the-boxes. They looked irritated. 'Where have you been? Aren't you following our Telegram channel? Ever since the frats got blacklisted, they've gone underground. The parties are now happening off campus.'

Valentina placed her fingers on her chin. *It isn't worth missing wrestling practice to party with strangers in Fort Lauderdale.* 'Jackie, Vicky, Rosie,' she called to the women, 'you're dolls for inviting me to this gig. But Fort Lauderdale's an hour away and I've got to study for my midterms. I'm going to pass on this.'

Jackie shook her head like a disapproving professor from the University of Gentility. 'V, this is an exclusive party with a VIP guest list. I've already told Marco you'll be coming. If you don't go, I'll lose face. Then I can't invite you to stuff anymore.'

Valentina realized she'd pay a steep price for alienating Jackie and her gang of girls. *Get uninvited from the hottest parties on campus? Hell no! I'm going to look like a loser and a loner in the eyes of my peers. I guess I'll have to reschedule my workout to tomorrow.* She turned around to look at her phone lying on her bed. It was streaming a workout video onto her TV set. She looked ruefully at the paused instructional video by a legendary female wrestler, closed her eyes and whispered her wish aloud. 'Rhonda, please be my fairy godmother and whisk me away to your world . . . right now. The world of wrestling. The world where I really, truly belong.'

At that moment, her mind rewound to a wrestling match at the school athletics centre during her final year of high school. She was in the thick of a match during the finals of the National Female Wrestling Championships. The last round had commenced. Her opponent, a hefty girl five feet, ten inches tall and weighing seventy five kilograms, advanced menacingly and grabbed her in a vice-like grip. She squeezed Valentina with her massive thighs—almost pinning her down and leaving her gasping for breath. The judge noticed that her resistance was fading fast. He raised one arm slowly and was about to bring it down when Valentina somehow managed to escape the chokehold and flip over her rival. She quickly executed a leg-sweep and pinned the rival onto the mat. A collective gasp went around the auditorium before the crowd erupted into cheers of celebration. Valentina stared in disbelief, first at the opponent, and then at the audience. She had won.

Valentina gazed at a framed photo showing her being fêted with a gold medal at a grand public ceremony, and smiled wistfully. *That was my greatest triumph. A fitting culmination to five years of hard work in the school sandpit.* A second framed picture showed her wearing the gold medal and posing with her coach and her mother. The smile disappeared and she addressed the empty room. 'Why is my passion so uncool?' She flipped open her class yearbook to a picture of her with a group of school students and stared resentfully at the picture. *After I won the medal and earned a public commendation from the principal, I received an invitation to a party hosted by the popular crowd of my school. These were the same people who'd never noticed me until that day. I was so happy they'd recognized me for the first time in my life. I was so excited to earn their validation. But when I showed them my medal, they laughed at me and said that wrestling was for social rejects. I should quit the sport because no sane person wrestles . . . only lesbians and mentally unstable men cared about female wrestling. I should stop acting like a degenerate and join them at Aventura Mall for shopping, grooming and exchanging life tips.* She tossed the yearbook back into the box of memories below her bed. *I wish my friends were more supportive of my passion. I wish they accepted me for who I am.*

Outside, the honks got louder. Jackie's shrill, impatient voice sliced through the neighbourhood's silence like a car speaker blasting music in the middle of the night. 'V! You're taking forever. Come on.'

Valentina shrugged her shoulders and whispered to her coach in the photo. 'Mr Martinez, we've got to keep my wrestling dream a secret from my friends. I know we've had this conversation before. I want to go pro. But I don't want to alienate my friends. You told me to dump them like toxic waste. But how can I do that and lose access to all those hot parties, cool people and exciting things? I can't go back to being the faceless person I once was. I guess I'll have to train in secret. No way Jackie Inc. can know that I'm training for the regionals.' The coach continued to look at her impassively.

Valentina threw out her arms. 'That's my life. There's nothing I can do.' She quickly changed into a short-sleeved black dress and sky-high Louboutin stilettos and rushed downstairs.

She squeezed herself into the backseat of the car. Her dress rolled up. Vicky—a tall blonde with skinny legs and breasts that were popping out of a golden slip dress—looked at her exposed legs and frowned. 'Hey! What's up with the thighs, babe? They look huge. Looks like you just did heavy squats or something.'

Rosie, a petite woman of African-American descent with surgically enhanced derrière and lips, rolled up the sleeves of Valentina's dress and looked shocked. 'V, your arms are so thick. Have you been lifting heavy dumbbells or what?'

Valentina could see Rosie's absurdly defined abs through her low-cut crop top and wondered why these women even bothered with her. At that moment, Valentina recalled what had happened two months earlier.

It was the first day of her sophomore year at Miami University. The previous night, she had partied hard and crashed in bed at 5 a.m. At 8 a.m., she was awakened by the alarm. Half-asleep and hungover, Valentina staggered to the dining room and poured herself a glass of orange juice. Her mother—a petite, forty-five-year-old woman wearing a nurse's uniform and a nametag that read 'FLORENTINA PEREZ'—was sipping from a cup of coffee. She put it down on the table and handed Valentina an envelope. Valentina tore it open and saw an invitation letter from the American Female Wrestling Association. Drowsiness dispelled, her eyes began to sparkle.

> Dear Valentina,
>
> Based on your superlative performance at the national high school championship two years ago, we are pleased to award you a wildcard entry into the regional selections of the American Female Wrestling Assocation (AFWA) championships, to be held in Miami this June. Should you qualify in the regionals, you'll be selected to join our Federation as a fully paid member. You'll earn an annual stipend of $100,000 plus benefits and be able to access opportunities to compete for professional trophies around the world. If you're interested in this opportunity, please enroll on our website and pay the registration fee of $5,000. This amount will be fully refunded to you, should you fail to qualify.

Valentina read the fine print and looked out through the window. *It's been two years since I quit wrestling and joined the*

Miami University party scene. Why did I do that? Because I wanted to hang out with the 'it' crowd on campus. I wanted to be seen as popular and beautiful. I wanted to have a fashionable image too. But what did I get by compromising on my passion?

Florentina wondered what her daughter was worried about. She snatched the letter from her hand and read it. She set it down a moment later and looked at Valentina thoughtfully. 'You know, I understand what you're going through. I wanted to be a singer before you were born. But just before my big audition, your dad died at the construction site.' She paused for a moment. 'I was so overcome with grief that I couldn't bring myself to attend the rehearsal. That was a lost opportunity to pursue my passion. Soon after, I found myself with all these bills to pay. My friends and relatives told me to get a qualification and find a skilled job. I listened to them and made up an excuse in my head that the pursuit of music was not a viable option. Today, after years of intensive training and work experience in nursing, I make a good living, but not a day goes by when I don't think about what I could have achieved pursuing my passion.'

She stroked Valentina's arm and smiled sympathetically. 'There are moments in life when a window opens, ever so briefly. Those are the moments when we have to be brave and fly out towards the sun.'

Valentina looked at her mom with embarrassment, before diverting her gaze to outside the window. *What did I get from these two years of college? Weekly hangovers. Naked strangers lying next to me in bed, pawing me all over. Opulent bedrooms littered with coke. Friends interested only in attending hot parties, being seen and photographed. Friends who only cared about making shopping expeditions to different malls . . . buying expensive cosmetics, jewellery and clothing with money from some sugar daddy.*

Florentina suddenly noticed a faint residue of white powder on Valentina's lips and assumed that had come from the previous night's exploits. Her eyes widened and she let out a gasp before quickly composing herself. Tissue in hand, she gently wiped off the tell-tale residue. 'Baby, this isn't you. You know that!'

Valentina choked back her tears. 'No, Mom. You're right. It's peer pressure. I've felt it since high school. I have to look beautiful all the time. I have to be successful. I have to be popular. Right now, I feel so deflated . . . so hollow . . . like an empty piñata.'

'Do you remember that day when you won the wrestling trophy? I was so proud of you. You were so happy.'

Valentina recalled that moment when the principal had garlanded her with the gold medal. She nodded. 'Yes, I do. I still feel your pride and love. I still feel the love and appreciation of the school community; who for once, saw me for who I really am, a wrestler with great potential. But what did I do? I succumbed to my fear of exclusion and became what others wanted me to be—a glamorous party girl. Six months ago, I cashed my award of $2,000 to pay the advance deposit for a breast augmentation surgery. An operation I have to pay in full by the end of today.'

Florentina smiled and placed her hand on her forearm. 'If that's what makes you happy, then do it. But let me share a tidbit. Do you know what's the most joyful moment in my life every month? No, not the quarterly visit to the tanning salon. It's the monthly karaoke night at the old-age home where I work on the weekends. Why? Because on these nights, I get to sing my own songs. The ones I sang so many years ago as a crooner at bars in Tijuana, Mexico.'

'Mom, thanks for reminding me what makes me happy. I'll put the rest of my funds towards wrestling. Towards training, conditioning and registration. But I'll have to do it in secret. None of my friends can ever learn about it.'

Florentina gave her a warm hug and laughed. 'I know these girls. You think they can't accept who you are. But actually, they can't accept who they've become.'

'Please don't say a word about this to anyone. You know how judgmental people are. They'll think I'm a weirdo or a butch. They'll spread rumours about me and I'll be excluded from all the parties. I will go back to being invisible. I can't live like that.'

Mom put a finger on her lips. 'You're special, my darling. Don't worry. Your secret's safe with me.'

The memory of that day faded like ripples in a pond. Valentina stretched out her legs a bit to relax the muscles. Her quads now looked a bit blobby, but not as vascular. 'Umm . . . no. I guess I feel bloated . . . that's all.'

Jackie handed her a strip of Midol. 'Take this. It will work like a charm.'

Valentina was about to put the pills in the outer pocket of her clutch bag, however, her friends kept looking at her. Vicky handed her a bottle of water. Valentina popped a pill into her mouth and washed it down.

Jackie turned around in the driver's seat and flashed a thumbs-up sign. 'Your tummy will be as flat as a washboard in twenty minutes.'

An hour later, Jackie steered the car through the main entrance of a mansion in Las Olas, Fort Lauderdale. After they got out of the car, Jackie handed the keys to a valet. Valentina heard pulsating music coming from inside. At the door, they were greeted by a tanned man in his early twenties, whose shaved head was painted with the word 'MESSIAH'. He wore a white tank top that revealed a chiselled physique. He gave Jackie a kiss on her cheeks and squeezed her bum. Then he looked the other women up and down and gave them a lascivious grin. 'You ladies are looking fine tonight.'

Jackie slapped him lightly and looked at him, annoyed. 'Look but don't touch, Marco. We're way out of your league.'

Marco bowed in mock reverence, his expression filled with false hurt. He gestured to the women. 'Come on in, ponies. My players are all here, waiting for you.'

Valentina followed her gang into the living room. She saw twelve leatherbound sofas. Ten couples were seated on them. Some were sipping champagne. A few were feeding each other olives. Others were making out. Not one person gave the newbies so much as a glance. A man in his sixties placed a diamond tiara on an eighteen-year-old's head, and Jackie watched the girl's eyes light up with excitement.

Valentina frowned. Jackie placed a comforting hand on her shoulder. 'Relax. The cops aren't coming anytime soon. That's Giuseppe Bigotti, an Italian racecar dealer. Filthy rich. This is his mansion, and he's opened it up for these parties so that he can mingle with the hottest young women in the city.'

Jackie smirked as she saw the ageing paramour kiss and fondle a young woman. She brought her mouth close to Valentina's ear. Her extra minty, alpine-flavoured breath reminded Valentina of a frat house jerk at a college party who had tried to get her drunk and pass her around with his friends. Valentina strained to hear Jackie's voice amid the somewhat monotonous din.

'He sponsors the ones he really likes. He pays their college fees, puts them up in his house, covers all their expenses, provides them with a stipend for clothing and fashion. In return . . . ' she paused and winked at the young woman who was bending down to undo the magnate's belt. 'He expects total devotion.'

The living room was connected to an outdoor pool via a sliding door. Through the glass panel, Valentina saw a hundred people dancing to a DJ's tracks. Jackie peered at the far corner of the deck that surrounded an Olympic-sized pool. A huge, muscular man with a long ponytail, who looked like the wrestler HHH, was surrounded by five young men and women around a cocktail table. Their heads were all bowed as if they were bending to read something. She pointed in their direction.

'Jonas Beauchamp. The chairman of Beauchamp Enterprises. He's worth $500 million and has a monopoly over the shipping trade between the east coast of the US and Cuba. Rumours are that he wants to divorce his wife, who's suffering from cancer. But he can't because he'll end up losing half his fortune. So he's waiting for her to die by not funding her cancer treatment,' she reported in a matter-of-fact tone.

Valentina observed the brawny man laughing and blabbering away, gesticulating wildly with his right hand holding a cocktail glass. He was waving it around so vigorously that she expected it to either drench or injure someone. 'What a psychopath!'

Jackie shrugged her shoulders. 'Well, tough luck. It's my philosophy to always seize the moment. After my dad had an affair with his assistant and walked out on us, Mom told me, "Jackie, life's cruel and petty. Relationships are never permanent or selfless. Keep that in mind, and get the most out of people before they inevitably let you down."'

Valentina was aghast at Jackie's flippant, calculated attitude towards relationships. A tear welled up in her eye. She concealed it by quickly wiping it off.

Jackie noticed and shook her head slowly. She then patted Valentina on the shoulder. 'The only way to survive in a filthy swamp is by turning into a jellyfish. Don't worry, babe. Cheer up! You'll get used to this.'

Her accomplices, Rosie and Vicky, stood behind the distressed woman and rubbed Valentina's shoulders like trained massage therapists. 'Come on, babe. You'll feel a lot better once you meet these guys. They aren't all that bad . . . only rough edges. That's all!'

Just then, a young woman in the shipping tycoon's group spotted Jackie and her friends and waved enthusiastically at them. 'Come on, guys. What are you waiting for? We're running out of gold dust.'

Valentina raised her right hand with a puzzled look. 'What's she talking about?'

Vicky laughed. 'Haha! She's as high as a kite.'

Jackie rushed towards the group, turning around and ushering her pals to keep pace. 'Hey, guys! Really selfish of you to start without us. Now, give me a dose of that.'

Valentina stayed behind the party trio and advanced tentatively towards the table. Three women and two guys from her campus were huddled around the cocktail table next to the beefy guy. In between sips from their drinks, they all snorted lines of white powder scattered on the table. In a trance-like state, they flailed their arms around, smiling and singing.

Valentina observed the crystalline texture of the powder. She noted its hallucinogenic, trance-like effects on them. She remembered a story that had been circulating around the campus last fall, and gasped. *Ketamine. I need to draw the line and avoid this. A year ago, Claire from our group became so addicted to it that she had to be admitted to a rehab clinic. Then Jackie cut her off because she was afraid of her reputation being tarnished by the association.*

Aloud, she said firmly, 'Go ahead, guys. I'll pass.'

Jackie's ears perked up like a startled rabbit. She raised her head, wiped off some powder from her nose, and offered her friend an extra cocktail from the table. 'All right, but at least have a Bloody Geisha. Be a part of the group.'

Valentina hesitated, but quickly gulped down the drink. Hoots and cheers from the crowd followed.

Jonas winked and flashed a smug 'come hither' smile at her. 'Your party animal creds are restored. Maybe you can join me at my pad later?'

Valentina was just about to rebuff the proposition when she started to feel dizzy. The glass fell from her hand and smashed on the turf. She staggered but held on to the edge of the table. Suddenly, she saw a strange glittering light appearing around all objects and people. The guests' faces started glowing. The drugs on the table sparkled like a pile of diamond-encrusted feathers. 'They're so beautiful. Can I touch them?' she giggled and plunged her face into the drugs.

'Oh wow! She's in Toon Town,' joked Vicky.

Jonas slipped Jackie a wad of $100 bills and whispered, 'She's really cute, in a thick America Ferrara sort of way. Can you bring her to my room on the top floor for some private time?' Jackie's eyes lit up on earning the instant fortune. He winked at her. 'You know what I mean?'

Jackie gave him a kiss and gestured to her friends quietly, 'Take her upstairs so she can recover.' They responded to her orders by hauling Valentina past the living room, up the stairs, and to a room at the far end of the corridor.

Sometime later, Valentina awoke, finding herself lying on a bed wearing just her bra and thong. The room was pitch dark; she felt groggy and nauseous. She turned around and spotted a faint glow of light entering through the window behind her, concealed by a curtain. Upon drawing the curtain, sunlight streamed in. 'What time is it?' she asked herself. She lifted her wrist to check her watch. It was gone. She bent over the side of the bed to search for it, found it behind the curtain, and gave a sigh of relief.

She picked it up and looked at the time. 'It's noon!' she shrieked. 'I've been out for almost twelve hours. I have to get out of here.'

She looked around the room and saw her clothes dumped on a chair by the side of the bed. She moved towards it to put them on, but suddenly stopped. She glanced over at the bed. There was a man sleeping next to her. He had a massive letter X tattooed on his muscular back, and his long hair was tied up in a ponytail. She tiptoed to his side of the bed and looked at his face. She gasped. *Oh my God! It's that sleazy shipping tycoon. I didn't talk to him last night, so how did we end up sleeping together? I can't remember a thing.*

She looked around the room for clues and spotted a glass of alcohol by her side of the bed. *Hmm . . . I just had one shot. How come I was out for so long?* She peered at the glass and detected a white powder bed at the bottom. Curious, she dabbed her finger and tasted it. Immediately, she gagged and threw up on the floor. *It's ketamine. My drink was spiked.* Right then, the memories of the previous night became clearer. A beefy man had come into the room and removed her clothes.

She was about to lose consciousness when she caught a glimpse of his face. Jonas. Suddenly, a horrible thought formed in her head. She lifted her panty and saw a damp, sticky substance deposited around her inner thighs. She screamed, but the man on the bed didn't stir. *Oh my God! I've been raped.* She quickly took out a wet tissue from her handbag to clean herself up. The man remained fast asleep. Valentina dressed quickly, collected her belongings, ran up the corridor, then down the stairs into the living room. There were twenty people, all fast asleep and totally naked. She tiptoed past the unconscious bodies and made her way towards the door. She put her hand on the doorknob and turned it. But, from the corner of her eye, she saw somebody move. She turned around nervously and saw Jackie's head briefly pop up before dropping back onto the floor.

'That's the last time I'm hanging out with you creeps,' Valentina muttered. She closed the door behind her and ran towards the nearest bus stop at Seven Isles. Five minutes later, she was on a bus bound for Little Havana.

Florentina was about to leave for work when Valentina returned with a runny nose, dilated pupils and watery eyes. She immediately recognized the symptoms of a common condition which brought people in for admission at her hospital. *V's taken hard drugs again. She must have been coerced because she's been training for the wrestling contest for some time now, there's no way my baby would do such a stupid thing herself!* She put her arm around her daughter's shoulder and waist and helped her stabilize. 'Baby, you don't look well at all. Can I get you something?'

Valentina could barely stand upright. 'I'm gonna puke,' she groaned, and stumbled into the guest toilet. Florentina lifted the toilet seat quickly. V threw up into the bowl. Several minutes later, Florentina helped her stand and gave her a saline rinse. After she'd rinsed Valentina's nose, Florentina wiped her daughter's face with a warm cloth.

'That feels so good, Ma. You're an angel, you know that?' Valentina said before plonking onto the living room sofa. She shut her eyes. A couple of minutes later, Florentina woke her up and handed her a beverage. 'Don't sleep yet. Drink this ginger tea first.'

Valentina sipped the drink with a look of satisfaction. Her mom stroked her hand. 'So, what happened?'

Valentina put down the cup. She shook her head and looked ashamed. 'Something really bad. Someone laced my drink with ketamine. Then, while I was drugged, someone took me into a room and a strange man raped me.'

Florentina's mouth opened wide and her fingers extended. 'What! You must go to the hospital right now.'

Valentina nodded her head.

An hour later, a doctor looked up at her after reviewing the blood work and toxicology report. 'You are lucky, Ms Perez. There was an awfully high amount of ketamine in your system when you were admitted. Thanks to the blocker we administered immediately, there are now only traces of the compound left in your bloodstream. In a day or two, you'll be completely clean. We also found traces of semen on your body. Fortunately, there's no sign of infection . . . yet.'

He glanced at Florentina. She had a grim look on her face. 'I'll watch for warning signs and bring her in if I see anything.' The doctor closed his folder and proceeded towards the door. Florentina tapped him on the shoulder. 'So can we file a police report regarding the rape?'

The doctor shook his head and looked at her in regret. 'I empathize with your ordeal. Unfortunately, there's no physical evidence confirming she had sexual intercourse at all, or that she was assaulted. You can go to the police station if you want, but the forensic examiners will probably say the same thing.'

'You're saying that there's nothing we can do? The people who did this will go scot-free?' Florentina waved her hands in furious protest.

The doctor snapped his fingers. 'Perhaps if you can show the police a video recording of the whole thing, maybe they'll take action.'

Florentina glared at him in helplessness and rage. Valentina touched her arm and begged, 'Mom, it's not the end of the world. I'll live. Just drop it.' She gazed at the doctor with an imploring look. 'Can I go home now, please?'

The doctor signed the release forms and gave Valentina his business card. 'Get some rest. Call me if there's anything urgent.'

Florentina escorted her daughter from the examination room towards the main entrance of the hospital. They reached a massive emergency ward—filled with a hundred patients—located midway on the passage.

Florentina stopped and squeezed her daughter's hands. 'Baby, your friends aren't good people. They'll do anything to get their way. That includes hurting you.'

For a moment, Florentina's body looked super buff and draped in a multi-coloured leotard. Valentina hugged her mom. 'Thanks, Mom, for being such an angel. I don't know what I would have done without you. You're absolutely right. I won't hang out with them anymore. In fact, I'm going home and making the payment for the wrestling competition.'

Florentina kissed her on the forehead. 'This is your moment. Don't look back.'

The moment Valentina returned home, she called the cosmetic surgery clinic and cancelled her upcoming appointment. Her deposit was refunded immediately. Then she transferred $5,000 to the AFWA and locked in her registration. Once the website flashed a confirmation, she looked up at the cosmic motif on her ceiling and heaved a sigh of relief. She stared at the glow-in-the-dark rendition of a constellation and saw a shooting star. *Finally, I'm on the path that I should have taken all along. Now there's just one more thing to do.* She clenched her teeth and launched all of her social media accounts at once on her computer. Then, she posted the same message on each one: 'Friends who don't look out for their own when they're drugged or raped, aren't real friends.' Without a moment of hesitation, she unfriended Jackie and her troublemaking associates. 'Out of my life, you creeps.'

The next day, as Valentina entered the main building of Miami University, she was greeted by a number of students who gave her the thumbs-up. One of her new fans—a muscular, red-haired woman with glasses, wearing a Rhonda Roussey T-shirt with the slogan 'REVIVE YOUR INNER DEMON', gave her a high five and laughed. 'Hey! Did you walk out of Jackie's group?'

Valentina gritted her teeth. 'I was drugged and raped. So I left that backstabbing group! I'm sick of peer pressure. I'm sick of being someone I'm not. A gullible party animal. An unthinking proponent of the superficial lifestyle. I want to follow my passion. I want to be a professional wrestler. That's who I want to be.'

The woman slapped her back in delight. 'I never liked those bitches. You go, girl! Don't let anyone stop you from *being* you.'

At that moment, a catty voice snarled in the background, 'So you think we are backstabbers, huh?'

Valentina turned around. Jackie and her friends had assembled by the building entrance. An army of students had gathered behind them, at a distance, eager to witness the face-off. Jackie greeted her with an angry, condescending gaze.

Her lips curled into a sneer that would make Anna Wintour proud. 'Two years ago, you were a freshman. You came to me and pleaded to join my group. You were desperate to get in on the party scene. You were desperate to be noticed. I saw your innocent face and I pitied you. But I also saw in you the potential to be a bona fide diva. So I helped you out by giving you access to the hottest parties in the city . . . by loaning you money to buy fashionable clothes and accessories. All I wanted from you was loyalty. All I wanted you to do was to be an ambassador for my angels. But what did you do instead?' She approached Valentina and caressed her face with her nails like a tigress preparing to gut a goat. 'You exploited your VIP access to serve your selfish ends. You slept with random men. You took money from them. And then, you backstabbed us by walking out on us, and then blaming us for your sins. You ungrateful, two-faced whore!' Jackie snarled, presenting her version of the sordid saga.

The gathered audience gasped with horror. Valentina's face turned red at the allegation. 'I slept around with random men? That's a lie. I was drugged. You know I'm right.'

'Is that so?' Jackie asked snidely, taking out her phone and showing Valentina a series of pictures and videos from the previous night. They showed Valentina doing drugs, kissing the shipping tycoon, sprawled naked on the bed with drugs on her belly.

Valentina's face turned white and she shook her head vehemently. 'No, this isn't me. These are photoshopped. That's not what happened.'

Jackie smiled and whispered like some criminal mastermind, 'These will go public today. You will rue the day you crossed paths with me.' She strutted down the corridor towards the elevator like an empress. Before she got on, she turned around and raised a finger as if she'd forgotten to mention something. 'Oh! And before I forget, you can flush your wrestling dreams down the toilet.'

Dazed and confused, Valentina staggered into her classroom. Her mind buzzed with many horrific consequences of Jackie acting out her threat, but they seemed too farfetched. *The photos don't prove anything. I'm sure nobody will believe her.*

At the start time, the classroom was agog with excitement. Nearly all the students were looking into their phones and whispering to each other. One of them, a young man in a suit, stared at her and pointed her out to his neighbour. 'That's her. That's V. The slut!'

Immediately, the entire classroom looked at her and sniggered. 'Latino trash! Crawl back into the gutter where you came from,' hollered a student. 'Yuck! Look at her arms and thighs. They're so huge and disgusting, makes me wanna puke,' mocked another, pretending to vomit. 'Look at that guy snorting drugs from her huge belly. I heard she wants to be a wrestler. She's definitely got the build for it,' chortled another. 'Whoa! The dude just paid her to be his bitch. His sugar baby! That's hysterical,' roared a student, doubling over with laughter. 'Hahaha! Look at that picture. Muscle Fairy. Isn't that hilarious?' joked another.

Amid the uproar, Valentina scrolled through her phone to see what they were talking about. She was horrified to find a series of images, videos and memes featuring her in various states of undress and intoxication.

The first image was of her snorting ketamine at the poolside table. She shrieked, 'Oh my God! That didn't even happen!' She scrolled through a couple of photos of her dancing in an inebriated state before pausing a video. This one showed her kissing and dancing with the tycoon in the bedroom before lying dazed on the bed—a sheaf of dollar bills placed on her torso. She felt a horrible sinking feeling in her stomach. *These must have been taken when I was cuckoo.* She quickly browsed the rest of the feed—each photo presenting a more incriminating and embarrassing portrait of her than the last—and stopped at the final one. It was a doctored photo of her in a party dress with muscular arms, huge thighs and a pair of angel wings, bearing the caption, 'Muscle Fairy'. Her chewing gum fell out of her mouth and her face turned beetroot red. She rose from her seat and shouted, 'These pictures have been manipulated to make me look ugly and slutty. They aren't real. This is not what happened out there. You've got to believe me.' Boos and chuckles went around the classroom. Her eyes filled with tears as she gesticulated wildly. 'Please listen to me! These are all fake. Things didn't happen the way they've been shown. I'm not that kind of a person. Please believe me.'

A section of students created a cacophony of horse-like sounds drowning out her plea. One of them flashed two thumbs down. 'That's really funny coming from a greedy, social-climbing slut!'

The professor finally discovered his voice. He raised his hands to restore order. 'All right! That's enough. It's time to begin our class.'

The rest of the day passed like a terrible nightmare. Everywhere she went, Valentina saw students whispering and sniggering at her and then looking at their phones, ostensibly sharing and commenting on the photos and videos. At the end of the day, she slumped on her living room sofa and burst into tears.

Florentina raced out of the kitchen and sat next to her daughter. 'What happened, darling?' Amid a deluge of tears, Valentina shared the events of the day. Her mom furrowed her eyebrows. Her lips curved downwards and she gnashed her teeth. 'Lying, manipulative snakes. Someone's got to put them in their proper places.'

Valentina shrugged her shoulders. 'How? I have no evidence to counter them.'

Florentina looked at the floor in silence. The look in her eyes alternated from helplessness to profound rage. Suddenly, Valentina's phone flashed an email alert. It was from the AFWA.

> We regret to inform you that in light of the incriminating evidence about your behaviour at a recent public event, we are forced to terminate your application. However, we cannot refund your deposit. You will be eligible to apply after two years. At that time, you may use the same funds towards a fresh application.

She looked at Florentina in dismay. 'Wrestling is over for me! The AFWA has cancelled my application because of the photos. I feel like someone just bulldozed my house.'

Florentina stood up and paced the length of the living room, 'They can't do that.'

Valentina went silent. *God! What's the matter with them? Why are they ruining my life?* She tried hard to make sense of the madness that had wrecked her life. But logic came at a premium. Her thoughts were interrupted by her ringing phone.

'Hello, Ms Perez. This is Audrey Isaac, the secretary to the dean of Miami University. Mr John Patrick Robertson would like to speak to you,' said a curt female voice.

After a few moments, Dean Robertson came on the line. 'Ms Perez, information has just surfaced that you've engaged in activities that violate the university's code of conduct for its students. We will have to expel you unless you can provide a valid justification for your actions. You will get a chance to defend yourself at a university committee hearing tomorrow.'

Valentina listened silently and then hung up. She gazed at her mother with a look that could make 100 per cent dark chocolate seem sweet. 'They are going to expel me unless I can present convincing contrary evidence.' She paused and took a deep breath. 'Now a battering ram is following the bulldozer and smashing my dreams to pieces.'

Florentina clenched her fists and brought them down in the air as if she were smacking their skulls with hammers. Her voice grated with steely determination and fighting spirit. 'They can't do this to you. Not as long as I'm alive.'

Valentina waved her hands dismissively. 'Mom, sit down. There's nothing we can do. There's no evidence to disprove what they're saying.'

Florentina waved her hands around in frustration. 'But—'

Her daughter stormed out of the living room before she could complete her statement.

That night, as she lay in bed, Valentina looked up at the ceiling and imagined herself bouncing from one star to the next like a ray of light. Her heart felt heavy when she saw the ray flitting aimlessly from one place to the next, unable to secure a home for itself. *My future is over. I can never follow my passion after all this. I can't even graduate from university with a major in biology. I guess I'll have to go to a crappy community college and start all over again. What will become of my life now? Have I lost my chance to be happy?*

The next day, she went to the dean's office and met the secretary. 'I'm Valentina Perez. I've come for the inquiry by the dean's committee.'

She was led down the hallway into a crowded, spacious room used for PhD oral exams. A single empty chair stood in front of a row of twelve seats already occupied by members of the faculty and the administration. A large projection screen was fixed to the wall in front of her, right behind the committee. Next to her, twenty people were seated in a theatre-style configuration. Valentina sat down on the hard aluminum chair, about six feet away from Jackie, Rosie, Vicky and the rest of the witnesses.

Jackie was sniggering and telling her friends, 'Bye bye, university. Hello, Walmart.'

Valentina looked at the judge and jurors. They were whispering to each other and throwing accusatory looks at her. She felt her heart dragged down to her stomach by a massive iron block and chains. *It's a fucking parole hearing.*

The dean called for silence and then addressed the gathering. 'Ms Perez has been implicated in actions that are considered unbecoming of the university community. You will be presented with evidence that suggests she took part in illegal activities. After analysing the evidence, we will issue a collective verdict.'

For the next hour, the gathering was exposed to a litany of pictures and videos showing Valentina in different compromising positions. Then the dean summoned Jackie, Rosie, Vicky and ten other college students who'd attended the party. All confirmed the veracity of the information.

Valentina recognized the corroborators as followers of Jackie's group. 'Fucking cronies,' she growled under her breath.

After the evidence was presented, the dean looked at Valentina sternly. 'Do you have anything to say about these allegations?'

Valentina cleared her throat. 'What can I say about these pictures and videos?' She paused and gazed at Jackie. She was staring at her with an 'I told you not to mess with me' look. A surge of defiance permeated her voice, 'They are all a big lie and an invasion of my privacy.'

Robertson responded, 'You should be aware, Ms Perez, that the behaviour of all students, even off campus, must comply with legal and ethical norms. You agreed to these terms the day you became a student at this university.' Valentina did not respond. The dean repeated, 'Do you have any evidence that can disprove these allegations?' Valentina shook her head. Robertson looked satisfied with the proceedings and turned to the jury. 'May I have your verdict, please?'

A commotion outside the door caused all heads to turn and a loud female voice shouted, 'Let me pass. I have something to show this kangaroo court.'

The security guard entered the room, seeming flustered. 'There's a lady outside who says she has new evidence.'

Robertson looked intrigued. He nodded his head. 'Okay. Let her in.'

Valentina's jaw dropped when she saw the visitor striding into the room. 'Who are you?' asked the dean, puzzled.

The lady pointed to Valentina and introduced herself. 'That's my daughter, and I'm not letting you destroy her reputation.' She looked at Jackie and her brigade with an expression of disgust. 'And I'm not letting peer pressure stop her from following her passion.'

Several whispers circulated around the room, building up to a humming crescendo. Robertson smacked his fist on his table. 'Silence! What evidence do you have to clear her of the charges?'

Florentina handed him a USB drive. 'It's all here.'

After the device was plugged in, a video recording played on the screen. It showed a group of six men and women snorting ketamine. They were joined in a little while by Jackie, her buddies and Valentina. The audience watched Jackie offering drugs to Valentina, who refused. Then Jackie spiked a drink and coerced Valentina to consume it. Initially, Valentina reeled. Before she could fall, however, her friends steadied her. Appearing to be in a state of intoxication, completely out of control of her senses, Valentina danced with the tycoon, who was aroused instantly, kissing her and squeezing her buttocks. Gasps of astonishment went around the room.

Florentina cleared her throat like an expert defense attorney to summon the audience's attention again. She pointed to Jackie's gang. 'All of them took advantage of her vulnerability.'

Next, the recording showed the tycoon whispering something in Jackie's ears and then slipping a wad of cash into her hands. Florentina froze that image. 'You can all see that Jackie took the money. Let's find out what for.'

The next segment of the video recording showed Valentina being hauled into a bedroom by Jackie, her friends and the tycoon. The wealthy businessman smirked slyly at Jackie. 'Can I take pictures of her naked?'

Jackie gave him a deep kiss in return and addressed him with a fake Southern drawl. 'Babe, you paid me. You can do whatever you want with her.'

Then the gang stripped Valentina naked and laid her on the bed. Jackie threw the wad of dollars on her body and licked the tycoon's Adam's apple. 'She's all yours.' Before the video could showcase a litany of acts of debasement and defilement, Florentina turned it off. 'So you can see that my daughter was drugged, pimped and raped by a stranger. These are grounds to press criminal charges against the perpetrators.'

Jackie jumped up from her chair and stretched out her arms. Her face had the look of a high-street burglar caught red-handed. 'No! Please don't do this to me.' She burst into tears and ran towards Valentina. She got down on her knees and held Valentina's hand. Tears flowed from her eyes. 'V! Please! Forgive me. Remember, I was your friend from the start. Your best friend. Your only friend.'

Valentina looked away from her ex-friend and gazed at a single, unoccupied chair that stood against the back wall. Its body was made of glistening white marble. The cushion comprised of lavish, lime green felt. Its legs were sawed off for some reason. She turned her attention back to the cowering Jackie. 'You disguised yourself as my friend. You're a charlatan.'

The dean thumped his desk. 'It seems we have compelling evidence to revisit our decision. We will now try Jackie and her friends for Valentina's abasement. Issue your collective verdict.' After a five-minute silence, the audience submitted their written votes. The dean counted the votes and declared, 'Jacklyn Hernandez, Rosalyn Chestnut, Victoria Lourdes, you are all guilty of violating the dignity of Valentina Perez. You are hereby expelled from the institution.'

The room erupted into cheers. The security guard removed the three women from the room. Valentina ran to her mother and gave her a mighty hug. 'How did you get this information?'

Florentina smiled and handed her the tape. 'Yesterday, I nursed a patient at the hospital who was suffering from internal bleeding and nausea. After his test results came back, I saw he'd overdosed on ketamine. He was slurring and could not walk properly or sit upright. I suspected he'd been at the party. I checked his ID. His name was Marco Ramirez. I chatted with him and learned he was an event promoter who'd organized a party the previous night. An out-of-control party. According to a guest at the venue, a woman had been raped, he said. I figured he'd have access to evidence of the crime. I revealed that you are my daughter and that I needed to unearth this information to save your reputation. After much prodding, he told me about a centralized recording system at the house connected to hidden cameras placed in every corner of the property, that must have captured all the events of the day. He agreed to help me exonerate you by finding the relevant tapes.

But how could we get it? He said he could access the video recording system because he was friendly with the owner, who happened to be unaware of the rape. This morning, we went over to the house. To help me gain access, he introduced me to the owner as his cousin. Then, he said he'd left behind a storage device with footage from the party that he needed to promote the next party on social media. We entered the video recording room and accessed the raw camera feed from the previous day.

There, we saw . . . in full gory detail . . . the horrific things you'd suffered. We captured all this on the USB drive.'

Valentina clapped adoringly. 'You saved my reputation. I don't know how I can ever thank you.'

Meanwhile, the security guard had just opened the lone window at the end of the room. The colours of the rainbow swathed the dark space—performing a magical light show on the white walls. Florentina pointed to the rainbow on the horizon. 'You can thank me by following your passion.'

Valentina gave her mom another hug. Her eyes fell on the rainbow. It was so radiant that it compelled her to close her eyes for a moment.

Florentina stroked her daughter's shoulder. 'It's beautiful, isn't it?' she whispered.

Valentina's voice was choked with emotion. 'You've always told me to follow my heart. Instead, I got distracted by the noise around me. From today, I'll never allow myself to be sidetracked again.'

On the strength of the video evidence, the billionaire car dealer and the shipping magnate were arrested for sexual assault, criminal abetment and drug proliferation. They were tried, found guilty, and sentenced to twenty-five years of hard time at the Federal Detention Centre in Miami.

After the university had revoked the accusations and issued a public letter of apology, Valentina's social reputation was restored. Subsequently, the AFWA reversed their judgment and enrolled her in the wrestling regionals. Three months later, in front of her beaming mother, Valentina crushed all pretenders and emerged as the leading rookie at the contest. She was awarded a three-year contract to become a full-time professional wrestler.

Six months later, after a whirlwind global tour, she returned home. Florentina gave her a hug and smiled with a mischievous look. 'You're so brawny now. I can barely wrap my arms around you.'

Valentina removed her superhero costume wings and smiled. 'Thank you for reminding me I have wings.'

REFLECTION: REMEMBER, YOU HAVE WINGS

Were you ever forced to mould yourself into an image acceptable to your peers?

Social pressure is a force akin to that of a screwdriver, which compels us to fit into our circles and prevents us from expressing our individuality. It is intended to foster homogenous behaviour so the unity of the group may be preserved. To make people fit in, alternative expressions of thought and action are often ignored or condemned by group members. Whenever our ideas, aspirations or actions are rebuked for being out of line with the principles of our peer group, we tend to feel humiliated. In these moments, we might even feel small and insignificant, like a mere screw at a construction site, surrounded by big, heavy machinery. We might think our thoughts and opinions don't matter to anyone because they fail to capture the imagination of our peers. As if we didn't matter to anyone in the entire world because we don't matter to our peers. In those moments, we tend to overlook the fact that we have wings of our own.

We forget that we have the power of technology at our disposal to transmit our thoughts to mankind—the ultimate peer group. We forget that we have the power of intellect to inspire strangers to listen to us, to follow us. We forget that we have the inner strength to change things by simply working to make things happen. We forget that a lone traveller on a road can someday nourish a land. We forget that we have the power to fly.

It is during those moments of utter rejection and abject humiliation that we most urgently need our wings—wings to help us soar above the low tide of public opinion. Wings to help us smash through the barriers to our dreams. Wings to help us reach our goals.

In this darkest hour, when our individuality is threatened by the maddening crowd, let us unleash our wings to rise above them all.

The protagonist in this story overcame the suffocating pressure from her peers to mould herself into their image. Understand how she did it, and you will believe that you can too.

4

OVERCOMING FINANCIAL STRESS

UNDERSTANDING FINANCIAL STRESS

To lead a quality life, we must have the resources to meet our needs. The only way to access these resources is by having a stable stream of income. However, there are times when our earned wealth is inadequate to satisfy our needs. During those moments, we are often hounded by stress.

Financial stress is the inner negativity we experience when we try to solve our resource constraints. We require resources to fulfill a variety of needs: shelter, transportation, health, nutrition, education, careers and relationships, to name just a few. These resources may be in the form of goods or services, to access which, we need to pay. Most of us might find ourselves without a partner or a guide to help us in this process and trying to solve the challenge alone can produce a negative web of thoughts and feelings which might further isolate us. This is how we experience financial stress. Here's a metaphor to better illustrate how financial stress plays out in the mind.

Initially, when we first set out to address our resource constraints, our minds may be clear. We may see a dimly lit path in front of us and that might make us nervous—we might ask ourselves if we can travel alone on this path. It seems to get darker the further ahead we move. Now we might feel too scared to continue walking on it alone. We may think about who could join us on this journey and may not be able to think of anyone. We will likely become even more afraid as more dark paths seem to diverge from the one we're on, forming many scary crossroads. A clear decision about which path to follow becomes more and more complicated. Fear and anxiety envelop us. Then we might start seeing potholes appear on all of these paths. Now we might ask, which path is the safest? We don't know the answer. So doubt starts to cloud our mind. We ask ourselves unnecessary questions. To our horror, the paths multiply further and further in all directions in response to our questions. The potholes seem to increase manifold, too. The web of fear, anxiety and confusion takes hold of our minds. What a terrible price to pay for doubting ourselves!

To give you my own real-life encounter with financial stress, I'd like to share my experience of raising funds for my company during the coronavirus pandemic. At the beginning of 2020, I was extremely upbeat about the prospects of my digital startup, MeVero. The social media app had garnered strong reviews from customers and gained significant traction in just eight months since its launch. Impressed by the results, an angel investor had signed an agreement to bankroll us for a full year. Buoyed by these developments, I thought that nothing could go wrong. Success was just a hop-skip away.

I couldn't have been more delusional!

It took just a few weeks for the pandemic to decimate the prospects of millions of entrepreneurs and working professionals. I was one of them. Three weeks into March—ten days before we were supposed to receive our first tranche of funds—our investor pulled out of the deal we'd agreed upon. In a tone of regret, he informed me that he couldn't go through with it because his own business had completely tanked, and he was almost out of cash. Shocked, I begged him to reconsider. He could not. Fortunately, he threw me a slim chance at a lifeline by extending funding by a month. But after that, I would be on my own. So I had to raise funds amid the worst financial crisis imaginable.

The next eight months proved to be the most stressful period of my life. India was in the midst of a strict lockdown—a total shutdown of almost all businesses around the nation, including Kolkata, my city of residence. In this warlike scenario, I had to somehow find and woo investors for my startup. It seemed like an impossible task.

Between April and May, I contacted more than 5,000 investors from different countries, both personal contacts and complete strangers. To my horror, I found that no one was even willing to talk, let alone invest. The common refrains I kept hearing were, 'You're too early' and 'This is a bad time for me'. During that phase, I had funds for only two more months. Meanwhile, rejections from banks and private investors also started to pour in. Time was running out and my options were highly limited. I tried to maintain a brave face, but internally, I was a nervous wreck. Financial stress had me by the balls.

Every night, I'd toss and turn in bed, unable to sleep . . . racked with doubt and anxiety. During the day, I'd wait to hear from the few who'd responded to my initial outreach. They never called back. On many occasions, I'd curl up in bed midday, debilitated by the tension. I couldn't bring myself to continue with my physical fitness regimen. To take my mind off my problems, I started binge-eating sweets and junk food.

These gave me a temporary sugar high, but I gained a lot of weight and sustained tooth decay in the bargain. A fusillade of anxious thoughts blasted my mind. 'What will happen to me if the company shuts down? What will I do next? How will I live with failure?' I despaired, my heart buffeted by a tornado of negativity.

This is a classic experience of financial stress. Our desperation to rid ourselves of it can further force us to take drastic decisions with adverse, long-term consequences. Financial stress would not have been so suffocating had we had easy access to a community support system—as people did in the past.

In the analogue industrial era (pre-1990), most people lived in neighbourhoods with a deep sense of community spirit and shared values. These communities provided members with support and camaraderie. People trusted each other and it was usually easy to get help. Moreover, the world felt like a smaller place because the reach, frequency and volume of media were limited. In those times, it was easier for people to fulfill their needs and aspirations. There wasn't a huge gap between one's aspirations and the means required to achieve them, as a result. Life was simpler and much less stressful.

In the digital, globalized age, the migration of people to different parts of the world has increased exponentially. Technology has disrupted old-world manufacturing industries, causing the decline of many towns and cities. Erstwhile homogeneous neighbourhoods have either been hollowed out or repopulated with people professing different value systems. Thus, communities have become more diverse in terms of identity, making it harder for people to discover things in common. Social bonding has, overall, declined and people have become more isolated. Social trust—the glue that keeps communities together—has been frayed. At the same time, people are better exposed to information and trends through advances in technology. Aspirations have skyrocketed. However, with the decay of social trust, people cannot easily find help on their journey to fulfill their aspirations. With the gap between aspirations and means widening, resource constraints have become more acute, making financial stress inescapable for the majority.

The protagonist in this next story experienced acute stress caused by financial constraints. Will he overcome this barrier and find peace of mind?

WE CAN BE LEGENDS

The problem of dirty drinking water was an inconvenience that many residents of Flint, Michigan had learned to live with. But for Carmelo Jones and his mother, it was a descent into a living nightmare.

On a Monday morning, Carmelo Jones turned on the kitchen tap to pour himself a glass of water. A pool of brown, polluted liquid collected in the basin. He hastily turned off the tap and hollered to his mother, who was sitting outside on the porch. 'Mom! Where's the bottled water? There's so much lead out here that the water's as brown as mud.'

His mother, a slender, frail, sixty-year-old woman—nicknamed 'Granny' by her friends because her hair had greyed more than any of them—sat in a rocking chair, drinking coffee. She put down her cup and shouted back, 'There's no more bottled water left. I set aside the last lot, half a bucket, for you to take a shower today.'

Carmelo shook his head and filled up a glass with the lead-contaminated tap water. He then poured it into a $15 water filter. It took a few minutes for the dark brown load to lighten through the removal of iron and other impurities.

He took a swig from the glass as if it were a tall, cool mug of beer and wiped his lips with a towel. The starch white fabric got considerably darkened with sediments and impurities of various sorts. Carmelo looked at the dirty towel and scoffed. 'Well, it's great that our cheap water pitcher removes iron and arsenic. At least it's drinkable. The best I can do is settle for lead poisoning.'

His mother spat out the final dregs of her morning beverage onto the floor. She turned her head and looked into the kitchen with a displeased expression. 'Watch your mouth, Carmelo! I don't see *you* doing anything about it. I don't see you following your passion, making enough money and getting us out of this contaminated, crime-infested neighbourhood.'

Next to the basin, on the countertop, lay a two-page pamphlet advertising a district-level town hall meeting with the municipal administrators of the city to be held a few days later. The second page was a photocopy of an attendance sheet containing his signature. Carmelo slammed the document with his fist. 'Mom! It hurts me that you think I'm a passive bum in this crisis and that I'm not contributing to our better future!' He glanced at a corner in the living room. There was a carton filled with spare parts from cars, computers and various other devices. He smiled wistfully. *Way back in middle school, I once built a world of smart, connected devices with Mom. But how can I dream of following my passion now when we are so strapped for cash? A hassle-free degree in nutrition is my best bet.*

He raised his voice. 'How can I be somebody in this hellhole? How can I dream of pursuing a demanding course in automobile engineering when I'm struggling to support us financially? How can I be just a college student now that Dad's gone and you have chronic bone and kidney diseases?'

Carmelo's mother rolled up the long sleeves of her dress and stared at her prosthetic hands regretfully. *Prolonged exposure to this contaminated water has ruined my life.* She looked up at the heavens in anguish and raised her arms. 'Lord, why did you punish Daisy Jones so badly? I have done some bad things, but were they so bad as to deserve this awful fate? Why did you take away my hands? Why did you compromise my knees? Why did you snatch my nursing job at the Flint Community Hospital . . . my only window to repentance . . . my only window to a decent wage? Why? Why?'

Carmelo came outside and gave her a hug. 'Don't worry, Mom. We've taken some hard knocks. But we're not down yet. There's still a chance we can bounce back from this financial mess.'

His mother wiped a tear from her eyes. 'How? Carmelo? How? There are days when we don't even have enough food on our table. How are we going to cope with the situation?'

Carmelo stroked the top of her head. 'Mom, I'm working part-time at the auto repair shop. I know it's only $10 an hour. But if I work hard for the next two years and put in ten hours of overtime every week, I'll make enough to move us out of this place and take care of your health.' He packed his water bottle—full of light brown water—and zipped his backpack. 'And I will definitely buy a decent water filter.'

'My joint pain is so bad now that it's difficult to take the stairs in the mornings.' His mother moaned and pointed to a used Chevy Spark she'd bought seven years earlier. Its paint was peeling off, its body was heavily damaged. 'I can hardly get into that beaten-up, creaking, secondhand junk. I can hardly drive to the hospital for my weekly checkup. I can hardly push a grocery cart down the aisle to use my food stamps. The doctor said I need surgery on my limbs in six months, otherwise I'll become a paraplegic. Medicare won't cover it completely. Tell me, Carmelo. How can we ever afford this operation and buy ourselves a new house?'

Daisy winced in pain as she shifted in her hard rocking chair. Carmelo noticed exposed pieces of the worn-out cushion's stuffing, which had been ripped out by two feuding neighbourhood cats. He helped her up, handed her a bent walking stick and assisted her to the driveway. On the way, he spotted his next-door neighbour, a young woman in her early twenties—wearing a sharp business suit. She was about to get into a spanking new blue BMW 7-series sedan.

She smiled and waved her hands towards them, 'Hi, Carmelo. Hi, Mrs Woods! How ya doin'?'

Carmelo smiled back. 'Real good, Lakisha.'

She flashed a thumbs-up. 'Good to hear that. I'm starting today as a real estate broker with Truman and Lepinsky. I'd love to tell you how I earned it. But I'm late.' She got into her car and drove off.

The pair watched the car speeding along Industrial Drive, the pot-holed neighbourhood road, past rows of dilapidated houses occupied by former employees of GM's closed car factory. After it had disappeared down a side street, Daisy looked at Lakisha's freshly painted, six-bedroom mansion across the street ruefully. 'Some people seem to be doing fine. Why can't we?'

Carmelo lowered his voice. 'Her dad is Lebron Adams. He makes a living supplying guns and drugs to the gangs of the city. It's rumoured he works with the police.'

Daisy Jones glanced at the tony house with bitterness. She immediately turned her head and looked at the cloudy horizon. An old story formed in her mental horizon. 'After your dad got laid off from GM, he joined the illegal drugs and guns trade, the only thriving business in these parts. I suppose it's a good thing he abandoned us for good. There was too much heat on him . . . from the cops . . . from other gang members . . . all for the money he owed. He decided it was better to leave us than to put our lives at risk.' She looked at the façade of their own house. The wood had chipped off in several places. The roof had been battered by a recent storm. The paint was black in patches from the August humidity. She sighed, 'Oh well! We should be thankful that he left us money to buy this place and get a fresh start.'

At that moment, a strong gust of wind blew in and rustled the fragile, plastic roof shingles that Carmelo had installed the previous month. Ten roof shingles came crashing down on the front porch. Daisy picked one up that lay at her feet and her lips curled into a sneer. 'There we go! Some start!'

She looked up to see where the tiles had blown from and spotted a multicoloured pigeon sitting on the dilapidated roof. It was watching them with rapt attention.

Carmelo noticed its unusual gold-and-red striped feathers and his eyes widened. 'Wow! I've never seen such a pretty bird out here before. It must have escaped from the Wilderness Trails Zoo. I should call the officials to come and rescue it.'

Daisy wasn't interested in appearing on the cover of *National Geographic*. 'Get the hell out of here, you demonic spy,' she yelled and hurled the plastic shingle at the avian. Fortunately, the sharp object missed the bird and landed in a neighbouring tree. Without as much as a squawk, the pigeon flew away toward the horizon.

A large delivery truck emblazoned with the logo 'MICHIGAN WATER DEPARTMENT' appeared in front of their house. A uniformed man approached them. He wheeled two gallons of water on a trolley. 'Water delivery,' he said, handing over a receipt for Daisy to sign. Afterwards, he dumped the cases of water in front of the door.

Carmelo pointed to the van. 'When are you coming next?'

The man shrugged. 'No idea. The water honchos plan the schedule at the start of every week. It's all politics, you know.'

Carmelo looked at him with an enquiring expression. Silently, he entreated the man to provide inside information about the Michigan Water Department's makeshift plans to provide Flint's households with clean water until the town's supply was fully restored.

The delivery man winked. He came close to Carmelo and whispered in his ear, 'I can turn this sporadic weekly delivery into a sure thing every month if you pay me $200.' He stood for a moment, waiting to see if the family would take the bait. They looked back at him coldly. The delivery man flicked his right hand dismissively. 'Whatever. Loads of families are taking me up on this offer.' He glanced at Daisy, who was looking at him with dagger eyes, and held up his hands in mock defense. 'Hey! Stop looking at me like that, Miss Goody-Two-Shoes. This is the only way a public servant can earn a living wage these days.'

Once he'd left, Carmelo kissed his mother goodbye and drove for half an hour to reach a vast, abandoned GM car factory that had once hummed with the bustling noise of automobile production machinery. He then took a side road for another mile to a car repair shop, Flint Auto Works. The modestly sized store was located in a large area with a parking lot, a big crumbling building and a discount superstore. He parked just outside the second building, a place that used to accommodate twenty vehicles for various repairs but was now an abandoned warehouse in the centre of a discount superstore parking lot. Inside the main workshop were only two cars, waiting to be fixed. He donned his overalls and slid beneath the undercarriage of a Nissan Altima.

His coworker was working underneath the adjacent vehicle, humming a song. He saw Carmelo under the car, stopped singing and looked furtively to his right. A corner office was located there, bearing the sign 'Director'. He lowered his voice. 'Hey, Carmelo! I heard the shop is closing down. One month, max.'

Carmelo's brow furrowed. 'Canon, you must be mistaken. This place has been around for fifty years. It's gone through so many ups and downs. But, it's always found a way to survive.'

The coworker was a beefy, thirty-five-year-old with a goatee. He took a piece of paper from his pocket and read aloud. 'Dear Mortimer, Revenue at the site has declined continuously over the last three years. Despite shutting down the second workshop and turning it into a parking lot, the additional income has not been enough to offset the fall in the auto repair business. It seems the death of the auto industry in the rust belt is imminent. To protect our investment, I recommend we wind up our company and sell our property to the discount chain 50 Cents. Regards, Zack Renfro.'

Carmelo listened to the intentions of the founders of the auto repair franchise with disbelief. *What! They are shutting down? The once proud owners of twenty locations throughout the states of Ohio, Michigan and Pennsylvania? This can't be happening!* He tried his best to maintain composure. 'How do you know we'll shut down in a month?'

Canon continued reading in response. 'Dear Zack: our families have been in business together for twenty-five years now. We've attended each other's weddings, bar mitzvahs, and birthdays. However, the situation you describe is truly alarming. Let's meet on March 30 and take a final call on the future of our company. Best, Mortimer.'

Carmelo felt a number of micro-needles piercing his back at the same time. *Oh no! They're doing it! Their decision to sell the firm is final.* He looked to his left at the broken windowpanes, which had remained in that condition for the last six months. All of a sudden, the pins turned into thick blades digging into his flesh. 'In a month? Oh my God! In a month, this place will shut down.'

Canon nodded. Carmelo jumped up on his haunches. He stared at Canon with an entreating look. 'I need this job, man. I really, desperately need this. I can't afford to lose it at this time.'

Canon got up from under the car and hugged his mate. 'I hear you, bro. I'm in the same boat. I guess we have no option but to look for another job.'

Carmelo shook his head and pushed his friend's hand away. 'Another job? Are you out of your mind? There's no job around here in manufacturing. The only places that are hiring in Flint are hospitals, restaurants, supermarkets and barbershops. Their pay? Abysmal. I'll have to drop out of college. Work full-time in retail for six bucks an hour. At that rate, it'll take me five years to pay for my mom's operation. Ten years to move out of our shithole on Industrial Drive. And five years . . .'

He paused momentarily and went over to a display rack in the corner. It showcased various trinkets, awards and medals. Carmelo picked up a framed photograph taken on his first day at the job, a year ago. He was posing with Canon and the owners. Everyone had smiles on their faces. 'My mom won't live for five years unless she has an operation.' A tear escaped and trickled down his cheek.

Canon hugged his friend again. 'I feel your pain, bro. I've been there. When Westbury Steel—my dad's employer—went bust, he lost his medical insurance. He was no longer covered for a lung infection he'd suffered from inhaling toxic dust at the plant. Financially stressed, my mother was forced to sell her body to make ends meet. That's how she put me through high school and then two years of community college. I was on the road to graduation. However, in my junior year of studying to be an electronics engineer, she was killed in a drive-by shooting. That was when I dropped out of college and got a job here. This has been my home for the last ten years.'

Carmelo shook his head and looked down mournfully, Canon whispered in his ear, 'Hey, there's a way out of this mess. Meet me at six tonight outside the abandoned warehouse of Zeno Construction. It's at 8035 Fenton Road.'

'What will we do there?'

Canon flashed a half-smile and created a circle with his arms. 'Turn our lives around.'

Canon told the owner, Mortimer Gluckman, that he wasn't feeling well, and left work early. After completing his regular nine-to-five shift, Carmelo popped into the owner's office. 'Hey, Mort. Need me for anything?'

The office was a cramped space of 100 square feet. Most of the area was cluttered with furniture in disrepair—a cupboard with a broken lock and five filing cabinets with drawers so damaged that they didn't close properly. Several dusty files and documents were strewn on the floor. A one-foot-high glass case occupied a prime spot in the office, directly opposite the owner's desk. It stood on top of a three-foot-high pedestal. Inside it was a wooden box—six inches long, four inches wide and three inches high. From his position at the door, Carmelo saw Mortimer perusing a rather large document intently, oblivious to his presence.

What's he staring at?

A minute later, the proprietor looked up. He was a short, paunchy, sixty-five-year-old man with sad, tired eyes, a silver beard, thinning hair, and wearing a wrinkled business suit. He hastily folded the document and placed a book on top of it.

Carmel glanced at the glass case to his right. 'That thing's been sitting here unopened since the day I joined. Sure you don't want my help on your secret project?' He laughed. 'I'm pretty good with alien technology, you know.'

The owner waved his right hand and gave his employee an evasive smile. 'Oh, Carmelo! You're such an amazing technician. I wish I could engage you more meaningfully than for the odd paint job or engine replacement. However, there's very little business at the moment. Go home.'

Carmelo nodded his head. He was about to leave when he spotted a portion of the document sticking from beneath the book on Mortimer's desk. From of the corner of his eye, he thought he saw the drawing of a futuristic-looking car with wings. 'Is that the blueprint of a new car?'

The embarrassed owner moved to hide the schematic completely. 'Oh! It's nothing! Just something I'd once set my heart on finishing. Something . . . ' His voice trailed away as he glanced at the wooden box in the glass case. He looked out through the window at the crumbling, abandoned warehouse at the centre of the parking lot. Carmelo saw Mortimer looking at a multicoloured pigeon perched on top of the decrepit building, its lively, richly coloured feathers in stark contrast to the dark, fading exterior of the workshop. Regret filled his eyes, spilling into his voice, 'Something that's no longer there.'

Carmelo noted the pigeon had the same red-and-gold striped feathers as the one on his roof earlier that day. 'Hey! I just saw that bird this morning. It must be a rare species gone AWOL. I thought about calling the zoo folks to rescue it, but I was running late.'

Mortimer turned around and looked at the derelict warehouse to check if the bird was still around. It wasn't. 'Haha. Rare? That's an overstatement. The ancestors of that bird—a male and a female—were gifted to the CEO of GM by the Mexican government way back in the eighties. A special aviary was even prepared to house them. But guess what?' Carmelo looked at him inquiringly. 'They escaped when the layoffs and closures started.' Mortimer roared with laughter. He pointed to the warehouse. 'The runaway birds reproduced and expanded their population for a decade. However, during the last twenty-five years, they became a favourite target for hunters and poachers—many of whom were laid-off factory workers. That bird you saw is one of the last survivors of a glorious species.'

Carmelo shook his head. 'That's really sad. But I suppose necessity is the mother of crap.'

Mortimer responded with a nod. 'Yep. Human nature for you. Back in those days, I used to be a production manager. I remember that bird's ancestor perched on top of the factory roof at midday, its eyes fixated on the activities on the premises. In fact, . . .' Mortimer paused for a moment and closed his eyes.

He loved that job. He must really miss that life.

He opened his eyes again. For a moment, there was a sparkle, but then it faded away. 'In fact, its feathers were the same colour as . . .'

'Same as what?'

Mortimer swallowed what seemed to be a lump in his throat. 'Oh! Never mind. I'd rather not talk about it. Anyway, you should leave now.' His voice quivered as he dismissed his helper with a wave of his hand.

Once his shift was over, Carmelo drove towards Zeno Construction in Grand Blanc Township. After a thirty-minute drive, he pulled over near a scrapyard for abandoned construction equipment. A barbed-wire fence formed the complex's mile-long perimeter. A signboard outside cautioned, 'TRESPASSERS WILL BE PROSECUTED'.

Carmelo looked for an opening in the fence. *How do I get in?* He soon spotted a hole cut into the fence. He bent down and squeezed his body carefully through the gap. A lightly forested area lay ahead. He walked through the woods for five minutes before stumbling upon an embankment. He slipped and slid twenty feet down the earthy, grassy side of a pit. He got up and dusted off the dirt that had gathered on him. 'What the hell is this?' He was standing in a pit about fifty feet long and twenty-five feet deep, that had been dug for the purpose of housing junk equipment. A scissor lift stood at the opposite end of the space, providing the only feasible exit to the surface.

'Welcome to the rehab clinic.' The greeting was delivered by a familiar voice.

Carmelo looked at his buddy disapprovingly. 'Canon! You could have told me that you were hosting a meet-up in a pit full of junk equipment.' He pointed to six broken vehicles that included an excavator, a crane and a dump truck. Six guys were leaning against a massive, rusted water pipe.

Canon laughed. The young men were all in their late twenties and early thirties. 'Jamal, Kareem, Joseph, Michael, Ronnie, meet my coworker at the auto works, Carmelo.

Carmelo, these guys are all former employees at the GM plant that got shut down three years ago.'

'What are you people doing here?' Carmelo narrowed his eyebrows.

The men laughed. Jamal—a short, skinny person with a goatee and dreadlocks—lit up a cigarette. After a puff, he answered, 'Planning our escape from poverty.'

Carmelo flailed his arms as if he was staving off a bunch of mosquitoes. 'I've been hearing such nonsensical comments from Canon all day. Now, unless you have something to say that's useful and concrete, I'm outta here.'

'Nobody's leaving.' A gruff voice boomed from behind him.

Carmelo turned around. A nattily dressed, clean-shaven man in his late fifties faced him. He was wearing a purple suit and a top hat, and carrying what appeared to be a cane. 'Mr Le—Lebron . . . Adams?' he stuttered, recognizing the father of his neighbour, Lakisha.

Lebron laughed and patted Carmelo's back. 'Welcome to our club, The Homies. Canon's been talking you up a fair bit, you know. I understand you have financial problems?'

Carmelo nodded. 'That's right. My ma's really sick and needs an operation soon.'

Lebron's voice mellowed with a sprinkling of compassion juice. 'I've seen her often, and it breaks my heart. No one should suffer like that. Everyone you see around here . . .' He pointed to the group of men. 'All these boys were laid off from that car factory. So was I. We had lives . . . dreams . . . prospects. Those went kaput once GM decided to shut down its plant and move it offshore to China. Unfortunately, like you, none of us can leave this town. We have roots in this place, people to take care of. People who've fallen sick from the sewage water served up by our corrupt system. Now that the factories are gone, there's only one way to earn a decent living out here.'

Right then, a man wearing a suit descended to the pit on the scissor lift. The man carried a black trunk, and when he opened it to reveal the contents, Carmelo's jaw dropped. Inside were twenty packets of white power and ten handguns.

Lebron placed an avuncular arm on his shoulder. 'After the auto companies shut shop, many former workers joined gangs. Today, there are twenty criminal rings running amok in this region.'

Carmelo scratched his head.

'And what do these gangs need to thrive? Drugs and guns. That's what we supply.'

Carmelo backed away a few steps, slinking away from the hand. 'I can't be a part of this.'

Lebron advanced towards him. 'Carmelo, be smart. How are you going to rehabilitate your mother in six months?' He paused, looked sideways with a furtive glance and broke out into laughter. 'The police? Heck, no. You don't have to worry about them. They're all getting a cut.'

The other men wore threatening expressions and began to close in on him. Carmelo looked around and found no way of cutting through. *There's no way I'm getting out of this alive. I'm trapped. I have to go along*. He took a deep breath and cleared his throat. 'Okay, Mr Adams, I'm in. What do you need me to do?'

'Go with Canon to the Goo Goo Dolls Club on Atherton East. Drop off this consignment at the Jersey gang's; they operate from there. They'll pay you $100,000 in cash. The two of you will get $1,000 apiece. You will return the rest to my house tonight.'

Carmelo and Canon proceeded to the lift. 'Load the merchandise in the back of his car,' Lebron gestured the bearer of the trunk to accompany the two.

With the trunk loaded in his car, Carmelo drove down the Dort Highway to Atherton East. The fading light could not conceal a zone full of permanently shuttered hardware and auto repair stores now chock-a-block with 24/7 liquor shops.

Canon glanced at his watch. 'It's five past seven. The light's totally out now.' He directed Carmelo for five minutes through winding, dark roads with lampposts whose bulbs had been shot out by bullets, and houses that had signs for foreclosure or sale. Many façades were sheathed in a cloak of blackness. Half their exteriors were visible in the faint illumination from the working streetlights while the other half were dark. Carmelo noticed their semi-dark, semi-lit appearance. They resembled unfinished paintings. He slowed down the car in front of a house and peered through his car window. Something was moving around in the dark portion of the façade. He flashed the car's headlights at the segment and gasped. A huge colony of termites was crawling all over the building. Canon looked grimly at the site of infestation. 'The entire area is infested because the sanitation department only visits on a monthly basis. None of the residents can afford to get their houses fixed or to call pest control.' Canon shuddered. *Damn! People actually live like this?* He quickly hit the accelerator.

Ten minutes later, they drove into the parking lot of a building bearing a neon sign, 'Goo Goo Dolls Strip Club'. Canon pointed to a heavyset man manning the front entrance. 'The gang members are inside. We've got to tell the bouncer to inform them we are here.' They got out of the car and approached him. He eyed them up and down suspiciously. Then, he stood like a wall in front of them, arms folded across his chest. 'We are closed at the moment.'

Canon tiptoed close and whispered into the man's ear. 'Tell Shawn Patrick I have a delivery.'

'Wait here,' the security guard replied and went inside the club.

Five minutes later, he emerged from the club with a group of ten men, all wearing leather vests and torn jeans. Their arms and necks were heavily tattooed. The leader—a limping, reed-thin bald guy in his early fifties with a pierced tongue and a soft moustache—inquired, 'So, you are Lebron's boys, huh?' Canon glanced at Carmelo. 'That guy is Shawn Patrick.'

'What happened to his legs?' Carmelo asked under his breath.

'Shh! He suffered an accident years ago at the auto plant.' Canon bowed his head deferentially before the gang leader and smiled obsequiously. 'Yes. This is our new guy. Carmelo. He'll be servicing you.'

'I don't trust this guy, boss. He looks like a snitch.' One of Shawn's comrades—a burly, bearded man with a bandana painted with the Latin words 'Declines Pacis' (decline of peace)—smirked at the two friends.

Shawn growled sarcastically, 'Bulldog, you know this from your career in psychotherapy, huh?' He pointed at the parked car and looked sternly at the two visitors. 'Show me what you've got.'

Bulldog inspected the guns in the trunk and flashed a thumbs-up. 'Ten brand-new TEC-9 semiautomatic handguns. Straight from the PD warehouse.'

He placed his hands on the trunk. Shawn clenched his jaw. 'Idiot! You forgot to check the drugs.'

Bulldog quickly apologized for the omission. He tasted a sample of powder from a 100-gram sachet and nodded. 'This is heroin, all right.' Once again, he closed the trunk and lifted it by the handle. Shawn's face had turned red. 'Weigh it, you moron! All of it.'

A short, portly associate with a shaved head and a tattoo on his neck that read 'ANGEL KILLER' handed Bulldog a scale. He chuckled. 'Don't worry, Bulldog. This scale is accurate up to a margin of error of 1 per cent. That's enough for you to live.'

Bulldog grumbled with irritation, but weighed every packet. When the task was over, he wore the look of a harangued porter at an airport. 'Ten packs. Amounting to 1 kilo in total. Can we go now?'

Shawn looked relieved and snapped his fingers. 'All right, boys. Let's get outta here. Pay the man here a hundred grand.' The gang leader handed Carmelo a thick envelope, shook his hand, and said, 'Good doing business with you.'

One of the Jersey gang members lifted the trunk from the car. Suddenly, gunshots rang through the air. The guy was startled and dropped the case back to its place. 'On your hands and knees! You are all under arrest!' A police officer, brandishing a gun, emerged from a car parked in the distance.

Almost immediately, a police van screeched to a halt in front of the strip club. Ten heavily armed officers jumped out of the vehicle. 'Drop your weapons, or we'll shoot!'

Carmelo looked around. They were surrounded by officers. Beads of sweat rolled down his forehead. He quickly bent down and hid near the hood of his car. From his vantage point, he saw Shawn take out a gun and shoot at the posse. Two officers were down in an instant. A full-blown assault commenced. Sounds of gunfire echoed everywhere.

Bodies of both criminals and cops riddled with bullets slumped to the ground in every direction. Carmelo slid underneath the car and crawled to a spot below the backseat—right beneath the trunk. He nearly bit off his tongue. There was Canon's body on the ground. His face was turned toward Carmelo. His eyes were wide with shock and horror. His head was drenched in a pool of blood. Carmelo looked to his right. A few gang members who'd survived the onslaught ran to the dark space behind the side entrance of the club. They signalled to each other to shoot anyone who came close.

Several police officers converged on the crime scene. A cop looked nervously at the slumped bodies. 'We need backup. Six dead.'

'How many of our own?' asked another police officer.

A third keyed in the mic of the radio. 'Three down. Three down.'

A static-y voice blared through the device. 'Paramedics are on their way.'

The first officer spotted some movement by the side entrance. 'Proceed carefully,' he indicated to the others to follow him in that direction.

Carefully and quietly, guns cocked, the police approached the side entrance. Two minutes later, they disappeared into the darkness. Silence followed for what seemed like an eternity. Carmelo shivered. Suddenly, he heard the sounds of guns and several screams. After a five-minute shootout, silence ensued again. Carmelo heaved a sigh of relief. *Finally, it's over!* Four survivors of the carnage stepped out of the darkness into the dimly lit parking lot. Carmelo gasped. They were Shawn, Bulldog and two associates.

They'll kill me. I've gotta get out of here! Carmelo crawled backwards on his hands and knees to reach the front of the car.

Bulldog gestured for his men to hurry up and pointed to the back of the car where the contraband merchandise was still stored. 'Get the stash and let's get outta here.'

I have to make a run for it. Now! Or they'll find me. Carmelo observed he was bathed with bright light from an adjacent street lamp—a light that was visible to anyone six feet away. The gang approached until they were about ten feet from him. *Now!* He closed his eyes and jumped out from below the car.

Shawn reeled and almost fell on his back. 'What the fuck! The kid's alive. I'm gonna kill him.'

The gang members took out their weapons and pointed them at Carmelo. He closed his eyes and prayed to God. *Look after Mom for me.* Suddenly, the door to the strip club door blasted wide open. Dozens of people—customers, employees, and dancers—rushed out. Screams of terror rent the air. The escaping patrons raced between the shooters and their intended victim. The criminals lowered their weapons. *It's now or never!* Carmelo jumped into his car and drove off like the wind.

He reached home at 11 p.m. Breathless, he wrestled the trunk out of the car and into the house, where he dumped its contents on the kitchen floor. Then he poured a glass of water from the pitcher. He immediately spat out his drink and threw up all over the sink. 'Damn! The water tastes filthy,' he growled. He put his hand into the broken fridge and grabbed a half-eaten ham sandwich his mom had made for him yesterday. He swatted the flies frolicking in the fridge and devoured his first meal in thirty-six hours. *Man! What a night! But, I'm so glad that it's over . . . that I'm alive . . . that we don't have to worry about food, clean water and medicine anymore.*

A tired moan interrupted his meditation. 'Carmelo, you're back? It's so late. Have you eaten?' His mother limped into the kitchen.

'Ma, I've been really busy all day. And yes, I've eaten. Go to bed.'

Daisy placed her hand on her hips and contorted her face in anguish. 'I can't sleep, boy. The pain's too much.'

Carmelo held her elbow. 'Come on. It's time to go upstairs.'

She suddenly stopped in her tracks. 'What is that, Carmelo?' She pointed to the odd-looking black trunk lying on the floor.

'Nothing . . . it's nothing.'

Daisy shook her head and mumbled. 'I smell a rat. A big fat rat.' She knelt on the floor and opened the suitcase. The sight of drugs and guns gave her a royal shock. 'Good heavens, Carmelo. What have you dragged yourself into?'

Carmelo shook his head and looked nervous. 'Err . . . it's nothing. Just something I had to do today. An assignment that went south.'

Daisy leaned on the kitchen counter and got up, groaning with pain the whole time. 'You think I'm stupid? I can see what you're doing. You've joined a gang—peddling drugs and arms. Are you insane, Carmelo? What do you think is going to happen to you?'

Carmelo picked up two empty prescription bottles. He placed one of them right in front of her face. 'How can we afford your medications on my pitiful salary? How can we perform your operation when I become unemployed?'

His mom pushed away the bottle. 'Unemployed? I thought you were due for a raise!'

'A raise? Mom, wake up! The shop will close next month. My only option then would be to work at a discount retailer, where the pay's even lower. It would take me six years, not three, as I had envisioned, before I can afford your operation. But this heist—' He took out a brown paper bag from his inside jacket pocket and raised it triumphantly above his head. 'There's $100,000 in this bag, Mom. It's enough for us to leave this wretched place right now and start afresh somewhere else. You can get your operation and be healthy again. I can enroll in university and become an engineer. That's who I've always wanted to be.'

Daisy touched his face lovingly. 'An engineer. That's who I hoped you'd become. As a child, you were so good with your hands . . . tinkering around with things . . . building cars from spare parts your father and I collected from the dump yards of the car companies.'

Carmelo nodded. 'That's right, Ma. But then reality hit us. Dad left. You fell sick. That's why I had to reduce my hours at community college. That's why I had to work at the auto repair shop. After two years of compromising on my education, I'm so behind in my studies that there's no way I can ever graduate with any degree, let alone engineering, in the near future.'

He squeezed the money bag as if it were his sole lifeline. 'Ma . . . this money . . . this money is our salvation. It's the road to my passion. It's the ointment for your pain.'

His mother slapped his face. 'Did I raise you to be a thief . . . a rat that snatches at scraps and escapes into the dead of night?'

Carmelo staggered and nearly hit his head against a cabinet. 'Why did you hit me, Ma? Why? Why?'

Daisy smacked him again and again. Her face was as red as a tomato. 'I don't care what you did. I don't want to know about it. This is blood money. You've just brought the demon of greed into this house. The same demon that consumed your father and expelled him. You too have fallen prey to this demon.'

Carmelo burst into tears. 'Ma! I was only trying to help you. I meant no wrong. What should I do now?'

Daisy wore a look of steely determination. 'We're staying right here. You'll return this ill-gotten wealth to its owners.'

Carmelo bit his lips repeatedly and fidgeted his fingers. 'But Mom . . . how can I do that? They'll kill me.'

For an instant, Daisy thought she was looking into a mirror. *His eyes. The confusion and anxiety from doing the wrong thing. Don't I know a thing or two about that!*

Greased Lightning

At that moment, a feeling of déjà vu enveloped Daisy's being as she rewound to a time thirty years ago . . . before she became a nurse . . . before Carmelo was born. She was a lead engineer at the GM factory in Flint. She was in-charge of completing the final technical evaluation of the latest Thunderbolt model with a spanking new V8 engine. The appraisal had to be completed before a showcase in front of the senior management. She stroked the engine like a pet cat and turned to a man wearing overalls with the badge, 'Production Supervisor'. 'Are the pistons good to go?'

The subordinate brought his face close to her ear. 'Hailey Automotive—the company that provides spare parts for Ford's cars—wants us to test its pistons in this engine.'

Daisy shrugged her shoulders. 'Tough luck! We've already tested their parts and they've failed the trial.' A stern look appeared on her face. She crossed her fingers. 'You shouldn't be asking for such things. This is corruption . . . your request is both immoral and unethical.'

The engineer folded his hands. 'They've promised to pay us each a handsome commission if the Thunderbird engine passes all the safety tests. Please do this for us workers! It's a risk-free trade-off. All the employees here have been desperate for this, ever since our bonuses were cancelled. I can't make my house payments without this.'

She peered into his pleading eyes. *He's right. Auto industry workers are in dire straits this year. Competition with Japanese companies is forcing US corporations to slash costs. To cut back on innovation.* She looked at a scale model of a winged car encased in a glass display. A blueprint of a futuristic flying vehicle—controlled by computer sensors—was framed on the wall above it.

The subordinate saw her staring at the official comment, 'TO BE COMMISSIONED AT A FUTURE DATE', with longing eyes. 'This is your vision. You designed it. Together, we were supposed to build it. It would have been our venture . . . a company where all the workmen would have been shareholders.' He spotted a janitor in the distance mopping the floor. He pointed at the man. 'In fact, he's the one who suggested this measure to our project's finance guy. But corporate killed it. They killed our dream.'

She gritted her teeth in anger and bitterness. *All they care about is short-term profits. Not building something great. Not taking care of their own people. Thousands of workers were laid off last year. My husband was among them. When these companies treat their staff like junk to be trashed in the neighbourhood dump yard, why should I protect their shareholders' interests over those of ordinary workers, especially in times like this?* Her gaze settled on the steel appendages of a line worker on the production floor whose legs had been sucked into a malfunctioning assembly line and crushed. *I'll do what I can to alleviate the suffering of these workers.*

I'll do what I can to help my own family overcome financial distress. She turned her attention back to her subordinate. 'Okay, Mo. You're on. Get this done.'

Horns of a Dilemma

Carmelo saw his mom lost in thought. 'Mom, what's on your mind?'

'Son, I never told you this, but before I became a nurse, I was a lead engineer at GM. My name back then was Daisy Paradis. That was before you were born. My marriage was in its early days. Your father worked at the same company . . . in supply chain manufacturing.'

'What? Why didn't you tell me this?'

Daisy rubbed his shoulder. 'I did something really bad. Something I'm terribly ashamed of. I took a bribe from a rival auto component manufacturer to place its parts in a new model. It withstood the crash tests and got released in the market. However, the model was a disaster on the roads. It often spun out of control due to a faulty piston and caused hundreds of deaths . . . including the CEO's daughter's. I took personal responsibility for this debacle and resigned from the company. Because of me, my entire team was let go. 500 people lost their jobs. I burned with guilt. Every night, I was haunted by the dead faces of the victims and the laid-off workers. People I'd sent to death's door . . . whom I'd plunged into bankruptcy and crime . . . all because I'd succumbed to greed. Wrecked by guilt, I changed my name. I quit the auto industry and swore never to work as an engineer again.'

She paused momentarily and sipped on a glass of brown water. 'In any event, who'd hire a corrupt engineer after all this?' She coughed repeatedly, struggling to finish her words. 'To atone for my sins, I promised to heal lives. So I became a nurse.' She grabbed his hand and led him to the living room. There, she pointed to his collection of toy vehicles displayed on a wall cabinet, a collection she'd helped him gather since childhood. 'You were my sole window to my passion. I tried to live it through you. That was my one solace over the years.'

Carmelo gave her a warm hug. 'Thanks, Mom, for telling me this. It's not worth selling my soul in exchange for fear and unhappiness. I know now what I must do. I must return these goods to Lebron tomorrow. I must return the money to the Jerseys. My hands must be clean of this crime once and for all.'

The next morning before going to work, he stopped by Lebron Adams's house and rang the bell. 'I have something for you.' Carmelo showed him the trunk.

Lebron looked around furtively. 'Not here. Not now. Meet me at the site in half an hour.' He pointed in the direction of Atherton East.

Carmelo placed the case in the trunk of his car and drove down to the Zeno site. Then he took the box down to the sandpit. Lebron and his henchmen were already there. They were engaged in what appeared to be a heated discussion.

Lebron saw Carmelo and gestured for him to come close. 'Hey, Carmelo, you were there. Tell them what happened.'

Carmelo approached the group and looked at them nervously. 'The deal went south. Cops knew about the transaction and ambushed us. Several officers and Jersey gang members were killed in the mayhem. Canon, too.'

Lebron removed his top hat and asked his lackeys to observe a moment of silence in honour of their departed brother. He tapped Carmelo's shoulder. 'I know what happened yesterday.

You got caught in the crossfire. The deal couldn't be completed. However, you escaped with the merchandise intact. You're brave and committed.'

Jamal audited the contents of the trunk. 'Everything's here. No damage.'

Lebron patted Carmelo on the back. 'Good boy. We'd have a disaster on our hands if the merchandise had been stolen or confiscated. Now that there's no deal, we'll have to start all over.'

Carmelo's mind streamed a ticker tape of questions. *Should I tell him about the money or not? If I tell him I received money from them, he'll demand it right now. And then the Jerseys will kill me. But, if I don't hand it over, he may slaughter me right here.* The Homies pointed their fingers at him and fired mock shots. *I'd better stay quiet about this. I'll go back to Goo Goo Dolls tonight and return the money to the Jerseys.*

After the meeting, Carmelo drove to Flint Auto Works. When he reached the entrance, he found Mortimer standing outside. 'Haven't you heard? Canon's dead. The police just stopped by and informed me that he had a side hustle as a gang member,' Mortimer said, his voice filled with dread.

'I really had no clue. This is terrible,' Carmelo said, looking away from Mortimer's piercing gaze.

'Carmelo, I need to tell you something. Can you come inside?' Mortimer led the young man into his office and motioned for him to sit down. 'Carmelo, business has been really bad this year. My partner and I have decided to shut this place down—'

Carmelo interrupted with a shout. 'Mort! Your trusted associate's just died, and you want to bury his legacy! Despicable!'

Mortimer brought his palms out forward. 'Canon's death is horrible, I know. No one will miss him like I will. But you've got to understand an important lesson, son. If you do bad things, they'll always come back to haunt you. Canon was a good man, but he did the wrong thing to escape his woes. He was destined to—'

The sound of gunshots interrupted him. 'What . . . what the hell?' He drew up his window blinds to see what was going on outside. Twelve armed intruders had entered his property. His eyes grew wide with terror. The insurgents pointed to the open window and fired. 'Vandals! We're under attack!' Mortimer ducked and hid below his desk.

Carmelo crouched on the ground below the window. His heart pumped even faster than last night. 'Do you have a gun?'

The terrified proprietor shook his head. A hail of bullets ravaged the cabinets, cupboards and chairs, smashing the glass casing of the mysterious exhibit. An eerie silence reigned momentarily. Five minutes later, the victims of the incursion heard the stomping of heavy boots in the adjoining work area.

'Game's over for me, kid. Save yourself.' Mortimer pointed to a large hole in a portion of the wooden wall that could be used as an escape hatch.

Carmelo shook his head. 'No. I'm not going anywhere. You gave me a life. An escape from my financial troubles. I'm staying put.'

The door crashed open and several men burst in. 'There he is! The rat! That lying snake.' A familiar voice was heard shouting as Carmelo was dragged from the shop.

'Lebron! Shawn!' He gasped in horror upon seeing ten men from both gangs standing shoulder-to-shoulder against the backdrop of the parking lot.

Lebron made Carmelo kneel outside the shop's entrance with his hands on his head, and shoved a gun into his mouth.

'You lied. You stole from them.' He pointed to Shawn Patrick's men.

Carmelo's fingers trembled as he took out the bag of cash from his back pocket. 'Here . . . take it.' He handed the largesse to Shawn with quivering hands.

Shawn gently removed his ally's gun from Carmelo's mouth and pointed his own gun at his eyes instead. He clenched his teeth and growled ferociously. 'Apology not accepted. Because of you, we almost traded blows today. Fortunately, cooler heads prevailed. We figured out you were just trying to two-time us. The question is, should you be shot in the mouth or in the head? Actually, I prefer the eyes. There's a chance you'll live and feel the pain of your treachery for the rest of your life.' Lebron pushed Mortimer to the ground and forced him to kneel next to his apprentice. He pointed his gun at the owner's temple and addressed him in an ominous tone. 'Know the price of betrayal, Carmelo. Because of you, this innocent man has to die.'

A sudden gunshot from the adjoining parking lot halted the impending executions. A bullet whizzed past Lebron's head, just missing his ear. 'Take cover, boys.' He shrieked and leaped to his right. A barrage of shots rent the air. Within three minutes, dozens of holes were drilled into the aluminum exterior of the repair shop.

A grating female voice reverberated the surroundings. 'If anyone touches my boy, I'll shoot him like a dog.' From fifty metres away, an elderly woman wearing a ripped, muddy dress hobbled towards them, armed with an assault rifle. 'Nobody moves.'

Carmelo's eyeballs nearly popped out of their sockets. 'Ma, what are you doing here?'

'What do you think? Saving your ass. I had a nasty feeling in my bowels the minute you left the house today. So I packed my gun, got into a taxi, and followed you to the Zeno site. I then hid behind a disgusting, filthy heap of shit—where I learned how deep the hole is that you've fallen into!' She scowled and brushed a dirty twig off her dress.

Shawn's associate, Bulldog, laughed. 'Hahaha! Carmelo, is that your bodyguard? Your mom? Jesus. Boss, shall I finish her?'

Shawn, who was in the direct line of fire, looked circumspect. He shook his head. 'No. Let's hear what she has to say.'

Daisy squinted at an old man with a silver beard kneeling on the ground next to Carmelo. *He must be the owner of this place. His face is so familiar. Where have I seen him before?* A couple of minutes later, she reached fifty feet from the hostages who were both kneeling on the floor with guns to their heads. Suddenly, she spotted a sudden movement in a clump of bushes near the entrance of the workshop. A bullet whizzed over her head and crashed into a billboard on the approach road. She turned to see a sniper hiding in the shrub.

Daisy glared at the assailant. 'Clumsy ass! Can't even shoot straight.' She ground her teeth and fired at the culprit.

He ducked, and the bullet smashed into the workshop. He then raised his arms and emerged from his hideout. Daisy lowered her guard momentarily. The hoodlum jumped to his left and popped out a pistol like a Western gunslinger. However, Daisy was more Trinity than Rose. She nimbly bent her body to the left and dodged the bullet. Then, she fired a rapid round. With the first few bullets, she accidentally blew out a sizeable chunk of the wall. 'I should have taken that damned shooting range membership,' she grumbled, annoyed at missing her target. The last shot felled the hidden shooter. 'Definitely after my knee replacement surgery.' She decided to give herself an irresistible Christmas present.

Carmelo's heart fell when he saw the gangster slump to the ground. *Their retaliation will be far more brutal.*

Daisy, however, continued to advance at the gangsters. 'Let my boy go . . . or I'll blow each of your heads off like scarecrows.'

Nonplussed and shaken up, Shawn Patrick, Lebron and their men raised their guns in the air. Daisy pointed her rifle at the ground. 'Guns on the ground . . . NOW!' She raised her voice and shot another barrage of bullets into the tin shed.

Carmelo raised his hand in the air. 'Ma. Enough. No more Django. Drop your weapon now.' He worried his mother's bravado would come to naught as she was heavily outgunned.

Daisy shook her head and looked at him angrily. '*You* caused this mess. Now you're telling me what to do? What gall!'

Right then, a bird flew towards them from the top of the abandoned building. Out of the corner of his eye, Carmelo could just about identify it. It was the multicoloured pigeon he'd seen on the roofs of the derelict warehouse and his home. The bird darted towards the gap in the wall with a mysterious sense of purpose.

What the hell does it want?

The shooters forgot about the conflict for a moment and gazed vacuously at the pigeon. Everyone except Bulldog, who had a marked preference for target shooting over ornithology. He chuckled sarcastically, and fired at the bird. He missed. The bird disappeared into the warehouse. A moment later, a loud thud was heard . . . like a heavy object hitting the floor.

Daisy directed her gun at Shawn's henchman. The gunmen, in turn, pointed their weapons at Daisy simultaneously.

Lebron gritted his teeth. 'Enough playtime, Granny! You've got ten seconds to drop your weapon. I wouldn't be so forgiving if you weren't my neighbour.'

Daisy scoffed and spat on the ground. 'Lebron, do you take me for a fool? I know everything about you. Your vile criminal activities. Your family. Where you live. If you harm a single hair on Carmelo's head, I'm gonna finish you and your baby girl.'

A red dot flashed across Lebron's right pupil. 'That's it. You're done.'

Shawn Patrick nodded and gazed at Carmelo with hate. He picked up a clump of soil from the ground with his left hand, squeezed it like putty and smeared it on Carmelo's temple. He looked at Daisy and smirked. 'Right after he finishes you off, I'm gonna wipe this gravel with your son's blood.'

The glare of the midday sun was so strong that Carmelo's shirt was drenched with sweat. Any moment now, lots of blood would be spilled needlessly. *This is all my fault. I wish I hadn't been seduced to the dark side by financial stress.* He looked up at the blazing sun, closed his eyes, and prayed for forgiveness. *I'm sorry I acted out of need and desperation. Let me set things right. Show me a sign. Please.*

Magically, the world froze like a YouTube video on pause. Everyone stood still—guns pointed, expressions locked in determination, anger and hate. Dust and various other particles hung in the air, forming a gravel path along the stationary sunbeam that stretched diagonally from the adjacent roof to the workshop. Time stood still. Carmelo couldn't hear a sound. He couldn't detect a single movement. Everybody and everything became immobile, like wax sculptures. His mother stood transfixed, her teeth clenched, glaring at Bulldog. Shawn Patrick continued to stare at him, eyes red and unflinching, his right hand clasping his gun firmly. A fly remained motionless right above Lebron's hat while he pointed his weapon at Mortimer. Then, to Carmelo's surprise, the renegade pigeon flew out from the workshop, completely unscathed, and transformed into his mother, thirty years younger.

What Ifs and Maybes

'Ma! Ma! What's going on? How's this possible?' He stared alternately at the frozen version of the old lady with the torn dress and her younger, mobile doppelganger wearing a pink business suit. While the elder Daisy looked tired—with thick creases on her forehead, her skin wrinkled and blotched, and hollow, sunken eyes—the younger one had thick, curly hair, a blemish-free complexion and piercing eyes.

Young Daisy flashed a radiant smile and reached out her right hand. 'Come, kiddo. I want to show you something.'

Carmelo felt dazed and disoriented. 'Huh? What? Where?'

With a wave of her hand, she transformed the desolate landscape into the vast factory floor of an auto manufacturing hub. The frozen people were erased and replaced by a thousand employees spread out over the large enclosure housing two dozen car variants. Carmelo looked flummoxed. 'Where are we?'

Daisy pointed to a large nameplate high up on the second floor of the hangar-like building. 'GM, Research and Development wing. The place where I worked, back in the eighties. I was the lead engineer here. We developed so many pathbreaking projects.'

Carmelo looked around at all the vehicles and assorted machinery in the area. There were quite a few cars with technical features way ahead of their time. He saw a worker charging a vehicle with an electric battery at a station. Another prototype had an LCD panel behind its front seat and played live TV. A third car, an SUV, had a collapsible toilet in its trunk. Carmelo clapped his hands. 'So cool. I can't believe you actually worked on this stuff!'

A sanguine expression filled Daisy's face. 'Yes! It was exciting work. Sadly, very few of them got commercialized.'

'Why?'

'Oh! There were many different reasons. A narrow focus on short-term profits. Corporate politics. A disdain for workers' welfare. Increased competition from international companies.' Daisy let out a deep sigh.

Carmelo shook his head. 'I can't believe those schmucks! They'd call a peacock a pheasant if it were up to them. I wish you had more support. You could have been Elon, well before Musk.'

Daisy shrugged her shoulders. Her voice became matter-of-fact and resigned to reality. 'Oh well! Success isn't everyone's sparring partner. Some things just aren't meant to happen.' She paused for a moment to clear her throat. 'I want to show you the grand prize.' She pointed to the middle of the facility.

She directed Carmelo past the vehicles to a space in the centre of the premises. He saw a car with the name 'ICARUS' painted in gold and red stripes. *Hmm! Very unusual. The same colours as the pigeon.* Next to the car was a pedestal that held a glass box. A miniature version of the car was displayed inside it. A remote control sat on top of the exhibit, and next to it was a podium with a microphone.

A gaggle of workers surrounded the car. They smiled. Their eyes sparkled with anticipation; something big was about to happen. Six men in their sixties, wearing identical suits affixed with identical badges labelled 'CORPORATE', conducted the proceedings.

Carmelo frowned. 'What's happening?'

Daisy smiled at him mischievously. 'Wait and see.' She closed her eyes.

What's going on? Wait! Carmelo gasped. A replica of young Daisy emerged from her body and walked towards the podium.

'Wait a minute! What . . . how . . . who . . . ?'

'I'm running this show.' Daisy chuckled and turned into a static hologram.

Carmelo stared at his mom's body double and felt his hair standing on end. She looked like a character out of a Jordan Peele movie. She reached the glass box, took the remote and clicked on a button.

The car's engine revved up and floated up to the top of the warehouse. Then, it jetted towards the entrance 150 feet away. The airborne vehicle spun, rotated and performed several flips. Finally, it returned to its original spot without a scratch or a bump.

'Get out of here!' yelled Carmelo.

The Daisy double suddenly zipped back and merged inside Daisy, and the hologram reverted to its spiritual form.

The reconstructed younger Daisy had a smile on her lips and pain in her eyes. 'My life's work. I wanted you to see this.'

Carmelo furrowed his eyebrows. 'Why are you showing me this, Mom?'

Daisy could not find an appropriate reply to the question. *Maybe he's not old enough to understand my compromise.* She looked at the throng of onlookers inspecting the car in awe, and felt a tremendous urge to touch her creation. 'I have to touch her face. I have to stroke her hair. I have to look in this car's eyes one last time before she vanishes from my memory.' She passed through the bodies of the employees to reach her baby. For a moment, she stood still and stroked its hood as if it were a human child. She then closed her eyes for a second. When she reopened them, they were filled with tears.

Carmelo's mind recalled a day from when he was ten years old. He remembered his mother laying out an assortment of rubber strips, screws, plastic sheets and batteries on the floor. He remembered her drawing a chart with the various components of a car, neatly labelled and described. He remembered her saying, 'You can build anything with patience and diligence.'

His eyes lit up. 'Mom. Mom. You've always told me to follow my passion, no matter what. I never understood why you kept harping on this. But now, I do. All that time, you wanted me to finish what you'd started.'

Daisy stroked his hair. 'Our journeys are unique. But they may intersect. I wanted to show you my path. As for yours? You've got to find it yourself.'

Carmelo felt torn. *How can I think of pursuing my passion at a moment when the spectre of death looms before me? Isn't it necessary to survive before I can even think about growth?*

Daisy gave him an enigmatic smile. 'Let your passion be the guide to your conscience.'

'What do you mean by that, Mom?' But just when he'd completed the question, the high-tech development centre disappeared. The desolate landscape of shuttered automobile plants, decrepit warehouses and discount superstores re-emerged. The frozen characters of the surreal drama then returned and occupied their previous positions on the metaphysical stage.

The Height of Noon

The surroundings remained fuzzy for a few moments. Suddenly, the sun appeared and blinded him. The glare subsided after a few seconds. Carmelo rubbed his eyes. Everything and everyone in the original landscape had been restored, but still frozen in time. The younger Daisy's image flickered in front of him like an out-of-focus video. He reached his right hand towards her and shouted plaintively. 'Mom!' The image stabilized. 'I . . .' he began, as if about to make a promise. However, Daisy's younger avatar reverted to its original form, the pigeon. It followed the path of the sunbeam and flew back to its original shelter in the abandoned building. 'Wait! Mom! Wait! I have so many questions.' The bird didn't turn back.

The ethereal calm was quickly dispelled by the whirring sound of propellers. *What the hell is that?* Carmelo turned around to look at the battered workshop. The sound came from Mortimer's office. The next moment, a second object hurtled through the yawning cavity in the wall.

Everything returned to normal instantly. Startled by the whirring noise, everyone regained their senses. Carmelo observed a flying object circling thirty feet above the ground. He placed his hand on his forehead and looked up. 'Is that a drone?' The UFO rotated for ten seconds at that height. Then its propellers sputtered and it descended rapidly, crash-landing on the ground, just in front of Mortimer.

The gang gathered to view the object. Mortimer was the first to get to it. He cradled the contraption as if it were an injured baby. 'Oh God! My passion. Don't tell me it's dead.'

Daisy finally lowered her gun and approached the object. 'It can't be. Th—that's . . .' she stammered, struggling to string together a coherent sentence.

The strange object aligned with the memories from Carmelo's paranormal and childhood experiences allowing him to finish the thought lodged in the recesses of his mother's mind. 'A car. A flying car.'

Mortimer nodded. 'This is the model hidden in the box. It's one of a kind. I didn't want anyone to see it or touch it. I was afraid it would be stolen or damaged.'

The criminals dropped their guns and took turns inspecting the model. Mortimer quickly repossessed it. He gazed at Lebron with a pleading look. 'Take everything. Take my money. My bonds. Hell, take the deed of this godforsaken property if you want. But don't take this. This is all I have to remind me of who I once was.'

Before the gang leader could respond to his plea, Carmelo's mother, keen to verify an old link, was determined to have her say. 'Give that to me.' Daisy stretched out her hand towards Mortimer.

The auto shop owner glanced at her finger on the trigger of the gun still pointed at him and slowly handed over the grounded vehicle. 'Okay! Here it is! But please . . . please don't break it.'

Daisy turned it around and inspected the undercarriage. There was a sticker with the words 'GM demo 9/9/89'. She looked up in astonishment. 'Good God! The exact day!'

Mortimer observed the old lady's curiosity for the car. She seemed to be so familiar, but he couldn't quite place her. *Who's this lady? Why's she so fascinated by this model? What's her connection to the date on the sticker?*

Meanwhile, Daisy raised the hood to check the engine. Her mouth opened wide. 'The V9. The very same engine that we modified back in the day. God Almighty!'

There's only one woman in the world who's familiar with that engine, Mortimer thought. He looked closely at the elderly woman who stood before him. She was thin—110 pounds, hunched, five feet in height. Her silver hair was thin and she had a significant bald spot. *That can't be her. She looked totally different back then.* He pictured a woman with long, lustrous hair who weighed closer to 140 pounds and stood reed straight in flat shoes, making her seem significantly taller than her diminutive stature now.

Daisy held the car, eyes sparkling like a kid in a toy shop. She let out a hoarse laugh. 'Hehehe. I'll be damned. My little flying baby.'

That look in her eyes, and the sound of her laughter struck a chord in Mortimer's memory. *Wait a minute* . . . He deliberated internally, noting a couple of defining features. *That glint in her eyes. That rasping voice. It must be her.* 'Daisy? Daisy Paradis?' he asked, hesitantly.

Daisy peered closely at the proprietor's face, and her eyes widened with familiarity. 'Nobody's called me that in years. Wait! Mortimer! Is that you? You're as fat as a toad.'

'Daisy Paradis. It can't be.' Mortimer gasped in disbelief. 'Carmelo's your son?'

The gunslinging lady nodded. 'Yes. And I've changed my name. I'm Daisy Jones now.'

Carmelo looked at his mom with puzzlement. 'Mom, you've never worked around here. You've never even been here. So how do you know Mortimer?'

Mortimer looked at Daisy with admiration. 'In the eighties, she was the lead engineer at GM. I was her chief production officer. She'd developed a revolutionary car, one that reduced carbon emissions by 75 per cent. One that could fly, communicate with electronic devices and reach a top speed of 200 miles per hour.'

Daisy reached over and smacked her former coworker's head in not-so-mock affection. 'Until an act of corruption ended our plans.'

At that moment, something stirred in Shawn's mind. 'Wait a minute! I know them. I know that world,' he remembered.

His mind returned to a day thirty years earlier. He was in his early twenties, working as a production executive on the shop floor of GM's plant in Flint. A thousand factory workers and managers had gathered to witness the showcase of a new high-tech car. The full-scale model—named Icarus—stood in regal glory before the excited gathering. A miniature version was placed in a glass box that stood on a short pedestal. A remote control was placed on top of it. A chart—etched with the blueprint of the car—was pasted on a whiteboard that stood on an easel.

A man in his fifties, wearing a business suit and a company badge with the letters 'CTO' printed on it, addressed the gathering. 'I'm delighted to invite you to the demo of our revolutionary model, the Icarus. Note, this is just an early showcase. It will need to go through multiple inspections and iterations before a full commercial release. And now, without further ado, here's Daisy Paradis—the mastermind behind this marvellous vehicle—to demonstrate and explain the science behind it.' He beckoned in Daisy's direction and handed over the remote to her. 'It's all yours.'

Daisy thanked the chief technological officer for his support and endorsement, and switched on the remote control. To the surprise of Shawn Patrick and everyone present at the site, the full-scale Icarus started up and lifted fifteen feet above the ground—halfway between the floor and the roof of the sprawling factory. A real-time camera feed of the car's interiors appeared on every security monitor installed in the facility.

'What the hell?' Shawn muttered, his eyes large with surprise.

Daisy chuckled at seeing the befuddled reactions of the audience and clarified the science behind the magic. 'The cameras in the car are connected to various electronic devices, such as the security cameras, through high-frequency radio waves.' The crowd whispered to each other, puzzled looks abound.

Daisy bowed dramatically. 'Enough with the boring dribbles. Time for the money shot.'

The vehicle flew towards the factory entrance about 150 feet away, turned ninety degrees, reached the ceiling, rotated counterclockwise, then clockwise, and finally made its way back to Daisy. The car landed gently at its original spot. Shawn clapped furiously. Celebratory chants of 'Go GM! Go Flint! Go Daisy!' rent the air.

After the memory of that day faded, Shawn looked carefully at the old lady's face. 'Wait a minute! Daisy Paradis? You're Daisy Paradis? I remember you. I was at GM, too. I didn't report to you, but you were a star. A hotshot who developed a pathbreaking new car. This one. It could fly and communicate with other vehicles via sensors. It could be powered by electric, hydrogen or solar energy sources. We, the workers, were supposed to be co-owners of that project. But the management killed it.'

'The last remains of a famous experiment,' Bulldog recalled. 'I hadn't joined GM then, so I never saw it live. But I heard everything about it from my colleagues. I mean, how could you not? How could you work at GM in the nineties and not be aware of the flying car project? I remember seeing the model once, at a distance, housed in a special display cabinet inside one of the labs.'

Daisy looked at Shawn's reconstructed legs and a lightbulb flashed inside her. 'Wait a minute! I remember you. You were always on the factory floor. You'd lost your legs in an accident, yet it didn't take long for you to return to work.'

Shawn looked at the silhouette of the shuttered plant in the distance and dropped his gun. He covered his face and fell to his knees. He pointed to the building, eyes filled with bitterness. 'Twenty-five years. That's how long I worked at that plant as an assembly line worker. That's how much of my life I gave to GM. Even after my accident, I never took a day off work. I hoped to be a manager someday. But then they laid us all off. They just shut down that goddamned plant.'

He glanced at the car. 'I saw that model one more time before I was let go. It was at the cafeteria before the car was dumped in the R&D division, far out of sight.' He paused and gulped down his tears. 'That venture was my ticket to better things. *Our* ticket. A ticket we *all* lost.' His voice quivered with disappointment.

'We had a dream,' Bulldog added. 'They killed it when they killed that project. We were a family. They tore us apart.'

Murmurs spread around. Lebron picked up the car and mumbled, 'Hey! I've seen this too.' His mind rewound to a day long, long ago. He was thirty years younger and considerably beefier. He was mopping the floor of a cafeteria when two men entered the employee dining area. They went towards an open wall cabinet bearing the words 'GM INNOVATIONS' printed on top. It contained numerous miniature showpieces developed by the engineering divisions. Lebron looked suspiciously at the men. One of them removed an object and placed it in a plastic bag. The janitor left his cleaning supplies and rushed towards them. He caught a glimpse of the piece they were looting. *They can't do that, can they?* He pointed his fingers at them. 'Hey! Stop it! What are you doing? You aren't supposed to touch that.'

The two men glared. One of them—a tall, bespectacled man in his forties wearing a white dress shirt and a tie—replied in a condescending tone, 'We're from Finance. This object is being moved under the CEO's directive. If you don't believe me, call his secretary.'

Lebron realized that this decision was above his pay grade. He started to walk back towards his cleaning cart. Suddenly, a question popped into his head: *Where are they moving the exhibit to?*

He turned around and asked one of the finance guys, 'Are you moving the flying car for good? Better tell me, or I'll have to make up bullshit excuses. Everyone likes to see that thing. It's really popular.'

'If anyone asks,' the man replied curtly, 'say it's being moved to R&D for better security.'

Lebron scratched his goatee. 'Why are you moving it? There's plenty of security here.'

The guy with the glasses placed his hands on Lebron's shoulders, glanced at his nametag, and said in a conspiratorial tone, 'Lebron, I shouldn't be telling you this. You look like a nice guy. Can you handle the truth?'

Lebron nodded his head sheepishly.

'Corporate's killed the project,' the man whispered.

With a crestfallen look, the sanitation worker inquired, 'Why? This is such an amazing project. The workers are supposed to co-own it with management and investors.'

The executive shrugged his shoulders. 'It's too ahead of its time. The market, the suppliers, the regulators . . . nobody's ready for it. I don't think they'll ever buy it.'

The second man—a bald, tubby guy in his thirties with a baby face—sniggered. 'This is a pipe dream that won't earn a return in a hundred years. Our company will become far more profitable by becoming leaner. How? By focusing on the core business and killing these woolly projects. By outsourcing to China where people work harder for way less than our stupid, entitled, working-class bums. Oops! You never heard me say that. In any event, some objects are better off in museums than in stores. I think it's a good decision to place this model in the R&D wing. Something about motivation, the CEO said. Better there than the dump yard!'

Lebron looked back and forth between the two men, feeling completely deflated. The bespectacled man continued, a cruel glint in his eyes. 'Why should losers with no college degrees get shares in our company? What good will that do?'

'But . . . but . . .' Lebron stammered. The men laughed as they removed the glass box from the cafeteria. The janitor waved his hands dismissively and shouted, 'Thanks for telling me where to find my stock options.'

They were already out of earshot.

As the memory crumbled into dust, Lebron saw the yarn that wove them together. 'No crime. Only passion,' he mumbled.

Shawn heard the unexpected word—passion. 'What are you mumbling about?'

Lebron shook his head. 'I've seen this before. I was a GM man too. Sanitation Services. Worked my way up to the mailroom. Got laid off in '95.' He pointed to his men. 'They're all GM men. Lost their jobs when the plant got shut down three years ago.'

The former auto-workers-turned-criminals looked at each other in befuddlement. Carmelo noticed a spark of electricity emanating from the car's undercarriage. 'Oh no! Don't tell me it's damaged,' he said. He picked up the car and tried to blow out the spark.

'Don't do that! You'll destroy it.' shouted a horrified Mortimer.

Suddenly, the short fuse turned into a blaze that gutted the body. Despondent, Mortimer and Daisy watched the burning vehicle. A rueful smile appeared briefly on her lips. *It would be wishful thinking to believe that some good could have come out of this mess.* The gang members stared, a morose expression on all their faces.

Shawn picked up his gun and beckoned his compatriots to do the same. He shrugged. 'Well, that's that. I guess we won't be seeing this again.'

Carmelo gazed at everyone's downcast expressions. *United in pain.* A thought entered his head. *This is important. It's a reminder of who we were. Notwithstanding what happens to me, we can't let this die. We'll only be killing ourselves.*

He raised his fist in the air. 'It doesn't have to end here. We can fix this.'

Shawn furrowed his eyebrows and scoffed, 'Fix this? Why should we fix it? Who do you think we are? Engineers?'

Daisy picked up her gun. She looked at the gathered men and placed her hand on her heart. 'All right! That's enough. It's good to know you all. But the grapes of that life have turned awfully sour. Carmelo, time to go.'

Shawn Patrick cocked his gun. 'Wait a minute! Your boy hasn't made amends for the scam he pulled.'

Lebron gave Carmelo a menacing look. 'He's right. I say you work for three months in our organizations. No pay. What do you think, Shawn?'

The rival gang leader nodded his head.

Daisy roared, 'Over my dead body! Let's go, Carmelo . . . NOW.'

Lebron grabbed Carmelo's hand and pointed a gun to his head. 'If you don't accept my offer, I'll—'

Daisy cocked her gun at Shawn. 'You think bullying us will work? One false move and your buddy will have a giant hole in his head.'

Carmelo's heart sank as he watched peace and dialogue rapidly unwind. *There's no way anyone's getting out of here alive. No way . . . unless . . .* His eyes fell on the charred model, and an idea for distraction flashed in his mind. *Unless the car's fixed. I have to fix it. I have to make it fly . . . but how can I repair a vehicle that's totally torched?* Then, he remembered an engineering course he'd attended briefly at his university. If the car's microprocessor was intact, it might—just might—still fly. And if it flew, then maybe—just maybe—they'd feel inspired enough to lay down their guns and let him live. Carmelo dashed ten feet forward to grab the car.

'What the hell!' Lebron yelled. He tried to smack Carmelo's head with his gun but only grazed the right shoulder.

Carmelo quickly grabbed the vehicle and reinserted two distended wires—blue and red—into open slots. Lebron rushed towards him and stretched out his hand to grab him by the scruff of his neck. Carmelo pressed a button on the car's underbelly. It took off vertically and reached a height of fifty feet. It hovered for ten seconds, then landed gently on the ground.

'I'll be damned,' Shawn exclaimed. 'The car still flies.' He looked at it in wonder. The rest of the crew nodded their heads. Jamal stared up at the car, his mouth agape. 'Yeah. It flies. It really flies.'

The crew gathered around in excitement to explore the car. Carmelo saw their weapons piled on the ground. *How long can Mom and I live? Today? Maybe. Tomorrow? Maybe. The day after? Maybe. But what about after that? As long as these people are around and engaging in crime, we'll always be vulnerable. How can we end this hostility . . . this hatred . . . once and for all?*

The gang members took turns flying the car—giggling like school kids. Carmelo spotted the pigeon on the roof of the adjoining building. It stared at him and squawked.

'What should I do, birdie? How can I get out of this mess for good?'

The bird transformed into a woman wearing a pink business suit and waved at him. 'Mom,' he yelled, spotting the younger Daisy once again.

The older Daisy looked at him, puzzled. 'What are you talking about?'

Bulldog frowned, turned around and looked at the roof of the warehouse. He saw absolutely nothing. 'Hehehe. The kid's seeing things. Maybe we've hit him on the head one too many times.'

Deaf to the gibes, Carmelo continued to peer at the figure on the rooftop. The younger Daisy outstretched her arms and flapped them like a bird. Then she reverted to her avian form and disappeared into the horizon. Carmelo's eyes widened with realization. 'I can see now. I can see now.'

'See what? What are you talking about?' Shawn shouted and rapped Carmelo on the head with his palm.

Carmelo ignored the strike and shouted ecstatically as if he'd solved a great mystery. 'Passion is the road to righteousness. Passion is the road to unity.' His reflection elicited roars of laughter from the criminals.

Jamal chuckled. 'I like his spirit.'

'Be careful! It's gonna cost ya at Sunday Mass.' Bulldog chortled.

Carmelo ignored them. *Mom, I'll make things right. I'll build what you conceived. I'll unite everybody.*

The men roared with laughter. Carmelo, undeterred by the mockery, fleshed out a larger, more durable idea for reconciliation. *Passion. Passion can bring an end to all this negativity. Passion can bring us together. We've been destroying ourselves for so long. Isn't it time to build ourselves?* He pointed to the workshop. 'Guys, before you drill a bullet into me, I want to show you something. It's in Mortimer's office.'

Bulldog's laugh turned to anger. He smacked Carmelo's head. 'Shut up, you lying sack of shit!'

Jamal growled. 'He's just trying to buy time.' The rest of Lebron's boys advanced on Carmelo.

A bullet hit the ground just below Jamal's feet. Daisy roared, 'Move your stinking guns away from my kid.'

Shawn raised his hand in an attempt at pacification. 'I want to see what the kid's blabbing about.'

Mortimer's office was a wreck. The cabinets were shot out. The drawers lay on the floor, totally crushed. The desk was riddled with bullet holes. The pedestal that bore the glass casement lay on the floor, cracked in two. The casement itself had been reduced to shards. Fragments of glass littered the ground. The wooden box housing the miniature car lay open.

Carmelo sidestepped the debris and directed the group to Mortimer's desk. He took out a piece of chart paper hidden below a book and laid it out flat on the desk.

'What's this?' asked Lebron. The rest of the men gathered around to study the schematic.

One look at the design that had been framed in the R&D centre at GM's factory thirty years earlier, and Daisy recalled that moment when she received a rapturous applause for the successful demo from the audience of workers and managers at the production centre. She gasped. 'It's the blueprint of the flying car. Our dream. The one that got away.'

Mortimer held her hand and sighed. 'It's the one we never built. After getting laid off in 2000, this model and its blueprint were the only items I took with me.'

Shawn perused it with the excitement of a kid in a candy store. His breath grew quicker. 'I was in the audience that day. As a production executive, I was excited to work on revolutionary technology. This is who I wanted to be.'

Lebron remembered his connection to the blueprint and a faint smile appeared on his lips. 'Me too. Long ago, I was delivering a memo to the VP of finance about a new venture. I jokingly mentioned to him that the organization should spin it off as a new company and make its employees shareholders. He pointed to a photocopy of the blueprint framed on his wall and said I should be part of it.'

Mortimer's and Daisy's jaws dropped in astonishment. 'What? You were the janitor,' they both said.

Lebron nodded and smiled. 'I believe my suggestion was included in that presentation. I wasn't invited. But I remember the work floor buzzing with excitement that day. Everyone was dreaming of becoming an entrepreneur. Everyone thought, "This is the gateway to my passion".'

Carmelo watched the gang silently poring over the blueprint, their eyes sparkling with wonder. He was now convinced of their true purpose in life. *This is where we really belong. I see this. Do they? They must.*

'How much will it cost to build a full-scale model? I believe there's an annual expo in Detroit later this year. The World Car Show or something. The most innovative vehicles will win prizes and rich contracts.'

Mortimer tapped his forehead. '$100,000 for a full demo model. I had estimated this years ago, in a flight of fantasy.'

Everyone paused and considered an impossible scenario. Then, the thought of *actually* building the car appeared as absurd as a pink elephant with wings. They burst out laughing. 'Hahaha! Let's sell this one to Disney,' Jamal said. 'Maybe they'll give us a share of the profits!' He roared with laughter.

Carmelo was the only one not laughing. He gazed at the motley crew and saw their weapons transformed into laptops, their grungy clothing substituted by workmen's overalls. *We can do it. We have the blueprint. We have the passion. We have the skills. All we need is the inner fire and the finances to make this happen. We are too good to be degenerates. We can be legends.*

Carmelo faced the group and pointed to every person. 'Each of us has expertise in automobiles. Mom, you're an engineer. Mortimer, you're a production specialist and a line manager. I know about electronics and computer software. Lebron, Shawn, all you guys . . . all of you . . . have considerable manufacturing experience and entrepreneurial skills. But most importantly, you've got passion. We can build this thing together.'

'I hear you,' Shawn said, 'but, it's been so many years. We're all into different things. We no longer have the belief.'

Lebron shook his head. 'We've got mouths to feed. Accepted, we don't enjoy our way of life. But it's too late to change now.'

Carmelo pointed to the broken toy box. 'Financial stress? That's what brought us into this mess. That's what forced us to make these choices. But what if we'd listened to our hearts? What if we'd done something we truly cared about? What if we were guided by our passions, not our needs?'

Carmelo's words triggered an identical question in both the gang leaders' minds. *I ventured into a life of crime when I couldn't afford to cover my rehab costs. But what has this life of greed and crime given me? Uncertainty, suspicion and fear. Is this a life worth holding on to?* Shawn wondered.

Lebron stared at the blueprint. A tree of life decisions and alternative choices appeared on it. *After I lost my job, I became a criminal to pay my bills . . . only because I didn't have an education. What I got in the bargain was a lifetime of deceit, of near deaths. Why did I choose this life? Because I was blinded by the fear of financial distress.*

The underlings noticed their bosses in deep contemplation. They got curious and looked at the blueprint more closely. The car came to life in their collective imagination—generating a surge of excitement that flowed through their eyes and veins.

'It's time to be legends, not criminals. It's time to make great things again,' Carmelo exhorted, his statement greeted by whoops of joy and encouragement.

Two weeks later, Lebron and Shawn voluntarily divested their illegal businesses and invested all their proceeds in the auto repair shop, thereby rescuing it from bankruptcy. Flush with funds, Flint Legend, Inc. embarked on a six-month project to build the revolutionary flying car. After much brainstorming, the team decided to update the blueprint to add features such as self-driving and nuclear fuel cells. The first model—Flint Legend—debuted at the Detroit Auto Expo. It garnered rave reviews from the media and the public and attracted the attention of investors. Greedy companies tried to buy out the intellectual properties but to no avail. The Legend team was determined to go it alone. Buoyed by the excitement around the innovative product, hundreds of entrepreneurs and investors poured their energies into the auto sector. Many products, services and ventures got launched.

A year later, a brand-new factory was inaugurated by the governor of Michigan at Autoville, a sprawling new industrial complex teeming with factories and ancillary shops all humming with the sweet sound of production. A crowd of 10,000 had assembled to witness the first global rollout of the connected, flying cars. As the first lot sailed into the horizon, the fully healed CTO kissed the cheeks of her son and CEO. 'How does it feel to exchange your gun for a dream?' she whispered in his ear.

REFLECTION: LET YOUR PASSION BE THE GUIDE TO YOUR CONSCIENCE

Were you ever forced to do the wrong thing because of financial constraints?

In times of plenty, we seem to have many chances to do the right thing. We are always in a flow and find it easy to figure out the right thing to do. However, in times of need or distress, when our backs are pinned to the wall, we see a limited set of options, each one more unpalatable than the other. In these circumstances, figuring out the right thing to do can be an extremely confusing process because we usually have to make a decision within a short time frame. As a result, we may feel terribly stressed.

In situations of duress and deprivation, we are often tempted to do things that provide quick returns and can salvage us from our mess. These actions may be against our principles and may involve lying, cheating or cutting corners. However, the need to urgently resolve resource constraints often tempts us to step in a negative direction. It is a direction that often leads to harm and unhappiness. Fortunately, these negative actions aren't inevitable.

In difficult times, if we are guided by our passion rather than our need, we are not so easily tempted to stray into a harmful direction. The call of our passion helps us focus on our long-term happiness while equipping us with a positive mindset to tackle short-term obstacles. A mindset free from fear. A mindset to explore new opportunities and connections. A mindset geared towards the pursuit of happiness.

I am happy to report that I underwent just such a mental shift during the pandemic. This change in outlook not only helped me keep the demon of financial stress at bay, but also eventually banish it from my consciousness altogether.

When I was plagued by the lack of access to investor capital, I asked myself two questions to de-stress: 'What can I control?' and 'What do I love to do?' The answer to the first question was my relationship. My girlfriend and I live in different countries. The pandemic not only prevented us from physically meeting each other or our friends, but also devastated our professional prospects. As a self-employed professional, she saw her business shrink to zero during this difficult period. Consequently, her personal finances were battered. Fortunately, my personal bank balance was a bit healthier, although the pandemic had devastated my business.

I took on a manageable goal to shore up as much financing as I possibly could to support my companion during this difficult time. I pulled out all the stops. I sold my mutual funds. I cut back on discretionary expenses; massages and home-delivered food were the first to go. I even withdrew a sum from my retirement fund. After four months of belt-tightening and saving, my personal bank balance was stronger than before. It was enough to help my girlfriend keep afloat during this difficult period. This achievement imbued me with the inner discipline to overcome personal financial challenges. It made me feel confident that I could cultivate mental resilience to overcome the hurdle of fundraising—an altogether different and more complex challenge.

The most significant internal challenge I faced during the sourcing of funds was managing the continuous web of negative thoughts, feelings, and impulses that kept spinning in my head. One of these was the temptation to do whatever it took to gather funds, even if unethical or illegal. I was presented with one such perverse opportunity as well. Through a broker, I'd applied for a business loan at a government bank. The middleman assured me that the loan would be approved only if I paid a bribe to the senior banking official. Although the amount was affordable, the very thought of paying a bribe made my stomach churn. I was taught by my parents and teachers to always do the right thing . . . to be honest, transparent . . . to conduct myself with integrity and dignity. This act would have violated my moral code. At the same time, my funding situation was looking really bleak, and I needed a quick solution. A similar conundrum faced Carmelo Jones. While he succumbed to the temptation of doing the wrong thing, I benefited from the experience of writing the story as it reinforced my moral compass. In the process, my conscience told me that accepting a bribe would lead to destructive long-term consequences, and I was able to walk away from temptation, even in the face of financial duress.

Notwithstanding my discovery of the moral high ground, I was still no closer to unlocking funds, in spite of applying for scores of loans and private deals. Each day felt like ascending a steep mountain, then plummeting to earth upon reaching the halfway mark. I needed a way to manage my stress levels. So I asked myself, 'What do I love to do?' The answer: tell stories.

I've been a writer for a decade now. For the last three years, I've been working on a series of books on the barriers to the pursuit of happiness. This book is the most recent addition to it. A close family friend, who is like a sister to me, suggested that I host a series of online storytelling events. She'd organized a digital forum where a handful of artists from around the world would perform live for a charitable cause. 'You should join our group. You'll be a really effective storyteller and provide hope, inspiration and healing. What's more, you'll discover inner calm that will silence the din in your mind,' she cajoled.

I thought about her offer but I said no, though I instantly felt guilty. There were millions of people in worse straits than me. Was I so self-obsessed that I couldn't spare an hour to do something positive for others? So I was spurred to start a series of online storytelling sessions, 'Life Lessons in the Time of Corona'. Initially, I had conceived the events to last for a month. But when we garnered a regular audience, I ended up continuing the show for almost a year.

The programme wasn't personally lucrative for me, in the sense that I didn't earn fame or fortune through it. Yet I was able to disconnect from my grim life and engage with positivity at least once a week. Every weekday, I looked forward to the next Sunday's talk. I found a forum for raising my voice against financial stress and contributing to a platform for healing people through inspirational stories and practical wisdom. I must confess that the small following I built was a far cry from what is enjoyed by the leading motivational speakers of the world. However, I felt very happy because I knew that I was performing a vital service. Despite the absence of material rewards, my corporate fundraising initiative benefited surprisingly from the positive energy I generated through the events. Here's a curious story of a serendipitous event that occurred during one session.

It was the middle of June. I was in the midst of a Facebook live event when I received an SMS alert. It was a bank—one among 100 where I'd applied for a loan for my company. I had received ninety-nine rejections to date. But this message was different. The message said that my business loan had been approved and would be disbursed in a few days. I was euphoric! This bank had been sitting on my application for several weeks. My company was left with a scant two weeks of funding. Had I not done the event, I'd have been pacing my room, lying in bed or chewing my nails anxiously. But lo and behold! There it was—the priceless message: 'Your loan has been approved'. That was the beginning of an incredible turnaround in my fortunes. That loan created a four-month runway for my company. During that time, we signed up our first cohort of investors. That chain grew slowly but steadily until we were finally able to raise sufficient investments. This is an illustration of how passion can help us overcome financial stress by keeping us connected to our moral compasses and helping us think and act in a positive way.

When trying to overcome financial constraints, ask yourself, 'What is the right thing to do?' The answer will direct you towards a set of ethical and moral principles. While this code may differ from one person to the next, everyone has a set buried inside. You may be aware of it, or you may not be. You may be fuzzy because you haven't spent time introspecting, but the code is embedded deep within you. During moments of acute distress, such as a financial crisis, it's important that you try to discover these principles instead of pushing them aside. It is in these dark times that they will be your true guiding light.

Let us follow the path of passion and discover our conscience. Doing the right thing in life will become much easier.

The characters in this story experienced severe financial stress caused by resource constraints. Learn how they overcame this barrier, and you will believe that you can too.

5

OVERCOMING HEALTH STRESS

UNDERSTANDING HEALTH STRESS

To lead life to its full potential, it's very important to be sound in mind, body and spirit. This means taking care of ourselves in a holistic fashion by working on nutrition, exercise, mental agility and spiritual upliftment. Neglecting any of these aspects can lead to unbalanced or stunted development, as well as a state of physical and emotional atrophy, marked by pain and stress.

Health stress can cloud our minds and prevent us from moving forward in life. It might manifest as a persistent and recurring pain in our body, which often mutates into disease. On the surface, the pain might seem to stem from the impairment of certain components of our body, preventing them from performing physical functions—such as breathing, eating, mobility and sleeping—to their normal capacity. This dysfunction causes persistent pain and mental stress.

Although a physical condition, health stress often stems from an underlying cause that might be linked to the lack of overall well-being in other aspects, or a lack of harmony of mind, body and spirit. This harmony can be maintained only through consistent efforts to improve physically, mentally and spiritually—holistic self-development entails the parallel undertaking of several initiatives. Enabling one's mental and emotional development, socialization, creativity, and compassion is just as vital as proper nutrition, rest and exercise. When all of these initiatives are undertaken with sincere intent, one can hope to someday attain a state of perfect well-being—a state where one is free of all forms of stress and is at peace with oneself and the world.

Adverse circumstances in one's life can compromise their journey towards harmony. A breakup, lay-off, financial crisis, or personal loss can fill a person with such negativity that they may be rendered incapable of focusing on personal development. As a result, they may lose inner balance; they may even adopt unhealthy habits to plug an emotional void and unconsciously inflict lasting damage to themselves.

Here's an example of how an adverse life circumstance can lead to health stress.

A middle-aged shop floor manager had stagnated professionally after working for twenty-five years in the same industry. He was filled with depression and self-loathing. Unable to stand his negative attitude, his girlfriend left him, his friends shunned him and he became even more isolated. He filled the void by overeating and drinking too much alcohol. His weight shot up. In an attempt to shed flab, he started a home fitness programme. But in the absence of a trainer to motivate him, his regimen was short-lived. Moreover, he was reluctant to attend a weight-loss programme at a gym for fear of judgment by leaner and fitter members. In the absence of a good diet and fitness regimen, he developed severe cardiac and liver issues and his mind became further plagued by anxiety, paranoia and depression.

Health stress can follow when we get derailed from our self-development path by a setback. It can be overcome by rediscovering that road and consequently, our inner balance.

The characters in the next story suffered great stress because of health issues. Will they regain their well-being?

THE DAYLIGHT PROGRAMME

Charles had neglected his physical health to the point of no return. He needed a different kind of medicine—a dose of soulful inspiration—to save him.

Charles Martin Smith had just finished lunch at Westlake Supplies—a hardware shop in North Oklahoma City—when the store bell rang. He glanced at the wall clock and noticed that two minutes remained before the store would reopen after lunch. 'Damn! Nobody respects off-duty hours anymore.' He stepped out from behind the sales counter and released the door. A slender woman in her early fifties with coiffed hair entered the shop. She wore a tan Gucci jacket and black trousers, and carried a Louis Vuitton satchel. She placed her eyeshades on the countertop and gave him an inquiring look. 'Hi! I'm looking for a wrench, pliers, and screwdrivers.'

Charles squeezed his portly figure through the narrow space behind the counter and went over to the relevant section of the store. He found the most premium brand of supplies and handed her a box. His eyes sparkled, eyeing a handsome commission from the sale. 'These are the best in class. Suitable for heavy-duty repair work.'

The woman gave the packaging a keen inspection. Finally, she looked back at Charles. 'Are you confident in this brand?'

The salesman shrugged his shoulders. 'Sure. It's our bestselling brand. What do you need it for?'

'To replace a toilet.'

Charles gave a wry laugh and shook his index finger upwards and downwards. 'This is the perfect kit for that. Plumbers come in all the time asking for it.'

The woman studied the product specifications closely. Charles' mind buzzed with various options on how to close the sale. *She must be buying this set for her plumber so she can negotiate a cheaper service contract. But she doesn't know that they get a special discount here. If I open an account for her plumber, that will net me recurring sales. I should discourage her from buying the hardware herself.*

A few minutes later, he cleared his throat. 'Are you buying the equipment for a plumber?'

She nodded.

He quickly took out a form labelled 'PLUMBER REGISTRATION' and asked her to fill in the contact details for her contractor.

She removed a pair of reading glasses from her designer handbag, quickly filled in the appropriate details and handed the form back to Charles. He opened a drawer and prepared to file the form in a folder.

An earnest question from the lady froze his hand in place. 'Aren't you going to give me a discount?'

Charles furrowed his eyebrows. 'This offer is for your plumber.'

With a smile, she took out an ID that read 'OKLAHOMA PLUMBING SOCIETY'. 'I'm a plumber.'

Charles looked her up and down. 'You? You're a plumber? No way!'

The woman removed her glasses and brought her face closer to his. 'You haven't seen a female plumber before?'

Oops! Hope I haven't offended her. Charles gulped and a hang-dog look appeared on his face. 'Well . . . err . . . sure. Of course, we've got quite a few ladies registered with the plumbing association. However, I've . . . I've . . . never seen anyone—'

'Anyone who looks like me?' She twirled around like a diva. 'Elderly? Fashionable?'

Charles nodded his head. His voice stuttered. 'I . . . I . . . guess so.'

The woman broke into a hoarse laugh. 'Hahaha. I get this reaction all the time when I buy supplies. When I first got my license, I went shopping to this store on North Council Road. The owner literally fell off his chair when I told him that I was recently registered.'

He shook his head apologetically. 'My bad. Now that you've created an account, I'm gonna give you a 20 per cent discount on this merchandise and on any items you buy in the future.'

The woman looked at him with a twinkle in her eye—behooving someone who's successfully eked out a good deal. From the corner of his eye, Charles saw a white cat walk past the store. 'So, how long have you been a plumber?'

She did not respond immediately; instead, she turned her gaze to the shelves exhibiting a wide assortment of devices and equipment. It seemed she couldn't find what she was looking for. She turned back to look at him with an expression of resignation.

'A year ago, my twenty-year marriage ended. Once the divorce was finalized, I knew I had to do something to keep my mind occupied and stay positive. One day, after a heavy overnight downpour, I found my toilet leaking incessantly. It was a Sunday, and I just couldn't get hold of a plumber. The sight and sound of the dripping latrine was unbearable. So, I decided to take charge and fix it myself. I looked up many websites and figured out how to do it. After I repaired the toilet, I felt a tremendous sense of accomplishment. I asked myself, can I practise this as a vocation? I looked at the greasy tools on the floor and felt that I could, so I took up a course and got certified. Today, I'm a licensed plumber.'

Charles beamed at her appreciatively. 'It's amazing you took positive steps to move forward in your life. I wish I could do that.'

'Why do you say that?' Her voice was soft. There was an ocean of kindness in her eyes.

It gets pretty lonely out here, I guess.

He took out a picture of a much younger version of himself. He was locked in an embrace with a woman in her twenties who had curly red hair and a chubby face. He smiled ruefully. 'This is Marge, my ex-girlfriend. This photo was taken on a trip to the Florida Keys about fifteen years ago. We dated for twenty years. Last year, we were supposed to get married, but we suddenly broke up. Since then, my life's been in free fall.'

'What happened?' The woman's tone was soft and sympathetic.

Dreams. A lot like unsolved riddles.

Charles glanced at a framed picture sitting on the counter. He sported a wide grin and a certificate from a senior corporate manager. He pointed to the award in the photo.

'I've been in retail my whole life. Employed by Walmart at its megastore on North May Avenue, I worked my way up from the cashier's to the office of the store manager. Twenty years! That's how long it took me to get there. Then last year, just three months after my promotion, the store downsized its operations, and I was laid off.' His tone was sardonic. 'I couldn't find another opening in big-box retail, so my only options were to move to another state or settle for a lower-paying position. Since my elderly, sick mother lives all alone here, I couldn't move. So, I ended up working at this store at half my previous salary . . . with no benefits.'

He paused momentarily, looking at his substantial belly protruding out of his trousers. 'I became really depressed and angry after the company threw me out. They never even bothered to help me find another job. So I drowned my sorrows in food and drink and kept complaining about my sorry plight to Marge. I suppose all that negativity was too much for her.' He looked morose.

The woman nodded in solidarity. 'I guess that's what happened to my friendships too. I'd constantly complain about my husband's infidelity until a time came when they no longer cared to listen.'

'It seems you found a way to stay positive all through that bleak period, though.' Charles's tone brimmed with admiration. 'Look at you now. You're in great shape. Being healthy helped you discover a passion and made it possible for you to rise above your mess. As for me?' He pinched a thick roll of flab on his belly. 'My body's a mess. Excess fat. Liver and cardiac problems. You name the medical issue; I have it. It's a good day if I can sleep without pain.' He shook his head in abject disappointment.

The woman looked at the red patches filling his neck. Her eyes grew wide. *Diabetes. I can see it in his skin. Heart disease . . . who knows what else he might be suffering from? If he doesn't get help now, I don't think he'll live for too long.*

As if verifying her assessment, Charles pulled out a bloodwork report and confessed, 'You see my latest report? Blood cholesterol and kidney markers are totally out of whack. My doc said, "Charles, you're forty-eight and no more a spring chicken. You've got to change your lifestyle. You've got to take all these medications . . . change your diet to include organic lean chicken, fruits and vegetables. You've got to start exercising seriously." But how can I do all this? It costs money. Money I have to take out of my mom's account. Money I don't have.'

The woman considered his downcast and forlorn expression. She carefully opened her bag and peeked at a stack of profile photos concealed in an inner pocket. The topmost one was that of Charles. *Mariana was right. He needs help*. 'Look,' she told him, 'I can help you get your health in order. I was a naturopath when I was married.'

Charles asked, 'Why didn't you continue with that field instead of becoming a plumber?'

The woman waved her hands dismissively. 'Oh, well! That's life, you know. Priorities can change after a breakup or a setback. After my divorce, I couldn't bear to return to my old profession and face my former clients.' She noticed Charles's puzzled expression. 'Why? They all knew me. I couldn't stand the constant whispers, looks of pity and irritating chatter. I had to get a fresh start. So I decided to start my life all over again.'

'Can you really help someone like me lose weight?'

The woman nodded her head. 'Of course. I used to do it all the time. And, I must add . . .' She paused momentarily and flipped through the photo album on her phone to showcase the 'before' and 'after' pictures of a man in his fifties. She turned her phone so Charles could see them.

Charles' eyes popped wide open. 'What! You got this dude to lose over 100 pounds?'

The woman laughed and nodded. 'Of course. That was two years ago. I put him on a six-month programme . . . purely natural, I must tell you . . . no drugs, no chemicals.'

Charles frowned and leaned forward. 'Why do you want to help me . . . a total stranger?'

The woman handed him a business card wordlessly. She replied with a smile, 'Because that's what I do. I help those who really need it. And it's free of charge.'

Charles scratched his head and stared at the card that read 'ESMERALDA FOSTER, FIXER UPPER'. Meanwhile, she made her way towards the door. As she was about to leave the store, Esmeralda turned around and said, 'Charles, be at my place tomorrow at 6 p.m. for your first consultation. The address is on the back of my card.'

That night over dinner, Charles informed his mother about the unexpected offer of rejuvenation. Mom gazed at him suspiciously. 'It sounds like a scam. Why would anyone do this for free?'

Charles helped himself to a third portion of meatloaf and slathered it with an extra dressing of gravy. He looked at her combatively. 'Mom, who knows what her intentions are? Do they even matter? What's the harm in going to her place and checking out what she has in store? We both know I really need it. If she tries to pull a fast one, I'll just leave.'

The next day, Charles headed to Esmeralda's home in Nichols Hills—a twenty-minute drive from his low-income, subsidized apartment on North Rockwell Avenue. He drove a beat-up Ford pickup truck. On the way, he passed a sprawling golf club receiving cold stares from several members. A wave of doubts submerged his mind. He stopped the vehicle by the side of the I-44 highway and stared pensively at the large signboard that read, 'Nichols Hills. 10 miles'.

This lady must be rich to be able to live in this neighbourhood. Will I feel out of sorts at her place? Will her family, friends or whoever's there, mock me, a blue-collar worker without the airs and graces of high society? Should I turn around now?

His thoughts were interrupted by an elderly man's voice on his left. 'Where's the Foster House?' He turned to see a heavyset man in his mid-sixties. He sported a thick white beard, cowboy hat, and rotting teeth. His vehicle was a Nissan Frontier pickup truck with a heavily dented front passenger door. The song 'City of New Orleans' by Willie Nelson was blasting in the background.

Charles pointed down the highway and said, 'I think it's ten miles this way in Nichols Hills. I'm heading there, too.'

The crusty badger gave a swift thumbs-up and then sped past him like a torpedo.

'Maybe I'm not the only unhealthy schmuck she's seeing today,' Charles muttered and stepped on the gas.

Ten minutes later, he arrived in front of a massive gate with the sign FOSTER HOUSE. A deep, masculine voice blared through the speaker at the front gate. 'Who are you?'

'Charles Martin Smith. I'm here for a counselling session with Ms Esmeralda Foster.'

The gate opened and a mansion designed like an English manor loomed in front of him. It was surrounded by trees—pine, oak, apple and maple—and flanked by a sprawling lawn. At the main door, he was welcomed by a short, muscular, uniformed man in his late thirties and a petite woman in her twenties with short, cropped hair. 'Welcome, Mr Smith. My name is Darius. I'll park your car for you,' offered the brawny valet.

Charles looked around and couldn't see an enclosure for cars. 'Where? I didn't see a garage.' The valet pointed to his right at a discreet parking space just behind the massive lawn. 'Over there. Your car will be easily accessible from the house.'

Charles looked in that direction and saw twenty cars parked there. He recognized the vehicle of the old fogey he'd encountered on the road. Charles looked at the welcome party inquiringly. 'I'm not alone, am I?'

The woman standing next to the valet handed him a drink. 'Welcome to the Foster estate, Mr Smith. Here's a drink to refresh you after the drive. I'm Mariana, the housekeeper. Ms Esmeralda is waiting for you with her guests.'

He gulped down the drink. Instantly, Charles felt a cooling sensation in his tummy. 'Wow! That feels like a dozen antacids.'

'Coconut and ginseng. It's all natural.' Mariana smiled.

She led him down the lobby of the house. Charles saw portraits of various noblemen hanging on the walls. Mariana saw him looking curiously at the artwork. 'They are the ancestors of George Nichols, the architect who designed this house in 1929. Ms Esmeralda's ex-husband, Douglas Foster, bought this place about thirty years ago. After the divorce, she got the house as part of her settlement.'

She led him past the living room filled with sculptures and exhibits from various European countries, to a glass door that led to the lawn. It opened automatically. At a distance, he saw a group of men and women seated on yoga mats. They wore identical white trousers and kaftans. A woman was giving them instructions. He peered into the distance and recognized the instructor as Esmeralda.

Mariana pointed to a locker room to his right. 'You'll find an outfit and slippers there. Hurry! The lady is waiting.'

It took him ten minutes to change into a robe. His heart was filled with eager anticipation. He stepped onto the manicured lawn. Esmeralda waved at him from a distance. 'Hi! Come join us. So glad you could make it.'

Charles observed the other guests—he thought there were about twenty of them—seated in a circle on yoga mats, with Esmeralda at the centre. Their eyes were closed, and they were breathing in and out.

'We've just started the session,' Esmeralda whispered as she ushered him to a position on a mat. 'Close your eyes and breathe deeply for a couple of minutes.'

Charles tried to mimic the others' seated positions. Soon, he discovered he couldn't fold his legs into a lotus formation. He heaved his body to get into an upright position on the mat and winced in pain. *Oh God! This is so painful. I can't do this for more than five minutes. I'm gonna look stupid.*

He looked around and noticed that everyone was as out of shape as him. *Most of them look just like me . . . overweight . . . probably with similar sorts of health problems. Yet, they're performing this routine like pros. I have to do the same.* He closed his eyes and listened to the soft voice of the mentor.

'Imagine a happy place. Now, picture yourself enjoying a moment in that world,' she said, softly.

Charles closed his eyes. He saw a vision of himself from the past. A considerably leaner version. That version stood near the cashier section of a supermarket. The date and time on the giant wall-mounted clock behind the checkout aisles showed 11 December 2001, 7 a.m. He was surrounded by a throng of workers wearing uniforms branded with the Walmart logo.

A grey-haired man wearing a business suit came forward and felicitated him.

The gentleman handed him a certificate embossed with the commendation, 'Employee of the Year'. He shook Charles's hand and gave him a beaming smile. 'Thanks to Charles, this store has become the highest grossing outlet of our company. The award is a special recognition on behalf of the company for your outstanding performance. Congratulations!' Cheers resounded all around the giant store. An employee popped a champagne bottle and doused Charles in its frothy foam. He winced in pleasant discomfort amid claps and whoops of joy.

The memory of his finest hour was interrupted by Esmeralda's voice directing the group to open their eyes. Charles did as instructed, surprised to find himself sitting upright fairly comfortably. Although he couldn't fold his legs in a lotus formation, he discovered that he could cross them without discomfort. His eyes lit up. *That's weird! I feel calm. Relaxed. No pain while sitting do*wn. He looked around to get a peek at the others. His eyes fixed on the crusty badger, who greeted him with a smile and a thumbs-up.

Esmeralda addressed the gathering. 'Welcome to the Daylight Centre. I hope you enjoyed the initial orientation. How do you feel now?'

A 250 pound woman in her fifties with short red hair beamed with excitement. 'I swear I could never sit on the floor for more than five minutes. My knees always caved in. But right now, I feel no pain. This is incredible.'

A bald, mustachioed man in his early thirties who weighed 350 pounds and wore a T-shirt labeled DEADLY DUKE looked equally astonished. 'Damn! I can't believe it. I can sit upright for the first time without pain.'

One by one, the members of the group voiced their wonder at the healing after-effects of the session. Esmeralda waved her hands in a circular motion. 'It's wonderful to be free of pain for the first time in years, right?' Cries of confirmation went around like soulful chants.

Esmeralda handed each person a pin with a red flower. 'You are now permanent members of this centre. Wear this pin at all times while you're on this property. The red eucalyptus flower has a positive, healing aura that will help you in your efforts to regain your health.'

Charles held his chin. *What's her methodology for weight loss?* He raised his hand. 'So what are we going to do here?'

Esmeralda looked at everyone with a smile. 'That's exactly the question on everyone's mind, right? "What will I do here?"'

The red-haired woman nodded her head. 'That's right. When we met at the laundromat two days ago, you told me you were a service technician and that you'd help me fix some of those malfunctioning parts. We struck a really nice rapport. You said, "Annie, I'm gonna help you lose weight." Now I'm wondering how you are going to achieve that. Only through group activities like this?'

The crusty old badger rubbed his eyes and glanced sideways at the redhead. 'Yeah! That's right. Last week, you approached me at the auto repair store where I work as a mechanic and offered, "Hey, Billy Bob, I'm a supplier of lubricants. I'd love to do business with you. And, by the way, I want to help you lose weight." Hell, you even flaunted your business card as a self-employed dealer of auto supplies. Tell me, lady, who are you?'

The members whispered among themselves the apprehension that Esmeralda had tricked them into coming for underlying motives. Charles scratched his nose. 'You said you were a certified plumber. But here you are . . . a yoga teacher . . . a health coach. Who are you, lady?'

The attendees looked at Esmeralda with cold expressions.

Esmeralda put her hands up in the air. 'You're right. I impersonated those individuals in order to strike a rapport with you. The truth is that I'm a holistic health practitioner. A naturopath. This centre specializes in holistic well-being. I offer a nutritional programme allied with fitness and community activities. I would like to invite all of you to try out a six-week programme for free.'

Annie looked around at the sprawling acres wide lawn and grand mansion. 'What's in it for you, lady? You could be selling these services to rich folks. Why are you wasting your time with junk-food-eating slobs like us?'

A glow of sincerity lit Esmeralda's eyes. 'I've been a health coach my whole life. I aided only the rich and the famous. All the while, I saw the poorer sections of society suffering from the debilitating effects of poor nutrition and lifestyle. It seemed unfair that the knowledge and practice of good health would be out of reach for the majority of our nation's citizens. For a long time, this concern pricked my conscience, yet I didn't do anything about it. Then, a personal loss forced me to change my attitude. Last year, Juan—my chauffeur for ten years—collapsed from a heart attack while driving. He was obese and had been experiencing various complications: diabetes and high blood pressure, for many years. He'd been taking medications for these. But over time, they caused terrible side effects'.

She paused for a minute and wiped a tear that trickled from her eye. 'He was Mariana's father. I blamed myself for not doing enough to safeguard his health, especially since I had all this knowledge, tools, and connections at my disposal . . .

since I knew how to address obesity with the help of natural remedies, and—'

Mariana walked into the garden and placed a hand on her shoulder. 'After Papa died, Madame embarked on a mission to spread the philosophy of wellness to the struggling sections of society. She was determined to bring joy and good health back to the silent classes. But we had to start the health movement somewhere. So, we went around the city identifying people who needed help the most. People who were in the pits of death but couldn't afford a safety harness. How could we find you? At first, I thought of putting an ad in the paper. But we were afraid we'd be inundated with replies and wouldn't be able to identify the neediest. So, we went to corner shops, supermarkets, restaurants to find the most desperate. Once we identified you, we had to figure out how interested you'd be in improving your health. We also had to earn your trust to sell you on the programme. So, she disguised herself as a professional from a related industry in order to strike a rapport. I know all this sounds sneaky. But I promise you on my father's grave, that the mission is for real.'

Annie stood up and hugged Esmeralda. Then she broke down sobbing. 'My whole life, my weight stopped me from doing the things I really wanted to. You're an angel for caring.'

Esmeralda stroked her hair and kissed the top of her head. 'Annie. You should know it's not your weight that's the problem.' Annie looked at her, puzzled. 'It's your physical health. Your journey's about to begin. Wait until you see what you're capable of.'

Very quickly, the emotions of the others changed from rank suspicion to bemusement, and finally to tearful joy. Esmeralda raised her hand like a pilgrim about to begin a holy mission.

'I won't rest until each and every one of you overcome health stress, until each and every one of you regain the vitality you deserve. All I ask is trust. Trust me. Trust each other. Trust the process we're about to begin.'

The members broke out into whoops of hope and joy. 'We trust you.' 'We want to change ourselves.'

The naturopath then gathered the group to a greenhouse situated at the end of the lawn. Charles saw a patch of plants, vegetables, and fruit-bearing trees; his mouth gaped with incredulity. 'You've grown all this?'

Esmeralda pointed to a platter full of what appeared to be cut melons. 'Homegrown cantaloupes. Try them.'

Charles dug in. The sweet and fresh aroma of the fruit reminded him of a high school trip to Sacramento he'd taken when he was twelve. He'd gone on the excursion with twenty-five members of his sixth-grade class. Its purpose was the exploration of the agriculture and botany of the region. At the end of the seven-day field trip, every student had to submit a detailed project report to get their final semester grade.

On the second day of the field trip, Charles took detailed pictures of a fruit-bearing tree at an orchard fifty miles outside of Sacramento. At the same time, the owner of the farm explained how the weather and soil patterns of the region influenced the development of the fruits. Charles looked hungrily at a basket of cantaloupes, all neatly sealed and packaged and awaiting their transport to the nearest farmer's market. A bespectacled, auburn-haired girl watched him eyeing the fruit greedily while he furiously jotted notes. She came up to him and flashed a teasing smile. 'Are you thinking about food or the assignment?'

Charles blushed. 'Err . . . Marge . . . no way . . . it's not like that at all.'

The girl giggled. She brought her face close to his ears. 'Hehehe! I can hear your tummy growling.'

'I guess so. But lunch is in two hours, and we aren't supposed to touch or eat anything out here. Teacher's orders.'

Their teacher—a woman in her late forties with jet-black hair tied in a bun, a portly figure, and severe, dark glasses—saw the two in private chat mode. She raised her eyebrows. 'Keep quiet and pay attention to Mr Kelly. You have the rare opportunity to learn from a legend of the farming world. He has twenty-five years of experience in agriculture. His insights on soil cultivation are more valuable than anything you'll ever find in textbooks. If this talk doesn't interest you, at least show respect to those who want to learn.'

Charles buried his head sheepishly in his notebook and scribbled a scrawly diagram of the tree. He was suddenly jolted from his stupor by a pat on his shoulder. Before he could turn around, he felt something being inserted in his trouser pocket. He faced the perpetrator of the mischief. It was Marge. She placed a finger on her lips and gestured for him to check his pocket. Furtively, he pushed the object from his trousers . . . ever-so-slightly, with his fingers. His eyes widened with surprise and anxiety when he saw a fruit from the forbidden basket. He looked around to make sure nobody was watching and tiptoed a few inches towards the fruit basket. A peck on the cheek stopped him. He gazed at Marge's loving eyes. 'Eat it. I can't bear to see you hungry.'

That fateful day passed through his memory like a sepia-tinted card scented with rose water. *All those years, I never had the courage to talk to Marge even though we'd been in the same class since we were seven. I never thought she'd notice me. Her gesture made me realize that she felt about me the way I felt about her.* He bit into the fruit unleashing a symphony of flavourful recollections. *After that day, we became inseparable. Right through high school, through vocational training institute, until we became steady.* The aroma of the sweet memory filled his consciousness with the scent of lavender and honey. *I still remember the taste of that fruit. My first cantaloupe.*

Meanwhile, Billy Bob, the crusty old badger, bit into the fruit. His face immediately contorted, and he spat it out with a yell. 'Yuck! It's too sour.'

Esmeralda put her arm on his shoulder. 'We always reject at first that which is unfamiliar to us. But once we get used to it, we want nothing else.'

Annie's reaction mimicked Billy Bob's. 'This is so disgusting. It tastes like stale syrup.'

Charles shook his head. *They don't know what's good for them even if it's staring them in the face.* He pointed to the bald, obese man with the moustache. 'Hey . . . Deadly Duke . . . when was the last time you ate a fruit? An actual fresh fruit?'

The embarrassed member shrugged and furrowed his brows. 'Oh! I can't remember.'

'For the past twenty years of my life, I've lived on a diet of frozen meat, chips, french fries, and doughnuts.' Charles paused as several others gathered around him. 'Plus plenty of Coke and beer to keep me company. I haven't touched a single fresh fruit, vegetable, or natural juice in all these years.'

Billy Bob nodded his head. 'I've followed an almost identical diet. With a few exceptions. I prefer rare steak to cheeseburgers. And whisky to beer.'

Another member—a twenty-five-year-old man with a swollen abdomen, bruises, and swellings on his neck and shoulders—sighed and looked defeated. 'The only things I can taste these days are tobacco and liquor. I drank too much in college and developed liver cirrhosis as a result. These days, I have to force myself to eat anything. There's no way I can touch this fruit.'

Charles held out a cantaloupe. 'You think you can't taste this fruit, right? Err . . . what's your name?'

'My friends call me Sallow Hal,' replied the gaunt youth.

The audience broke into laughter. Esmeralda looked cross and interrupted them. 'Visualize yourself as a picture of health, not decay. We'll call you Hal.'

Charles tapped Hal's shoulder. 'So, Hal, you say you can't taste anything? No food? No drinks? Nothing?' Hal nodded in agreement. Charles turned his gaze to Annie first and then Billy Bob. 'And as for you guys . . . y'all find the taste of natural fruits and vegetables repulsive, right?'

A loud chorus of yeses could be heard all around.

Charles closed his eyes momentarily and recalled the sensation he'd experienced a little while ago. 'When I bit into this fruit, at first I couldn't taste its texture or its flavour. Then, I saw something. A memory.'

Esmeralda's eyes widened with surprise. 'What did you see?'

'A simple life. A better life. A life that got away from me.' Charles looked wistfully at the basket of cut melons.

Esmeralda gazed at his sad eyes. *The fruit reminds me of my father. We used to go to the farmers' market together. The first time we went, he bought me a cantaloupe. Like me, Charles associates this fruit with a bittersweet memory. Perhaps the others will do the same.* She glanced at each person individually in the group. 'Close your eyes. Think of a moment when you really and truly loved someone. I mean, loved someone with all your heart. Then, place yourselves in that moment.'

For ten minutes, everyone stood with their eyes closed. Suddenly, the greenhouse disappeared.

After a moment of darkness, Charles saw the trunk of an enormous tree right in front of his nose. He looked around and saw that he was behind a large oak in the middle of a community fairground. A huge sign by the carnival entrance read, ADAIR COUNTRY FAIR.

'Adair? It's where I grew up. This is a place I loved to frequent,' he exclaimed. He noticed a Ferris wheel, carousel, and concession stands. Hundreds of people were gathered there enjoying treats. He raised his eyebrows. 'I remember the slight nip in the air, typical of late March. I remember the massive crowds. I remember—' His recounting was interrupted by the chiming of a makeshift clock tower perched atop a haunted house attraction.

'I remember that clock. It's 7 p.m.,' he said breathlessly. At that moment, a skinny boy with freckles and a red-haired girl wearing glasses, both appearing to be about thirteen years old, sat on a bench thirty feet behind the tree. He gasped. 'This can't be. That was my . . . my first kiss.' The couple's lips got close to each other and had nearly locked when the fairground disappeared abruptly.

Charles returned to reality holding half a piece of cantaloupe. Its juice dripped liberally from his mouth.

Esmeralda handed him a napkin. There was a twinkle in her eye. 'Did you get lost in your memory?'

'Uh-uh . . . I . . . ' Charles looked around. The surroundings and the people seemed blurry. He looked around to see how the others were reacting. They all seemed a little woozy.

Annie's dazed voice shattered the silence. 'I feel light-headed.'

Esmeralda rushed to her aid, held her hand, and offered a glass of water. Annie drank it down in an instant. Her face was flushed and her voice quivered with emotion. 'Broken Bow. Thirty-five years ago. I was right there with my husband on our honeymoon. We were scuba diving together. I can still taste the salty water on my lips.' Her voice cracked. 'That was our first and last trip together before he died in a shark attack. The very next year. I was so deep in that moment that I felt every emotion racing through my heart.'

Billy Bob was the next to relate his experience. 'It felt like I was right there. Just outside the Tallgrass Prairie Reserve in 1965. I was standing on a truck with my brother, posing for pictures with a dead bison. I remember that day so clearly. It was the day before Bernie shipped out to Vietnam.'

The rest of the group went on to share their moments of love. At the end of the outpouring, Esmeralda pointed to the empty plate, which was loaded with fruit just a little while ago. 'You were so caught up in your memories that you didn't notice you'd eaten the fruit.'

She offered them the platter. 'Now, try another one.'

The members tucked into their second helping, and this time, their faces brightened with satisfaction.

Hal's face glowed. 'I can't believe it! My taste is back! When I eat this fruit, I can see my sister's face lighting up with joy as she read aloud her admission letter from Yale University. An offer she secured through my relentless SAT prep. An offer I could never crack myself because I drowned in a well of alcohol.'

They made a beeline for the remaining cantaloupes and helped themselves to a third and then fourth round. Esmeralda applauded. 'Now, cherish these memories. You've taken the first step towards changing your eating habits.'

After their reintroduction to natural foods, Esmeralda escorted them to the north side of the lawn near the entrance of the house. Charles was surprised to see two identical lines of objects and barriers laid out like obstacle courses. A book on the ground marked the start of each line. Sixty feet ahead of it stood a table. A net and a plate filled with ten apples lay on it. A brick wall stood sixty feet ahead of the table. It was ten feet high, six feet wide, and mounted on a metallic platform with wheels. A rope ladder stretched from the base of the wall to its peak. A watermelon was placed there. Another sixty feet away was something that looked like a water pipeline, thirty feet in length, three feet in diameter, and three feet in height. An icebox was perched about halfway on the top of its surface. Next to it was a timer clock with the count, thirty minutes. Another sixty feet away, he saw a blender plugged into the boundary wall of the estate. The blender had a timer too. It displayed the same count as the clock.

Annie stared at the intricate arrangement and frowned. 'What are we doing?' Esmeralda took out her phone and played a video.

Accompanied by a dance soundtrack, the title of the video—*Smoothie Run Challenge*—appeared on the screen in disco fonts. The group watched as a man in the video picked up the book and ran towards the table. Then, he bent his body below the table and wriggled under it. Once he'd passed it, he turned around and placed the book on the table. Then, he packed the apples into the net and ran towards the brick wall. He climbed up the rope ladder to reach the peak and placed the bag of apples carefully on the top of the wall. Then, he grasped the twenty-pound watermelon and climbed down. Next, holding the fruit, he crawled through the pipe like an escaping convict until he reached its midpoint. A vase—slightly shorter than three feet—was fixed to the base. It concealed an electronic push button, which was pointed out to the viewers.

The participant knelt on the floor and heaved the watermelon through the funnel of the container. The heavy fruit landed hard on the push button and released an opening on the pipe's ceiling—an opening that was big enough for a person to squeeze his torso through and access the icebox. The man wriggled his upper body through the aperture, opened the box, and found ten sealed pouches. He grabbed one of them, bent down, and slithered to the end of the pipe. He stood up and ran towards the blender by the corner of the garden. Then, he ripped the pouch and dunked its contents into the blender: one ice cube, one slice of banana, and one slice of watermelon.

The video raked up an ancient memory in Charles' mind. *This looks like an obstacle course similar to one I competed in as a ninth-grader. Although I wasn't heavy back then, I wasn't particularly athletic and never excelled in traditional sports. On the annual sports day, the school authorities planned an obstacle race to allow everyone to participate. To my surprise, I won. That day, I celebrated my victory by taking Marge out to a club for the first time. We used these fake IDs and sneaked in. We partied all night and returned at 3 a.m. I'll never forget that day.*

Esmeralda interrupted his fond recollection. She pointed to the blender at the opposite end of the lawn. 'There's only one blender at the far end of the grounds by the wall. However, there are two identical rows of obstacles and barriers.'

Billy Bob adopted the posture of a 100m sprinter in jest and laughed at Esmeralda. 'I suppose we have to race each other to prepare the highest quantity of smoothie.'

'A race? Yes. Individual competition? No.' Esmeralda shook her head. Bob looked perplexed. 'You'll form two groups of ten. Each of you will run the obstacle course, then pour the ingredients from your pouch into the blender. Only after all of you have completed the course and emptied your pouches will the blender's process button work. Only then will you be able to make the smoothie.'

Hal peered at the circuitous obstacle course and made a face. 'What if we take a long time to finish it? The ingredients would just sit in the blender and may spoil.'

Esmeralda let out a mischievous laugh. 'Hehe. I figured that would be an issue. So, I've added an extra dimension to this game.' Hal looked at her, confused. There was a cheeky glint in her eye. 'The ingredients can sit in the blender for only thirty minutes. After that, the blender will activate a capsule of ink, which will ruin all the materials. However, if the mixer is filled with the contents of all twenty pouches within thirty minutes and that primary button is pressed, water will release automatically, and the smoothie will be blended.'

Charles' mind processed different scenarios of the game. The other members looked at each other, confused, wondering what their roles would be.

Darius arrived with two fresh iceboxes and planted one on top of each pipe. He also placed a clock with a timer set at thirty minutes. He winked and pumped his fist in the air. 'All right, guys. You've got half an hour to drink the most delicious smoothie of your lives.'

The gang split into two teams of ten. Billy Bob took the position of a sprinter and goaded Esmeralda. 'Aren't you going to blow the whistle?'

She gestured for him to begin, saying, 'Ready whenever you are.' She took out her phone and clicked on the screen. Immediately, the clock counted down.

Billy Bob dashed a step forward, but Charles stopped him and indicated the members of both sides to huddle. 'Remember, we aren't competing against each other. We have to help each other out. So, we need a game plan. Now, only a few of us can run the course at the same time. Each of us has weaknesses. For instance, I can't wriggle through a pipe. It would take me ten minutes to crawl through that sewer on my own. By the time I'd do so, the contest would be over.'

Annie bent forward, but barely managed to lower her shoulders. 'I can't bend forward even by ten degrees. My lower back hurts every time I try.'

Another member—a long-white-haired, slender man in his sixties—held his right kneecap. 'My knees are really bony. I've got arthritis. I can't crawl or bend down. I even have a nickname: Stick Leg Stan.'

Another participant—a woman in her thirties with olive skin and dark-brown patches on her neck—jiggled her midriff like a belly dancer. 'Hi! I'm Yu Yan. People called me 'Doughnut' for years because of the way I look. I can do everything except climb.'

Charles pointed to the top of the wall. 'On the other hand, we all have strengths. I, for one, am a good climber.'

The others nodded their heads and looked at each other nervously. Charles glanced at the clock and saw that four minutes had already elapsed. "We need to work as a team to harness our strengths and complement each other's weaknesses. For example, Annie can climb, but Yu Yan can't, so Annie can help Yu Yan go up the ladder. Then, when Annie has to bend down to pick up the book, Yu Yan will help her do so without straining her lower back.'

Billy Bob performed a jog standing in one place. 'C'mon, stop talking.'

Stick Leg Stan stared at him, looking cross. 'Going to war without a plan is pointless. Look at what happened to our soldiers in Vietnam, Afghanistan, and Iraq.'

Charles asked Esmeralda for a notebook. He tore out a bunch of pages and handed everyone four pieces of paper. 'Label each of the four activities—knee stretch, table bending, pipe crawling, climbing—A, B, C, and D. Then, rate your skill in each activity in terms of a number . . . one or two. One means 'I need help'. Two means 'I can help'.'

Everyone filled out their forms. Esmeralda reminded, 'Twenty five minutes left.'

Charles held out his flash cards. 'Every time you need help on an activity, display that activity card. Then yell out your code, say A-one. Anyone who isn't busy with an activity at that time and has the complimentary card, A-two, will help you. On the other hand, once you've finished an activity on your own, you must show that activity card and yell, 'A-two'. At that time, anybody who's about to start that activity and needs help should shout, 'A-one'.'

Billy Bob's eyes sparkled like a farmer who spotted a UFO in the middle of the prairie. 'Only ask for help when you really need it because it may cost the other person valuable time.'

By the time they took their position, eleven minutes had elapsed. Charles realized they had an average of a minute and a half to complete the whole routine. He bit his lip. *Did I waste too much time talking instead of acting?* However, the participants began the race by forming a network of partnerships. Billy Bob helped Hal crawl through the pipe; Annie helped Billy Bob wriggle under the table; Stick Leg Stan helped Hal to climb. Charles helped everyone to climb and bend.

In this phase, eighteen members finished the exercise and dumped their pouches into the blender. With two minutes to go, Yu Yan and Charles were the only ones left. Charles closed his eyes. *It's now or never.* He quickly bent over and picked up the book. He wriggled underneath the table, placed the book on top, and bagged the apples. A surge of pain shot through his spine. He breathed heavily. Determination filled his eyes. 'You've done this before, Charles. Piece of cake.' He gritted his teeth and somehow, completed every activity, and ran to the mouth of the pipe—his bugbear—with the watermelon.

Yu Yan was standing by the wall on the other track. She yelled out D1.

Should I offer help, or should I ask for it? He looked at Yu Yan. She was panting heavily. *She probably needs my help more than I need hers.*

He rushed to her aid. 'Lace your legs carefully on the rope.'

Yu Yan yelled. 'No. I can't. I'll fall.'

'Hold on tight. I'm behind you.'

Yu Yan utilized Charles's support as minimal leverage and clambered up the rope ladder like a monkey. In no time, she hefted the watermelon and climbed down with it. After that, it didn't take long for her to acquire a pouch from the top of the pipe and dump its contents into the blender.

Charles' eyes almost popped out of their sockets. 'Wow! Where did that come from?'

Yu Yan smiled. 'For ten years, I tried out for the Chinese gymnastics team. I never made the cut. But I guess some of the training rubbed off on me for good.' She gazed at Charles's next challenge ground. The pipe.

Charles glanced at the countdown clock, which read one minute and twenty seconds. *I did the crawl successfully in high school. I feel good today. I can make it on my own. There's no point in dragging Yu Yan down.* He shook his head at Yu Yan. 'No. You go on. Dump your sachet.'

Charles crawled laboriously through the tube for what seemed like an infinite period. At a distance, he heard faint voices of exhortation. 'Charles, forty-five seconds to go. You can do it.' His entire lower body felt almost paralyzed from the waist down. Suddenly, he spotted the vase about thirty feet away. A gentle breeze blew past his face. 'No fear. No pain.' He gasped for breath, but somehow managed to crawl to the middle of the pipe. He heaved the watermelon and hoisted it into the vase. A narrow segment of the ceiling opened up. *The icebox. I can see it.* He grabbed the last pouch from the icebox and crawled furiously through the pipe. He emerged on the other side and raised his arms triumphantly, unable to get up.

The countdown chorus of 'Ten . . . 9 . . . 8 . . . ' rent the air. His eyes fell on Esmeralda. She shook her fingers from side-to-side. *Oh no! I still have work to do.* He took a deep breath, jumped up, and sprinted towards the far end of the lawn. The voices counted down— '4, 3, 2 . . . ' He dumped the contents of the sachet into the blender. When the crowd chanted '1', he pressed the process button on the mixer. A stream of water filled the device, and the blender revved up.

The group gathered around Charles and gave him more high-fives and embraces than he had ever received in his life. *I can't begin to describe this feeling. Achievement. How long since I've been recognized for anything? Too long.*

Esmeralda handed him a glass filled to the brim with the nutrient-rich drink. 'How does this feel?'

Charles gulped it down in a flash. He panted like a swimmer coming up for air after a record underwater session. 'Victory's sweet.'

A friendly slap on his shoulder made him turn around. Annie looked at him with feigned annoyance. 'Are you gonna just stand there? Or will you dance?' She pulled his hand and made him join the rest of the group that had formed two circles.

'Only if she does,' he joked. He reached his hand out to Esmeralda.

Esmeralda accepted it. 'What are we dancing?' Suddenly, she looked out-of-sorts.

Annie played the song *Soldier's Joy* by Zip Wilson on her phone. 'We're square dancing.'

Esmeralda looked confused. 'Oh! I'm so sorry. I grew up in California. I don't know how to do that.'

Annie grabbed her elbow. 'Oh, come on! I'm from Idaho, sweetie. We do things differently there, too.'

Esmeralda stared at Annie with an expression suggesting, 'Honey, have all the smoothies you like, but leave me out of this kitsch.'

Annie pointed to Yu Yan—who was performing the dance steps with ease. 'She's from China. Come on. You'll be fine.'

Esmeralda looked a bit self-conscious during her initial dancing steps with Charles. But then she saw everyone in full dancing mode. Nobody directed as much as a glance at her. Her breathing relaxed and her body got loose. She swayed more vigorously and tapped her feet with greater energy. Her discomfort melted away, and she moved in harmony with the rest.

Charles saw her in sync with everyone, and playfully threw her question back at her, 'So how does this feel?'

She smiled and cupped her mouth. 'Victory's sweet. But partnership's even sweeter.'

Half an hour later, a sweaty and happy Billy Bob raised his hands in celebration. 'If this is what health improvement's all about, count me in every day. Twenty-four-seven if need be.'

Annie wiped a tear. 'After God took my husband, I let myself go. All these years, I had no zeal for life. I couldn't find happiness in anything. Today, you changed that. Today, you made me feel life is worth living.'

Esmeralda hugged her. 'I'm so glad you trusted me and the process.'

Esmeralda gazed at the folks—who were strangers a few hours ago—hugging, celebrating and talking excitedly. She swallowed her tears. *Come on, Es. You've got to remember these are clients, not personal friends. You've got to be professional. This is just the beginning of a journey. Many of them will drop out in the coming weeks despite their current enthusiasm. That's just how it goes, and you know it. But, you can't forget the coaching mantra. Be personal, humane, but always maintain a slight distance. You can't get too caught up in your clients' feelings.*

Stan looked at her with expectation. 'So, what are we doing tomorrow?'

Esmeralda felt the tears re-emerging. 'This has been . . . gosh . . . uplifting . . . for me as much as it's been for all of you.' Her voice choked with emotion.

At that point, she noticed Charles' gesture that seemed to suggest she had something below her right eye. She took out a handkerchief, quickly wiped the tears and cleared her throat. 'Umm . . . Today was your first day at the Daylight Centre.

Every day for the next six weeks, we'll do different activities around nutrition, fitness and meditation. You'll arrive here in the evenings at 6 p.m. We'll continue our activities until 9 p.m. and then finish off with a healthy dinner. Every three weeks, you'll undergo bloodwork and a body composition analysis to check your progress. Throughout the programme, you can consult my network of experts in medicine, fitness and lifestyle. What goal shall we set? I want to whip you in the best shape of your lives in six weeks and then equip you with a mindset to maintain it.'

For a moment, there was silence. A clap broke the silence and someone moved to the centre of the gathering. It was Charles who faced the crowd. 'There's nothing more important to me than overcoming health stress. Come hail, hurricane, or heat, I'll be at the centre every day.'

The remaining members gave a resounding ovation. Their collective voice reverberated the surroundings. 'We'll be here every day. We'll all overcome health stress.'

Everyone proceeded to the changing rooms before their homeward journeys. Charles turned around, gazed at Esmeralda and placed his hand on his chest. 'In mind, body and spirit, I will become a new person.'

That night, over dinner, Charles related the events of the day with great excitement. Substituting a tuna salad for the meatloaf his mother offered, he waved his cutlery with fanfare. 'Mom! This programme will change my life. I'm gonna get my life back.'

His mother furrowed her eyebrows. 'Humph! So this woman told you to exchange homecooked food full of love for this nauseating bowl of grass?' She sniffed the tuna and turned up her face. Her voice was layered with disgusted skepticism.

'You really think you'll eat this smelly, slimy paste every single day for six weeks?'

Charles nodded his head. 'I will, Mom. I have to. Don't you remember what I looked like before I moved in with Marge? God! That must have been twenty-five years ago! I was slim and joyful.'

His mom shook her head. 'I think you were a bit too skinny back then. As for your mindset?' She paused and pointed to an old, framed photo of the couple posing on a bridge over a lake in the nearby town of Carmen. 'Do I see you smiling or glaring on that vacation? It's obvious you weren't happy.'

'Come on, Ma. That's unfair and you know it. Of course, we had bad moments. But there were good ones too.' His mom looked at him disapprovingly. 'All I remember when I think of that period is how much I enjoyed life. How much energy I had. How much stuff I did. But over the years, I lost my mojo. And then my health went downhill. Even my doctor says I need to change my lifestyle.'

She looked at her own reflection on the scratched mirror installed in the dining room with dismay. *Look at me. Those heavy jowls are pig's cheeks. Those baggy eyes are a donkey's drooping orbs. That wrinkled forehead is a map with silted rivers. Those saggy boobs are punctured tires. That fat stomach is a mountain of molten cheese. Those thick legs are a hippo's attachments. All controlled by a heart that never stops palpitating. By kidneys that never stop urinating. By lungs that never stop wheezing. Ain't I a beast?*

She stared at her son as he slowly ate his salad. *As long as he stays like this, I can be comfortable with the fact that I'm not the only one who looks and feels as such. But if he pursues this madness, he may very well change himself. Would I be able to recognize him? What role would I have in his life?*

She threw her arms up. 'It's your life. You know what you've got to do. Just ask yourself, is it worth giving up the simple joys . . . meatloaf, cornbread and beans, biscuits with gravy, and fried pecan pie—all those wholesome things made with love?'

A look of clarity and determination appeared in Charles' eyes. 'These things have been making me fat, ruining my health. I need to quit them cold turkey. I need to eat lots of fruits, veggies, and lean proteins. That's what Es said.'

Mother slapped her forehead and moaned. 'Oh God! That witch doctor put *some* spell on you.'

The next day, Charles reached the Daylight Centre ten minutes late. Mariana ushered him into the kitchen. The group was already assembled, intently viewing a cooking demonstration. A man in his fifties with a goatee was in charge. He wore an apron and a toque—and applied what looked like breading on a burger patty. Mariana caught Charles's perplexed expression. 'A healthy cooking lesson by MasterChef Rodrigo Santoro. A celebrity chef who worked for many Hollywood superstars before setting up a chain of natural food restaurants across the country.'

'What's he doing in this neck of the woods?'

Mariana did not reply to his question. Instead, she handed him a business card from a pile on a counter. The restaurant's name, 'NATURE'S GRUB' and its locations were printed on it. She pointed to the branch in Oklahoma City. 'He's in the city to open his latest branch. As an old friend, he took up Esmeralda's request to offer a lesson.'

Esmeralda beckoned Charles to stand by the prep table. 'We are learning how to make a healthy burger.'

Charles looked around. 'Where are the buns?'

Rodrigo showed Charles several dainty ramekins neatly arranged on the table; each contained different condiments. 'Usually, we eat cheeseburgers made from processed red meat, high fat cheese and white flour buns. But there are equally delicious options that are way healthier.' He took a spoon and scooped up some beans. 'Chickpeas, beans, eggs, onions, garlic, soy protein, bulgur wheat for the breading. Now, you can substitute the starchy bread with flavourful and healthy whole grain flour as a topping. Here's everything you need to make a delicious plant-based burger in fifteen minutes.'

Charles shook his head vigorously. 'That's impossible for regular people to do. Only a master chef like yourself can make that.'

Billy Bob wielded his fork like a wannabe serial killer of munchies. 'Come on! I'm a meat-and-potatoes guy, just like everybody here. How can a veggie burger taste good?'

The chef flashed a mischievous smile. 'Well, you'll never know unless you try it, right? First, let me show you how it's made.'

He mashed up the ingredients in a mixing bowl, scooped out a clump of the mixture and placed it on a tray. Manually, he formed a circle and then sprinkled the wheat on top. 'Voilà! Next, I'm gonna put it in the oven on high for ten minutes. After that, we'll all taste it.' His voice was bursting with enthusiasm.

Ten minutes later, the timer sounded an alert. Rodrigo removed the patty from the oven and placed it on the table with a triumphant, 'Here we go.'

Charles saw a perfectly brown burger patty and stroked his chin. *Hmm. This looks like a real burger. But surely it can't taste the same.*

Esmeralda then sliced the patty into twenty small pieces. Using toothpicks, she passed the nibbles around.

Charles placed the morsel in his mouth. All of a sudden, the kitchen disappeared and it got dark for an instant. When the light returned, he was standing by a vegetable patch in the middle of a farm. There were veggies of all sorts: snow peas, kale, spinach, onions and lettuce. *Hey, I remember this place. I must have been fifteen. This is—*

His thoughts were interrupted by the sound of heavy boots. He turned around. Two people stepped out of a shack about 600 feet away and approached him. One of them was a tall man in his fifties. Next to him was a teenage boy with an empty wicker basket. Charles peered to get a good look and his mouth opened wide. *Good lord. That's me. I remember this day.*

Oblivious to the presence of the otherworldly entity, the two picked the vegetables and sorted them in the basket. The older gentleman patted Charles Junior on his back. 'Charles, I never imagined you'd have such a flair for farming. Without your help, these veggies would never have turned out so perfect.'

The younger Charles smiled and looked at the man appreciatively. 'That's really nice of you, Mr Berger. I wish my high school botany teacher felt the same way.'

Mr Berger snorted. 'What does that idiot know about farming? Gardening. Agriculture. These pursuits can never be taught in classrooms. You gotta sweat it out in the fields if you wanna be good.' He paused and held a rich green clump of vegetables. 'These are the freshest spring onions I've ever seen. And to think six months ago, those damned Nation Fresh buyers cancelled my contract because one batch was rotten.' Mr Berger's eyes were filled with tears. He gave Charles a hug. 'You saved us from financial ruin. How can I ever repay you?'

Charles filled up the basket with an assortment of perfectly ripe vegetables. 'Don't thank me. Thank Marge. When she told me her father was financially stressed because the drought had ruined his crop, how could I stand by? How could I not offer my limited expertise in botany and agriculture? How could I not draw on my passion?'

The middle-aged man looked at young Charles as if he were a messiah; the surroundings changed and Charles found himself back in the kitchen. *Farming was my passion. It's something I never took up seriously.* He considered the plant-based burger he'd tasted. 'This is great. Way better than regular burgers.'

Billy Bob slobbered all over the treat. 'I can't believe this. I just had a flashback of Bernie, my brother, and me stealing vegetables from a neighbour's farm.'

Deadly Duke had the look of a punter whose favourite NASCAR team had just won. 'Wow! This is the first time I've eaten vegetables in years. I always had a phobia I'd throw up because they're so bland and tasteless. But I was wrong! This is just great!'

The rest of the group shared their experiences. Esmeralda's face lit up with satisfaction. *This was the hardest part of all, getting them to try out fruits and veggies. Their biggest bugbear. I'm so happy they crossed this barrier.* She got up from her stool and proceeded to roll some of the fillings. 'Now, let's learn to make this ourselves.'

The members eagerly teamed up to prepare two dozen burgers. Charles put one of them in his mouth. It melted instantly in a puddle of aromatic flavours. *This is amazing. It's simple to make, yet so tasty. Changing my eating habits will now be a breeze.*

The next morning at 8 a.m., Charles's mother put on her jacket and went towards the door. 'I'm going to the doctor's office for some tests. My muscles and joints are aching like crazy. I think the thyroid's acting up.'

Charles got up from the sofa. 'Let me drive you.'

She smiled sweetly and squeezed his cheeks. 'That's really thoughtful of you. You're truly like your father.'

Charles looked at her coldly. 'I should hope not. Dad abandoned us when I was ten. You had to raise me on your own. I definitely hope I'm nothing like him.'

Tears welled in her eyes. 'I know you hate him. He hurt us real bad. But things are complicated. He would have come back to us had he not made that one huge mistake.'

'Oh, come on!' Charles snapped. 'He tried to pull off a scam at the Cherokee Casino in Fort Gibson. And why? Because he owed a hundred grand to some shady loan shark. Well, he got caught and sentenced to ten years. And then, during his imprisonment, he got embroiled in a racketeering operation and received another forty years. He'll die in Oklahoma State Penitentiary. How stupid is that!'

His mother wiped her tears. 'Please don't bring this up again. You know how badly it hurts. You know how I feel after visiting him every month in prison.' Charles was about to issue a stinging riposte. But she quickly pointed to the fridge. 'Your lunch is ready. Just heat it. I'll be back later this afternoon.' She turned and headed out the door.

Charles looked inside the fridge and found a plate of sausages and mashed potatoes. He pulled his ear. *I can't eat this stuff anymore. I'll have to prepare myself one of those veggie burgers from last night.* He looked through the bag of condiments he'd brought back from Esmeralda's house. *There's enough raw material to make burgers for a week. I'll make lunch for my mom for a change. The rest, I'll distribute among my buddies.*

He mixed the ingredients and formed twenty patties. Looking at the sizeable number of flat minces on the table, Charles smirked. *That'll be enough to fill the tummies of my cavemen clan.*

After ten minutes in the oven, the patties were ready. He gazed at their perfect golden-brown condition with wonder. 'My God! This looks like the real thing.' He put one in his mouth and closed his eyes. Instantly, the dining room transformed into a farm. Branches of trees laden with juicy apples swayed in the wind. 'It's definitely the real thing. Let me have another.'

Suddenly, an alarm rang in his head. *Damn! I've got to be careful about portion control.* He took the tray with nineteen burger patties and put it away in the fridge. At that moment, the door opened.

'Mom! You're back early!'

She dumped her handbag on the living room sofa. 'Good news. The doctor said my thyroid is stable.' Her voice was upbeat.

She entered the dining room and looked around. 'Have you had lunch yet? Wait . . .' She paused and sniffed the air like a guard dog. 'What's that?'

Charles opened the fridge and showed the platter. 'Burgers. Healthy and plant-based.' His voice throbbed with excitement. 'I made them for the two of us. A helluva burger party.'

His mom furrowed her eyebrows. 'Burgers? You made burgers when I've got such delicious food? There's enough for a whole family.'

Charles patted her lightly on the shoulder. 'Didn't you listen? I made it for us.' He put two patties on a serving plate and handed it to her. 'Try it.'

His mom stared at the object in disgust. She slowly reached her hand out and held one patty. She gazed at it for a whole minute. Then, in slow motion, the burger approached her mouth. In the time it would take to detonate a nuclear device, a corner of the burger went down her gullet.

Charles looked at her with eager anticipation. 'Isn't it yummy?'

Mom made a face and spat the piece out on the plate. Her face turned red and her nostrils flared like an angry hippo. 'You made this piece of shit? From some voodoo recipe by a crazy woman? In my kitchen?'

She looked disdainfully at the tray lying on the counter top. Charles frowned. 'But, Ma . . .'

With the hand speed of a TGI Fridays waitress, she grabbed the tray and dumped all its contents in the trashcan. 'Never again. If I ever see this shit again in my house, I'll throw you out.'

Charles tossed and turned in bed that night, trying to figure out how to practise his new healthy food religion without interference from the family mandarin. 'It sure looks like Mom doesn't approve of my healthy food choices. Well, tough luck. I can't make myself sick by eating that comfort food. I need to take control of my own body . . . of my own health. I guess I'll be eating at the centre from now on.'

The next morning, after finishing a bowl of oats, he looked at his mother apologetically. 'Look, Ma. I'm sorry I upset you by cooking the burgers without telling you. But you've got to understand. I need to improve my health right now, or I'll be in big trouble in a few years.'

His mother studied him with a stern expression. 'I see. So what are you planning to do?'

'For six weeks, I have to follow the programme to the letter. Don't worry about my meals. I'll prepare them myself.'

That evening at the centre, after the programme was over, the group assembled for a buffet dinner arranged at Esmeralda's sprawling dining room. Charles helped himself to a plate filled with salmon with salsa, beans and steamed veggies, and proceeded towards an unoccupied chair.

Esmeralda's voice stopped him in his tracks. 'Many of you have told me you are finding it difficult to follow healthy nutrition at home. This is a problem. Unless you're fully committed 24x7 for six weeks, your health will not improve. Can we try to work out a solution?' Her tone was dense with concern.

Several members shared the difficulties they were facing in eating healthy food at home. Annie's voice was pensive. 'I live with my dad, who suffers from a serious heart condition. I work two part-time jobs to make ends meet. After preparing his specific diet, I have no time, money or energy to buy special ingredients for my breakfast and lunch.'

Hal looked concerned. 'I live in the Flatiron district. There are no supermarkets there stocking these items. I have to travel an hour away to the nearest specialty food store. As a night watch at the Mercy City Hospital, how can I find time to buy the items and prepare the stuff myself?'

Six other members reported different issues that hampered their adoption of the healthy lifestyle—ranging from job stress to family to social pressure. Esmeralda stood uneasily, twiddling her fingers. Charles stood up. 'Maybe you can provide us with ingredients and recipes for breakfast and lunch. We could all prepare them together and carry them home each night after the session.'

Esmeralda relaxed. *Better to bypass the dietary gatekeepers, for now. Hopefully, they'll come around in time.*

Esmeralda turned to Mariana with an inquiring look. Her housekeeper gave her a worried frown. Esmeralda hurriedly put on a disarming smile. 'That's an amazing idea. From tomorrow, one of our daily activities will be to prepare our meals together.' She instructed Mariana, 'You must ensure we have enough ingredients each day to prepare forty takeout meals. This is important.'

Over the next three weeks, every day was spent on the holistic health improvement programme, incorporating an array of fitness, nutrition, and meditation options. Each activity was adapted to the lifestyle and interests of the collective and administered by an expert practitioner. Instead of performing a traditional weight-training drill, the members participated in cross-fit exercises with ropes and a 'strong man' drill involving real-world objects like tires, buckets and bricks. Dance became the bellwether of the aerobics classes. Yoga sessions turned into 'silent sitting' sessions with God. The daily menu included popular items like burgers, chips, steaks and pie, albeit in healthier forms. To encourage people to consume fruits and water, a contest was instituted whereby points were awarded to those who consumed at least six servings of fruits and a gallon of water per day. Those winning a minimum number of points by the end of the programme would be included in a lucky draw.

Three weeks later, a visiting doctor performed a comprehensive physical evaluation of every member. He handed over the medical report to Charles with an appreciative smile. 'Charles, you are making very good progress. Your weight is 230 pounds, and your BMI is around 35. Your blood cholesterol and sugar levels are slightly outside the normal range, but I'm confident that these will normalize in three weeks, if you continue with the programme. Your kidney and liver readings are perfectly normal.'

Charles studied the report and jumped with glee. 'What! This can't be right. My weight was 250 at the start of the programme. BMI? A complete joke. All other physical indicators? Really bad when measured only six weeks ago.'

The doctor beamed at him. 'You know something? Everyone here has said the same thing. Too bad I didn't test you folks at the beginning of the programme. You'd have been able to compare the readings.'

A question cropped in Charles' head about the prescription drug programme recommended by his family doctor. 'Doctor Park, I want to ask you something. I'm on a list of meds that include Flomax for kidney stones and Lipitor for cholesterol. These cost me a fortune and leave me with headaches, nausea, chest pain and blurry vision. However, my doctor says that I should continue taking them. What's your opinion?'

The thirty-something doctor put his arm around Charles' shoulder. 'Charles, your star is rising. You don't have to take meds you don't need. At this time, it's clear to me you have no genetic predisposition towards diabetes, heart disease or liver disease. If you did, your body wouldn't respond so effectively to the wellness programme. It's my firm opinion your physical condition was brought about by poor lifestyle choices.'

Charles looked shocked. 'You can't be serious! I don't have to take prescription medications anymore?'

Park handed him two bottles of pills. 'You could probably do without the meds entirely at this stage. However, if you must take something, try these natural supplements. Milk thistle and CoQ10. They will augment your nutrition programme by regulating your liver and kidney functions.'

Two weeks later, Charles accompanied his mother to the doctor's office for their monthly checkups. The doctor asked Mrs Smith to wait in the reception and escorted Charles to his chamber. He appeared surprised by Charles's slimmer build.

'You've lost weight. What have you been doing?'

Charles looked like he'd just won the power ball jackpot. 'Doc Ashby, I've joined a holistic health programme at the Daylight Centre, a wellness clinic in Nichols Hills. The owner, Esmeralda Foster, has me on a healthy eating and exercise programme. I met many people who suffered from similar health-related problems, such as obesity and heart diseases. At the start of this programme, we were all stressed,' he broke into a smile and snapped his fingers, 'but in three weeks, all of our health indicators have changed for the better. I feel great. I'm running, jumping and climbing like I'm twenty. Most special of all, we've got this sense of community. A feeling that we're all in it together.'

'That's great,' the doctor said, with a half-smile. 'But I hope you're still taking your medications. After all, I've been treating you since you were fifteen. Over the years, I've seen your health deteriorate in front of my eyes. Had I not prescribed those medications, you would have been far worse off.' He looked at him like a doctor who accused another of practising without a medical license.

Charles slammed the table with his palm. 'You're right, doc. I stopped taking the meds two weeks ago, and I feel great.'

The doctor turned his attention to the bloodwork analysis done at the Daylight Centre. 'This report is barely two weeks old. When I compare it to your last report, I do see a remarkable improvement. But I'm not sure you'll be able to sustain it. I'm really worried you'll develop further complications if you continue to avoid your medications.'

Charles pushed his hands in front of his body. 'Don't worry, doc. I haven't gone cold turkey. I'm taking some supplements that Dr Park recommended.' He showed the two supplement bottles.

The geriatric doctor's mouth widened and a look of horror appeared on his face, as if he'd seen the devil. 'I've got to tell you, doc. I've never felt better.' Charles jumped up and exited the room with a spring in his steps.

Elevation

On the penultimate day of the programme and after an intense muscle conditioning class, Charles headed towards the locker room with the other guys. A woman's voice called his name. He turned around. It was Annie. She looked disappointed.

'Tomorrow's our last day. After that, it's back to waitressing three days a week at Popeye's and another three days at the Walmart cash register. Back to my nest with only my invalid dad for company. I'm really going to miss this place. I'm going to miss everyone.' She sighed.

Charles hugged her. 'It's the same story for me. Back to Ma, my friends and the job at the hardware store. Back to my old routines . . . couch surfing, comfort eating . . . because I don't think I'll be able to motivate myself without everyone here.'

Billy Bob jumped into the conversation. 'After all these fun activities and enriching food, I can't imagine returning to my joyless job at the auto repair shop. I can't imagine reverting to my greasy, unappetizing lifestyle. Without you folks to spur me on, I'm afraid I'll have to.'

Yu Yan overheard their conversation. 'As an immigrant from China, few residents of this city treat me with love and respect. You're the first locals who've ever welcomed me as a friend. Who've ever treated me as your own. I'm so afraid I'll lose you. I'm terrified of facing the wolves once more.'

Hal placed a comforting arm on her shoulder. 'Yu Yan, we'll always be friends.' He pointed to his belly. 'The things I'll miss most about this place are the cantaloupes. The first natural food I've tasted in years. I worry my tastebuds will cease to function once again.'

Stan had a hang-dog look. 'My knees don't hurt anymore. I can walk normally without limping. But for how long?'

Charles looked at the dejected faces and then at the greenhouse in the open field with longing eyes. *The programme's almost over. But there's so much left to work on. My body needs to be leaner, stronger, and healthier. My mind needs to be more agile. I need to discover inner calm and balance. If only I could stay longer.*

Esmeralda walked in on their chatter. She looked aggrieved and moved her hands vertically in front of her body. 'Folks! Don't think for a moment that just because this programme is about to be over, we'll never see each other again. Definitely not! We'll always stay in touch. You may visit the centre anytime. In any event, tomorrow hasn't come yet. That's when you'll get your final physical reports and realize how far you've come.'

Everyone headed towards the changing rooms. Mariana, who was standing outside the locker area, handed Charles a towel. 'So Charles, how do you feel after six weeks? What can we do to improve the programme?'

'I'm in the best shape in years, thanks to Es. She's been so warm and attentive. I only wish she thought of us as her family.'

Mariana looked perplexed. 'What do you mean?'

He looked wistfully at the obstacle course placed on the lawn. 'To me, this place feels like home. But to her, I'm a guest, not family.'

That evening, after dinner, Esmeralda joined Mariana in the kitchen to do the dishes.

Mariana took out her phone and showed her a collection of photos of the members performing various activities in an atmosphere of bonding. 'Look at them! Here, at this speed cycling race, they could be at the Tour de France. Here, at this aerobics dance class, they could be at the Oklahoma Dance Festival. Here, at dinner, they could be at a Horton's Sunday brunch.'

Esmeralda observed the pictures with a rueful smile. 'They look like they've known each other for years.'

'They feel that way about each other. They feel the same way about you.'

'How do they feel that about me?' Esmeralda looked surprised.

'This place . . . you, me, Darius, everyone . . . To them, we're all family.'

'Family? They think we're a family?' Esmeralda's eyes widened with astonishment.

'Yes. Their hearts are broken because they have to leave tomorrow.' Mariana nodded slowly.

That night, Esmeralda tossed and turned in bed. She thought about all those pleasant memories. About how everyone was feeling. *I could never have imagined how close we'd become. I've organized so many wellness programmes before. Participants got close. Formed friendships. Created lasting bonds. But family? I can't recall anyone saying we've become a family. I can't recall any group of people that depended on the programme for their happiness.* She stared at her bedroom ceiling, which was painted with the Renaissance fresco of a woman lying in a field with a hundred infants. *We've forged such a deep connection. After tomorrow, will it be severed? Will they plunge into depression as a result? Will they lapse into their old routines to cope with their sadness?*

A beam of moonlight entered the room through an open window and illuminated a single infant on the far side of the painted ceiling. Its face was contorted with anguish as it desperately reached out its hands towards the woman but found its way obstructed by a hundred others. Suddenly, a feeling of guilt enveloped Esmeralda. *I thought they'd feel joyful at the end of the programme, not heartbroken. How can I abandon them now? Not when we've come so far. Not when we have so much to do. But how can I sustain the programme free of cost? Oh God! Have I unleashed a genie?* She tossed and turned, trying to figure out the right decision. *For now, I've got to continue the programme. In time, I'll figure out how to sustain it.*

Seed

The next day, the final day of the programme, the members were inconsolable, wailing, hugging each other and bidding their goodbyes. A teary Annie turned towards Billy Bob. 'I'll miss your jokes about liberals and the media.'

The badger gave her a kiss on the cheek. 'I'll miss your tasteless cupcake recipes.'

Yu Yan hugged Charles. 'I've never had more fun on an obstacle course than with you as a partner.'

Charles kissed her cheek. 'We must have won five in a row. I can never partner with anyone else.'

Stan greeted Hal with a handshake. 'My friend, if I ever net a bonanza, I'll thank you. I never met anyone with so much knowledge about fishing.'

'You're the finest expert in camping I've ever met. Your advice saved me at least nine lives and a thousand bucks.'

Deadly Duke high-fived Charles. 'Man, I thought I was the expert on racecar driving. But after listening to all your anecdotes about drivers, I know I'm a total novice.'

Charles chuckled. 'How about a trip to Daytona for the NASCAR playoffs?'

'You're on, bro.'

After the goodbyes, Annie wiped away her tears and wished everyone. 'We must meet every month and stay in touch with the programme.'

The members all murmured. 'Sure, that's . . . that's a good idea . . . we definitely need to stay in touch.'

Charles noticed them looking at each other hesitantly and then at the floor. *This six-week programme has been like a vacation. Very soon, all my time will be eaten up by my job, my mom and my friends. How can I possibly meet? I'm sure most people feel this way.*

A loud, shrill voice interrupted their morose thoughts. 'It's time for dinner, followed by the lucky draw.' Mariana's announcement elicited excited whoops from the group.

At the start of the sumptuous Southern buffet, Esmeralda gave a short speech. 'Over the past six weeks, each one of you has undergone a remarkable transformation. Your passion and dedication have brought you closer to good health. As long as you stay motivated, I know you'll keep on improving.' She paused for a moment and gazed at the sad faces in the audience. 'During our time here, we became not only colleagues, but close friends. From strangers, we became passion-mates.' She suppressed a tear.

Billy Bob stood up and raised his voice. 'Health nuts! That's who we are! The Daylight Health Nuts!'

A roar of laughter dissipated the somber mood. Esmeralda gazed at Mariana standing by the buffet station. There was a look of expectation in her eyes as she waited for Esmeralda to say something.

'It's time to dispense with conventional client–therapist protocols,' Esmeralda whispered. Suddenly, a heavy iron ball formed in her heart. Her voice choked up. 'At the beginning of this programme, I thought of myself as your therapist and guide. In my mind, the role had to be cloaked with formality. I felt I had to keep an emotional distance from you to be an effective therapist. I'm sorry to say . . .' She took out a handkerchief and sobbed into it. 'I failed. I'm so sorry.'

Her sudden display of emotion perplexed the group, but finally, Annie shouted, 'Aww! We love you, Es.'

Yu Yan joined in with, 'You're the best, Es.'

Esmeralda's tears poured as liberally as the rain during the Indian monsoon. 'I'm sorry because I no longer feel like a therapist . . . and you no longer feel like clients.'

'What do you mean?' Deadly Duke asked.

'Family. You're my family. The only one in the whole world.' The dining room became silent with shock. Esmeralda blew into the hanky. 'The programme can't end right now. Not when we have so much to do. It must continue.'

The stunned silence in the dining room gave way to unbridled joy. The members rose from their seats and hugged each other. Amidst the claps and shouts, Charles looked at Annie with a frown. He motioned for her to follow him.

They weaved past their dancing, cheering compatriots in the dining room and went outside to the lawn.

'I don't think this is right,' Annie told Charles.

'Do you know how much it will cost to run this programme indefinitely? The cost of food alone would be enormous.'

Annie looked at the lavish spread on the tables and shook her head. 'My dad taught me you should never take anyone's gifts for granted. It would be wrong of us to take advantage of her like this. I can't stay in the programme.'

The words 'Me too' formed in Charles' mouth but couldn't quite make their way out. His eyes focused on a basket of fresh uncut vegetables placed on the buffet table. Immediately, the dining room transformed into a farmers' market. He now stood at a stall labelled 'ADAIR FRESH', next to Mr Berger, Marge's father. A long line of customers thronged their stall, desperate to buy the produce. With a sigh of contentment, the middle-aged man ran his hand through young Charles' tousled hair. 'Charlie boy, you're a magician. It's one thing to be a fantastic cultivator. A very different thing . . .' he paused and pointed to the flyers several customers held that read 'BRING A FRIEND AND GET 10% OFF', 'a very different thing to be a great salesman. Son, someday, you'll be a great food entrepreneur.'

The seed of a question planted itself in Charles' mind. *What if this programme could be run sustainably? What if we could recover the costs in some way?* He looked at an apple tree about twenty feet away and saw a single fruit fall on the ground and roll down the grassy slope to his feet. Pure red, its surface sparkled intermittently with orange, white and other shades of the late evening glow. He picked it up and turned it around. Its shape, colour and texture seemed magical. 'The last time I saw one so perfect was at the farmers' market in Adair,' he said under his breath. Then, he was filled with an irresistible impulse to taste it. He bit into its sweet, mushy centre. 'So pure. So fresh. How tragic that we can't get this anymore at the supermarket!'

Suddenly, an idea sparked in his head. *Wait a minute! Who says we can't? Surely, it's possible to grow fresh, natural fruits like this! After all, with all this fertile land around, we can grow heaps and heaps of them. Organic farming. My one true passion. This is my chance to follow it. This is our chance to save the programme.* He gazed excitedly at the vast, untilled land.

Charles shared the idea with Annie. 'Do you think it's possible to turn this programme into a business?'

'Huh? What sort of business?'

Charles led her farther onto the lawn and pointed at the vast grounds. 'You see all that land? All that space? Much of it is unused. But, I know the soil is fertile. We can grow lots of fruits, vegetables and other produce out here.'

'What does that have to do with our programme?'

'We can develop a whole range of natural products out here. Fresh fruits and vegetables. Herbs. Maybe, we can develop natural food recipes. Supplements. Body products and creams. A whole range of products under the banner of the Daylight Centre.'

Annie frowned for a moment. *Hmm! Could he have a point? We have enough people to help out with this initiative. Sure beats working two shifts at Walmart. Es has access to so many experts and scientists.* She shook his hand. 'You're on. Let's propose this and see how others respond.'

At the dining hall, everyone had calmed down. Charles raised his voice. 'Annie and I have something to say.' Esmeralda raised her eyebrows and invited them to approach her. Charles had a look of determination on his face. 'I want to take this moment to thank you all for supporting me and for being such good friends throughout this process. I also want to thank Es for her persistence and devotion.' He cleared his throat, glanced at Esmeralda, and then looked at the audience. 'While I feel incredibly happy to resume this programme, I know that this will prove to be a huge financial burden on you.'

'It's a burden we can't possibly ignore,' Annie added.

The looks of elation on everyone's faces faded considerably. Esmeralda placed her hand on Annie's shoulder. 'Oh! You don't have to worry. We'll manage.'

'We can and we will . . . if we work together,' Charles said. Esmeralda looked baffled, so he continued. 'What if we don't have to run the programme for free? What if we created something together? A company. One that tries to bring affordable health and wellness solutions to ordinary folks. That's your vision, isn't it? Isn't that the reason you started this programme in the first place?'

Esmeralda nodded. Charles pointed to several members in the audience. 'There are twenty of us here. Twenty unhealthy buffoons who are now twenty able-bodied individuals. Most of us have experience in agriculture or manufacturing. We can all build things with our hands. We all know how to nurture life from the soil. We can work together to create a line of natural food products that can change people's lives.'

Annie added, 'We can earn enough money from all of this, enough to keep this programme running for as long as we want. Without any extra burden on Es.'

Stick Leg Stan jumped up. 'I have a suggestion too. Why don't we sell programme memberships to the public?' The folks looked at him puzzled.

Yu Yan beamed. 'Brilliant! We can be trainers. Each of us can specialize in an area. Something we really enjoy. Something playing to our strengths. I'd love to teach yoga.'

Billy Bob motioned to himself, then to Charles, and then to Annie. 'We can do it. We've been here for a year. I've done every activity so many times that I know them all by heart.'

'I can be a sports and athletics coach,' Stick Leg Stan pointed to his knees that no longer required braces.

The rest of the group articulated their passions. Esmeralda asked them to gather around in a circle. 'I've seen every one of you grow to become proficient in the activities of the programme. You've all evolved from hating wellness to becoming passionate about it. Now, we must begin the next phase in your evolution. Your transformation from hobbyists to instructors.' The members voiced their excitement at the change of tack. Esmeralda's eyes twinkled with excitement. 'Identify your passion. From tomorrow, we'll begin a training programme to turn you into coaches.'

Esmeralda's eyes gleamed with possibility. *This is what I've wanted to do for many years. But didn't.* She paused momentarily and gazed at the faces in the crowd, all of which were looking at her with eager expectation. *They are my family. They believe in me. I must believe in myself.* Her face radiated with quiet confidence. 'From today, we'll no longer be called the Daylight Centre.' Faces fell as people braced themselves for the worst. 'From today, we'll be known as the Daylight Company,' she shouted as a cacophony of triumphant cheers rent the air.

Flowering

Over the next three months, the venture turned into a reality. The mission of the Daylight Company was to deliver affordable wellness solutions to all. Initially, the company focused on healthy snacks, natural juices, daily essentials, supplements and a wellness programme. Everyone was made a shareholder of the firm. Even though the company couldn't pay full-time wages, most of the group joined as part-timers. The few who joined permanently, like Billy Bob and Charles, quit their regular jobs.

Notwithstanding the energy, infrastructure had to be created. Esmeralda dipped into her $20 million settlement account and remodelled her estate. A shed was built for R&D on supplements, snacks and juices, with a three year launch target. A significant part of the greenery was converted into agricultural land—with a vegetable garden, cowshed and poultry farm. Fortunately, no effort was needed to grow fruits because the area was naturally endowed with a plethora of fruit and nut trees: black cherries, plums, prairie apples, pecans and many more.

Esmeralda also instituted rigorous training regimens across the fields of fitness, yoga, sports conditioning, Pilates, organic farming and osteopathy. She drew on her contacts in the wellness industry and the state government, and was able to acquire accreditation for the Daylight Programme. She hosted ten renowned experts and mentors at the centre for six months. During that time, they personally groomed Daylight members to become wellness instructors.

Six months later, Charles was at the vegetable garden. He sat on the ground and arranged a basket filled with snow peas, kale, spring onions, lettuce and squash. Next to him stood a Hispanic man in his thirties. The man scrutinized a sample of each vegetable and burst into a smile.

'You've done it, my man. These are perfect now. So ripe, they'll taste better raw than in any cooked recipe.'

Charles high-fived him. 'Maybe now they're good enough for your Uncle Pepe's farm? Perhaps you can promote them at the global organic fair in Mexico City?' They burst into giggles.

Pepe slapped him on the back. 'I wouldn't go that far.'

Annie rushed towards them and disrupted the banter. 'What are you guys doing here?' She looked frantic and pointed to the main dining room. 'You're going to be late for the ceremony.'

Half an hour later, the twenty members of the Daylight community received their certifications. The dining room was filled with claps and whoops. Charles' mother cheered from the front row along with the families and well-wishers of the other members. But there was one particular person who caught Charles' eye.

'Marge? What are you doing here?' She came down from the back row and stood next to his mother.

Marge glanced at his mom. 'Linda told me how you'd turned yourself around.' She wiped a tear from her eye. 'I'm so happy for you, Charles.'

Charles wrapped his arms around her. 'I know I wasn't there for you. Most of the time, I wasn't even there for myself.' His voice choked with regret.

She kissed him on his cheek. 'But you've done it now. You've put yourself back together.'

At the compliment he'd never imagined he would receive, his cheeks got even rosier.

'Now, I want to follow your path.' Marge gazed at him with love and admiration.

Linda's eyes welled up with tears. 'That smile? That glow? They're back after all these years,' she whispered under her breath as he saw them hug each other like they'd never hugged before. *All this time, I've dragged him down. No point denying it.*

I should have encouraged him to eat healthy. Yet, I kept feeding him junk. I should have encouraged him to join the programme. Yet, I kept talking him out of it. Why? To give me a sense of purpose. A purpose I'd lost when my husband went to jail.

She squeezed her son's hand affectionately. 'Now go, be the man you're meant to be.'

The Harvest

Three years later, the Daylight Centre was the go-to wellness camp for the people of Oklahoma. It pioneered a voluntary membership scheme where people paid what they could afford. It also catered to the poorest of the poor. The facility offered a unique set of activities rooted in the cultural traditions of the state. It attracted patrons from all walks of life—industrialists, working professionals, construction walkers, homeless migrants, even children. A large number were Daylight-accredited instructors and practitioners. Several new sites opened under franchise, supplementing the Foster Estate. The wellness movement was ubiquitous in Oklahoma; obesity and lifestyle diseases were significantly down.

On the launch day of its products, exactly three years and three days after the group first met, the Daylight community visited the Walmart Supercentre on North May Avenue.

A man in his fifties approached Charles. He wore a badge that read 'TERRY LIM, STORE MANAGER'.

'Hi, Terry! Long time. The place is still the same.'

Terry looked Charles up and down. His eyes were full of awe. 'Yep. This place hasn't changed one bit. But you certainly have. You look good, my man.' He turned his attention to the rest of the group. 'You must all be from Daylight. We've created a special aisle just for your products—number ten.' He escorted them to the specific section. 'There's so much demand for your stuff. I've never seen anything like it.'

The members were astounded to see an entire row of Daylight products. Charles picked up a packet of plantain chips, turned it around and showed Annie. 'Hey, Annie. They've got the story of my transformation right here. It says, "Charles Martin Smith. Once a vegetable. Now a master cultivator." What does yours say?'

Annie turned around a can of organic tomato sauce. Her 'before' and 'after' pictures bore the blurb, 'Anne Francis. Once a restless spirit. Now a mindful warrior'.

With wide-eyed wonder, each original Daylight member looked at a product depicting their individual journeys from crisis to good health. Esmeralda gazed at the back of a box of dried cantaloupes, and a smile spread across her face.

Her pictures were the only ones that did not show a discernible physical transformation. However, her story said, 'Esmeralda Foster. Once a fixer-upper. Now an inspirational leader'.

REFLECTION: CHANNEL YOUR PASSION INTO A HEALING FORCE

Have you faced a health problem that sapped your vitality?

There are times in life when we might experience serious health problems. During those times, we may suffer a great degree of pain and consequently, lose our vitality. In those moments, relieving our pain becomes our only concern. This pain is present in both the body and the mind. And we are usually prepared to go to any lengths to mitigate it. To counter the pain in our bodies, we may decide to take drugs—pharmaceutical, or even illicit. For temporary emotional upliftment, we might indulge in comfort food and drinks. The cumulative long-term effects of these behaviours are highly destructive.

Pharmaceutical products have long-term negative side effects on our bodies that can override their healing properties. A diet of processed food and drinks may cause obesity, lifestyle diseases and mental health issues at the expense of producing an instant emotional rush. The best way to manage the side effects of these aberrant behaviours is to address the root cause of the health problem.

Often, the root cause of health stress lies not in one's biology but psychology. There may be certain experiences in our lives that fill us with negativity. Perhaps because we never dealt with these dark feelings and they continued to fester deep inside us, our minds became infected, prompting us to act in ways that are harmful and self-defeating. We may even have learned these behaviours so well that we enter a 'bad health trap', a vicious loop of harmful actions and consequences that feed into one another and destroy our well-being. Thirteen years ago, I experienced these negative feelings myself, during a health crisis.

I've been a fitness freak since my college days. However, lust was my driving force to get ripped. I felt that if I acquired that huge, muscular physique I saw in the glossy pages of men's magazines, I'd be flooded with overtures from attractive women. Even after I got married, I never really grew out of this mindset. I invested thousands of dollars in expensive bodybuilding supplements. I ate tons of protein every day—chicken, steak, fish; you name it, I've probably ingested it. All in the quest for the perfect physique!

For fifteen years, I kept up this vacuous routine, despite not seeing significant improvements in muscle mass. At the same time, my weight kept increasing, shooting well above the recommended Body Mass Index (BMI) for my age and height. Every day, I'd stare in the mirror, hoping to be greeted by the reflection of a ripped Viking warrior. Instead, I was disappointed by what I saw—an overweight, bulky wrestler. Unfortunately, this was only the tip of a large, very unhealthy iceberg. My regimen was causing long-term damage to my health.

Most days, I'd wake up bloated and suffering from diarrhea. After a punishing, two-hour workout routine, I'd report to work, exhausted. My muscles and joints constantly ached. Low on energy, I'd perform my official duties like a zombie, then return home and crash on the couch. My wife at the time would try to make conversation, but I would always be too distant and disengaged, my mind preoccupied with selfish priorities like gaining five pounds of muscle by the end of the month—a target I never managed to hit anyway! I would have ended up in a hospital with a serious medical ailment had my ex-wife not proposed a medical intervention.

In 2008, she suggested we visit a spa resort called the Pritikin Longevity Centre, located in Miami, for a summer vacation. I was intrigued by her choice because it was far off the beaten track from the usual island resorts, cruises and city tours that we'd opt for. At the Pritikin Centre, we underwent a battery of medical tests that measured our vital markers, such as cholesterol, thyroid, blood sugar and hormonal profiles. Additionally, the experts there assessed my flexibility, cardiovascular capacity and other attributes of athletic performance. I remember boasting to my companion that I'd beat her so badly in all the health parameters that she'd have to pay for three expensive steak dinners in a row. Sadly, the joke was on me!

On the third day of our stay, the medical counsellor delivered a series of damning reports. With a serious look, he informed me that my cholesterol and sugar levels were way out of range. I was not building muscle because my hormonal profile was below the range of a healthy male of my age. My cardiovascular capacity was poor. My joints were getting worn out due to the endless pounding with heavy weights. In the tone of an earnest school principal, he informed me that I had a

50 per cent chance of suffering from heart disease and arthritis if these conditions persist for the next fifteen to twenty years. 'What should I do?' I asked, aghast. He replied that I needed to change my food and exercise habits dramatically. I had to greatly reduce my protein intake and consume more fruits and vegetables. This way, he said, I'd be reducing calories and the stress on my kidneys. 'But what about my muscle mass? Wouldn't that get compromised?' I asked.

There was a grave look on his face. 'Don't worry. You're getting enough protein from one shake and two meals per day. Anything above that is purely excessive. It will only get converted to fat.'

When I made the devastating discovery that my body wasn't converting all the protein into muscle, I asked myself, 'Is it worth chasing the illusion of physical perfection?' In response, my conscience responded, 'Look, Aritra. Bodybuilding isn't your true passion. You're a generally active, healthy guy. You love books, films, philosophy and writing. So go spend time doing the things that you love. Work on yourself. Be a caring, compassionate, mindful person. Focus your energy on something that you're really, truly passionate about.' At that moment, I recognized that I'd pursued bodybuilding and physique-sculpting only to feed my ego. Vanity comes at an exorbitant cost, I realized.

Thereafter, I made major changes to my diet and fitness programme. Out went the endless chicken breasts and weight-gainer shakes. In their place, I started consuming salads and fresh fruits. I even added more rice to my diet and reduced my intake of fish. On the fitness front, I dropped my weights and introduced high-intensity interval training into my routine. Remembering the Pritikin expert's advice to be patient, I kept up this routine for some time. By the end of that period, I was a transformed man.

Two years after I'd made those changes, I finally felt satisfied with my reflection. No, it wasn't a muscular, Adonis-type figure that gave me goosebumps. It was a body I felt comfortable inhabiting. Most importantly, all my health markers showed tremendous improvement. Overall, I felt energized, refreshed, nimble and lithe—an eager panther ready to pounce on opportunities, and not a sloth that lies in waiting.

In *The Daylight Programme*, Charles and his compatriots suffered from various compulsions that prevented them from achieving optimal health. Like me, they overcame their psychological barriers to experience well-being for the first time in their lives.

To break out of our health rut, it is important to unlock the thoughts and feelings that underpin our destructive behaviours. This is difficult to do directly, because many of these feelings are so unpleasant that we bury them in the basement of our consciousness. Is it possible to resolve them in a manner that isn't painful? And if so, how?

Deep inside our hearts lies a desire to do good things. This desire for life or passion, is the first impulse that gets sidelined by the negativity arising from health stress. However, passion can never be fully destroyed because it leaves an indelible stamp on our identity. Somehow, if we can awaken our inner passion, we can use it to escape the traumatic and debilitating chokehold of health stress.

The pursuit of your passion will enable you to form healthy relationships and make a positive impact on the world. As a result of these initiatives, you'll feel emotionally supported and validated for your talent—this love and support will give you the confidence and courage to deal with your inner demons. As you overcome your barriers, you'll realize that there's nothing to fear. Your mind will become clearer and more positive. You'll start loving yourself and your actions will be driven by a desire to improve yourself, not cause harm. Consequently, the sensations of pain and discomfort that crowded your consciousness will slowly ebb away and you'll be able to reclaim your life and your health.

During times of ill health, try to find the passion that's buried deep within you. Open up a brief window in your day to follow it in any small or big way. That's all you need to do to ensure your well-being.

The characters in the previous story suffered immense stress from health issues. Learn how they overcame this barrier, and you will believe that you can too.

6

OVERCOMING JOB STRESS

UNDERSTANDING JOB STRESS

These days, our jobs have become extremely demanding. In an age of 24x7 mobile communication, it is quite common for work to follow us to bed. While we benefit from the higher growth opportunities that result from being more engaged with our work, this is often detrimental to our mental well-being.

Job stress refers to the negative thoughts and feelings we experience when we do not meet our standards of performance at work. These standards may have been foisted upon us by our employers, or they may be our own creations. Whatever the origin, we often feel a compulsion to meet them at all costs. This desire can lead to a vicious cycle of doubt and half-hearted actions that beget unsatisfying results. This cycle can often spin out of control—sapping our self-belief and plunging us into a dark well of depression.

Here's an example of how the relentless pursuit of performance standards can lead to job stress.

A front office executive at a hotel was desperate to earn a promotion and get into the accelerated leadership programme at her company. However, she didn't enjoy being in Sales and felt overwhelmed by her revenue targets. She was reluctant to seek help from her peers because she didn't want to share credit with anyone or be perceived as incompetent. Without support and guidance, she fell further behind on her targets. She responded to the crisis by working longer hours. In the bargain, she cut back on time for studies, health and friendships. This decision affected her life adversely. Her friends and family distanced themselves from her—at the same time, she was no closer to earning a promotion. Due to the dip in her fortunes, she fell into depression.

As you may discern, the root cause of job stress often stems from an obsessive focus on numerical targets. While a target is useful to drive us in a disciplined way towards a chosen direction in our lives, we must remember that it's just a milestone, not the final destination. The final destination, in fact, is not even a point we can reach in a given time frame. It is a state of mind that we must constantly strive to attain. A state of mind that's fearless, empathetic and open. A state of mind that will bring us perennial happiness, regardless of our circumstances. We can attain this mindset by being in Oneness—a state of perfect spiritual alignment with the universe, which we can achieve by pursuing any path of conscious growth to reach a permanent meditative state. This includes a field we may be passionate about, a practice of any faith, meditation or spiritual practices, or even just the daily activities of life. When we are in a state of Oneness, we are always in the moment—constantly overcoming barriers, learning from our experiences, emitting love and improving ourselves, without being attached to the outcome of our actions.

The protagonist of the following story faced severe stress from trying to do well at her job. How will she overcome this barrier?

LIGHTNING IN A BOTTLE

Agata's performance targets at work were unattainable. Her boss knew it. Her colleagues knew it. Even she knew it. Despite this, failure was not an option for her.

At the staff offices of the Ace Hotel in London, when Agata Kowalski spotted an anomaly in her real-time performance data on a computer screen, she accidentally bit her tongue.

'Ouch!' There was a significant disparity between the two leading metrics of her monthly targets. 'My customer satisfaction score is a solid nine out of ten. But my revenue score is a measly five.' She placed her hands on her head.

A woman of Indian origin in her mid-twenties approached her. Just an hour ago, at a company party, she was in the audience, watching Agata performing in a dance show with great enthusiasm. She looked at Agata with concern. 'Hey, Agata! Why the sad face after such a sassy show? I never imagined anyone would perform "Rhythm Is a Dancer" at my birthday party! What's wrong, babe?'

Agata leaned back in her chair and looked at the ceiling in despair. 'Oh, Meghna! Your suggestion didn't work. Management didn't consider my effort to land a bulk deal with that Warsaw travel agency. Now I'm so behind on my revenue targets!'

A flicker of a smile appeared on Meghna's lips, but she was quick to douse it. *What an idiot! She actually fell for my ruse! When I told her to find travel agents to bulk-sell rooms, she gullibly bought my suggestion without bothering to find out that our hotel doesn't incentivize staff to sell to third parties. Hahaha! I can't believe that only five months ago, I thought she was a serious contender for the fast-track programme.*

Meghna noticed that Agata's screen was frozen on a digital dashboard headlined ACE HOTEL REAL-TIME PERFORMANCE MANAGEMENT SYSTEM and put on an affected tone. 'Oh! Don't be so hard on yourself! Third-party sales are always a crapshoot. Sometimes, when business is tough, the management decides to go all out and woo the travel agents. But when times are good, they see them as undesirable drags on our yields. And, oh! Don't worry about those revenue targets. Everybody underachieves in their first year. In time, you'll figure out what guests really want. You'll know which buttons to push. Anyway, look at the bright side! Everyone loves your sunny attitude.'

Agata stared at the screen and shook her head. Two heavy, ugly badgers—Disappointment and Frustration—plonked themselves on her slender shoulders. 'According to this data, I'm rated highly for my customer service at the reception desk. At the same time, though, I'm rated poorly for not upselling services during their stay. For not generating enough revenue for the company. And, since revenue management appraisal is such an important factor for being inducted into the fast-track programme . . .' She sighed and pointed to a chart filled with her annual targets pasted on the wall of her cubicle.

Meghna noted Agata needed to triple her sales figures in the next three months to meet the benchmarks for the fast-track programme. She bent down and looked at her sympathetically, while forming a thumbs-up sign with her left hand behind her back. 'Yes, darling! It's difficult, but not impossible. But even if you don't get on the programme this year, it's not the end of the world. After all, nobody in their first year of employment has ever made it.'

Agata continued to sulk, in no way comforted by Meghna's words.

The conversation was cut short by a phone call for Meghna from the duty manager. She spoke for a couple of minutes with a saccharine smile, and hung up. 'Hey, Danny wants to see me. Look, babe. Let me buy you lunch one of these days, and I'll explain how things work over here.'

Agata looked at the target sheet again and remembered the day when it was given to her, six months ago. She'd joined Ace as a new recruit after graduating with a diploma in hospitality management from Advancements, a vocational training institute in London. She first attended a group orientation session highlighting the company's vision and future plans. Then the manager of the hotel, Ron Dexter, chatted with every newbie before handing each one a sheet filled with business targets. He sat down with Agata and circled a heading on the paragraph entitled, 'Goals'.

'Only a few who joined today will achieve their targets by the end of the year. Those who don't will stagnate like frogs in a stinking well of low pay. But those who do? Aha! A world of opportunities awaits them. Those high performers will become the thoroughbreds of this place. They'll be inducted into our prestigious fast-track leadership programme. They'll be groomed for leadership roles. They'll have their pick of properties around the world. Tell me, Miss Kowalski, are you a frog or a steed?'

Agata looked at him with eagle-eyed determination. 'Mr Dexter, my whole life, I've had to push myself to the limit. When my mother contracted cancer five years ago, I had to drop out of Warsaw University and get a full-time job as a retail assistant to support her and my young brother. Two years ago, when her treatment costs increased beyond the scope of my meager salary, I was forced to migrate to London with my brother. I had to juggle two part-time jobs to pay for her medical expenses, my brother's education, food on the table and a diploma course in hospitality . . . all this while being a mother to my brother. You asked me whether I was a frog or a steed. I think you have the answer.'

Dexter raised his eyebrows in surprise. 'Excellent! That's the attitude we value here. I'm impressed.'

Agata took his pencil and wrote the number 1 on the performance sheet. 'In the next five years, I'll be the hardest-working employee in this company. I'll be the top performer in the industry. I'll save enough money to ultimately pursue a full-time degree at a leading university.'

'I appreciate your drive. But this is a lot for a young person to put on her plate. Aren't you setting yourself up for failure?'

'I have to do this. For my brother's education. For my mom's treatment. For my dreams.'

'Who do you want to be?' Ron looked curious.

Agata removed a textbook titled *Advanced Molecular Biochemistry* from her backpack and placed it on her lap. There was a look of longing in her eyes. 'Biochemistry. That's my passion.'

Ron shook her hand. 'Welcome to Ace, Agata. Here, we encourage our employees to shoot for the stars.' He walked towards his office, but midway, turned around and looked contemptuously at the biochemistry book. 'Hmph! As long as the stars fall in our universe,' Agata heard him mutter softly.

The memory of her first day of employment faded. She opened her desk drawer, took out the biochemistry textbook and turned to a dog-eared chapter titled 'Genomic Organization of Coronaviruses'. A note was enclosed inside depicting the drawing of a molecule with the headline 'TREATMENT FOR THE MERS-CoV VIRUS'. *Five years ago when I was a college student in Warsaw, I got the opportunity of a lifetime. I participated in a Europe-wide science contest to develop a treatment for a contagious respiratory disease affecting residents of the Middle East.* It was a very prestigious contest and its purpose was to identify top scientific talent in biochemistry. In the first round, contestants had to submit a paper outlining a treatment method. In the second round, selected candidates would be taken to a GoLife laboratory in Dubai to develop their formulations in collaboration with company biochemists. These solutions would then be tested through human trials. The most successful formulation would be commercialized into a vaccine. The winning student would receive a full scholarship to a college of her choice and a job with GoLife Pharmaceuticals upon graduation.

At the end of the rumination, her scrawly handwriting magically vanished and was replaced by a formal typed letter dated 19 June 2017. It was addressed to her from the Director of Strategic Initiatives, EU Science Foundation.

Dear Ms Kowalski,

It is my pleasure to inform you that your paper has been shortlisted for the final round of the EUSF-GoLife Science

Contest. You are now eligible to take part in the second round of our contest to develop a vaccine for the MERS-CoV virus. You and nineteen other talented individuals from various countries will get a chance to develop your formulas in collaboration with GoLife's research team. Please confirm your participation in the programme by June 26.

Regards,
Sabine Schmidt

She gazed at the letter. A painful itch developed on her back. *It was the opportunity of a lifetime. An opportunity . . .*

The logo of the EUSF Foundation was instantly replaced by that of the Warsaw State Hospital, and the letter by a medical report. The title of the page now read BREAST CANCER TEST FOR AGNIESZKA KOWALSKI. The test results showed that the patient's breast tumour marker was at the high end of the range. On the basis of this result, the clinician concluded that the patient had contracted breast cancer. The date on the report was 26 June 2017.

. . . that wasn't meant to be after my mother contracted cancer.

Next, the medical report vanished to be replaced by a picture of her as a fifteen-year-old along with a five-year-old boy and a thirty-five-year-old woman. They posed in front of the Eiffel Tower in Paris. Her brows tightened. *My last family vacation, after Father left us . . .*

The image of a fifty-five-year-old bearded man kissing a young woman in her twenties flashed across her mind. She gnashed her teeth in anger. 'For a medical student.' She forced that image to leave and replaced it with the one of her family vacation. *Health. Wealth. Peace. We've lost so much. I must recover all of these. I must do everything in my power to restore our happiness.*

The pictures in her imaginary canvas morphed back to the original image of the molecule. She hit that spot with a pencil butt, leaving a mark on the drawing. 'I must make enough money to pay for my mom's care at a leading private cancer treatment centre,' she mumbled aloud. 'I must make enough money to pay for my brother's education. I must make enough money to pursue biochemistry at university. This job is my stepping-stone to wealth. This job is the stepping-stone to my passion. I must qualify for the fast-track programme by the end of the year so I can rapidly move into the upper echelons of management. This is my only goal.'

Her musings were interrupted by a colleague. It was a man of similar age. 'Agata, your shift at the front desk starts now.' He pointed to the time on his $2,000 Rolex Oyster watch.

She glanced at the silver dial of his watch, noticing how well the expensive watch complemented the young African man's suit.

'Agata, there you go again, taking your eye off the ball. You've got to focus, girl. Be at the desk five minutes before time, in plain view of the duty manager so he can see your professionalism. These signals do matter.'

Her peer strolled back to his desk. On the way, he high-fived Meghna. 'Mamadou the Senegalese bull is on fire. I exceeded the revenue targets once again.'

Agata got up to head to the reception desk. From the corner of her eye, she caught the dazzling gleam of the watch and couldn't help but stand and stare. *Some people seem to be acing their targets and earning big bonuses. What do I have to do?*

Her first client at the reception was a heavyset, middle-aged man with silver hair and a beard. He let out a pronounced yawn and threw his credit card on the reception counter. 'Hey! I've just landed after a ten-hour flight from Cambodia. Can I have my room now?'

She looked at her watch. It was only 11.45 a.m. . . . three hours before the official check-in time. *Hmm! I could offer him a premium upgrade package and get him checked into a deluxe room right now. That way, I'll be closer to my revenue targets.* She swiped his credit card and smiled. 'Welcome to Ace, Mr Lundgren. Unfortunately, the check-in time at the hotel is 3 p.m.'

'You mean to say you can't check me in right now? I'm a platinum honours member, for God's sake!' The tired guest's nostrils flared.

Agata shook her head. 'Unfortunately, we're totally booked out of the standard rooms at the moment. But I can offer you a paid upgrade to a deluxe room. It's ready now.'

The guest went silent and slapped the reception counter several times with his palm. Then, he waved his hands dismissively and nodded. 'All right. I can't wait for three hours in the lobby. I'm dead tired after the flight. I'll take the room.'

Agata gave him a registration form to sign. She then handed him the keys and her business card. 'If you need anything, sir. Please don't hesitate to call me personally.'

Two hours and fifty guest registrations later, the duty manager, Daniel, came out of the staff room and whispered into Agata's ears. 'I need to speak to you urgently.'

She requested her current check-in guest to wait. 'What's wrong, Mr Wyman?' she whispered.

Wyman pointed to Agata's colleague, Meghna, to take over for a bit. He escorted her to the staff boiler room.

'Is there something you need me to do?' Agata looked puzzled.

Daniel looked at her, his expression stern. 'Are you lacking common sense? You checked in Peter Lundgren earlier today. He's a platinum honours member. Didn't you know that?'

Agata furrowed her eyebrows. *Of course I saw that detail, and he mentioned it, too. But I can't exactly throw out someone from his room and check him in instead. Neither can I give him a deluxe room for free. I know the hotel policies.*

'I checked his membership details. He's entitled to a special rate for a room upgrade. That's what I offered him. Have I done anything wrong?' An anxious look darkened her face.

Daniel logged into the guest's membership account on his computer and showed her the perks and privileges he was entitled to enjoy. 'Lundgren has 10,001 points. According to the membership terms of the platinum account, when a member reaches 10,000 points, he's entitled to a free room upgrade. You did not give him his rightful reward.'

She smacked her head in shame. 'I'm so sorry. That's really silly of me, Daniel. I swear I didn't do it on purpose.'

The duty manager raised his voice. 'You almost lost me an important customer. When Lundgren realized his reward had not been honoured, he called me up personally and gave me a roasting. He threatened to write to the CEO and get me fired. To placate him, I had to give him a free night instead of just an upgrade. You cost me £200 today because of your stupid mistake. What do you have to say for yourself?'

Agata hung her head. 'I'm so sorry. I didn't know about this.' Her voice was down to a squeaky whimper.

'On your first day at work, you had to take a test about the tasks and procedures of this hotel. You were told to learn every detail of every process relevant to your job. How can you stand there and claim you didn't know?'

Agata looked down on the floor and saw a fly menacingly circle an ant. She shifted her attention back to Wyman's glaring eyes when the winged predator grabbed its lunch. 'I'm sorry, sir. I'm so sorry. It won't happen again. I promise to be a master of every process in the hotel industry.'

Daniel waved his hands in exasperation, dismissing her from his bullpen. Agata slinked back to her cubicle, feeling totally deflated, and logged into her performance dashboard. She saw her updated score, and threw her arms up. 'Oh God! Once again, I didn't get credit for the revenue I earned for the company. What's worse, my customer satisfaction score has fallen from 9 to 7.5.'

Meghna came over to her desk in the management office. 'Don't worry, Agata. It's no big deal, really. The guest will be fine once he's sloshed at the bar tonight.'

She looked behind her at Mamadou, who was fist-thumping another associate for breaking his sales record—again. Her voice filled with despair. 'I'm trying so hard. But I come up short every time. I'm never going to be a winner like him. I'm never going to get on the fast-track programme.'

Meghna exhaled like a meditation expert and stroked Agata's hair. 'You're trying too hard. Maybe that's your problem. You never relax. You're always so wound up. Just let go.'

Agata shook her head emphatically. 'That's exactly what I can't do. I can't relax. I have too much to lose. I need to hunker down and focus even more on my job. That's what I'm going to do.'

Steep Incline

The next day, Agata extended her daily work schedule by two hours. After two months of sticking to this gruelling regime, she returned home one day to her residence in Hackney—a 1,000 sq. ft., two-bedroom flat in a council estate on Albion Drive—owned by her mother's school friend, Jan Nowak, and his wife, Hanna.

Filip was waiting for her in their shared room. She changed into her nightclothes and got into bed. 'You forgot about the carnival at Fitzroy's Park.' His face had an upside-down smile.

'Oh God! It's your birthday today. I'm so sorry for missing it.'

Filip turned his head away in a huff. 'Never mind. Hanna and Jan took me there.'

Agata kissed him on his cheeks. 'I'm so stressed. I'm having to put in all these extra hours at work. But I promise to make it up to you soon.'

'Two months ago, we used to play video games. You would read to me until I fell asleep. You even helped me with my homework. Lately, we've stopped doing those things. Why?' Filip looked genuinely puzzled.

Agata launched her phone's browser and surfed to a page on a real estate portal titled 'Rental Apartments in Chelsea'. She flicked through pictures of a spare two-bedroom flat and turned the phone toward him. 'Don't you like this flat? Isn't it so much nicer than this one?'

Filip nodded and smiled. 'It's pretty and so big. But I like this place too. Aunt Hanna and Uncle Jan are really nice people. They're always so kind to me.'

Agata sat up with her back straight and gazed at him in excitement. 'That flat is much bigger than this one. You'll have your own room. And, most important of all . . .' She paused and browsed through pictures of facilities and amenities in the neighbourhood. Finally, she stopped at the local school's website, at a page that showed students playing video games in an arcade. Her eyes sparkled with hope and longing. 'This is the school you'll be attending. It even has an arcade. How cool is that?'

Filip smiled. *Unlimited access to a gaming arcade? I'll be damned!* However, his face contorted into a frown when he saw the apartment's details. 'How are we going to afford this place? It costs £2,500 a month.'

Agata gave her brother a warm hug. 'Of course we can afford it . . . very soon. I wouldn't have mentioned it otherwise, would I, silly-billy? That's why I've got to work hard for the next few months. I've got to save up. I've got to make something of myself. I've got to impress these snooty managers so they promote me by the end of the year.'

She scrolled to a web page about the Ace Hotel's fast-track leadership programme. 'Fast-track managers are the thoroughbreds of our company. They earn a starting salary of sixty-thousand pounds per year. They get opportunities to work at different sites around the world and are offered exclusive assignments. From the time of induction, they are groomed for senior management roles.' Her voice bubbled with glee.

Filip looked confused. 'But sis, I thought your passion was biochemistry, not hotel management.'

She gave a wistful smile, as if reminiscing about a former flame. 'Biochemistry isn't something I can realistically pursue at this time. Biochemistry won't get us out of this place,' she paused, her eyes fixed on an image of a group of stylish, smiling managers featured on the programme's website, 'but hotel management will,' she concluded.

That night, Agata tossed and turned in bed, trying in vain to fall asleep. Her mind assailed her with many paranoid questions. *Who are my rivals in the company? What must I do to beat them?*

How can I present myself as a worthy candidate for the first-track programme? Sometime around 2 a.m., a buzzing notification on her phone woke her. She clicked on the message. It was from her friend and guide to London's social life, Katya Wojcik:

> Agata, Kelly and I observed that you haven't attended a single party or get-together in the last six months. It seems we don't fit into your life's priorities. Since we can't associate with people who aren't regulars on our party scene, we have to remove you from our group. Bye, Katya.

Agata felt like a person swimming inside an imploding submarine. The fragments of her personal life flew around her like shattered boiler room parts. Her thoughts were suffused with laments of despair. *My brother is upset with me. My friends have cut me off. All this because I'm so preoccupied with my targets. Is my obsession with this promotion destroying my relationships?*

The following day, she logged into her computer to check her real-time performance update, and saw that her cumulative score—encompassing both revenue and customer satisfaction indices—had increased marginally over the last six months. She analysed her performance graph over time. *Hmm! Ever since I started clocking in extra hours, my score has crept up from 6.8 to 7.4. It seems like I'm making some progress. But . . .* She turned around to look at the employee leaderboard stuck to the wall next to the staff water cooler. It featured the top performers of the month. *Look at their scores. Mamadou 9.2. Meghna 8.9. I'm way behind in the derby*, she thought and then grimaced.

At that moment, Daniel, the duty manager, approached her. He noticed her sullen expression. 'Agata, where's your smile? You're supposed to be at the front desk right now.'

Agata frowned. 'I'm always smiling.'

He gestured for her to follow him into his office for a private chat and closed the door. His eyes were lined with concern. 'I see you've been working long hours. Your diligence is commendable, and the results reflect your changed attitude. Your revenue figures have gone up. However, I must mention that a few guests have rated you negatively on customer service.'

'What do you mean? What feedback have they given?'

'Some have described you as cold, clinical and robotic. While they thought you were helpful and efficient, they also found you impersonal and somewhat commercially motivated.'

Agata put a palm on the back of her neck. *Ugh! Do they expect me to be a therapist? I can't seem to play this right one way or the other. What will it take for me to shine here*? She put her hands in front of her body. 'I was just following the principles of hotel management that were communicated to me on the day of my orientation. Be swift, smart, silent.'

Daniel gave an irritated grunt. 'Hmph! It seems you've chosen to internalize the less important principles while ignoring the most important lesson in the company handbook.' He noted her puzzled expression and ticked off his fingers. 'Customer first. That's our credo. The principles you cited have to be balanced against this sacred motto. You would have figured this out if you'd gone through the company's website in detail instead of performing your tasks like a mindless robot. You would have been steeped in our company's philosophy if you'd memorized its vision, mission, and values statement. You would have been fully aware of our industry's standards of performance if you'd read *The Essential Hotelier's Handbook* by our founder. You would have developed a greater passion for this art if you'd not buried your head in that useless chemistry textbook . . . the one you keep hidden under your desk.'

Agata swore that smoke was coming out of his nostrils towards the end of the recitation. She waved her right hand dismissively. 'Oh! That's nothing. Just something to dabble with during my downtime.'

'Downtime? There's no downtime for junior associates here. Everyone is supposed to be engaged, alert and committed on their shifts. I am beginning to question if your heart is in the right place. Is hotel management even your passion? Because if it was, you would not be making such stupid mistakes.'

Agata felt tears welling beneath the surface. She swiped a tissue across her eyes. 'I'm sorry, Mr Wyman. Biochemistry is something I intend to take up in the distant future. Right now, there's nothing more important to me than to perform well in this job.'

Daniel shook his head like a disapproving professor. 'Your mind is constantly wavering from your task at hand. Focus, Agata. I want to see you relentlessly focused from now on.' He shooed her from his office with an impatient wave of his hand.

Agata ran into the toilet and locked herself in. Tears flowed from her eyes. *I'm running so hard. But still, I'm going nowhere. I can't let my mom and brother down. There's only one thing I can do now.* She washed her face and applied some fresh makeup. Then she returned to her cubicle and picked up the biochemistry book. On her way to the reception, she dumped it in a trashcan near the hotel entrance.

It was around 3 p.m. when she took her position at the reception desk. A large number of visitors had congregated in the lobby. She noticed a sixty-five-year-old man wearing a light brown suit and holding a placard that read BMA MEDICAL

Conference on Respiratory Illnesses. *This must be one of the conference groups. I'll approach that liaison officer and get their identification documents.* She stepped out of the reception area. Suddenly, a familiar figure barged in front of the queue of guests and handed her his passport.

'Welcome back, Mr Lundgren. I'll check you in right away.' She recognized the surly platinum member who'd gotten her into trouble a couple of months earlier. *I have to make amends for my earlier faux pas or I'll be in trouble.* She smiled at him sheepishly. 'Would you like a free upgrade to a room in the premium wing?'

'Nope. That room you put me in last time was a pile of shit. Wasn't worth the extra price even though I got comped eventually. I think I'll stick with a standard room this time.'

She quickly activated a set of electronic keys and handed those to him along with her business card. 'I'm sorry for your bad experience last time, Mr Lundgren. If there's anything you need, please call me personally.'

The gentleman with the tour group waved at her. 'Hey! What's taking you so long?' He sounded impatient. She approached him and shook his hand. 'Welcome to Ace. I'm Agata Kowalski. I'll help you today. Are you representing one of the participating organizations at the medical conference that starts today?'

The man nodded. 'My name is Xander Roche. I work for Reed, the company that organized the conference. This is the group of biochemists from Novartis. There are sixty-five of them in all. Can you check us in right away?'

'Of course.' He put his handbag on the floor, bent down and took out a folder with documents. Agata looked at him with a curious glint. 'May I ask you what this conference is all about?'

Roche's face reflected his puzzlement over her question. 'It's about developing a vaccine for a mysterious virus that just originated in Burma. It's highly contagious and deadly. It's killed 100 people in that country during the last two days. Five cases have also emerged in neighbouring Thailand. And one in Boston.'

Agata recalled a BBC news report from the night before about a respiratory illness that had surfaced in Southeast Asia.

'It's a respiratory illness, right? Similar to COVID-19, the virus that had locked down the world?' Her voice was fearful. Xander's expression turned grim. He brought his face close to her ears. 'It's a member of the same family of SARS-CoV virus specimens. However, this one is much worse.'

'Worse? Surely no infection can be worse than the coronavirus.'

He rolled his eyes and pointed to the conference attendees. 'If you want to know how bad this mutation is, just ask them yourself. They've all flown in from Burma, where they studied the infection.'

Agata changed the subject with a diplomatic smile. 'Your colleagues must be very tired. Why don't you hand me their IDs? I'll check them in right away,' she offered, and then waited while he handed the folder to her.

She took the folder that held a bunch of passports and documents pertaining to their reservations. Right then, someone shrieked in the back of the lobby. Every head turned to see what was happening. The biochemists had formed a circle. Curious to see what was going on, Agata left the reception desk, and approached the throng. 'What's wrong? What's going on?'

No one answered her question. A slim woman in her mid-thirties, of medium height and wearing a purple scarf, looked at her with terror and pointed to the floor. Agata screamed. One of the young male biochemists was writhing on the floor in agony.

'What's wrong with him?'

'Is he sick?'

'Call the ambulance NOW.'

The lobby guests were chattering amongst themselves. Their eyes were full of anxiety.

Agata looked behind her at the reception desk; the receptionists were making frantic calls from their phones. Her eyes met those of the slender woman. This time, she had a clear answer to Agata's questions. 'He's infected,' she gasped with horror, pointing to the folder in Agata's hands.

Agata looked at the documents in the folder. The registration document of every guest had a form stapled to it that read 'COVID-99 STUDY GROUP'. At that moment, the victim's screams got louder as he gasped for breath.

'He needs a ventilator, *now*.' The woman backed off a few paces from him.

His body contorted in pain and he signalled his inability to breathe. A red substance trickled from his nose and his mouth. It was blood laced with a slimy fluid. Then, his body curved on the floor like a man possessed by a demon. He emitted a piercing scream and opened his mouth very wide. Pieces of his respiratory organs ejected on the bodies of the surrounding guests. His body went limp and in a few moments, completely lifeless. A guest placed a finger on his pulse. 'He's dead.'

The woman in the purple scarf brushed off the remains from her overcoat with her fingers. 'His respiratory system has imploded,' she stuttered.

Agata checked for any of the remains on herself and observed she was clean. 'I've got to get help.' She ran towards the reception desk, but stopped in her tracks after going three-quarters of the way. Xander, who was in front of her, collapsed on the floor squirming. The slender woman followed suit. In a matter of minutes, all the guests waiting to check in at the lobby . . . about 100 of them . . . collapsed on the floor. Then, the entire front office staff including Meghna, Mamadou, and five other associates suffered the same fate.

A pile of mangled carcasses lay all around her. But, only one thought came to her head: *I've got to protect Filip.*

However, the call would not go through. A current of panic seared through her veins. *I must go home.* She ran towards the door, gingerly sidestepping the mortal remains splattered all over the lobby floor like the set of a ghastly slasher film. She reached the entrance and saw an ambulance standing just outside on the main road. Suddenly, a ray of sunlight hit her left eye and blinded her momentarily. She rubbed it and turned her head in the direction of the light. She saw a trashcan. The upper part of a book stuck out from inside. The biochemistry book she'd tossed out earlier. *Can I afford to wait by the sidelines while millions die?*

The sunlight fell on the book, making the golden font of the title, *Advanced Molecular Biochemistry*, coruscate like a jewel. 'I know who I must be.' Agata picked up the book and dashed out of the hotel and into the streets of London like an Olympic runner.

She passed many cars and buses stranded in the middle of the street, their drivers and passengers slumped dead in their vehicles. There was not a living person in sight. Nervously, she peeked into a double-decker bus that had crashed into the side of a building. The driver was dead.

There were twenty passengers on the lower deck, their heads tilted back, their organs splattered all over the seats. 'Oh my God! They are all dead. The infection has spread throughout the city.' She scampered to the door. Suddenly, a shrill female voice screamed from the upper deck, 'Help me! Help me! Please!'

Oh my God! Someone's survived! Agata climbed the stairs to find only two people sitting upstairs. One of them—a child—was alive. She was about eight years old with braided hair and wearing a white dress. Her dark skin was pale with terror. She pointed to a woman in her early forties sitting next to her, she cried to Agata, 'Mommy. My mommy's dead. Everybody. Everybody's dead.'

Agata waved the child to come towards her and kneeled on the floor. 'I'm so sorry, honey. But you must leave now, or you're gonna get sick.'

'I can't leave Mommy here.'

Agata caressed her long hair with a reassuring stroke. 'Honey, there's nothing you or anyone else can do. The medics will come for her. But you aren't safe by staying here. You have to come with me.'

They got off the bus; Agata introduced herself. 'What's your name?'

'I'm Abbo from Kampala, Uganda. My mom and I came on a week-long vacation by winning an online contest.' The girl sniffled repeatedly and her voice came down to a whimper.

Agata looked at her anxiously. 'Is there anyone else at home?'

The girl shook her head. 'There's only me.' She pointed to a hotel on the opposite side of the road with the signage 'MARBLE MANSIONS'. 'That's where I'm staying.'

Agata looked to where the girl indicated and saw several bodies lying outside the entrance . . . including that of the doorman. *Everyone's probably dead or infected there. There's no way she can go back. I'd better take her to my place. We can then regroup and figure out the next steps.*

She gazed at Abbo reassuringly. 'Abbo, you can't go back to your hotel now. Come with me. I'll take care of you.' She handed over her phone to the girl. 'Is there someone you can call back in Kampala?'

The girl nodded her head and dialed a number. Someone answered. 'Dad, something bad just happened. Mom and I were on the bus when she suddenly started to cough and shake. I asked her, "What's wrong? Are you sick?" and she choked, "I can't breathe, baby," so I ran down the stairs to tell the driver to stop, but he was choking too. Very soon, everybody on the bus groaned, twisted their bodies and gasped for air. I screamed and rushed towards my seat. But Mom just shook her head. She held my hand and whispered with a hoarse voice, "Girl, get out of here." But I couldn't. The next minute, she was gone.'

The girl cried inconsolably. Agata offered the sobbing child a handkerchief, and wiped her tears. Abbo said to the caller, 'Dad. There's a very nice lady who has offered to help me for now.' A long and teary exchange of reassurance from her father followed. 'Yes, Dad. I'll be strong. For us. Please send the connection to this number.' She turned her attention to Agata. 'Is it okay if Dad texts you the details for the Ugandan embassy's liaison officer? You may speak to him later to send me home.'

Agata nodded her head.

The two trundled down Central London's commercial thoroughfares. They saw a mass of devastation. Bodies were strewn everywhere. They stopped at Piccadilly Circus. Agata gasped in horror. A bike had crashed into the Shaftesbury fountain. The rider's body was slumped on the base of the statue, right above a mass of dead tourists. Abbo held Agata's hand tightly. 'What's happening? I'm scared.'

'I don't know.' Agata squeezed the girl's shoulders. She launched the Facebook app on her phone and scrolled past dozens of videos and images of death. She chanced upon the video of a BBC news show. The anchor reported that a mysterious virus—a deadlier mutation of COVID-19 than anything previously reported—was sweeping the US, UK, Burma, and Thailand. Its pattern seemed to be to kill 70 per cent of the infected population within specific clusters before migrating to another community.

'COVID-99 is more contagious than COVID-19 because it can be transmitted through contact between humans, between humans and animals, between humans and plants. It can be transmitted through the air up to a distance of 70 feet and through water. It can pass through microscopic pores in clothing and render hazmat and medical contamination suits ineffective. Its genetic mutation enables it to camouflage itself as a known alpha coronavirus, thereby evading detection and nullifying the COVID-19 vaccine. Symptoms appear within thirty minutes for infected individuals, and death follows instantaneously. The virus kills a human being by infecting the respiratory system, rupturing the organs and causing asphyxiation.'

The news anchor suddenly stopped her broadcast. Her face contorted in pain. She coughed, choked and gasped for breath. Her eyes growing wide with horror. Then, she fell to the floor and squirmed like an eel. In an instant, she was dead.

Agata shivered with fear. 'I don't know what's causing this menace. But luckily, we seem to be immune to it. Let's get to safety first. We'll think of something later.' Right then, her phone rang. She gave a sigh of relief. 'Filip. I was so scared. I couldn't reach you.'

Her brother's voice was tense and desperate. 'Sis, you've got to come home. Something really bad has happened.'

An hour later, the two of them reached home. Agata saw Jan and Hanna dead on the living room sofa. Their heads were tilted back, and their mouths were open like goldfishes gasping for air in vain when removed from their fishbowl. A mass of guts was piled up on the table, swimming in a pool of blood in front of the TV. The BBC was on—playing the afternoon news. A series of Polish graphic novels—about a lone hitchhiker traversing an apocalyptic world—lay on the floor, dislodged from a wall-mounted bookshelf. Filip was crouched on the floor, covering his face and weeping uncontrollably.

Agata felt as if her legs had been felled by a hammer blow. She grew faint, her knees weak. Abbo squeezed her hand. 'You have to be strong for all of us now.'

Agata saw the look of quiet determination in the little girl's eyes. *I asked her to be strong and calm in the face of her mother's death. Now, I must live up to my own preaching*. She stroked Filip's head.

Filip removed his hands from his wet, red eyes and looked first at his sister, and then at the stranger with her. 'Who is she? Why did you bring her here? She could kill us.' His voice was loud and bursting with a sense of outrage.

Agata raised her arms out in front of her body. 'Don't worry. We're all immune to this; if we weren't, we'd be dead already.' Abbo raised her hand forward towards him. 'This is Abbo. I found her on a bus as I was running back from the hotel. Her mother's dead.'

Filip accepted her hand hesitatingly. 'I'm—I'm . . . sorry. Didn't mean to be rude. My name is Filip. I'm Agata's brother.'

Abbo smiled. 'All of us have lost so much today. Let's be strong together.'

At that moment, the BBC news programme showed live footage outside the Ugandan embassy on Trafalgar Square. The camera zoomed in on the front entrance and showed a pile of dead bodies. It then panned into the building. The reporter's expression was grim. 'Despite stringent precautions, London's foreign embassies have not been spared from the virus. This is the Ugandan Consulate. They have suffered the most devastating blow of all. Fifty people used to work here. The police and Home office have confirmed that all have died from COVID-99, including High Commissioner Sanyu Barya, and Director Mukisa Obote. Since Mr Obote was in charge of repatriating Ugandan citizens, it isn't clear who'll take responsibility for evacuating a thousand citizens, including tourists and residents.'

Agata grabbed her phone and checked the name of the contact that Abbo's father had texted. It was Obote. She looked at Abbo helplessly, but the young girl stared at the TV set, a singular focus in her eyes. 'Don't worry about helping me right now. It's important we find a way out of this together.'

'How?' Filip threw his hands at his sides.

Agata remained silent. *I need to come up with a solution*. Right then, the newscaster issued a chilling update. 'Parliament has authorized the prime minister to declare a national emergency and impose martial law across all of England. The army and air force have been called into action to strictly implement this order. For your safety, please stay inside your homes until you are told it's safe to venture out. If you break the curfew, you may be shot on sight by patrolling officers.'

The three sat still and pensive trying to figure out a plan for riding out the storm. Agata's mom called from her hospital in Warsaw to check up on her kids.

'Agata, I just woke up now and heard about a virus raging all over London. Are you okay?' She sounded dazed and petrified.

Agata swallowed her tears. 'I'm fine, Mom. The virus didn't affect me; neither did it hurt Filip.'

Filip overhead the conversation. 'But Uncle Jan, Aunt Hanna and Aggie's coworkers are all—'

Agata covered the receiver with her hand and silenced him with a furious wave of her hand. 'Shh! You know that she's in a very sensitive condition right now. She's all alone on a hospital bed at the ICU in a very crappy government treatment centre. If she hears about their deaths, she may well suffer a nervous breakdown.'

Agata put her mouth back against the speaker. 'Mom, don't worry about us. Jan and Hanna have prepared for this. We have enough food to last us for months. As soon as this crisis passes, everything will go back to normal.'

'I hope so.' Agnieszka sounded forlorn.

'Ma, I swear I'll get you out of that horrible government centre by the end of next month. That's when I'll get my promotion. I'll admit you into a top private care facility. You'll be cured. Just hang in there.' Her voice was infused with much-needed pep.

'I know you will, my baby. I believe in you. Stay safe.' Her mother's voice sounded feeble.

Agata hung up. 'Do we have enough food?' She looked at Filip inquiringly.

He nodded his head and opened the fridge. There was a large stock of eggs, milk, fruits, and meat. 'It will last us a week, I think.'

'Let's stay here for now. When the curfew's lifted, we can figure out our next step.' Agata pursed her lips.

Abbo held her nose and pointed to the decomposing bodies in the room. 'What do we do with them?'

Agata stood up and walked over to the waiting area near the door. 'Let's cover the bodies with garbage bags and put them in the utilities and storage closet.' She opened the door of a thirty-six-square-foot enclosure near the front door housing the electrical circuits, boiler, and cleaning equipment. 'There's just enough space for the bodies to be concealed safely for the time being.' She looked at the others with a sense of conviction.

Filip found a number of garbage bags in the kitchen, which the three survivors used to cover the bodies. They sealed and dragged them to the storage chamber. Afterwards, they disposed of the entrails and thoroughly cleaned the room.

A tired Agata flung her blazer on the sofa. Abbo noticed the textbook Agata had stuffed into a pocket pop out from it; she picked it up and asked curiously, 'Are you a biochemist, or are you studying to be one?'

'Oh no!' Agata shook her head vehemently. 'That's just something I love to do in my free time. I'm a hotel receptionist.'

Filip smacked her shoulders. 'Yes. A receptionist who hates her job but is willing to put in long hours. A receptionist who's unhappy with her income yet accepts low pay and poor incentives. A receptionist who wants friends yet is willing to sacrifice them for a promotion.' He wore a mocking smile.

Agata's insides burned with irritation. *How dare he criticize my life choice!* She smacked his face. 'Shut your mouth, you troll. If I don't put in those long hours, how will you go to school? How will Mom get better? How will we live in that new flat?'

'A receptionist who can't bother to remember her own brother's birthday.' Tears formed in Filip's eyes.

Abbo's eyes perused the book, away from the feuding family members. She stumbled upon a handwritten page of notes bearing the diagram of a circle with spikes. She read the caption aloud. 'Genomic Organization of Coronaviruses. What is this?'

'Oh! It's nothing! Something I'd worked on at college,' Agata said evasively.

'She won a biochemistry prize,' Filip blurted out. 'It was a contest to develop a coronavirus vaccine. She was all set to go to Dubai. Then, Mom fell ill, and she quit uni and got a job to support her,' he revealed.

'Stop talking rubbish! How will this help us now?' Agata shouted angrily and slapped him again.

Filip whimpered and held his cheek. 'Maybe, if you'd gone to Dubai, you'd have become a biochemist. Maybe, you'd have developed a vaccine for this plague. Maybe, you could have helped Mom become better. Maybe—'

Agata raised her hand. 'I'm warning you. One more comment about my passion—'

Abbo's voice cut through the brother–sister conflict. 'So, is hotel management your passion or is biochemistry?'

Agata looked confused. Filip answered emphatically, 'Biochemistry. Biochemistry.'

Embarrassed, Agata looked away and toward the TV, where a newscaster interviewed a biochemist about the intricacies of the virus and its possible remedies. A diagram of the virus molecule was displayed in an inset panel. She peered at it closely. *Hmm! Is this mutation similar to the one I studied five years ago?* She opened the book to the relevant chapter to compare the genomic properties of the variants.

This virus molecule looks very similar to the one I worked on, albeit with a few mutations in its spike protein that appear to imbue it with a greater degree of resistance to existing vaccines as well as the ability to camouflage itself. A question suddenly triggered in her mind. *Can my formula for the coronavirus vaccine actually work in reality?*

She laughed, much to the surprise of her partners. Abbo pointed a finger to her heart. 'If you were in college today, would you have participated in that contest?'

Agata nodded. 'Yes. Not to win anything but to save lives. That's the need of the hour.'

Abbo held her hand. 'Then you know what you must do.'

Agata pulled her hand away. 'I don't know what you mean by that. It's not like I can simply put on a uniform and become a biochemist.'

Right then, her phone rang. 'Hi! This is Peter Lundgren, the guest from Room 301. Am I speaking to Agata Kowalski?' The masculine voice was low-pitched and trembling.

She remembered the face of the difficult guest she'd checked in earlier. 'Yes, Mr Lundgren. Are you okay?'

'Err . . . Agata. Just call me Peter. Ever since the infection broke out, I've been trying my best to contact someone on the outside.' The man's voice quivered with anxiety. 'But everyone I know is dead or unreachable. I'm trapped in my room.'

'You mustn't leave the room, Peter. That's your only refuge for the moment.'

Peter's voice now choked with sorrow and fear. 'If you look through the keyhole of my door, you'll see a dozen bodies fermenting in the corridor. Rats and flies have surrounded them and are feasting on their remains. I've called you because nobody out here's answering my call. Everybody's dead. Luckily, I found your business card in my wallet five minutes ago.'

'Peter, you've got to be calm in this moment of crisis. Try calling your friends and family. Get a stock of their situation. Assure them you'll ride out this storm. In a short while, things will return to normal.' Agata kept her tone light.

'Agata, I've done that already! My family in Boston . . . my friends . . . they are all dead. Everyone's dead,' he screamed in distress.

Abbo, who heard the distraught man's voice and saw Agata's lost expression, whispered, 'Tell him you're there to help. Put him at ease.'

Filip pushed Abbo. 'Are you crazy? How are we going to help him? We can't even go outside.'

Agata covered the speaker and scowled at her brother. 'Filip, Abbo's right. He's in trouble. He called me. I must hear him out and do the best I can.' She removed her hand and spoke into the receiver. 'Peter, how can I be of help?'

The guest broke out into sobs of despair. 'I'm the director of infectious diseases at the CDC in the US. I was supposed to meet research scientists to discuss a potential vaccine for COVID-99 at the BMA Conference today.'

Agata's jaw dropped in surprise. 'What! You're the person responsible for developing a global vaccine for this pandemic?'

'Yes . . . yes. But, my colleagues . . . all the scientists . . . they're dead or missing. I can't reach anyone. So I called the CDC. They're sending a special flight from the States to evacuate me. However, because of the national emergency, they can't get here for three days.'

Agata heaved a sigh of relief. 'That's wonderful. At least you have hope. Now sit tight.'

'I have no food or water. Even my bathroom tap is running empty. On top of that, I'm a diabetic. I called you with a faint hope that you'd still be in the building. Now I don't know what to do,' he explained, sounding hopeless.

Agata pondered how to help him. Her mind rewound to her orientation at the hotel. Ron Dexter had said, 'Always remember the motto of our hotel. Make the well-being of your guest your highest priority.'

She looked at the name pin on her blazer and those words resounded in her consciousness. *When I received this badge, I swore to uphold the welfare of our guests. My colleagues have died. The hotel is no longer functional. But I'm still wearing this badge. I've got to help him.*

She cleared her throat. 'Peter. I'm coming with food and water. We'll get out of this. Just hang on tight.'

'But this is madness! You'll never get here alive.' Peter was aghast.

'You're a guest,' Agata reassured him. 'I'm still an employee. That relationship is more sacred than life itself.'

'You're an angel. Just get here safe. I'll be praying for you,' he cried before hanging up.

'Sis. What's the matter with you? Are you crazy? We'll never make it there.' His voice throbbed with outrage and his eyes glowered at her.

'I've got to help him. I swore an oath at my orientation.' But she wasn't able to look Filip in the eye.

'What oath? A promise to a company you don't cherish? A commitment to a job you don't love? A bond with a community that exists only in theory?'

Agata struggled to explain why duty trumped survival. *It would be selfish of me to involve the two of them in my mission.* She looked at her brother sternly. 'I can't explain why I must go to him. But I must. Alone. You don't have to join me. Stay here with Abbo.'

'How can you abandon us at a time like this? Do you think we can make it on our own? How can you be so selfish and place these principles above us? How can you place the life of a stranger above your own brother?' Filip threw up his arms and turned his back towards her.

The heated exchange triggered a moment of reflection in Abo. *I should have rushed out and called for help the minute I saw my mom wheezing instead of staying put in my seat . . . quaking with fear. Agata's doing the right thing. But Filip's got a point too. Leaving us behind is not the right thing to do.* She held Filip's hand. 'Filip, in this difficult time, it's important for all of us to remain united, right?'

'Of course.' He pointed to his sister. 'But when she tries to pull off some scatterbrained scheme, some wild goose chase, I've got to put my foot down.'

Abbo held his other hand. 'But what if it's not a wild goose chase? What if this mission is our only hope for survival?' Her eyes were piercing, her look appealing.

Filip looked baffled. 'Huh? What do you mean?'

'Who knows when the curfew will be lifted?' Abbo smiled gently. 'Who knows how long our supplies will last? Who knows when we'll start showing symptoms?' She opened the window, and pointed to a crow perched on the windowsill of an apartment in the opposite building. Filip watched it eyeing the rotting body of the tenant. Abbo placed her hand on his shoulder.

'I'd rather die there fighting for something than die here doing nothing. Our only chance of survival is a vaccine. Peter Lundgren can develop it. If a plane is flying him out in seventy-two hours, I say—get him on that damned airship.'

At that moment, the crow flew into the neighbouring flat and picked on the dead resident's remains. Filip backed away from the window. His face turned white. 'Oh, okay. You . . . err . . . you're right. Let's go now.'

Agata shook her head emphatically. 'No. I really think you should stay here.'

'No,' Abbo insisted. 'We're all in this together. If you go, we go.'

Agata paused for a minute and then nodded slowly. 'Okay, let's do it. It's a fifteen-minute walk to the Dalston Junction train station. We can take an overground train to Highbury and Islington. Then, we can transfer there to the subway that goes directly to Marble Arch.'

Filip looked at her with trepidation. 'Isn't all public transport shut down?'

Agata flipped open the BBC news site on her phone and scanned a news headline: 'ONLY TRAINS AND UNDERGROUND SERVICES ARE RUNNING AT THE MOMENT FOR THE BENEFIT OF PEOPLE HEADING BACK HOME.' She pointed to the update. 'This is our chance.'

The three loaded their backpacks with a three-day stock of biscuits, nuts, canned tuna, water, tea and various survival essentials, enough for four people. Then, the trio ventured circumspectly out of their building. There wasn't a soul in sight. Not a sound could be heard. They quietly ran to the end of Albion Drive. The thud-thud of footsteps came from the far side of Holly Street, the road perpendicular to it. They hid behind the wall of a building at the junction of the two streets; its wall bore a World War II plaque with the memorial 'DEDICATED TO OUR ARMED SERVICES FOR DRIVING OUT THE INVADERS'.

Agata peeked to her left and spotted a battalion of soldiers marching towards them. 'Shit! The military's here already! The armed forces have taken over the city. How can we possibly slip past them?' Her voice betrayed her desperation.

Abbo pointed to a row of bushes and plants lining the road divider at the centre of the street. 'We have to hide there.'

The green space was about three feet in width and stretched from the Holly Street intersection to the end of Albion Drive. The three lay on their backs, each in front of the other, to ensure they stayed hidden amidst the greenery. The stomping of boots got louder and a man's shout could be heard. 'March all the way to the end of Albion Drive. If you see any people on the street, order them to go inside. If they don't comply, capture and interrogate them. If they make a run for it, fire tear gas and rubber bullets at them.'

Filip whispered to her partners. 'We've got five minutes to play possum or get turned into a frittata.'

Ten minutes later, the sound of boots faded away. Agata peeked out from the foliage and saw a group of soldiers near the end of the road, about 500 feet away. She beckoned the children to get up and ushered them to follow her lead. The trio managed to tiptoe towards the intersection without raising any heckles. Agata saw that the left turn on Holly Street lead to an empty road. At that moment, Filip stepped on an empty water bottle.

A soldier turned around at the sound and spotted the escaping group. 'Stop where you are. Get down on your knees. Now!'

Filip placed his hands on his head to surrender, but Abbo gave him a disapproving look and shook her head. At the same moment, Agata saw a train arriving at the Dalston Junction station in the distance. She figured it would take them five minutes to reach the station if they ran like the wind.

'We might just make it to the train. In any case, we've got to try.' She kept her voice low. The soldiers ran towards them. Within a few moments, the distance between the youngsters and the military had reduced to 300 feet. 'Run!' Agata made a dash for it.

Filip was paralysed on his spot. Abbo shook him by the shoulders. 'Come on, slowpoke. We've got to go.'

The three sped faster than they'd ever run before. Agata heard the hoarse cries of the soldiers ordering them to stop. She glanced behind her and was shocked to see that despite their speed, the men were gaining on them.

The platoon commander raised his rifle. 'Fire. Don't let them get away.'

Three teargas shells whizzed past Filip's face, crashed on a building to his right and exploded. They produced a mist of chemical vapour that seeped into his eyes and nose. He rubbed his eyes and screamed. 'I can't see.'

Agata grabbed his hand. 'Don't worry. You'll be fine on the train.'

They ran like wild hares escaping a fox, and arrived at the station steps that led directly to the platform of the outbound express. It was preparing to depart. Agata held the children's hands and quickly ran up the stairs. However, the soldiers arrived at the bottom of the steps.

'Stop!' The commander fired a rubber bullet at them. It missed the three of them and hit the station wall. The soldiers swiftly ran up the thirty steps.

Agata saw the door of the train about to close. She yelled, 'Jump!' and the three dove inside. The door closed, and the train sped away. Abbo looked out the window and behind her to see the furious faces of their pursuers.

On the train, Agata poured some water into Filip's eyes to negate the effects of the teargas. 'I still can't see.' He made a face.

'Don't worry. You'll feel better once we get to Islington Station,' Agata said.

It took half an hour to reach Islington and Highbury Stations, from where they would need to transfer to the Marble Arch-bound subway line.

Filip's face brightened. 'It worked. I can see now.' His voice sounded cheery.

The platform seemed to be abandoned. Agata saw a flight of stairs on the other end of the platform with an arrow on a sign that read 'VICTORIA LINE'. She looked around and observed there were no guards posted there. She heaved a sigh of relief.

Right then, Abbo spotted a homeless woman in her sixties. She wore gypsy clothing and squatted on the floor beside the door of the station's waiting room. She approached the woman. Filip noticed her leaving the group. 'What are you doing? We have to get out of here.'

Abbo ignored him. She looked at the woman with a sympathetic gaze. 'Why aren't you waiting inside?'

The woman's face seemed to have weathered a hundred storms. A tear rolled down her cheek. 'I'm hungry, and I have nowhere to go. I'm homeless. My country, Romania, just closed its borders.' She pointed to the waiting room. 'Waiting inside would only delay the inevitable. It's better I die out here, begging for food.'

With a smile, Abbo touched the dishevelled woman's face. 'No one's going hungry tonight. And, no one's going to die.'

Agata came up to them. 'What's wrong, Abbo?'

The girl pointed to the old lady. 'She's hungry, and we have all this food with us. Can't we spare her something?'

Agata looked around furtively and removed her backpack from her shoulders. She opened it and handed the lady a packet of cookies. The old woman's face beamed with pleasure, Agata unexpectedly reached out her hand. 'Come with us. You'll be safe.'

The old woman looked up at the sky with gratitude. She stood, raised her arms and closed her eyes. '*Lăudăt să fie Domnul*.' She said a prayer thanking the Lord for his munificence, and took her hand.

The four prepared to move towards the exit. Suddenly, the buzzing noise of an aerial chopper rent the air.

'Get down on your hands and knees, or we'll shoot,' a voice boomed from the helicopter. The four looked up. The mechanical flying beast circled its prey ominously.

Abbo stared at the staircase that led to the subway about 300 feet away, and whispered to her companions, 'We can make it.'

Agata shook her head. 'They'll fire real bullets this time. Let's not play hero.'

Abbo looked insistent. 'We've come so far. Isn't it worth that extra push to get us over the line?'

Agata remembered her commitment to the cause of service. *She's right. It's better to live for something than to die for nothing.* She looked down on the floor. 'Act like you're planning to kneel. Then, on my cue, run.' She kept her voice down to a whisper.

The helicopter pilot saw the four kneel and descended towards the platform. Within moments, it reached about fifteen feet above the platform's surface. Agata yelled, 'Now!'

Instantly, the four dashed towards the subway stairs. The soldiers fired a round of bullets at them. They sailed past their heads and hit the trees in the adjoining park.

They dashed through the passage of the subway station towards the Victoria Line and reached the platform. The whirring sound of the helicopter's blades faded. A minute later, the tube arrived. The quartet heaved a collective sigh of relief and boarded the express train to Marble Arch.

On the tube, the old woman devoured two cookies in one go with a bottle of water. 'My name's Lavinia. Twelve years ago, my family—along with a hundred members of the Roma gypsy community—were thrown out of our homes in Bala Mare, a city in the north of Romania, by radical right-wing extremists. The barbarians stole all our valuables, identity documents and occupied our home. My husband, daughter and I fled the country to the UK on a bus. En route, we suffered a horrific accident. My husband and daughter died. Thanks to the Lord's mercy, I survived with no life-threatening injuries. A good Samaritan, a doctor, rescued me and admitted me to a hospital. It took a week for me to heal. Then, he offered me a ride to London. The streets of this city have been my home for the last ten years.'

Their jaws dropped and their eyes grew wide with shock. Filip wiped a tear from his eye. 'I'm sorry I didn't see you.'

Lavinia ran her hand through his blond hair and smiled. 'There's so much beauty in the world. Sometimes, we don't see it. But if we stop for a moment and look within, we'll always find it.'

Twenty minutes later, they reached the exit at Marble Arch station. Agata pointed to Ace Business Hotel on the other side of the road. 'Now! We've got to make a run for it.' A minute later, the group had sprinted into the lobby of the hotel.

There were no people in the lobby. No healthcare workers. No military personnel. No police officers. All the bodies of the infected individuals had been removed.

Agata looked at the thick sheets of plastic covering everything in the vicinity, including the floor, the walls, and every piece of furniture. *The place has been sanitized.* At the same time, Abbo noticed a group of NHS workers with hazmat suits walking towards the hotel entrance.

'They're here. We've got to move.'

Agata led the group towards a flight of emergency stairs located next to the elevator. She gestured for them to keep an eye on every direction. They quietly walked up three flights of stairs, and reached the hallway of the third floor. A sign that read R300–306 pointed to their right. On the way to room 301, Filip shuddered. There were several cadavers with their organs ripped out . . . blood and guts soiling the Venetian carpet. Lavinia saw his terrified look and held his hands tightly.

They finally arrived in front of room 301. Agata's eyes filled with relief. She knocked. A bearded, silver-haired, heavyset man in his sixties opened the door. His face was red. His lips had cold sores. His eyes had the frightened look of a deer pursued by an invisible predator for miles. A look of astonishment appeared in his eyes. 'I can't believe it. You came. You kept your word.' He was beside himself with excitement.

The foursome entered the room. Agata took out a water bottle and a packet of biscuits, and handed them to him. 'Take this. You must be starving and thirsty.'

He gulped down the 1-litre bottle in no time. Then, he ripped open the packet of McVities Hobnobs and devoured four biscuits in one go. 'You don't know how relieved I am to see you,' Peter Lundgren mumbled as he chewed.

Agata introduced the rest of the group. 'Any news of your rescue operation?' She looked at him inquiringly.

Lundgren studied her pensively. 'They've reached the UK. However, security protocols are preventing them from getting here within seventy-two hours. When they do arrive, all of us will be airlifted out of here.'

'All of us? Are you sure?' Filip's eyes lit up.

Lundgren nodded his head emphatically. 'Of course. You've undertaken the most heroic mission that anybody could have imagined under these circumstances.'

Abbo high-fived Filip. 'Now are you glad that you came on this mission?' She tickled the palm of his hand.

Agata looked at him quizzically. 'So, we should wait now until the CDC officials come. Right?' She dumped her backpack on the floor. A book fell out from it.

Filip grabbed it, removed a piece of paper inserted between two of its pages and handed it to Lundgren. 'This mission isn't over.' His face had an enigmatic smile.

Agata saw the design of a molecule and ran towards him to snatch it away. 'You filthy imp! Give that to me right now.'

Lundgren took it and studied it for a moment. His eyes widened in astonishment. 'What is this? Is this—?'

Filip winked slyly at Agata. He turned his face towards Peter. His voice filled with excitement. 'My sis came up with this idea to tackle the coronavirus about five years ago. That was the time when the early form of the infection had emerged in the Middle East. She had enrolled in an international contest to develop a vaccine for the virus. Her paper was shortlisted. She would have been one of the twenty candidates selected to go to GoLife's labs in Dubai to work with leading scientists and develop a vaccine. But our mother got cancer, so she couldn't go. After that, she became a bitch towards me.'

Agata's face turned red and she raised her hand. Lavinia held it—stopping it from falling on Filip's cheek. 'He loves you, you know. He only wants the best for you.'

Agata looked at the hurt expression on her brother's face, and a tear welled in her eye. She gave him a warm hug. 'I love you so much. I'm sorry I never said this enough.'

Meanwhile, Peter Lundgren was completely immersed in studying the diagram of the virus blocker. *Agata's description of a process for replicating messenger RNA is intriguing . . . but . . .* He pointed his finger at the diagram. 'The process you describe here is currently one of the approaches adopted to develop vaccines for the COVID-19 virus. However, my team tested it on the COVID-99 mutation and discovered it didn't work.'

Agata sighed with regret and shook her head at Filip. 'That's the penalty for wishful thinking.'

Abbo listened to their exchanges. Her mind returned to the last moment she'd spent with her mother before the affliction took her life. 'Abbo, whatever happens, you must fight until your last breath. You must never give up. Even when things seem the most hopeless, there's always a way around the corner,' she recalled her mother telling her. She raised her voice. 'We don't know much about this virus. We don't know what's going to work or fail. Can't we try it out first? If it doesn't work, maybe we can try something else.'

Agata laughed. 'Oh, my sweet little Abbo! You need a fully equipped lab to try these things out. Where will we find one at this hour?'

Peter snapped his fingers. 'As a matter of fact, we do have one.' There was a 'Eureka!' look in his eyes. 'Right here in the hotel. It was set up for the medical conference that was supposed to be held today. The conference venue was converted into a makeshift lab for trying out different formulations of the vaccine. If that space is still intact, we could try it over there.'

Filip experienced a rare boost of bravado. 'Let's go down now and try to get this thing to work. Then, we can solve this virus thing and get the hell outta here.'

All of them proceeded towards the door. Agata suddenly remembered that going downstairs might prove to be a fatal misstep for the CDC director. 'Peter. It seems this virus is deadly to most people, except for a minority. The four of us . . . for some reason . . . appear to fall in this category. But I'm worried you might be vulnerable.'

'Right. You guys go ahead and try it out. Hook me up from the lab with a Zoom call.'

Agata nodded her head, and led the group down the stairs to the conference room located in the hotel lobby.

The room was padlocked. 'Oh God! How are we going to get in?' Filip's voice was whiny.

Lavinia smiled. 'If it's locked, then perhaps it's been sealed and everything is intact inside.'

Agata crossed her fingers. She told them to wait for a moment and ran down to the housekeeping section in the basement. She returned with a pair of pliers. 'Here goes.' Her voice was triumphant. The group exerted a mighty, collective heave and destroyed the lock.

'You're right!' Agata squeezed Lavinia's arm.

The conference room was in mint condition. A third of the 20,000 sq. ft. space was equipped with a hundred chairs in a theatre-style configuration. The room was fitted with a screen and a projector. Another third was an exhibition area with unmanned company booths for selling medical equipment, supplies and services to the research fraternity. The final section of the venue made Agata's jaw drop with astonishment.

'This is what I've always dreamed about. To someday work in my very own lab.' Agata stroked the brand-new crucibles, monitors, test tubes, microscopes and other supplies as if they were garments at a designer store.

Lavinia squeezed her hand. 'This is your destiny. You know that, right?'

Agata found a bunch of contamination-proof suits in a carton below a table. The four changed into them quickly. Agata detailed her plan on a whiteboard. 'According to my theory, we need to synthesize messenger RNA that can produce antibodies strong enough to counter the virus.'

Abbo looked puzzled. 'How are we going to do that?'

Agata looked around, and, spotted a freezer. She opened the door to discover a box labeled 'mRNA TRANSCRIPTION KIT'. Inside, she found eight neatly labeled test tubes containing different compounds. She read out the compounds she needed. 'Enzyme mix. 10x reaction buffer. Ammonium acetate buffer . . .' Her voice trailed off as she checked the remaining substances. 'Yep. Everything I need is here.'

Right then, Peter called from his room using the Zoom app. He saw the conference room in spanking condition and sighed with relief. 'Thank goodness the equipment's intact. Do you have everything you need?'

Agata looked confident 'Yes, I think so.' Suddenly, she remembered something. 'Except . . .' She looked at Abbo and then, Lavinia, with a look of anxiety.

Peter asked what was wrong.

'We need a sample of infected tissue. Then, I can make the reagent and combine it with the virus to see if my approach works. That would mean going upstairs and collecting tissue samples from—'

Abbo promptly produced a sealed Ziploc bag with a clump of mucus. 'I picked it up when both of you were fighting in the hallway. I figured it might come in handy at some point.'

Lavinia squeezed her cheeks. 'Clever one.' Brother and sister looked at her with a mix of surprise and disgust. She waved her right hand as if her act was normal. 'And don't worry. I wore disposal gloves to pick it up.' She held up a box of powder-free surgical gloves that the three had packed in each bag.

'Way to go.' Peter clapped.

Agata placed the infected tissue sample in a new test tube, and combined the substances from the transcription kit in accordance with her formula. Then, she mixed the compound with the tissue sample. For a moment, the mucus hissed and deflated. Its surface turned greyish.

'Wow! It's working!' Filip raised his hands in celebration. However, there was a popping sound, and the tissue split into ten smaller identical samples. Each resembled the original version.

'Oh, my God! The virus split and multiplied into many variants. Far from dying, it actually replicated.' Agata looked aghast.

Peter moved his palm up and down. 'Don't worry. I'm sure my chemists will figure out a solution. You aren't the first in the world who's tried and failed at this.'

She gazed at the proliferating virus specimen and felt as low, helpless, and worthless as an amoeba on the ocean floor. 'I suppose there's a reason why I'm not pursuing my passion. I'm just not good enough.' She covered her face. 'I'm so sorry I let you down. I raised your hopes that we could solve this thing together. But we can't. We're too small.'

Peter's tone was filled with encouragement. 'You did an incredibly brave thing today. All of you. Without your help, I'd be dead today. I'm proud of you.'

Lavinia put her arm around her shoulders. 'My dear, you remind me so much of my daughter. She got down on herself when she didn't perform according to her expectations.'

Agata wiped her eyes. 'What did you tell her in those times?'

'The answer is around you. It's in each and every one of us. No one person can ever know it all.' The gypsy woman smiled kindly.

Agata looked puzzled. 'So, how do we find it? The right answer?'

'Ask the question that's most important to you. The one you're most afraid to ask. Ask it without bias.' Lavinia caressed her cheek.

Hmm! What is it that I really want to have answered? What am I most afraid to ask for fear of humiliation or condescension? How do I ask this question without bias? Right then, the conference room turned into her high school chemistry lab from a decade ago. Her teacher demonstrated a protein synthesis experiment showing how antibodies could be generated to relieve illnesses. Thirteen-year-old Agata politely raised her hand and then suggested a different approach. 'Why must we always produce chemicals for everything? Can't eucalyptus oil or some natural extract be used instead?'

Her classmates roared with laughter, her teacher looked at her with contempt. 'No self-respecting chemist ever uses natural products or methods derived from natural substances. Homeopathy, naturopathy, ayurveda. They are all scams. An affront to the pursuit of medicine, to chemistry. Don't you dare ever mention this topic at a scientific gathering. You'll be mocked and jeered out of the room.'

Agata looked resolute. 'Maybe my method will work. Maybe not. But what's stopping you from asking everyone for their ideas and views? Who knows? Perhaps a new approach will emerge from an open discussion.'

'It takes real scientists and experts to come up with viable approaches to scientific problems. Not . . . humph . . . amateurs . . . or school kids,' the teacher scoffed.

The environs of her high school lab morphed back into the conference room and she found herself staring at the mutating compound. *I've never questioned the established ways of doing things. I've never questioned the opinions of experts and authority figures. It's time to challenge these taboos.* She huddled the group. 'Have you guys ever used natural substances, extracts, or solutions to cure illnesses?'

Peter looked perplexed. 'That's quite unconventional from a scientific standpoint.'

'When the problem is unknown, why restrict our approach to just the known?' Determination was etched in the set of her jaw.

Lavinia raised a finger in the air. 'My daughter once suffered from a lung infection after ingesting coke from a coal mine. To heal her, I gave her a homegrown remedy: bat's saliva.' She took out a tiny bottle full of a white sticky substance.

'Eww! That's so gross.' The kids turned up their noses.

'This is an age-old recipe used by the Roma community to cure serious illnesses.' Lavinia scolded them gently.

Filip removed a bottle of vitamin C powder. 'Mom always gave me this to ward off the flu. It works like a charm.'

Not to be undone, Abbo obtained some eucalyptus tea from her bag. 'Whenever I catch a fever or a sore throat, Mom makes me take this.'

'All right, I think we have what we need.' Agata closed her eyes. *Am I challenging the right taboos?*

For the next ten minutes, Agata adjusted the constituents of her formula to include the new additives. Next, she performed the mRNA synthesis as before. Then, she added the fresh additives to the synthesized compound. The compound took on a silverish hue. She then added it to the lump of infected tissue. For a minute, the mucus hissed and split into a dozen parts. 'Oh God! It failed again.' Agata's heart sank.

Peter shrugged his shoulders. 'Oh, well! It was always a long shot. A hole-in-one sort of thing. Lightning in a bottle. Stuff like that never happens.'

Agata turned her back to the table and removed her coat. 'Come on guys, let's go. It's over.'

Lavinia, who was in front of her, pointed at the table. The faces of Abbo and Filip were bright with smiles. Agata turned around to see what they were looking at.

The mucus sample had stopped replicating. It had turned into lifeless, colourless white strands. 'It worked!' Agata put her hands on her cheeks and gazed at the substance in wonder.

Filip hugged her for the first time in years. 'You did it, sis. You did it. I knew you would. You saved the world.' His voice burst with affection.

Peter inspected the readings from the experiment. 'Good God! You've done it! It's lightning in a bottle after all.'

Lavinia removed the shawl she was wearing, and offered it to Agata. 'This belonged to my daughter. I had made it for her when she was young. It's her only article I could retain,' the gypsy woman told her in a voice choked with emotion.

Agata gazed at the gift in shock. She shook her head. 'Oh no! I can't accept that. It's the only thing you have to remember her.'

The old lady wrapped it around Agata's neck. 'She lives inside you.' She had the look of one who wouldn't take no for an answer.

Regeneration

That day, thanks to expedited security clearances, a helicopter, with personnel from the CDC, whisked them away to the US Air Force Base in Lakenheath. There, a military attaché from the Pentagon, received them. She handed the four special diplomatic passports from the US stamped with 'INDEFINITE LEAVE TO REMAIN'. 'Welcome to the United States. Under a special presidential decree, you've been awarded citizenships.' She gave them a royal salute.

Agata, Filip, and Lavinia beamed with joy. Abbo returned her passport. 'I must go back to my country. My father needs me.' Abbo gave each of them a warm hug. 'We're friends for life. I'll see y'all soon.'

After she left on a flight bound for Entebbe, the three immigrants boarded an Air Force jet with Peter Lundgren to Washington, DC. Peter pulled strings and got Agata included in his team at the CDC, where she led a team of scientists to develop a vaccine for the COVID-99 virus. Thanks to expedited, AI-enhanced clinical trials, the vaccine hit the worldwide market in two months. Thirty days later, the contagion was beaten hollow. Humanity regrouped and the world returned to normal.

A year later, Agata—wearing a sweatshirt branded 'GEORGETOWN UNIVERSITY, BIOMEDICAL RESEARCH FELLOWSHIP'—was on her phone. She waited for her lunch at a health food restaurant, Caravan, designed to look like a gypsy carriage. Her head shook from side-to-side like a viewer at a tennis match. 'Abbo, I can't believe it! You'll be in DC next month? On a one-year student exchange programme to Sidwell? That's Filip's school! This is destiny!' She couldn't contain her excitement.

Agata beamed when the caller produced the details of her upcoming trip. 'You must stay with us. We've got an amazing three-bedroom apartment on Wisconsin Ave, just five minutes away from the school. Fully paid for by my university.' The caller accepted her offer joyously, and promised to share further info at a later date.

Agata looked content and sipped a drink of chilled fig and grapefruit juice—flavoured with bat's saliva. Suddenly, Filip ran in. 'Hey, Filip. Guess who's staying with us starting next month?'

However, Filip's mind was somewhere else. Breathless, he slammed his backpack on the chair opposite to her and knocked a badge labelled 'SIDWELL FRIENDS SCHOOL' off the bag and onto the floor.

Agata gestured him to pipe down. 'Hey, buster. You're gonna hurt somebody.'

Filip took out a document from his bag and handed it to her. 'Mom's better. Her cancer's gone.' Joy wafted out from every pore of his body.

Agata perused the copy of her mother's latest oncology report and saw her mother's cancer had indeed receded. She embraced her brother. 'They did it. The doctors at MCMCC Private Hospital in Warsaw helped her.'

She gazed at her brother's happy face, and felt her heart bursting with happiness and love. *Is this really happening to me? Do I deserve this?* At that moment, a woman wearing a badge titled 'LAVINIA, PROPRIETOR', came over to Agata's table carrying her lunch. Agata smiled. She offered her a lamb drob sandwich stuffed with avocado and sundried tomatoes. Agata licked her lips. The gypsy entrepreneur looked at her with a mock expression of anger. 'You made the lightning in the bottle. Don't you ever forget that!'

REFLECTION: CHALLENGE YOUR TABOOS

Have you been stressed by your performance targets?

At different moments in our lives, we are often guided by conventional wisdom when we have to take important decisions. This tends to be an accumulation of things we've heard from different sources: the people around us, the media and various other information channels. This bank of information sits inside our heads and turns into a codebook guiding our actions. During times of crisis, when we really feel uncertain about what steps to take, we seek comfort in the universe of the known. Unfortunately, this feeling of comfort in conventional wisdom is just an illusion.

At any moment in life, a decision we must take is always dependent on a unique set of parameters. Granted that our situation may be similar to those of others, but our situation is always unique and demands an individualized approach to decision-making for the best resolution. Relying on conventional wisdom during these moments is a recipe for disaster.

The work sphere is a toxic breeding ground for conventional behaviour. It is here that we tend to internalize obsolete principles and practices, as if we were horses competing in a race against our co-workers. At the same time, we become infected with the notion that running in—and winning—this horse race is the be-all and end-all of life. As if there was no higher goal than this—it becomes the only thing we know to aim for.

This sort of homogenous, competitive mindset is viewed desirably by many leaders who want to instill a strong performance culture in their organizations but are reluctant to change themselves by becoming more open, just and humane. Therefore, organizations invariably perceive that a horse race between its employees is the best way to foster high performance, and so employees are conditioned to believe in and aspire for success within the parameters of this race. The tragic irony of the competitive workplace model is that only a tiny fraction of employees end up progressing. The majority is doomed to stagnation or dejection. Most employees become stressed and dissatisfied, and become disillusioned with their working life. This inner resentment against work tends to seep into their private lives, polluting their relationships and home environments.

In those moments of darkness, it is important for us to challenge the beliefs and principles we've held since the time we started that job. The biggest taboo enforced upon ourselves by our inner moral police is, 'I feel passionate about what I'm doing'. We must be brave and question this taboo, and ask ourselves honestly, 'Is my job my passion?' If the answer is no, we must go a step further and ask, 'Why am I not following my passion?' and 'How can I follow my passion?'

When you try to answer these questions, you will find the clarity you need to embark upon a journey of self-discovery—a journey that will open up new possibilities and new frontiers. A journey that will reveal to you for the first time in your life, what it is you are truly capable of. A journey that will help you become a happier person.

Be brave and embrace this journey.

The character in the story you've just read experienced acute frustration and anxiety to perform well at work. Understand how she overcame job stress, and you will believe that you can too.

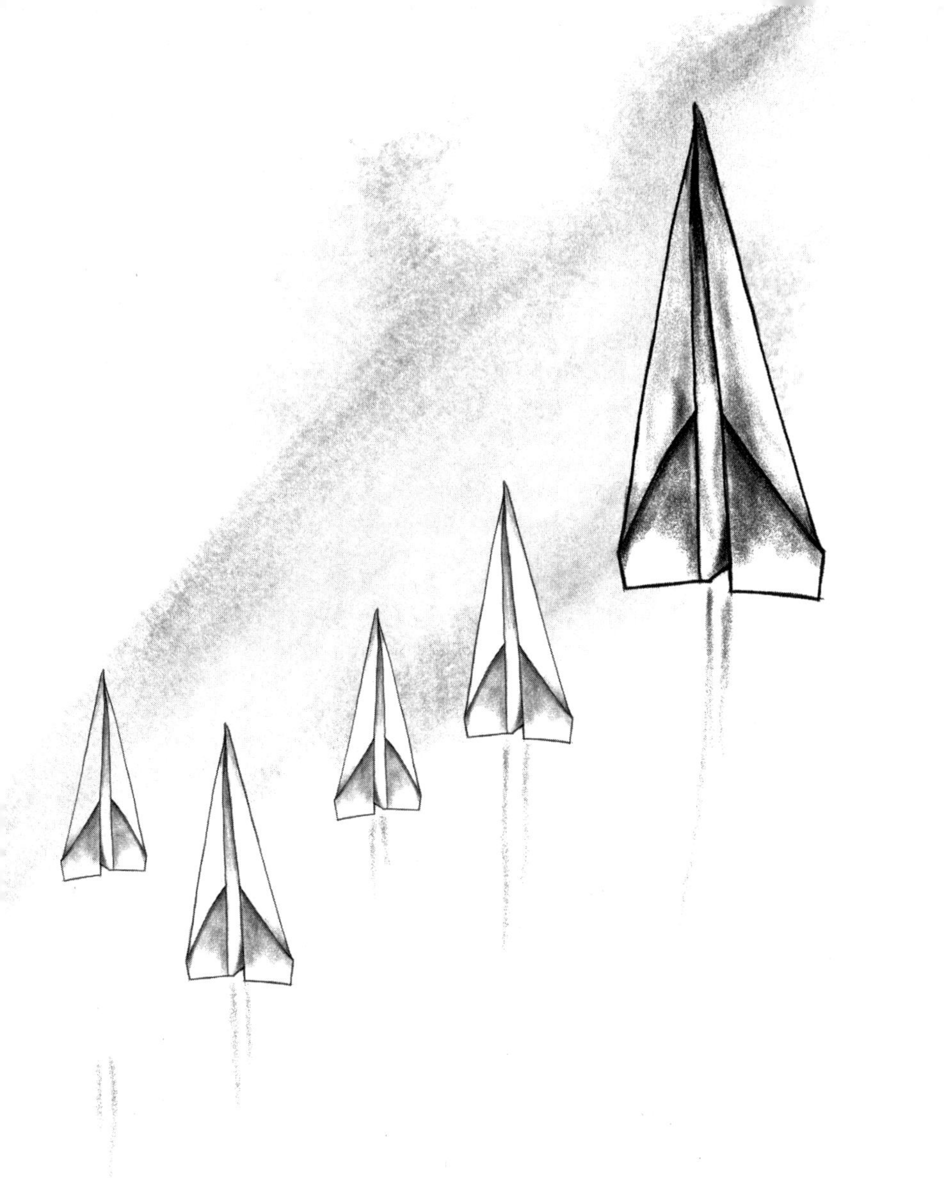

7

OVERCOMING COMPETITIVE PRESSURE

UNDERSTANDING COMPETITIVE PRESSURE

To progress in our education or career, it seems inevitable to have to compete with others. After all, plum jobs and admissions are highly sought-after in every corner of the world but are scant, making competition an inescapable reality of life. The belief that competition is good for society is deeply entrenched. Many pundits feel competition is healthy for the public because it drives people to perform and provides society with a method of identifying the most resourceful and talented. They argue that when these top talents are rewarded and nurtured, society progresses faster, benefitting from their innovation capacities. However, this rosy view of competition is tainted by its steep social costs. The pain inflicted upon the majority of the population far outweighs the benefits for a handful of winners.

Competitive pressure is experienced by a person when running in the race for wealth and power. This force compels an individual to strive for a singular outcome: victory at any cost. It conditions them to believe they will experience happiness only when that prize has been won. It colours their view of life as a death race; a state of existence in which everyone is either an enemy or an ally. When the participant races towards the finish line, they constantly see others forging ahead or setting traps to send them careening over the picket fences. So they're always suspicious, anxious or frustrated from having to constantly look out for themselves. They're never relaxed or at peace. If at the end of the race, they are anointed the winner, they set in motion plans to cement their position for good, blocking others wherever necessary. If the outcome is not to their liking, their self-belief wanes. Subsequently, they may plunge into deep depression.

Competitive pressure emerged due to a belief among social thinkers that not all human beings have the potential to excel, leading to a perception of limited talent within society. They feel that in this constrained environment, only those with the greatest potential to achieve should be nurtured. To ensure justice, though, the maximum number of people possible should be given a chance to qualify for a spot among the elite. Thus, competition is a sorting mechanism for identifying talent.

This Darwinian thinking has influenced organizations to treat competition as the primary driver of human progress. Fortunately for us, there's an escape from the cruel and endemic suffering brought upon us by competitive pressure. It is possible to free oneself from the chokehold of competition by changing one's cardinal life objective from acquiring material things to bettering oneself. The pursuit of one's passion is an example of such a high-minded life purpose. The experience of a person following their passion is very different from that of a person chasing wealth and power. A person coveting wealth and power derives happiness only from its acquisition. They find the process itself unsatisfying; a necessary evil. On the other hand, a person following their passion is focused on the growth of their inner self. They are bent on doing great work and forming partnerships towards that end. Thus, they experience happiness throughout the journey, not merely in fits and starts, and the outcome only enhances this feeling. Their potential for happiness is, therefore, greater because theirs is a journey of growth and self-discovery, not of attainment of material objects and social status.

The protagonist in this story faced great emotional hardship because of competitive pressure. Will he overcome this barrier?

REDEMPTION STATION

Asahi had applied to every undergraduate degree programme that provided a pathway to a desirable career. The problem was that he had no Plan B.

Asahi Saito was holding a stack of papers, waiting at the Hongo Sanchome station in Tokyo to board his homebound Tokyo Metro express, when a few drops of water fell from the ceiling onto the stack of documents made from the cheapest and worst-quality newsprint in existence. He looked up and noticed a prominent hole in the ceiling right above the place where he was standing. He glanced at the hundreds of commuters around him who were all waiting to board the evening train to Shinkoiwa and saw that they weren't affected.

'Are these tears or curses raining down on me?' he asked the Almighty with a grimace. He leafed through the ten wet pages, each bearing the logo of a different college and an identical headline: 'Undergraduate Engineering Admission Results 2020'. He looked at the wet spot that had formed on the paper from the University of Tokyo. It had fallen right on the word *Declined.* A tear rolled down his cheek and landed on the same spot—doubly drenching the sheet.

The station grew abuzz with the announcement that the train would arrive in one minute. 'Eleven colleges. Eleven entrance exams. Eleven failures.'

Asahi counted the misses and ran out of fingers. His ruminations were interrupted by a beggar without legs, his head shaven. He wore the robe of a Buddhist monk. He wheeled up to Asahi on a skateboard and begged for some change. Asahi threw a bunch of coins towards him and shooed him away.

'It's over for me.' He shook his head. 'This is the end of my engineering career. I can't afford to spend another year at the tutorial institute for a second shot at the exams.' He watched the paraplegic panhandler wheel his torso towards another commuter. Asahi wallowed in his misery. 'At least now, I can feel sorry for him. At least now, I can understand what he must be facing every day. No prospects. No hope. No respect.'

At that moment, the deafening roar of the incoming express interrupted his thoughts; a gust of wind slapped his face, and flicked several pebbles from the rail tracks on his backpack. 'No future.' He looked glumly at the graffiti on the opposite wall of the platform showing a dragon swallowing the sun. The bullet train charged towards the platform. He closed his eyes and hurled himself in front of it.

For a moment, there was darkness and complete silence. The quietude was broken by the screeching noise of a train trying to halt in its tracks. The sound that calibrated in volume from a sharp click to the deafening crescendo of a malfunctioning trumpet. Then, a force, similar to the kick from a heavy boot, hit him hard in the solar plexus and sent him flying through the tunnel.

'Help! What's happening?' he screamed, unable to see anything. There was no response. He continued to fly backwards, the loud noise gradually receded, and a faint light appeared in the vicinity. Asahi could see the edges of the platforms on either side and the shadowy outlines of people standing nearby. The light got brighter.

He stopped suddenly and felt himself being lifted, then rotated in mid-air like an astronaut in a zero-gravity space shuttle. 'Help! I'm falling!' he screamed as he felt himself hurtling down from a great height.

The next instant, he felt himself standing on a hard floor. Through the limited radiance, Asahi could see the faint outline of a train motionless in front of him and commuters standing all around. *Where am I?* The brightness of the light increased steadily. His question was answered shortly afterwards when the surrounding illumination was restored to the same level of brightness as before his suicidal jump.

He saw the train in vivid detail. His eyes grew wide with shock. 'I'm still on the platform.' The rush hour passengers were still there. 'Are these the same passengers?' He peered at them. Suddenly, he saw an empty skateboard about 150 feet in the distance. It rolled away and disappeared into a corridor on the far right. He sighed with relief. *That object is the property of the homeless man whom I just encountered. I'm still alive. I can't believe that I actually thought of killing myself.*

He was about to enter the train, when he noticed that the door wouldn't open. He banged on it. 'Open up. We're getting late.' There was no response. The door remained shut. Asahi turned around and voiced his frustration to an elderly woman with a walking stick. 'Another electronic malfunction during rush hour. That's three times this month. Unbelievable, isn't it?' Strangely, the woman did not react to his annoyed remark. Instead, she stood like a rock, gazing at something on her right.

Hmm! What's she looking at?

It seemed to him that she was staring at something near the front of the train, about sixty feet away. He walked slowly in that direction. He noticed, all the commuters were either peering at the same object or pointing at it. *Why is everyone like wax statues? What are they seeing?* A few yards before he reached the front of the train, his attention was captured by a ten-year-old boy whose eyes were wide with terror. His mouth was open as if he was screaming with shock and horror. His fingers were pointing at something in front of the engine.

'What's wrong? What are you . . . what's everyone staring at?' Asahi asked the question like a broken record, only to be greeted by silence from the petrified boy.

Asahi scratched his head and went to the front of the engine. Suddenly, a drop of water fell on his face. He looked up, and saw a leaking hole in the ceiling. *It's the same spot where I stood waiting for the train.* Right then, a heavy gust of wind blew through the tunnel, running a cold finger down his spine. 'Brr! What is that?' he asked, baffled, and then noticed a sheet of paper blowing in the breeze just above the roof of the train.

Curious, he jumped to grab it. However, the sheet eluded his grasp and blew away towards the locomotive until it unexpectedly stood still in the air, just in front of the engine in a state of suspended animation. 'What the hell?' he yelled in surprise. He positioned himself to leap and grab it, but stopped. His jaw dropped with astonishment and horror. A man was horizontally suspended in front of the train, right below the paper. It was him.

'Aaah! What's happening?'

'That's a gruesome way to die,' stated a gentle, masculine voice from the unknown.

'Who's that?' Asahi jumped and looked around for the speaker. But all he saw were dozens of mortified bystanders frozen in place. Everyone stared at his doppelganger suspended in front of the train.

He heard a *swoosh!* as somebody jumped from the opposite platform, grabbed the paper floating right above his suspended body, and landed next to him like a long jumper. Asahi's eyes became golf balls. 'It's you. Whatever happened to you?' It was the Buddhist monk to whom he'd donated spare change just a couple of minutes ago. Only this time, the monk had legs.

While the passersby remained mute bystanders to this surreal event, Asahi repeated his questions with desperation. 'Who are you? What's happening to me? Why are people frozen in their places? How can you walk?' His voice was frantic.

The monk handed him the paper. He was in his late thirties, about five feet three inches tall, and wearing a black robe with a yellow shawl wrapped around his right shoulder. 'Your questions will be answered in due course. But first, you need to understand why you are here. This is why.'

Puzzled, Asahi looked at the piece of paper. 'What is this, hmm? My admission result from the University of Tokyo! What does this mean?' he muttered, totally bamboozled.

The monk placed a hand on his shoulder. 'I'm sorry for your pain. You just killed yourself because you were filled with grief and disappointment over your competitive examination results.'

Asahi's head jerked backwards. 'Dead? You mean, I'm really dead?'

The monk pointed to the suspended body right in front of the locomotive. 'This is the point of impact. The moment just before that train smashed your body into pieces.'

The monk pointed to the crowd. 'You see the bystanders out here? They are all beside themselves with shock.'

Asahi glanced at the commuters and saw the monk was right.

The monk laughed and landed a friendly slap on Asahi's back. 'Hopefully, there won't be any heart attacks from the trauma.'

Asahi tried to wrap his mind around the supernatural facts. Suddenly, he felt the weight of his backpack. 'Wait a minute!' he beckoned and emptied the rucksack on the floor.

The monk spotted five heavy engineering textbooks and a dozen competitive examination guides. 'Goodness me! You really had a lot riding on these admissions.'

Asahi's voice grew defiant. 'If I'm dead, then how come my backpack is as heavy as before?'

'You may be dead, but the pressures of your previous life have followed you here,' the monk answered with a smile.

'If I'm dead, then how come I don't see a mountain of jewels and cash? How come I'm not holed up in a cozy arcade with an unlimited supply of video games?' Asahi's voice was filled with skepticism. 'How come I'm not in a sexy lounge, waited on by beautiful women? Or,' he pointed to a billboard on the wall next to him featuring an upcoming movie about a wrongfully incarcerated man, 'how come I'm not locked up in a jail being tortured and sodomized by my fellow inmates?'

The monk gazed at the poster of a man drenched in blood and trapped in a burning cell, a quarter-smile on his lips.

'If I'm dead, then how come I'm neither in Heaven nor Hell?'

The monk laughed and patted the young man's back. 'Hahaha! Is that your concept of death? Your imagination's really limited!'

'Huh?'

The monk gave his arm a reassuring squeeze. 'Relax. This is neither Heaven nor Hell. Just the afterlife. Here, there are no extremes like what you describe. No handouts or gifts. No penalties for sins. There's only one role that a person must fulfill out here. One task that he must complete.'

'What is that?'

He pointed to Asahi's stack of books, admission forms and competitive exam guides. 'Change yourself. Here, you have eternity to work on yourself . . . on your issues. Here, you have all the time in the world to dig deep . . . to identify and overcome the barrier that held you back, that stopped you from progressing in life. That compelled you to kill yourself.'

With a frown on his forehead, Asahi waved his hands towards his sides. 'Why? It's not like that will help me repair my previous life.'

The monk stared at the ceiling and finally pointed. 'You see that hole up there? It's leaking in the same way as before.'

Asahi looked up, saw the leaking hole and nodded.

The monk pointed at the people assembled around them. 'The folks you see out here? Their faces frozen with shock and distress? This platform frozen in a moment of indescribable pain, grief and horror?'

Asahi nodded again.

'This moment in time right before your deadly impact will become your reality for eons to come. This station, with its leaking roof . . . its frozen, horrified crowd . . . will be the only thing you will see or experience. Would you like to suffer this fate for eternity?'

Asahi watched the roof dripping incessantly. *I would prefer to fail my exams infinite times than to bear that dreadful drip, drip sound even for one night.* He shook his head and said emphatically, 'No. I can't imagine a fate worse than the suspension of this moment in time.'

'If you want to change your world, you must change yourself.'

Asahi looked irritated. 'Can you stop talking mumbo jumbo?'

The monk pointed first to the ceiling and then to the surrounding crowd. 'If you want to be free from this moment in time . . . if you want to escape this station . . . if you want to stop the leaking of that ceiling . . . if you want the crowds to move freely once again, you must overcome your barrier.'

Asahi rubbed his chin. *Hmm! He's right. There's no state of existence worse than being stuck here for eternity. That would be a living death. I suppose I must do what he says. What do I have to lose?* He looked at the monk inquiringly. 'If I do as you say, what will happen to me?'

'You should not ask what will happen to me. You should ask, "What will I make happen?"' Asahi gave him a confounded look, but the monk tapped his shoulder and walked towards the subway exit. 'Come with me if you want to find out who you really are.'

Asahi reached the flight of stairs and placed his front foot on the first step. He banged his head against a wall that emerged out of thin air, replacing the steps. 'Ow! What the hell! Where did the stairs go?' He rubbed his head.

'Hahaha! That's the stairway to the financial district. You don't want to go there. There are hundreds of bodies floating in the air.'

'Huh! What do you mean?'

The monk threw a devious wink. 'Jumpers from high-rises after last week's financial market meltdown,' he whispered.

'You've got a warped sense of humour, you know!' Asahi chided.

The monk parted his hands, and a corridor materialized in front of him; out of nowhere, a skateboard appeared.

Asahi looked surprised by its appearance. 'Hey! Isn't this the same one you were using at the station? And, anyway, you never told me how you got back your mobility.'

The monk balanced himself like an extreme sports specialist on the board. 'I'll tell you once we reach our destination. Now, get behind me and hold on tight.'

The skateboard revved up, Asahi struggled to find his balance and grabbed the monk's torso for dear life. 'Whoa! This is dangerous! Where are we going?'

The monk turned around. 'Redemption City.'

'There's no place like that.' Asahi shook his head.

The skateboard accelerated to 100 miles per hour, the monk shouted, 'Bunkyo. The place where you just came from.'

'Whoa! Slow down, buddy. This is way too rough.' The skateboard travelled ten times faster than the most extreme rollercoaster causing Asahi's heart to do a nosedive towards his gut.

'Relax. Go with the flow. You'll get used to the speed.' The monk's voice was as calm as a YouTube meditation guide's.

Asahi took a deep breath. He closed his eyes and pictured himself as an eight-year-old riding with his father on the Fujiyama roller coaster at the Fuji-Q Highland amusement park. He recalled that moment right before he plunged 250 feet down. *An excruciating sensation of terror ran through my body. Then, in an instant, that feeling transformed into unimaginable exhilaration. It was the most terrifying moment of my life. It was the most exhilarating experience of my life.* He opened his eyes and saw the corridor of the subway station flickering with fluorescent neon lights. The walls glowed with images of Tokyo's buildings . . . images that kept morphing from one era to another. Then, his terror changed to excitement, as it had done years ago on the rollercoaster. He removed his hands from the monk's chest, stretched them out and yelled, 'This is amazing!'

The monk chuckled. 'I told you, there's nothing to fear.'

They travelled for what felt like five minutes, then the skateboard stopped abruptly. The lights faded and were replaced by the glare of the midday sun. Asahi saw they were standing at the mouth of a major intersection in Bunkyo—home to the Tokyo Dome stadium—just outside the Hongo Sanchome station. He spotted the University of Tokyo museum about 300 feet ahead. 'Hey! I was right here ten minutes ago, just outside the station. Why didn't we take the exit like normal people instead of surfing on this weird device?' He looked down on the pavement searching for the skateboard, and was befuddled to discover that it had disappeared.

The monk noted his confusion. 'The board appears when we really need it. Right now, we don't.'

Asahi looked around the busy junction at the hordes of students and office workers pouring into the streets from various offices and campuses and thronging the food trucks and restaurants that dotted the neighbourhood. A massive traffic jam blocked the road in front of him and effectively sealed off all the cross streets. He spotted a huge electronic ticker running around the Softbank office building located on the opposite side of the road. Asahi put his hand above his eyes and peered at it. 'It says 12.30 p.m., Monday, 20 January 2020. That was earlier today.'

A twinkle appeared in the monk's eye. 'Now you know why we couldn't just take the stairs.'

The two crossed the road—squeezing past the vehicles. Asahi noticed the passersby looking right through him. *Am I a ghost?* He raised his arm to attract a police officer's attention. The officer didn't heed Asahi's signal and continued to direct traffic with a blaring whistle. A cavalier thought flashed in Asahi's head. *If I'm a ghost, I could probably walk through objects and people like a superhero. Let's check out if I've acquired superpowers*, and he stepped in front of a taxi. As expected, the driver didn't notice him and forged ahead, passing through him. However, instead of being impervious to the taxi's force like an invisible object, Asahi found himself lying on the road, squirming with pain . . . his legs crushed. 'I thought no one could see me out here,' he screamed.

The monk quickly pulled Asahi's body to the sidewalk before it was turned into ramen noodles by an oncoming truck. He ticked him off with his finger. 'Just because they can't see you, that doesn't mean they can't inflict pain. Remember, you felt that drop of water at the station.'

Asahi howled in pain. 'Oh God! How could I be so stupid? Now we've got to go to the hospital.'

The monk shook his head. 'Definitely not. Medical science can't help you here.'

Asahi held his fractured knees and winced in agony. 'Oh God! Then, what am I gonna do?'

The monk stretched out his hand towards the scorching sun. He spread his palm as if to grab something. A tiny hemisphere of light formed in his hand. The ball expanded until it became as large as a tennis ball. 'Open your mouth.' He placed his hand under Asahi's jaw like a doctor.

The luminous sphere entered his mouth. A spark of energy ran through his body and a pleasant tingling sensation seared past his legs. In a few moments, the pain melted away.

The monk offered his hand, to get up. Asahi stood up and moved his legs forwards, backwards and sideways. He found he could walk normally again. 'It's a miracle. I'm healed.'

'Heroes are made, not born. Don't try that again.'

The two walked ahead for a bit past the Softbank building. Asahi asked where they were going. The monk did not answer. He stood in front of the window of a fast casual restaurant serving Izakaya cuisine and gazed at the people dining inside. The restaurant was chock-a-block full of students grabbing a bite for lunch.

'Why are we stopping here?'

The monk continued to stare at the feasting crowd.

'Who are you looking at? Oh my God!' Asahi noticed two students sitting in a booth at the rear of the restaurant. 'It's Mako,' he shouted. He pointed to a woman who appeared to be about eighteen, slim and petite with olive skin and Eurasian features, and wearing a blue dress. She was sitting at a dining table with a slightly older young man who wore black metallic glasses and a business suit. The monk placed a finger on his lips and pointed towards the hostess, who was about to escort another young man towards the booth occupied by Mako and her companion.

Asahi noticed the man's bowl-cut hairstyle matched his own. *Who's he? He looks so familiar.* He peered through the window to get a closer look at the person's clothing. He was wearing a T-shirt etched with images of zombies rising from the graves. It was painted with the slogan 'Return of the Undead'. He checked out his own T-shirt, and jumped three feet vertically. 'Oh my God! I was here today. That's my T-shirt. That's me.'

The monk nodded his head in agreement.

For a minute, Asahi's alter ego stood transfixed. The doppelganger stared at Mako and her partner, ignoring the hostess's request to go to their table or to a separate one. He pursed his lips in anger and pushed the menu the hostess had offered him to the floor. The woman looked nonplussed and asked him something. But Asahi's alter ego stormed out of the restaurant and headed towards a park on the other side of the eatery.

The monk watched the departing young man sympathetically. 'You were here this afternoon. Everything happened just as we saw, right?'

Asahi confirmed with a nod. 'Yes. That's exactly how it happened. Now can we please figure out my barrier and take the skateboard back to the station? I'm in no mood right now to relive this moment.' His face was forlorn.

The monk squeezed his arm. 'It's important you understand why you felt so angry and humiliated.'

'Why? It's obvious. I was jilted. Now, let's go.'

'Come with me. Sometimes it's easier to rediscover a lost path by starting from the latest clue.' The monk walked towards the park, indicating Asahi should follow him.

The alternate Asahi sat on a bench. A cherry tree in full blossom stood in front of him. He stared at a squirrel sniffing an acorn at the base of the tree. Then, he took out a packet of nuts from his pocket and threw a few at the creature. He sighed ruefully and muttered aloud, 'I suppose it's too good to be true. A girl like Mako—an accomplished musician, star scholar, and committed social volunteer; not to mention beautiful and kind—what was I thinking when I asked her out on a date today? She's the daughter of an acclaimed author. Someone my parents and my friends would accept with open arms.'

He paused momentarily and looked down despondently. Meanwhile, the squirrel munched the peanuts heartily and directed a curious stare at its benefactor.

'It would take a special person to match up to her standards. Someone like Shujo. Another topper at my high school. Won a national award for "The Best Young Entrepreneur". The son of the CEO of Japan's leading industrial conglomerate. Did I actually believe she'd take me seriously? Did I actually believe she'd love me for myself? An ordinary guy without any significant accomplishments? I guess I was deluding myself all along.'

Asahi observed this bitter monologue by his alt self, and his face turned red. 'Come on. Let's get out of here. There's no point listening to this gut-churning drivel.'

The monk raised his palm. 'You must see what's going on in your mind. It's important you understand the feelings you've buried. Only by unblocking them will you be able to discover who you really are.'

'How can I see what's going on in my head?'

The monk glanced at the squirrel. 'You've developed a bond with that little creature. In your mind, you were having a conversation with it. Let's see how it played out in your consciousness.'

The monk pointed at the squirrel. Immediately, his thumb glowed. Then he touched the squirrel's head with the incandescent thumb. Instantly, the monk disappeared. The squirrel grew in size until it became as big as a bear. Asahi stumbled and nearly fell over a branch.

The squirrel placed a finger on its lips. 'Don't worry. This is what you saw earlier today.'

Asahi looked at the visitors in the park to ascertain if anybody had witnessed this strange event. Nobody looked at his alt self or the squirrel. Nobody saw it transform into a talking squirrelzilla. To his surprise, his alternate self smiled upon seeing the monster.

The monstrous rodent gave Alt Asahi a high-five and said empathetically, 'Girl trouble, right? I see it all the time here. Been through it a few times myself. But I always came out stronger in the end. You'll be fine too.'

Alt Asahi shook his head in dejection. 'I'll never get over Mako. She means everything to me.'

The squirrel placed its furry arm around his shoulder. 'Show me what she means to you.'

At that moment, Asahi's alternate self froze in his place. The squirrel placed a finger on his head, and four images appeared in the air. Each one was an animated image of Asahi at a different age.

'How did you do that? What are these?' asked a bemused Asahi.

The squirrel smiled. 'I'm tapping into your memories so you can assess your past actions. Each image is a gateway to a specific moment in your life. Each image is an access point to an incident that shaped your consciousness forever. Would you like to know more?'

Asahi felt intrigued. *Did something in my childhood influence my present dissatisfaction with life? I suppose there's no harm in finding out.* The creature tapped the first image with its six-inch-long claw, thc park disappeared and turned into a school classroom.

The bell rang, marking the end of the session. An eight-year-old girl with Eurasian features was about to pack her bags when she was approached by a boy of similar age. He handed her a T-shirt painted with superhero butterflies fighting an army of winged predators. His face brightened with a smile. 'Happy birthday, Mako. I made this for you.'

Her eyes lit up with surprise and joy. She hugged him. 'Thank you, Asahi. I'll be so happy if you attend my birthday party on Saturday.'

'I'd love to.' Asahi's smile could have been featured in a Colgate commercial.

Mako proceeded towards the exit. She turned around and waved. 'I'll bring an invitation card for you tomorrow.'

The boy looked at his reflection in the mirror on the door and smiled in satisfaction, the room changed once more, this time into a sprawling tatami living room.

A Japanese man in his early forties sat on a cushion at a low table, drinking tea. He was wearing a kimono paired with jeans. A heavyset Caucasian woman in her thirties, who wore a white dress with floral patterns, sat opposite him. She showed him the same T-shirt and smiled. 'Akihito, that boy in Mako's class, Asahi, is so sweet! He simply adores her, and he made this all by himself. I know we didn't include him in the guest list. But don't you think we should invite him and his parents to express our appreciation?' Her voice had a distinct French accent.

The man waved his left hand dismissively and scoffed, 'Humph! Asahi Saito? I know his family. His father's a line cook at a cheap diner. He's never held a steady job his entire life. His mother's a tailor at a local laundromat.'

The woman looked puzzled. 'Why does his family background matter?'

Akihito furrowed his eyebrows. 'Celine, don't be stupid. Who do you think will be at the party? CEOs. Politicians. Celebrities from art and entertainment. These are the people that Mako should befriend . . . not scum off the streets.' His words prickled with irritation.

Celine looked down despondently at the thirteenth-century tatami rug from the Muromachi era, Akihito grabbed the T-shirt and headed towards a sliding door. As he was about to leave the room, he dumped the T-shirt in a trashcan and shook his finger at the woman. 'Don't ever think of sending him a card.'

Asahi discovered he'd been cruelly ostracized. 'Stop! I don't want to listen anymore.'

The squirrel raised his paw and made the characters in this strange memory play freeze in their places.

'I had a feeling about this. But I never knew for sure. Mako's parents were always so polite and discreet. Now, I know they never accepted me. They manipulated Mako to stay away from me.' His voice resonated with sharp outrage.

'It looks like her father felt that way about you.' The squirrel nodded his head and removed a book from an extensive rack and showed the cover to Asahi; it read *The Parasites of Kyoto* by Akihito Morimoto. 'He may be a bestselling author known for his progressive stance on social issues. But in his heart of hearts, he doesn't believe in his own causes.'

The events smashed around in Asahi's head and formed a ghoulish Bento box. Suddenly, the room transformed once more into the classroom.

The students had assembled, and the class was set to start. The teacher spoke to the principal outside the room. During the hiatus, Mako approached Asahi, who was sketching a graphic image of a woman with a lightning rod and straddling a shark. He was so engrossed in his cartoon that he didn't notice the girl. He was jolted out from his imaginary world by a forlorn voice. 'I'm sorry, Asahi. But Mom said we've run out of invitation cards. As the party will be attended by many high-profile dignitaries, every invitee must have one. She said we'll keep you in mind for next year's party.'

With a look of disappointment, the young boy stuttered, 'Oh . . . okay, Mako. I hope you'll wear my T-shirt, though.'

The room disappeared and morphed back into the park, Asahi faced the squirrel, who sat next to his frozen self. 'She never invited me to any of her parties.'

The squirrel nodded its head with a mournful look. 'I know.'

A tear ran down Asahi's cheek. 'And she never, ever wore my T-shirt.'

'You now know you didn't do anything wrong. You didn't do anything to upset her. But can you recall how you dealt with those disappointments?'

The young man took a seat on the bench next to the squirrel and shook his head slowly. 'I really don't care anymore.'

'If you don't deal with the pain, the rejection and humiliation will fester inside you forever and make it impossible for you to change yourself,' the rodent encouraged him.

Asahi blew his nose. 'Okay. Show me how I reacted to her rejection.'

The second image, which floated above the frozen Asahi's head, turned into a school auditorium when the squirrel tapped it. Kids, parents, and friends were packed into the building, and 100 unformed children aged twelve and thirteen sat in the first ten rows. They listened in rapt attention to the speech by a bald, slender man in his fifties with a thin moustache.

'Welcome to the annual sixth-grade prize distribution ceremony at the Nishimachi International School. Today, we'll award the most exceptional performers in six streams of learning: the arts, mathematics, science, humanities, literature and sports. In my ten years as principal at this school, I've never seen a more talented and committed group of students. It gives me great hope that our school will someday be known as the birthplace of legends.'

He threw his arms in front of him like a conductor at the start of an orchestra.

'Now, it gives me great pleasure to announce the six champions of 2014. Mako Mirimoto, Shujo Watanabe, Seiko Yamaguchi, Yukiko Ishihara, Takuya Nakayami and Nozomi Fukada. Please step on stage to receive your awards.' He gestured a group of students seated in the front row to come on stage.

The six winners congregated on stage to receive their medals, accompanied by loud claps and cheers from the audience of a thousand parents and well-wishers. Asahi was standing in the front row. He whispered to his mother with breathless excitement. 'That's Mako. She's the first female gold medallist in science. Isn't that amazing?'

His mom nodded appreciatively and looked to her right. The man standing next to her looked like a well-known literary figure. She smiled and bowed her head deferentially. The man returned her smile with a condescending sneer, and placed his mouth close to the ears of a Caucasian woman standing next to him. 'That's the trash I told you about. Make sure you stay ten feet away from them.'

The next hour was devoted to mandatory speeches. Right after, Asahi, along with a hundred school friends, rushed on stage to congratulate the winners and take group pictures on their phones. He carried a bouquet of cherry blossoms and approached his love. 'I'm so happy for you, Mako! It feels like I've won tonight.'

Mako threw him a smile that melted his bones. 'Thank you. I've worked so hard for this award. I know there were many contenders. All I can say is . . . I'm really lucky.'

Asahi handed her the flowers. 'I bought these at the flower market today. The last cherry blossoms of the year. I was hoping we could hang out tonight and celebrate your victory.'

She was about to respond when a tall, bespectacled, twelve-year-old boy wearing a gold medal inscribed with the words 'MATHEMATICS CHAMPION' interrupted them. 'Hey, Mako! Aren't you joining us for celebrations at my place tonight?'

She turned around and replied with a tone of great excitement. 'Of course, Shujo. Let's go now.' She left Asahi in the lurch, holding the wreath of flowers, and departed hand-in-hand with her fellow gold medallist.

Right then, the stage turned into a bedroom filled with posters from manga such as *Akira* and *Full Metal Alchemist*. Young Asahi was curled up on his bed, sobbing. 'Why doesn't she like me? Why?'

The bedroom door opened, and a man walked in. He wore the greasy apron of a line cook. He noticed the boy in tears and rushed towards him. 'What's the matter, Asahi?'

The kid turned over to the other side. 'Dad, Mako doesn't like me. No one in school likes me. I don't know what I have to do to be accepted by them.'

Father hugged the kid, and stroked his cheeks. 'Asahi, you're a good boy. You've done nothing wrong.'

Asahi gazed at him with penetrating, grief-stricken eyes. 'What must I do to be seen?'

The cook ran his fingers lovingly through his son's hair. 'Let me tell you something about this world. I know you won't like it. But the world of Mako, Shujo and your peers isn't the one we inhabit.' His voice was sanguine.

'What do you mean, Dad?'

He took out an old photograph of himself posing with Asahi's mother and an elderly couple in the garden of a huge estate. 'Fifteen years ago, your mom and I worked for a very wealthy couple—the Fujimotos. I was their household cook. Your mom was the housekeeper. They were very fond of us and provided us with many benefits. However, during a foreign trip, they got sick and became bedridden for a year. During the convalescence, they realized they were terminally ill. To ensure we were financially secure after their deaths, they bought this apartment for us. But their most precious gifts weren't material objects. They were contacts. Contacts to jobs and schools. Through their contacts at a reputable labor agency, your mom and I landed full-time jobs. Through hard work, we achieved a modicum of financial stability. But their most special gift was a contact to the prestigious Nishimachi International School, an academy that normally accepts only the elites of Japan.'

He paused for a moment and returned the photo into his wallet. 'You see, Asahi, we aren't supposed to belong to their world. All these parents . . . their kids . . . they know who we are. They know where we come from. Secretly, they snigger behind our backs. They pretend to get along with us. They pretend to respect us. But deep inside, they see us as leeches feeding off their entitlement.'

'Dad, Mako isn't like that!'

Father kissed his face. 'I'm sure she's a very nice person. However, it's likely she's been conditioned to believe in the inherent superiority of her social class. It's not entirely hopeless, though. There's still a way for you to belong to their world.'

Asahi's eyes gleamed with hope. 'How can I belong to their world? How can I make Mako love me?'

Father gazed at him with a somber expression. 'You can't make someone love you. But you can earn their respect.' He brought his face close to the kid. 'You have to play by their rules. That's how I worked my way up from an assistant at a food cart to a second-line cook at a mid-range restaurant.'

'What rules must I play by?' Asahi looked puzzled.

His father held his hands and looked deep into his eyes. 'Academics. That's the world you must live in. Academic performance. It's the only thing your school community and the larger society value. You must get good grades in school. You must ace the college entrance exams. Only then can you attend an elite institution like the University of Tokyo. This is your only ticket to a good job. Your only ticket to financial security. Your only ticket to social respectability. You must earn this ticket. If you do that, only then will these people accept you.'

'Mako. Shujo. All their friends. They're really good at academics. I'm nowhere close to them. I need to up my level.' Asahi nodded with a sense of sobering realization.

Father opened a scrapbook next to his bed and wore a sanguine smile. 'I admire your will to succeed. But there can be no change without sacrifice. You must give up your pursuit of graphic art.'

'Why? I love to draw. I'm so good at it.'

'You're right. Your sketches are great. But manga art isn't taught at your school. Manga isn't recognized by employers at leading corporations. Manga won't help you crack competitive exams. Manga won't help you earn the respect of your peers. You must not waste your life on things that will get you nowhere.'

Asahi looked at his scrapbook with a forlorn expression. Father closed its pages. 'I wish I'd gone to a good school and then attended a good college. I could have made a better life for you and your mother. I could have earned a decent wage instead of begging my boss for a 5 per cent raise every year and settling for 1.5 per cent. I could have worked a decent schedule and spent more time with you. Instead, I spent my whole life working long hours with no overtime pay, no medical insurance, no benefits.' He wiped some sweat off his brow, which had formed because of the oppressive humidity and lack of air conditioning. 'No social respect. I wish I'd never been a cook.'

Asahi looked shocked. 'But Dad, I thought you loved to cook. Don't you feel happy when you do it?'

'I don't know what I feel anymore.' His father's voice was full of bitterness. 'Is it possible to find joy in doing something when the returns are hogged by someone else? Every day, I just bide my time until I can leave. You asked me if I am following my passion. The answer is, it doesn't matter. Because passion doesn't pay for zilch. It never will.'

He wished Asahi goodnight and left the bedroom, the boy dumped his scrapbook in the bottom of the bottom drawer of his bedside cabinet filled with old toys and useless memorabilia. 'From today, I'll be what they want me to be. An academic superstar. I won't rest until I crack the competitive exams and get into a top college. Perhaps then, she'll love me. Perhaps then they'll all love me.'

The bedroom morphed back to the park. The squirrel gazed at him sympathetically. 'So you see, you believed you needed to excel in academics to move up in life. You gave up your passion to pursue a life others wanted you to lead. Not one that you wanted to live.'

Asahi shrugged. 'So what? Everyone does the same thing. How else can I progress?'

The squirrel tapped on the third image. 'Let's see how your decision to follow the herd worked out for you.'

This time, the greenery changed into the school lobby. A gathering of fifteen-year-old students had formed by the announcement board located outside the principal's office. Several sheets of paper titled 'TENTH GRADE FINAL EXAMS' containing the names and scores of students were stapled to the bulletin board. Asahi and Mako were at the back of the group, peering over a sea of heads to view their results. Fifteen-year-old Asahi looked at her bullishly. 'Mako, I'm very confident of doing well this time. I studied so hard.'

Mako stood on tiptoes to check out her scores. 'I don't think I did well. I messed up a few questions.' Her voice was infused with anxiety.

'I'm sure you did fine. You always do. But, if we both do well, promise me that this time, we'll hang out and celebrate?'

'Of course, Asahi.'

At that moment, a young woman in the front row screamed with joy. She turned around, spotted Mako and flung her arms in the air. 'Mako, I got 92 per cent. That's way more than I'd hoped for. And you got 95 per cent. Congratulations! You're top of the class!'

Mako cupped her face in shock. 'No way!' She pushed through the crowd to reach the front row. Mako verified the results, and shrieked, 'Oh my God! I could never have imagined this.'

The two women jumped, hugged each other and produced whoops of joy. 'Let's go to the Peninsula Hotel right now and celebrate at the bar. My dad's college friend is the president. He won't mind that we're underage.'

The two girls ganged up with several high performers and ran excitedly towards a Maserati GranTurismo parked outside the school gate, Asahi shouted, 'Congratulations, Mako.'

His words were drowned out by the cacophony of the assembled students. When he managed to reach the front of the line, he looked for his name on the six lists printed with the results of 2,000 students. He noticed he had been listed on the third sheet—where candidates ranked from 200–350 out of 2000—were featured. *This can't be. I studied so hard. I expected so much more.* His face fell in shock. He checked out his scores in various exams, placed his hands on his head and sighed with disappointment. *Oh, my God! Not again! I got 90 per cent in all my subjects except for math and science. In both these tests, I scored a pitiful 50 per cent.* He looked up at the ceiling in despair. 'Why do I keep underperforming despite my best efforts?'

Right then, the school lobby changed into a small dining room of a flat. He sat with his mom and dad at the table, sipping despondently from a bowl of chicken noodle soup.

'What's the matter?' his father asked. 'You look upset.'

Asahi lifted his head, which was almost buried inside the bowl. 'The tenth-grade results just came in. I got 73 per cent.'

Mother flashed a beaming smile. 'That's wonderful. I'm so proud of you.'

Asahi threw the bowl of noodles against the fridge. An angry vein popped from his neck. 'Are you insane? I ranked 299 in my class. Do you know the minimum cutoff score to qualify for engineering courses at top colleges in the country?'

His father stood up. 'How dare you speak to your mom in that tone? Show respect. Tell us what's on your mind in a civilized way.' His voice was loud and stern.

Asahi rubbed the edges of the table hard with his fingers. 'I have to get 95 per cent in all my subjects to stand a chance at the competitive exams. This means I have to excel in math and science. Those mountains I've failed to conquer despite so much effort . . . despite so much preparation. How am I ever going to get into a good college?'

Asahi's father gestured for him to sit down. 'To conquer Mount Everest, it's not enough to practise at your local rock-climbing wall. You need professional equipment and high-level coaching to succeed.'

Asahi remained silent and looked down to see a hungry fly swimming in a puddle of soup on the floor.

'You think all your high-performing friends are succeeding only because of hard work and talent? Bullshit. It's coaching. They all have personal tutors who are top scholars in their fields.'

His mom nodded in agreement. 'Your father's right. Our neighbour works as a gardener at the Mirimotos' house. He told me that Mako learns math and science from a Nobel prize-winning scholar.'

He glanced at an old school photo of himself, Mako, and a group of friends at an official school picnic six years earlier. 'How can I ever compete with that?' His voice was filled with despair.

His father took out a copy of the *Tokyo Shimbun* and showed Asahi an advert.

'Fujioka Cramming Academy. Learn the tricks of competitive exam prep from the experts. 100 per cent success guaranteed. Early bird offers available,' read Asahi.

'This course may help you to win admission,' his father suggested.

'Dad, a six-month course costs 2 million yen. I have to take four such courses in the next three years to fully complete the requirements for the entrance exams. We can't afford that.'

'My son, it was I who suggested that you walk down this path.' He put his arm around the boy. 'I'm not going to ask you to backtrack now. Don't worry. I'll pay for this.'

Tears welled up in Asahi's eyes. 'Thank you, Dad. But we can't keep pouring all our savings into these admission sweepstakes. At what point do we ask ourselves if it's worth it?'

Father wiped his son's tears with a handkerchief. 'On the day you're hired as an executive at a top company, you'll know the answer.'

The dining room turned into the park; the squirrel commented sympathetically, 'After you abandoned your passion, you became obsessed with becoming a top student in order to ace the competitive exams. Unfortunately, you did not enjoy math and science. The most important papers at the entrance tests.'

Asahi shook his head and sobbed. 'I tried so hard. I really did. I enrolled in the cramming course for two years. All I did was eat, sleep, and breathe math and science. I improved a lot. But in the practice tests, I was always a little short of the level required to qualify for the exams. In spite of plateauing in performance, I hoped for a bit of luck on D-day. I hoped God would ultimately reward me for my effort and commitment.'

The squirrel gave him a warm hug. 'Now are you beginning to understand what held you back for so long?'

'It's me. I was my biggest enemy. I shouldn't have let Father bet his entire life savings on my competitive exam preparations. I should have stopped him.'

The squirrel clicked the last image in the hope he could persuade Asahi to let go of his self-blame.

The park's landscape morphed into the interiors of a hospital room. Asahi's father lay on a bed strapped to a dialysis machine. Both Asahi and his mother sat by his bedside. Their faces were white and sombre, their eyes red from crying. The GFR score—indicating the state of kidney function—fell with every minute. Abruptly, the reading fell several notches before leveling at a GFR score of twenty, slightly above the threshold for renal failure.

Asahi's mother covered her eyes and wept. 'Oh God! Why did you do this to us? I can't bear to watch him anymore.'

Asahi gave her a comforting hug. 'Mom, you shouldn't be here. Please go home.'

She dragged herself up, kissed her husband's face, and prayed aloud, 'My love, I'll see you in the next life.'

Asahi's father opened his eyes for a moment. 'I'll be waiting.' He smiled. Mom quickly left the room in tears.

Once his mother had gone, Asahi held his father's hand. 'Dad, please don't go. We need you more than ever before. Please fight this. I know you can do it.'

With his eyes half-closed, his father said, 'I know I pushed you hard towards a goal that wasn't natural to you. I did it to save you from a life of poverty and mediocrity. Today, I am at peace knowing that my support has reaped dividends. You are well on course to being the person you're meant to be. I wish I could be with you at the culmination of this phase in your journey. But I can't.'

Asahi shook his head and squeezed his father's hand tighter than ever before. 'No, Dad, fight this. Please don't go.'

Right then, the dialysis monitor registered a sharp drop in kidney function to below fifteen. Immediately, an alert sounded and a message: 'Warning! Renal failure!' filled the screen. The nurses rushed to administer the final lifesaving protocol. The dying man looked at him earnestly. 'Always hold your head up high. Don't let anyone take you for granted.'

Asahi kissed his father's hand one last time. 'Because of your support, I've been able to properly prepare for the admission tests next year. I swear I'll move mountains to ace them. I'll get into the best university in Japan. I'll make you proud of me.'

His father tried to say something, but his eyes shut, and his hands went limp. Yet a smile remained on his lips.

After the park reappeared, the squirrel had a philosophical look on its face. 'You felt you had to repay your father for everything he did for you. You felt the only way you could pay back your debt was by cracking the entrance exam.'

'He depleted his life savings to put me through that cramming course. As a result of that expenditure, he couldn't afford quality treatment for his long-term kidney disease. All these years, he kept shrugging it off. All these years, he kept reassuring us he'd be okay. But he wasn't. He felt he had to lie to keep me focused on the straight and narrow. He sacrificed his life so I could become successful.'

A wave of unimaginable grief overpowered him. He stood up and gazed at the sunny sky in anguish. 'I failed him. His sacrifice was for nothing.'

The squirrel reached for his hand. 'No. It wasn't. Not if you can understand yourself . . . finally. Can you see your barrier now?'

'No, I can't.'

The squirrel rose and tapped the frozen images above Alt Asahi's head. They vanished from his mind, then the rodent shrank to its cute and normal form. Right then, the frozen

Asahi woke up. He looked at his watch groggily and shrieked, 'Oh my God! It's 3.00 p.m. I must have fallen asleep. It's time to go.' He quickly put on his backpack and scampered off towards the main street.

The monk suddenly reappeared.

Asahi stared at him, startled. 'Did you turn into that squirrel?'

The monk winked. 'Let's say we formed a tag team.'

Asahi looked back at the squirrel, puzzled.

The monk ushered him to get moving. 'There's no time to waste. We have to follow him . . . I mean, you.'

The two tailed the doppelganger while maintaining a distance of thirty feet or so. Asahi turned his head towards the monk. 'Why don't we walk closer to him? After all, nobody can see us here.'

'Stand still for a bit. Let me show you why.'

At that moment, a six-year-old girl walking a Pomeranian came by. She looked at Asahi, and her eyes were filled with fear. It was almost as if she'd noticed him. The dog stopped in its tracks, faced the two, and barked loudly. Right then, bolts of electricity emanated from the girl and her dog. It surged through the veins of the two otherworldly characters—sending them reeling to the ground and squirming in pain. The dog and her walker proceeded onwards.

'What was that?' Asahi held his stomach and groaned.

The monk writhed in pain too. 'Empaths. People and creatures with extrasensory perceptions. They sense the presence of supernatural beings. When we encounter them, there's a chance we can be hurt by their supersensitive powers.'

Asahi slowly and painfully got back on his feet. 'Ouch! From now on, I'll keep a safe distance from everyone.'

After a five-minute walk, Asahi saw a museum to his right. 'There's the University of Tokyo museum. The campus is a short walk away.' He noticed his alter ego passing through a massive iron gate inscribed with the words 'UNIVERSITY OF TOKYO HONGO CAMPUS' and then walking up the steps of a building designed in the Uchida gothic tradition. 'Oh my God! I was here earlier today, right before I went to the station. I can't return there.'

The monk placed an arm on his shoulder. 'Trust me. There's nothing to fear. You must understand what really happened. Things are not as they seem.'

'Why must I revisit my pain? Why must I relive that awful moment?'

The monk smiled enigmatically and placed his hand on Asahi's heart. 'Because you need to change your world. To do that, you need to change yourself. You need to understand what held you back. You need to identify your barrier.'

'All right. We've come this far. Let's go all the way.' Asahi sighed.

As he gazed at the enormous sculpture of Descartes in the lobby, Asahi felt a shiver run down his spine. 'I remember this moment. The agony . . . the despair when I looked at the results,' he recalled with dread, reliving the heartbreaking emotions he'd experienced a short while ago. After what seemed like a ten-minute walk down the winding corridor, Asahi gestured for the monk to stop. A gaggle of students had formed outside a room that bore the nameplate 'UNDERGRADUATE ENGINEERING ADMISSIONS DEPARTMENT'. The alternate Asahi stood at the back of the line. His eyes were filled with anxious expectation as he awaited the results.

Ten minutes later, the door opened and the students were allowed to enter. The result forms were stacked neatly on tables, arranged by roll numbers. Alt Asahi reached his designated table, and asked for his form. 'My roll number is 100345,' he said to a proctor. The official handed him the sheet. Asahi closed his eyes and turned his head away. 'No! I can't bear to watch.'

The monk ran his hand down Asahi's back. 'There's nothing to fear.'

The alter ego stared at the result sheet, and a tear formed in his eye. Right then, Mako approached him. Her face shone with pride and the glow of achievement. 'I got into the University of Tokyo. Accepted by both engineering and social science departments. Shujo got in, too.'

The doppelganger curled his lips into a half-smile. 'Oh . . . that's . . . that's swell. Congrats!'

She saw the wetness in his eye and her voice changed. 'How did you do?' He did not answer. 'Oh! What's wrong?'

Alt Asahi showed her his results. The words 'ADMISSION DENIED' were printed in bold letters. She looked at him sympathetically. 'Oh . . . I'm sorry, Asahi. I'm so sorry.'

At that moment, Shujo—who was celebrating his triumph with his mates—came over and patted his back. 'Don't worry, bro. You're smart. You'll get into another good college. If you want, I'll tell Daddy to pull some strings.'

Before the alternate could thank them for their show of support, the otherworldly Asahi faced him and cried, 'Why did you fill a form created by others? Why did you ignore the voice of your heart? Why? Why?'

The doppelganger remained silent, unaware of the supernatural presence and his face buried in the script.

Asahi turned to the monk and shouted, 'Competitive pressure. That's my barrier. All my life, I filled someone else's form because I didn't have the guts to fill my own. All my life,

I've followed competition because I was too scared of following my passion.' The monk nodded his head and smiled knowingly. Asahi looked up at the ceiling and lifted his arms. 'Give me a second chance. I'll make things right. I'll overcome competitive pressure by following my passion.'

Suddenly, the lights dimmed. The din of triumphant whoops and devastated wails subsided. Everyone in the room froze. 'What's going on?' asked Asahi, puzzled.

'Redemption,' replied the monk as the lights faded and the sights and sounds of the ethereal domain vanished from existence.

A minute later, the lights came back on. Asahi felt a pail of water splash on his face. 'What the hell was that?' He squinted his eyes. He lay on a row of benches in the waiting room of a subway station. Mako and his mom were at his side. Mom held an empty half-litre bottle of water.

'Mako? What am I—what are you doing here?' He rubbed his eyes. 'I can't remember a thing.'

Mako wiped his face with a hand towel. 'You've had a long and eventful day. It's normal for anyone to be overwhelmed.'

Mom threw the bottle in the trashcan. 'Just as we were all about to board the train, you fainted on the platform. It was too much for you to handle. It would have been too much for anyone.'

'Huh? Why would I suddenly faint? The only thing I can remember is standing on this platform while a few drops of water leaked onto me from the ceiling . . .' He paused and tried to remember the events leading to that moment, but he couldn't.

Right then, a man arrived in a wheelchair, accompanied by a woman wearing medical overalls printed with the words 'HONGO

SANCHOME STATION DOCTOR'. 'He's had a very stressful day. So many turbulent emotions. So many important decisions. It was too much for his mind to process,' the paraplegic said to the doctor in a tone of urgency and worry.

'Dad? You're alive? It can't be!' Asahi shot upright, seeing his father alive and well, albeit without his legs.

Father tapped the metallic frame of the wheelchair, and smiled. 'You bet I'm alive. For twenty-five years since that accident in the restaurant kitchen, this steel monster's been my wingman.'

Asahi touched the old man's face. 'Dad! I can't believe you're alive. This is a miracle!'

Bemused, Asahi's father turned to the station doctor for an expert opinion about his son's medical condition. 'Can amnesia follow after studying for three days without a break?'

The doctor nodded her head. 'Yes, I see these types of cases all the time. After all, this is the most stressful time in a young person's life. The competitive exam season. So many students are suffering from nervous breakdowns.'

Father threw a concerned glance at Asahi. 'He seems to have memory loss too. You don't think he needs anxiety medication, right?'

'Oh no! Not at all. He's gone through a roller coaster of emotions over the last four hours. He'll be fine soon. Just make sure he rests well and has loads of fun starting tomorrow. Anything to take his mind off the stress he's endured during the last six weeks.'

Asahi frowned. 'Last six weeks? What happened to me during the last few weeks? I can't remember a thing.'

Mako slapped him playfully on his shoulder. 'Must I remind you of your kindness? Last month, I had a major blowup with

Shujo after discovering he'd been running an illicit ring—leaking test papers for money. I felt so betrayed, so humiliated. I had to dump him like radioactive nuclear waste. After that, I went through acute depression. You lent me your shoulder to cry on during that dark period. You took time out from your studies to listen to me. It was then that I realized what a special person you are. It was then that I realized we should have been together all these years. We've been a couple since then.'

'But what about your father? Surely, he'd object.'

Mako waved her hands and laughed. 'Dad would object? Hahaha! He's such a teddy bear. He wouldn't object if I went out with a serial killer.'

Asahi tried to raise his head, but he only managed to lift it halfway up before it came crashing down on the wooden benches.

'Oh! Be careful. Place your head on my lap,' offered his father.

Mako, Mom and the doctor pushed his body back so his legs were on the benches and his head on his father's lap. Asahi looked at his father with a sad expression in his eyes. 'I'm sorry for letting you down, Dad.'

His father looked totally bewildered. 'Let me down? What do you mean?'

'You didn't let anyone down,' Mako and Mom said in unison.

'I failed the competitive exams. I failed you all,' Asahi moaned.

The three looked somber for a moment, then they all burst into laughter. Father took out a bundle of torn papers from his fanny pack. He handed over the bunch—crudely reassembled with scotch tape—to Asahi. Each bore the logo of a different university with the headline, 'Undergraduate Engineering Admission Result 2020'. He saw the results of his efforts in the lower right-hand corner of the paper, and felt his heart pounding with shock and excitement. 'What!? I've been accepted by all these colleges? Even the University of Tokyo?' he exclaimed, breathlessly.

Father nodded his head. 'Exactly. Now you see . . . you're not a failure.'

Mako gave him a deep kiss. She then showed him her acceptance letter with sparkling eyes. 'We both got into the same elite university. How amazing is that?'

Asahi noticed that all his pages were torn down the middle, almost as if someone tried to rip his future to shreds. 'Why are these forms torn?'

Mako, Mom, and Dad looked at each other with befuddled expressions. Then, they turned to the station doctor for an additional expert analysis of Asahi's idiosyncratic behaviour.

'Temporary memory loss is a rare side effect of a nervous breakdown. It can last for a few days. The more you divulge details about the latest events in his life, the sooner his memory will slowly return.' The doctor's face was calm and reassuring.

Relieved no permanent damage had been inflicted on his son's mental faculties, Father narrated the events leading up to the torn documents. 'We accompanied you to the admission departments of all the universities where you'd applied. When you received your results, you were overwhelmed with joy and relief. But you were also seized by panic.'

'Why?' Asahi looked surprised.

Father pointed to the University of Tokyo form placed on the top of the heap. 'When you held that form . . . the last and most coveted of the day . . . you realized enrolling in the engineering stream meant a lifelong commitment to science. You realized you'd have to travel down a road you had no interest in charting. You realized you'd have to sail in a direction away from your heart. At the same time, you were racked with guilt because you feared you'd let me down if you didn't take up engineering. While you struggled to resolve your inner confusion, I made it easier for you to take the decision. In front of you, I tore up the scripts. I told you, "Son, it doesn't matter to me whether you become a high-profile manager at Toyota, a low-paid government clerk, or a struggling artist sketching portraits in Harajuku. I just want to see you happy."'

'What did I say in response?'

'With tears in your eyes, you said, "I know, if I walk down this path, I'll always be held hostage by competitive pressure. Thank you for accepting me as I am". To that, I said, "Go, follow your passion".'

The peculiar jumble of facts arrayed themselves in his mind. Mako took the forms from him and slipped them into her backpack. 'As you stood in the lobby of the University of Tokyo, considering your release from the prison of competitive pressure, you weren't fully able to let go of your guilt. Despite winning your father's support, you kept repeating the question, "Would it be wrong to renege on my original plan?" I detected your confusion and suggested you sleep on it. While the four of us walked to the station, I could see your face ashen with confusion and guilt. It was evident that the decision to abandon a path—a path you'd embraced your whole life—weighed heavily on your mind and prevented you from embracing the victory. Just as the train approached the station platform, the load of the decision became so unbearable that you buckled under its excruciating stress.'

The 'fact jumble' now formed a single word. RELAX. 'I want to go home,' he said.

The four helped him stand up and escorted him from the waiting room to the platform. He soon heard a familiar screeching sound and felt the kiss of a powerful breeze. Suddenly, he heard something behind him. The sound of wheels. Curious, he turned around and saw a man in his thirties without legs crouching against the wall and begging for alms. His head was shaved, and he was wearing a monk's robe. A skateboard lay in front of him along with a handful of loose change and a sign that read, 'HOMELESS. NO FOOD. PLEASE HELP.' He seemed familiar . . . like someone he'd fleetingly encountered years ago. *Have we met before?* Asahi couldn't place him in his timeline.

Meanwhile, the train had arrived. Asahi's parents boarded it. Mako saw Asahi lagging behind, staring intently at the panhandler. 'Do you know him?'

Asahi shrugged his shoulders and muttered, 'I don't know,' while continuing to stare at the stranger.

Mako thought that Asahi wanted to help the poor man out of the kindness of his heart but couldn't summon the mind–body coordination to do so. She quickly took out a few coins and handed them to the monk. 'Come on. We'll miss the train.' She ushered Asahi into the Shin-Koiwa-bound express train.

Asahi held on to her hand and got on the train, but he couldn't look away from the homeless man.

The monk noticed Asahi staring at him. He smiled and pointed with his index finger at something on the ceiling. The door closed, Asahi looked up to check it out.

The ceiling was perfectly smooth. There were no holes anywhere.

REFLECTION: CREATE YOUR OWN FORM

Have you faced pressure to perform in a field that was not your passion?

A competition is a race where we engage with others to earn a prize: wealth, a title, an award, or some other such benefit. The activity is like filling out a form. This is how it works: we are given a form with a list of questions or directions. We have to fill in the answers within a certain period of time. Our responses are compared to those of others by a panel of judges. The best respondents are granted rewards.

The process that I describe above is the methodology used by every type of competition to distribute rewards to the most proficient individuals. It is the gold-standard method deployed at university entrance examinations and corporate job appraisals to decide who gets admitted or promoted. To become adept at these competitions, we have to develop expertise in filling out forms in the manner demanded by the authorities.

How can we develop this skill?

We need to be familiar with the questions asked by people in positions of power. We need to anticipate what they may ask us to do. We need to become proficient in providing responses they may appreciate.

This entails cultivating a deep understanding of their motivations and decision-making patterns, a cut-throat attitude towards rivals and a mindset that prioritizes winning at all costs. Through social conditioning, we absorb these traits at an early age and inflict long-term damage on ourselves and society.

From an early age, we are conditioned to believe that the most attractive opportunities for a better life will be accessible only if we compete for them. Therefore, we end up devoting our lives to meeting the objectives defined by others instead of setting our own. We end up filling out forms created by others instead of designing and filling our own; hurting others in our desperation to stay ahead of the pack. We then end up unhappy when we ultimately realize that the rewards are hollow and ephemeral. I would like to share how I dealt with the disappointment of underachieving in my undergraduate admission tests.

Born into a family of academic whizzes, I was obsessed with securing admission into an Ivy League college in the US. I wanted to achieve because I had this need to prove that I was worthy of the family name, and not to follow my passion for a particular subject. So when I received rejection letters from all my top-choice colleges, I felt devastated. Like Asahi, I was terribly ashamed of myself because I felt I'd let my family down. I also felt that I'd never amount to anything in life. Fortunately, right before the end of the admission season, a kind uncle suggested that I apply to New York University (NYU). Back in the 1990s, the Violet Institute was ranked as a mid-tier school, and I wasn't keen on going there. However, I had few choices. I submitted an application and received an acceptance letter a month later.

In hindsight, I can certainly say that NYU had an amazing impact on my life. I got to experience student life in the most exciting city in the world. I discovered a passion for creative writing and philosophy. These two skills weren't tested on the SATs, but they have helped me complete this book. I got to launch my career with one of the most prestigious news organizations in the country. I made many close friends and fruitful associations. Significantly, over the last two decades, the institute has ascended the rankings to be numbered among the top ten universities in the US. So I ended up becoming an alumnus of a top-tier college without having to compete too hard to get in! This has taught me an important lesson in life. Sometimes, we lose an opportunity that we so, so badly desire. But then, all of a sudden, something new and unexpected appears on our horizon. This invariably leads to an outcome better than what we'd imagined for ourselves, so don't lose heart! If you happen to lose out on one occasion, remember one thing: it's never over till you decide it's over.

In that moment of defeat, don't beat yourself up. There are always possibilities to explore, new options to consider. Instead, ask yourself, 'What do I really want?' Ask yourself, 'Is this competition my passion?' What would the answer be?

If the answer is 'Yes, this competition is my passion', you need to understand why you feel this way. Is it because you're besotted with the thrill of winning; with the aphrodisiac that is victory? Or is it because you really and truly love the work you do? And if you do truly love your work, it wouldn't hurt to ask, 'Is there a happier way of following my passion?'

On the other hand, if the answer is 'No, I hate this competition', you must go a step further and ask yourself, 'What is my passion?' When you answer this question, you'll find many roads to pursue your passion. Not all roads require you to compete with others. It's possible to do things on your own terms, at your own pace, time and be led solely by your own level of interest. It's possible to set your own benchmarks for excellence. While the market may be the final arbiter of your work, you can always define the audience you'd like to serve. With all the tools available online, it's possible to discover an audience for your work anywhere—even in a remote corner of the world, or a place you wouldn't have known about, had you not followed your own path.

Let us not allow competition to dictate the course of our lives. Let us determine our own direction.

The identity of the protagonist was smothered by competitive pressure. Learn how he overcame this barrier, and you will believe that you can too.

THE LAST WORD: UNSHACKLE YOURSELF BY FOLLOWING YOUR PASSION

We've all been in adverse life situations. In these circumstances, we tend to feel powerless to impact the outcome. As a result, we may experience stress. With the passage of time, though, those negative feelings *always* recede from our mental shores like angry ocean waves after high tide. However, there may be times when the stress may recur and lash our minds like a tsunami smiting the earth. Just as nature's wrath can't always be justified by 'God's design', can stress *always* be attributed to misfortune? Can we honestly say we aren't *at all* responsible for fomenting stress, the same way we repeatedly deny abusing the environment?

Want to know the truth?

Adverse circumstances be damned, we're often guilty of unleashing our own stress monsters upon ourselves.

The absence of purpose in your life is a major cause of stress. Most of us who face continual stress, are caught in pursuit of activities that we find pointless or unpleasant. We stick to the path of drudgery and inauthenticity because we think that the alternative—changing our habits—is difficult and unpleasant. Like many people in our world, the characters in the stories I have related in this book were bereft of purpose. This made them vulnerable to both internal and external stress factors. Consequently, they acted out of desperation to meet various expectations—only to end up trapped in *Groundhog Day*-type loops of unproductive behaviours, inviting stress into their private lives. To our heroes' credit, though, they didn't just sit back and accept the inevitable. All of them took positive action to change their fate. All of them transformed their suffocating stress boa constrictors into fragrant garlands. What can we learn from their stories?

Recognize that stress is not your destiny. The path to breaking out of your rut and finding meaning begins with a focused pursuit of your passion. Start by asking yourself, 'What do I love to do?' Even if the answer has nothing to do with your present livelihood or scheme of things, even if you deem it a waste of time, give that activity a shot. Begin by dabbling in it as a hobby. It doesn't matter how much time, energy or committed you are to your passion. Even a minuscule effort can have a transformative effect on your mental state.

When you follow your passion, you produce something. This can be a tangible object or an idea. The very task of bringing something new into the world is a lot like giving birth—it will fill you with joy, instilling confidence in your abilities. It will help you look deep within and understand yourself. As incredible as it may sound, it will also ease your isolation by helping you to form kindred connections with the people in your life.

Your beautiful creation will attract the attention of various people, including acquaintances and strangers. Some of them will meet you for the first time and will be captivated by your energy. Some will reacquaint themselves with you later in life and marvel at your transformation. In other words, your idea or creation will trigger a community to form around you—a community that, in time, will bring out the best in you. This congregation of kindred souls will douse your dark spirits with a welcome shower of vibrancy and optimism. Its injection of positivity will help unshackle yourself from other people's expectations and your own, serving to dispel the dark clouds of stress hovering above you, endangering your peace.

In the stories that you've just read, the protagonists faced severe stress—filling their minds with a constant stream of anxiety, depression and dread of various kinds. Overwhelmed by these difficult emotions, they found it hard to take pleasure in the simple things in life. As for achieving their goals? Forget about it!

Learn how they discovered joy, and believe that you can, too.

ACKNOWLEDGEMENTS

I would like to thank everyone who has helped to turn this book into a reality.

I am indebted to the multifaceted artistic genius Sohini Roychowdhury Dasgupta and her husband, the musically-gifted, food connoisseur Sudipto, for inspiring me to reach out to the world with these stories and for their unquestioning support, love and delicious, home-cooked meals.

I will forever be mesmerized by the wizardry of Akangksha Sarmah and Anamaria Stefan, whose stunning cover design and captivating illustrations grace this book.

I would like to express my admiration for Candace Johnson, Cindy Davis and Udyotna Kumar, editors par extraordinaire, for their patient, meticulous and thoughtful work to make the manuscript true to its intent and authentic in its voice.

I feel privileged to have the support and belief of Randy Peyser, Founder of Author One Stop, who helped me to navigate the publishing industry and connected me to Cindy.

I am grateful to the Penguin Random House India team—led by Gaurav Shrinagesh, Ankit Juneja and Udyotna Kumar—

for giving my work a beautiful home and ensuring it shines brightly.

I am indebted to the team at Free Spirit Press for identifying my literary potential and being the first to feature 'The Daylight Programme' in the anthology, *Business Stories: Startups and More.*

My heart is always touched by the Oneness Family for their unconditional love and support.

Finally, I am left with no words to express my devotion to Sri Harit Ratna, whose Philosophy of Oneness has powered every word of this manuscript.

ABOUT THE AUTHOR

Aritra Sarkar is a storyteller with a social mission to enable all human beings to lead meaningful lives. His first publication, *Goliath of Shenzhen* (2016), inspired people to find their inner strength to overcome an authoritarian regime. It is the world's first dual-facing novel—told in both graphic and prose formats—where you can choose your reading experience. He has also scripted an audio drama, *Stilettos and Dentistry* (2018), to motivate people to overcome their financial challenges. This book is the first title in a series called *Parables for Growth*, containing stories that depict personal transformation from various forms of adversity, conveying vital life lessons to the reader.

Before becoming a full-time author, Aritra spent many years in the corporate world. He worked for two years in marketing research at *The Wall Street Journal* in New York (1999–2001) and then spent a decade working on corporate strategy at the ABP group in Kolkata. In 2014, he rolled up his sleeves and became an entrepreneur, launching MeVero, the world's first passion-based social networking platform.

Aritra has currently focused all his energies into literary pursuits and spiritual growth. He is an NYU graduate and is passionate about tennis, fitness, travelling, books and movies.

Scan QR code to access the
Penguin Random House India website